UNEARTHED

A DEATH SEEKER NOVEL

CECY ROBSON

D1520862

CECY ROBSON, LLC.

PRAISE FOR CECY ROBSON

New to Cecy Robson's novels? Here's what readers say...

"You know, I don't think I've ever read a book by Cecy Robson that I haven't just absolutely adored...She gives you characters you can identify with and a story that enthralls you." *-Two Girls With Books*

"I would devour anything that Ms. Robson writes. I strongly recommend [the Weird Girls] series to PNR/UF readers and fans of Larissa Ione, Kresley Cole and Gena Showalter. Cecy Robson is pretty up there, IMO." *- Under the Covers Book Blog*

"Cecy Robson is a phenomenal talent who knows just how to deliver a story filled with suspense, action, humor and romance...leaving you craving for more!" *-Romancing the Dark Side*

"Cecy Robson has been added to my favorite authors list and The Weird Girls series is one of my favorite urban fantasy series. Fans of Kim Harrison's the Hollows series and Patricia Brigg's Mercy Thompson series will devour Weird Girls." **- Caffeinated Book Reviewer**

"Like all of Robson's books, the characters of *Feel Me* are complex and dynamic, the emotions are raw and real, and the ending is sweet and heartwarming." *- The Book Disciple*

"Cecy Robson is one of my absolute favorite authors and each book that she writes becomes more gut-wrenching and brilliant than the last...I'm dying to read the next installment." - **Books-n-Kisses**

"Robson proves once again that she can sweep us off our feet with a fun, romantic tale... [*Once Kissed*] is another must-read. I thoroughly enjoyed this novel."- *Rainy Day Ramblings*

"Of Flame and Promise" is an absolutely amazing book. I laughed, I cried, I felt their pain. It's one of the best books I have read. While this was my first book by Cecy it won't be my last. -**Night Owl Reviews (Top Pick, 5 Stars!)**

"Cecy Robson has a talent for stepping outside of the classic fantasy and rebuilding the fairy-tale. Realism and connection are mighty weapons and she uses these to the fullest."
- *Hopeless Romantic*

"Already [Cecy] Robson was becoming one of my favorite authors but Inseverable sealed the deal. Inseverable shows Robson's different writing style and I couldn't get enough of this new setting and the new characters that were introduced."
- *Lush Book Reviews*

"Cecy Robson became an instant author to look out for with her great writing, loveable characters, good plot development and a story with just right pace wrapped up in sexy, sweet and swoony delightfulness, and *Crave Me* definitely delivered on all fronts."
- *TJ Loves to Read Romance Blog*

"Cecy has this fantastic ability to suck you into her stories. She takes difficult topics head on and doesn't cut corners in her portrayals...This is an auto-read author for me and she continues to earn that loyalty with every book she pens." - *Curvy and Nerdy*

"Ms. Robson has once again written a tale that I absolutely love. Both characters have captured my heart and the story is so well written and paced that I could not put it down." - *Cat's Reviews*

"Cecy Robson is a master when it comes to tugging your heartstrings but leaving you with a satisfied smile on your face."
- *Dog-Eared Daydreams*

ALSO BY CECY ROBSON

The Weird Girls Series

Gone Hunting

A Curse Awakened: A Novella

The Weird Girls: A Novella

Sealed with a Curse

A Cursed Embrace

Of Flame and Promise

A Cursed Moon: A Novella

Cursed by Destiny

A Cursed Bloodline

A Curse Unbroken

Of Flame and Light

Of Flame and Fate

Of Flame and Fury (coming soon)

The Shattered Past Series

Once Perfect

Once Loved

Once Pure

The O'Brien Family Novels

Once Kissed

Let Me

Crave Me

Feel Me

Save Me

The Carolina Beach Novels

Inseverable

Eternal

Infinite

In Too Far Novels

Salvatore

APPS

Crazy Maple's Chapters: Interactive Stories APP: The Shattered Past and Weird Girls Series

Radish Fiction APP: Union of Souls (exclusive); coming soon: The O'Brien Family Series

Also find Cecy writing as Rosalina San Tiago on *Hooked – Chat stories APP*

UNEARTHED

A DEATH SEEKER NOVEL

CECY ROBSON

Copyright Cecy Robson, 2019

Edited by Nicole Resciniti

Cover design © Rebecca Weeks, Dark Wish Designs

Formatting by DJW Formatting

Excerpt from *Gone Hunting* by Cecy Robson, copyright © Cecy Robson, 2018

This book contains an excerpt from *Gone Hunting* by Cecy Robson, a full-length novel in the Weird Girls urban fantasy romance series.

Published in the United States by Cecy Robson, L.L.C.

eBook ISBN: 978-1-947330-29-0

Print ISBN: 978-1-947330-31-3

To Mr. Harte, who taught me to believe in fairies.

ACKNOWLEDGMENTS

Unearthed is a novel I wrote many years ago. It's a story born from a necklace I purchased at a fair and a very overactive (and often frightening) imagination.

I dedicate this novel to the Harte family, James, Kay, Jimmy, and Johnny; and to Jim and Kathleen (Harte) Gilsenan. I also dedicate this novel to my brother, Douglas. Like me, he was blessed to have this family's love.

To my husband, Jamie, who knew the crazy he was marrying into and still said, "I do." Love you, babe.

To my agent, Nicole Resciniti. God placed you in my life to help my publishing dreams come true and placed you in my heart for so much more. Thank you for being my friend and for editing and loving this magical novel.

To my amazing assistant, Kimberly Costa, my wonderful artist, Rebecca Weeks of Dark Wish Designs, my meticulous formatter, Robin Covington, and to Tera Cuskaden, who had the absolute pleasure of proofreading this manuscript backward. Ladies, you are incredible. This novel would not be the same without your talents.

Lastly to Suzan Lacey. Olivia became Ryker's "little rainbow," in part because of you. Thank you for being such a wonderful fan of my work.

1

Ryker Scott, MacGregor and Santonelli's newest associate, prowls past my cubicle wearing a tailored black suit that hugs his broad shoulders. I swear he's not human. In the year he's worked here, he's represented a talk show host charged with having sex with multiple minors, a senator's son accused of sexually assaulting a young boy, and a Wall Street executive snagged in a cocaine smuggling ring. All were acquitted under his watch, despite the odds and endless charges. His latest victory was mere days ago when his client, a Broadway star one blow shy of beating his wife to death, was found not guilty.

Ryker's military haircut fits his serious persona. The guy doesn't smile, ever. I suppose when you represent walking pieces of filth, it's hard to pretend you'd skip through a field of daisies. I'd ask him how he sleeps at night, saving all those horrible people and releasing them back into society, but I don't know him, and I don't care to.

Ryker's ice-blue eyes dart in my direction when I glare. He knows I hate every inch of his hulking form. If I could flip him off, I would. Instead, I give him my back and return to my work, wishing he'd stay on his side of the office.

I sense him stalk around the corner to speak quietly to another paralegal. She's likely falling all over herself to please him. He has that effect on the staff, unlike my boss, who everyone avoids like shingles.

Speaking of the most irate man to ever wear a suit, Marco slams down the receiver to the phone, his booming voice loud enough to rattle the glass of his fishbowl office. "*Olivia*! Where the hell are my notes?"

My fingers fly across my keyboard, finishing the deposition Marco needs before that vein on his forehead finally pops. "In your briefcase, along with copies of the court documents," I reply.

My sensitive hearing picks up the *click, click* of the briefcase locks snapping open before the mad sound of rustling papers ensues. "I don't have—"

"You have three pens and two highlighters in the small zippered compartment and a new legal pad in the side pocket," I call out.

"My—"

"Your cell phone is charging on the table behind you," I remind him.

I hit *print* and swivel in my high-back office chair, working quickly to stack the copies neatly into a folder. After taking one last sip of tea, I lift the folder and an extra-large cup of coffee and hurry into my boss's office.

Marco welcomes me with a scowl, the motion joining his crazy caterpillar eyebrows. "You think you're so smart, don't you?" he asks.

"Yup. Happy Monday." I place the deposition on his desk and hand him the cup of coffee the new administrative assistant dropped off. So far, Marco is the only attorney she hasn't hit on.

"Drink up," I tell him. "You're due in court in an hour." I play with the talisman around my neck, reassuring myself that Death can't find me while I wear it.

I examine my boss and shake my head. Marco is roughly five feet, six inches tall, three hundred pounds and balding, and about as cuddly as a rabid raccoon living in a sewer. And here he sits, partner of the most prestigious law firm in the region and the best defense attorney in Jersey.

"What are you looking at?"

I motion to his face. "I told you to do something about your eyebrows."

"There's nothing wrong with my eyebrows." He tries to smooth them, but the motion only ruffles them further.

"Marco, they look ready to sprout teeth and bite." I push off the desk. "Let me trim them."

Marco is one second away from releasing the brows like Zeus did the Kraken. "*Do I strike you as someone who manscapes?*"

"No. That's part of the problem." I sigh when the vein on his forehead pulsates. "You need to take pride in your appearance. If I didn't have your suits and shirts dry-cleaned, you'd resemble a serial killer walking into court."

My voice trails when I take in the creases lining his gray suit. It's my turn to scowl. "Isn't this the suit you wore Friday?" He doesn't answer. "Marco!"

"You're one to talk. Look at you. Your hair is one pot of gold shy of a leprechaun."

I point a nasty finger at him. "Don't make fun of the hair."

As a pixie, I look human, the exception being my rain- bow-colored locks. That's right, blond hair intermixed with strands of pink, lavender, and blue. It's not on purpose. My hair was this color from birth, long before we crossed over from the dying realm of Fae. Many PTA moms scolded my mother for "doing this" to me. Mama tried to change the color, so I'd blend in better among humans, but nothing worked. Hair dyes dried my hair and faded in mere hours, and organic products made my hair shimmer like fairy dust.

Between my hair and the Celtic cross tat on the base of my skull, everyone in school assumed I was Goth. Truthfully, I prefer pretty clothes and music I can dance to without risking an elbow to the face.

"Why are you looking at me like that?" Marco snaps. "This suit cost two grand."

"It might as well cost two dollars by the way you take care of yourself."

I stomp in my pink kitten heels toward Marco's closet and whip out a fresh suit, tie, and set of underclothes. After taking a good whiff, I also grab a stick of Right Guard. I set everything neatly in his private bathroom and poke my head out. "You still have time to shower before court. Do you want me to turn on the water—"

The scuff of expensive shoes along the marble tile floor alert me we're no longer alone. Damn it. It's Ryker. Doesn't he have puppy kickers to defend?

Rock-hard muscles bulge against his designer suit. When he's not freeing predators back into society, he must spend his time in the gym.

Ryker squares his jaw hard enough to smooth the dimple on his chin. He's not pleased to see me or the glare I peg him with. Still, he tilts his head in polite acknowledgment. "Olivia."

I smooth the skirt of my long white sundress and walk toward Marco, ignoring Ryker. "Do you need anything else?"

Marco's features soften as he addresses Ryker. "Sorry you had to wait, son. I was negotiating the Andrews case with opposing counsel when you first stopped in."

That explains Marco's prior screaming and swearing. Marco is the type who prefers coercion to tact, which makes his interactions with Ryker odd. Marco smiles at him, as in, *genuinely smiles*.

"Congratulations on the acquittal, boy," Marco says to Ryker. "That was a hell of a job you did. Keep this up, and you'll make junior partner within a year."

"Thank you, sir. It was a challenging case, and I was grateful for the help."

"You can have all the help you want, anytime you want it." Marco's smile fades. "Is something wrong? You seem upset."

"I'm fine, sir," the leech answers.

"You don't seem fine. Would you like some coffee? Olivia would be happy to bring you a cup."

"No, she wouldn't," I mutter, walking toward the door. "You have fifty minutes, Marco. Take a shower."

I shut the door behind me, muffling their conversation. The glass offices may allow a full view in, but they're soundproof, except to my sensitive ears. Marco and Ryker glance in my direction before resuming their conversation. I was rude in there, and I'm embarrassed about my behavior. There's just something about Ryker that fires me up and puts me in a hideous mood...

I freeze when I glance toward Bill MacGregor's office. Bill is the other partner and a Fae like me. Right now, he's in serious trouble. The very slutty and *very human* admin is slinking closer to him. She leans over his desk, her tiny black skirt rising and exposing her butt cheeks.

Bill's eyes widen, and he tries to scramble away. The admin doesn't let him. She yanks him to her by his tie and stamps her lips to his.

Thunder booms, shaking the thirty-story building. Lightning blankets Bill's office in a painful blare of white light. As the light fades, so does Bill's glamour, revealing his true form.

Glistening mocha-colored skin envelops the boulder-sized muscles of the seven-foot-tall gargoyle. Dagger-length fangs, sleek and deadly, protrude from his terrifying maw as glider-sized wings expand, shadowing the terrified woman in darkness. She screams, loudly, the thick glass mercifully silencing her terror. I leap from my chair when she face-plants on Bill's mahogany desk and call to the administrative assistant in the cubicle beside mine. "Jane, clean up in aisle five."

Jane and I are both Fae and the only staff with a front and center view of Bill's office. We don't get a lot of traffic on this side of the building. Everyone avoids Marco, and no one wants to risk accidentally killing Jane.

Humans only see Jane's chosen glamor, that of a ninety-year-old woman with severe osteoporosis and one awkward step shy of a broken hip. For an eight-hundred-year-old druid priestess, Jane looks damn good. Unfortunately, she is ancient, and her hearing reflects it.

"Jane? Jane!"

I round back when she doesn't hear me and shake her shoulder. "Jane!"

She stops her two-finger typing and blinks her tiny black eyes at me, speaking in her two-pack-a-day smoker voice. "Whhhat?"

"Clean up in aisle five," I repeat.

I bolt to Bill's office, making quick work of drawing the privacy shades. Bill is freaking out. His mammoth wings snap irritably, and his clawed hands wave in distress. "Why dith thee havvvv to kitth meeth? Goth. Damnth ith!" he hisses through his fangs.

"Your glamour form is smoking hot," I remind him.

He scowls, his forked tongue dangling from his mouth.

"Did you have to pick *that* glamour?" I ask. I motion to the picture of him standing with the governor. "You resemble a young Laurence Fishburne with a goatee."

"I lithe Lawrenth Fishburth," he replies.

I pat his arm. "Try to relax and call it back."

I draw the last shade that blocks the view into his office and stick my head out the door to check on Jane. She's resumed her two-finger typing. On a good day, Jane can type ten words a minute. This doesn't appear to be a good day.

"Jane!"

"Whhhat?" she croaks.

"You're needed in Bill's office!" I holler. "Bring the big guns —*the big guns*, Jane!"

The slutty admin slides off Bill's desk and falls to the floor with a thump. She groans, her forehead crinkling.

"Sheeth wakingth," Bill says, panicking.

There's no way he can recall his glamour in this state. "Jane, haul ass, sistergirl!"

Jane glances over her shoulder and adjusts the black veil on her head. With the speed of molasses, she reaches for the candy-cane-striped wand she keeps in her pencil holder and shuffles toward us. Her black dress, two sizes too big, drags behind her tiny form.

The wand looks ridiculous clutched in her spotted hand. It's not just the red and white stripes, it's the red plastic heart complete with ribbons decorating the tip. Still, I wouldn't mess with Jane's wand. Our last temp tried to take it as a joke. Following a severe case of genital herpes and a beard so thick she looked ready to swing an ax, she was never heard from again.

Jane reaches Bill's office with all the grace and speed of a snail. Unlike Bill, Jane isn't panicked. She merely passes her wand over the admin, chanting in ancient Irish.

I try to make out the spell through her deep mumbles. It rings similar to the one she used to try to restore my magic.

Unlike the Fae who occupy this world, I don't possess magic.

My power and wings were ripped from me when my family and I crossed dimensions and into Earth's realm.

Although I was young, I remember the pain.

The last time Jane attempted to resurrect my magic, I cried with frustration. Jane wiped my tears, speaking slowly. "You have something, Livvie," she insisted. She smiled softly and pointed at my heart with her long, crooked finger. "What you seek is in there."

I want to believe her. My family comes from a powerful line of pixies. It's devastating to not possess even a wisp of their strength. It's not that I think I need magic to feel more Fae. I just want something—*anything*—to strike back at those who robbed me of my family. Until then, all I can do is hide beneath the veil and protection of my talisman, just like the rest of my kind.

Glitter sprinkles from Jane's wand as she shakes it over the admin's face, freezing her in place when she abruptly wakes and tries to scream.

I scoot around them and toward the large windows. "Please alter her memory, Jane, and kindly tell her to stop being such a skank— Oh, and if you could, help Bill recall his glamour. He's having a tough time settling."

My voice trails as I peer through the window. Across the Hudson River, dark clouds crawl along the New York skyline, expanding quickly and morphing day into night.

My blood chills to ice, threatening to snap my bones. Death has found us. It's coming. It's coming now. But *why*?

The growing cluster of ominous clouds inks the sky. Jane stops her chanting, training her beady eyes toward the ceiling when the lights flicker. "Livvie," she warns.

My fingers find my Celtic sister knot—the talisman that hides me from Death. It's still there. I look at Jane. Her talisman dangles from her neck. So then...

Bill whirls left and right, knocking books from the shelves

and sending the paperwork on his desk flying with the bat of his powerful wings. He falls to his knees when something on the floor catches his eye, the tips of his wings leaving deeps scrapes along the walls. Like a frantic cat, he scratches at the floor, trying to retrieve his broken watch.

I dive for the watch, *Bill's* talisman. The links snapped from his wrist when he resumed his true form, damaging the magical charge that gives the veiling spell its power.

In the distance, I hear them, the cavernous roars of the Cù-Sìth death hounds, the form of Death that devoured my family.

I drop the watch into his hand and cover it with my palm. It doesn't work. With each crash of encroaching thunder, the growls intensify. The Cù-Sìth are hungry. They need a soul, and it's Bill's they hunt.

The fluorescent bulbs explode, encasing the room in darkness. "Livvie…" Jane's throaty voice carries fear I've never seen in her. "Magic."

My pixie eyes adjust to the darkness, only to widen when I realize what Jane is asking. She wants me to call my lost mojo. Is she crazy? *Now*? We've spent countless hours trying to summon it only to fail each time.

Lightning flashes against the windows, illuminating the room. "Hurry," Jane urges.

The talisman can't conceal Bill from Death. It knows he's here. With sweat-soaked hands, I anchor the links around Bill's giant fingers, searching deep within me and attempting what feels impossible.

I scrunch my face, concentrating on cocooning us in my aura.

Emptiness is all that greets me. I hold my breath, focusing harder.

The emptiness grows more pronounced. I open my eyes. Bill

shakes his head, his pointy ears drooping as he motions for me to leave.

Tears blur my vision. "No, Bill." Magic or not, I won't leave him alone to die.

Thunder rattles the building, and the chorus of howls reach a mind-numbing crescendo. My eyes scan the office for something I can use to connect the links. I find a discarded roll of tape on the floor and lead Bill to it, both of us crouching low when we reach it.

I snap the roll from the dispenser, careful not to lose the end. With more speed than grace, I wind the tape around the watch and secure it to Bill's wrist.

I run out of tape just as the first Cù-Sìth arrives.

Tendrils of dark green smoke slink through the window and snake their way around the desk, widening and solidifying into a bear-sized hound with shaggy green fur and glowing red eyes. His long-braided tail snaps like a whip, cracking the tension-filled air while paws as big as my head scrape their long claws against the tile.

Jane doesn't move. I don't even think she breathes. I can't stop trembling, pleading for the good in the world to banish the hound from my sight.

Like the time I was ten, my pleas go unanswered.

The hound shoves his box-shaped head between Bill and me, his nose twitching until he latches onto a scent.

A hungry growl vibrates through the hound's immense chest. Slowly, he turns toward Bill, meeting him square in his eyes. Drool drips from his needle-length fangs, falling against Bill's shoulder and sizzling like acid. He licks the air near Bill's throat. My trembles turn into full out convulsions. He sniffs again. He's almost on top of us.

The hound's gaze cuts to me when a small cry breaks through my quivering lips. He pauses, drawing in a deep breath and trailing his scorching ember eyes down my body. I'm certain he can sense me, until he looks past me toward the metal door where claws scrape again, and again, and again. More death hounds have arrived.

The hound between us returns his attention to where Bill kneels, curling the lips of his long snout into a hideous snarl. He senses Bill's soul and wants it for himself. He sniffs again. He knows Bill is here. Like the strike of a cobra, the hound snaps at the air, puncturing through Bill's face.

The cords of Bill's neck strain as he struggles to contain his moans. I'm certain Bill is done for. But the magic from his talisman holds strong, veiling Bill's presence and masking the taste of his blood.

Dark blood dribbles from the hound's fangs, staining his dark green fur. I cup my hand over my mouth as the hound withdraws and I see what remains of my friend's face.

Mangled skin dangles in flaps against Bill's neck. It's all I can do to keep from screaming. Talismans muffle sounds, but they have their limits, and nothing on earth will be able to silence the horror shredding my insides if I let loose.

Bill's heavy hand encases my small one. He's trying to comfort me and encouraging me to be strong. But how can I be strong when Death has arrived to tear him apart?

I jump when roars bellow behind the door. The pack of Cù-Sìth lingering outside is growing more insistent.

I press my hand tighter against my mouth to stifle my sobs. It's not right for Bill to die this way. He's good and kind. It's not his time.

Two more hounds materialize like smoke through the door-jamb, silencing my cries. These are swathed in matted white fur. They stalk around the office, growling and frantic to eat. One of them knocks into the green one as if demanding food. The green one barrels her over, perceiving her actions as a challenge.

They fight like hungry beasts over a piece of meat, clawing, biting, and snarling.

More hounds arrive. They prowl restlessly, sniffing for prey and ignoring the fight. The white hound never stood a chance against the green. He dominates her, driving her into the opposite wall of the large office.

In one fierce move, the green hound flips over the female. He pins her to the floor and digs his fangs into her belly, tearing it open like rotting flesh. Souls spill from her gut in waves of translucent images. I recognize the faint forms of dwarves and fairies, their agonized faces pleading with me to help them.

Tears spill down my face. I wish I could help. But like the rest of my kind, there's nothing I can do except hide.

The dead try to flee, except the remaining Cù-Sìth are too fast. The pack sweeps through the door like a raging fog of white and green, mauling the already damaged souls.

Bill and I wrench our faces away, unable to stand the terror-filled cries and slurping noises of the feasting hounds.

I steal a glance as the last of the shrieks die out, hoping they're done. The hounds remain, raking their claws and scavenging for more. The spirits all are gone... except for one little Fae.

A sprite hides trembling in the corner of Bill's Juris Doctorate diploma. But just as I see her, so do the hounds.

The Alpha who bit Bill's face spots her first. He lunges, trampling over the others who try to intercept him. The little sprite shoots through the window, screaming in pain and fear.

In streams of white and dark green smoke, the hounds give chase. I want to race after her and help. But I no longer have wings to fly nor magic to save her. My pathetic attempts to summon my power proved as much.

I sniff meekly. The little sprite needs someone stronger than me.

I weep in silence for the souls that will never find peace and curse all forms of Death for filling their bellies instead of carrying their charge to eternal rest.

Bill and I rise carefully when the roars of the Cù-Sìth grow too faint to hear. He keeps his hand over mine until my trembling subsides and my tears stop falling, speaking kind words while his body mends his ravaged face and Jane's enchantments repair the damage to the office.

With Jane's help, Bill recalls his glamour. The moment his resemblance of Laurence Fishburne returns, Jane goes to work on repairing his talisman as only an Ancient can.

It takes time and an endless well of power to recharge damaged magic. Time Jane wouldn't have without the makeshift band the tape provided. Forged from rare copper, gold, and silver found only in Fae and triggered by rare gemstones and diamonds from Fae mountains, talismans are a wonder. They serve to hide us and open the portals between our homeland and earth. Yet to open the portal, you must remove your talisman and risk a direct call to Death.

My father took that risk, and it cost him his soul.

Jane nods to Bill and lifts her wand when she finishes. He walks naked to the opposite wall tugging on links to test her work. It's only when her magic seems to hold that the tension surrounding him eases.

Bill punches a small indiscriminate button hidden in the dark mahogany paneling. Two sets of doors part, unveiling a hidden bar. He pours a large helping of Irish whiskey into a glass and downs it, and another. He then removes a pair of pants and a fresh shirt from his closet. As soon as he dresses, he pours another drink and offers it to me.

"No, thank you, Bill."

"Cathasach," Jane spits through her teeth.

Bill nods. "I know."

My gaze dances between them. "What?"

"The green Cù-Sìth," he says. "The Alpha." Bill tips back the glass, this time only taking a small, hesitant sip. His hand is quivering. I didn't notice it before. I see it now despite the shots of courage he poured down his throat. "Cathasach is the father of all the death hounds and the first to taste Life. It was he who convinced the other forms of Death to feed on the souls of the living." He knocks back the glass, draining it of its amber fluid.

"The Cù-Sìth originally carried the souls of mountain Fae into the Afterlife," I say, my tears close to the surface. "They were peaceful. I don't understand how they became what we saw."

Bill's eyebrows knit tight, his anger momentarily shoving aside his fear. "It doesn't matter what they were, only what they are, creatures who lack souls of their own with no conscience or respect for the Fae they consume. Did you see their size? They're enormous from the plethora of spirits trapped within them. There's no rationale. No pity. No pardon. No loyalty. Like all forms of Death, they're selfish and their appetites insatiable. Look at how easily they turned on their own."

He pours a fresh shot and brings it to Jane. She takes a few gulps and resumes her wand waving over the admin. "Tell her she's fired," Bill says, his deep voice laced with resentment.

Jane nods and tosses the rest of the liquor down her throat. I retrieve her glass and return it to the bar. It seems wrong to end our conversation this way, without hope or gentle words to remind us we're safe. But this sense of safety is a momentary luxury, nothing that's guaranteed. Even with our talismans, Death is never far away.

I try to leave the office and this experience behind. Bill's deep baritone halts my sluggish steps, keeping me in place. "Olivia, Cathasach knew you were here. The way he took you in, somehow he knew."

My response is almost robotic. "We've met before. I just didn't know his name."

Jane stops chanting. Bill chokes on his next sip of whiskey. He rushes to me and grips my arms. "You met him before today?"

I nod, shaking from the force of his trembles. "Twice," I admit.

The color drains from his face. "Listen to me, Olivia. Do not remove your talisman, ever," he whispers tightly. "If you escape a hound more than once, you become more than prey, you become an obsession. He'll want you and not stop until he finds you."

This is the last thing I need to hear. I break free and run from the room. In my haste, I slam into Ryker.

I bounce off his broad torso and land hard on my ass. Shock parts my lips. Considering I'm the one sprawled on the marble tile, he seems plenty pissed.

Perspiration feathers his forehead and his chest rises and falls in furious bursts. He clenches his fists, his blue eyes searing as he looms over me.

By the way his imposing form takes me in, I should be terrified. Mostly, I'm baffled by his rage.

I try to stand, feeling vulnerable. Before I can make it to my feet, Ryker storms away.

2

Ryker disappears down the hall, his stride purposeful and threatening, sending the staff loitering in the halls to skitter from his path. Despite his gift for intimidation, the women home in on his backside like it's on sale and they have coupons. They can keep their coupons and chomp on his ass like bubble gum for all I care.

I return to my desk, passing my fingers along my talisman and praying to my ancestors for strength. As the cool metal slips from my hands, I force myself to work. Typing, filing, and copying means I'm still alive and breathing. It sounds irrational, perhaps, but it beats hiding under my desk in terror. I pause in the middle of arranging the stack of discovery documents opposing counsel requested, remembering my pathetic performance in Bill's office. Jane is certain I have something special. Can't she see how wrong she is?

With a defeated sigh, I resume my typing. I've only written a word or two when Marco flies out of his office. The gold tie around his thick neck is off-center, and what remains of his hair is dripping wet. Well, at least he showered.

"You forgot your briefcase," I call out.

With a curse, he rushes back into his office, slamming the door when he reappears with his briefcase.

"And your phone," I add.

More swearing, more rushing.

He flies past me. I pick up my office phone to warn his driver to be ready. Marco has fired six drivers in the year and a half I've worked at MacGregor and Santonelli. I don't have time to interview another. Patient, punctual, and ass-kissing drivers are hard to find in the Tri-State area.

Jane shuffles by a few minutes later and returns to her seat. She motions with a jerk of her narrow chin to Bill's office and holds up ten fingers. I hit the speed dial to Bill's line. It rings from his private bathroom. "Liv?"

"Jane says you owe her ten grand."

"*What*? All she did was alter a memory and clean up the office. A brownie would've done it for a few bills."

I look at Jane. She smacks her butt and hooks a thumb across her throat. With a rather smug grin, she shakes her talisman at me.

Jane is an Ancient of few words, only speaking when she feels it's absolutely necessary. Those of us who know her understand her well enough. I clear my throat. This is not a conversation I want to engage in with Bill. "Jane feels a brownie would have abandoned your ass at the first sign of Death and insists no brownie alive can fix your talisman."

"But—"

"Bill, take it up with the Hydra."

That's not a joke. Bill goes gargoyle with a human's kiss. Jane becomes the Hydra, a serpent-like beast with poisonous breath and multiple heads flailing wildly from her tiny black-swathed body.

A pause follows his defeated sigh. "Fine," Bill says, and disconnects.

I'm finally starting to get work done when a soft, flirty laugh rings a few feet away.

My roommate and best friend, Dahlia, shimmies down the hall. The associates and staff abandon their tasks, scrambling to gawk at her sensual beauty.

Her nymph-ness always guarantees attention, whether she wants to or not. It's not intentional. It's simply what Dahlia is.

When it comes to executing her bookkeeping and office manager duties, Dahlia always dresses somewhat conservatively, *somewhat*. After all, a nymph is a nymph and all that good stuff.

Today's outfit is a 50's-inspired navy baby doll dress. The wide white collar and bright red bow tied at the center suggests playful innocence. Dahlia might have pulled it off if the hem didn't stop above her knees and her hips didn't swing seductively.

An associate dives in front of her, anxious to strike up a conversation. Dahlia edges away from him as if he's doused with gasoline and he's offering her a match, not a date.

Fae are "allergic" to humans. Any level of physical intimacy be it a kiss, or something more, results in disaster. Some Fae lose their glamour, like Bill. Others morph into their dormant forms and sprout snakes for limbs, like Jane. Even more lose their magic for days.

Dahlia breaks out in head to toe boils.

I seem to be the only Fae immune to human intimacy. My lack of magic probably has something to do with it. I won't complain. Last time Dahlia broke out, she had to soak in a bathtub filled with swamp water for hours while enchanted frogs scrubbed down her skin.

Dahlia offers a pleasant smile and hurries down the rows of offices and cubicles. The associate scoffs. He's not used to rejection. Neither are the other young men and the occasional women who have attempted to get to know Dahlia. It's the reason she rarely leaves her office on the floor below. She doesn't want to be rude, but better rude than covered in boils.

She leans her tall form over Jane's cubicle, her midnight hair falling forward as she hands Jane a crisp new check. "Good morning, Jane," she says sweetly. "This is from Bill."

Jane takes it and shoves it through the collar of her black dress, tucking it in her bra located roughly at her waist. Dahlia straightens and opens the cover to her iPad. "We're ordering lunch from the deli. Would you like a sandwich, darling?"

Dahlia grins when Jane meets her gaze, teeth brilliant white against her ebony skin. "Roast beef on rye with ketchup it is." She frowns when Jane blinks twice. "Jane, I'm not ordering those prepackaged pies. They're bad for you—" Dahlia sighs when the skin around Jane's beady eyes crinkles. "Fine, Jane. But no more than two, missy."

Jane, now satisfied, resumes her two-finger typing. Dahlia flounces into my cubicle and sits with swan-like grace at the edge of my desk. "What would you like, darling?"

I'm not up to eating. I'm barely up to breathing. I start to tell her when she snatches my hands into hers, her long fingers frantically stroking me. "Livvie, you're shaking. What's wrong, darling?"

My nerves remain on edge, and my hands reflect as much, trembling violently as if I'm standing naked in the middle of an icy tundra. I withdraw my hands from hers and reach for my tea. The cup doesn't quite make it to my lips when I spill the tepid liquid on my dress.

Dahlia takes the cup from me and places it back on the desk. She grabs a small stack of tissues from the box and dabs the front of my dress. "Livvie, darling…."

"The Cù-Sìth were here," I manage.

Dahlia stills, then very slowly, turns from side to side. "It's all right," I say quietly. "They're gone."

Dahlia's chocolate-brown eyes shimmer with fear. She leans. "How did this happen?"

I take the wad of tissues from her grip and toss it in the trash, the effort resuming a sense of normalcy I wouldn't expect from such a mundane task. "Bill changed when the new hire's tongue met the back of his throat. His talisman is fixed to his watch. It snapped off when he went gargoyle."

Dahlia's long braids brush against her shoulders as she shakes her head. "I've told Bill more than once that he needs his talisman around his neck, not on that blessed watch."

"I know. His dormant form is too immense." I blow a breath hard enough to flutter my long bangs. "I suppose he never thought a human, especially one here, would be so bold."

Dahlia smiles sadly. "Humans are bolder than we give them credit for, darling."

"I've noticed," I reply, my small smile reflecting hers.

Dahlia has a way of calming me just by being her. Like the flower she's known for, she's vibrant and beautiful. She glances behind her to where Jane *tap... tap... tap*s on her keyboard. "Bill should have Jane incorporate his talisman into a long chain. Perhaps something with a spring capable of expanding."

"He should," I agree. "But I bet it will be pricey."

Jane stops typing and winks. Yup. It's going to cost Bill a fortune.

Dahlia plays with her talisman, running the strand of pearls it's fixed to between her fingers. "Darling," she says. "I didn't so much as sense them. No one did. I heard thunder but dismissed it as a passing storm."

"I think it's because you weren't in close proximity to Bill." I motion around. "Jane and I are the only Fae on this side of the building." My voice lowers. "We were with Bill when they manifested."

"Asshats," Jane croaks.

Dahlia gapes at me. "You saw them?" I nod. "My darling, of all the forms of Death that could have appeared…"

"It had to be the one who killed my family," I finish for her.

Fear pricks at my skin. This time, so does anger. I wish I possessed the power to destroy Death or, at the very least, enough to fight back.

I was only four years old when we crossed over from Fae. My father shut the portal behind us, protecting us from Cathasach and preventing his pack from following into Earth's realm. Father's talisman was the key to that portal. In removing it, he revealed himself to Death, and it cost him his life and soul.

Sometimes, I still hear his screams at night.

"Darling?"

I refocus on Dahlia, unsure how much time has passed. Tears I didn't realize I'd shed dampen my cheeks. "I'm sorry. What?"

She brushes the final tear that follows. Her fingertips are warm, and her touch is gentle against my skin. "I asked if you wanted to take the rest of the day off? I'm certain Bill will insist upon it given your state."

I smirk. "Are you saying you'll take over Marco duties when he returns from court?"

Dahlia makes a sour face and waves me off. "Pffft. Certainly not." She angles around, her smile magnetic. "Jane darling, do you think you could take care of Marco this afternoon? Nothing special. Perhaps just fetch his coffee and answer a few calls?"

Jane responds with a stiff middle finger. She's hated Marco since the time he held a mirror under her nose to make sure she was still breathing.

"He's not that bad," I insist. I reach into my bottom drawer and grab a stack of paper to load into the printer. "He just mourns differently than the rest of us."

For the most part, I lead a happy life, having learned long ago to shove my pain away where it can't debilitate me. Today, following the arrival of those hounds, my fear broke through the vault where I've locked it away. Marco hasn't quite mastered his grief. On days like this one, so close to his wedding anniversary, he's almost intolerable.

Well, to anyone but me.

"You think he still mourns his wife, darling." Dahlia isn't really asking. She knows that's exactly what I think. If anything, she's trying to change the subject for our benefit.

There isn't a Fae alive who doesn't fear Death. How can there be? With more than a dozen forms, all vicious, all hungry, all on the prowl, it's a wonder our kind has made it this long.

Humans are lucky. Their version of Death only claims those who've reached the end of their lives, are injured beyond help, or who fall terminally ill like Marco's wife, Marion. He did everything to save her, but it wasn't enough.

My gaze drifts to the silver frame on Marco's desk. Marco can't be more than thirty in that photo. He's a little leaner, his hair thicker, and his attire impeccable. Marion rests in his arms, her red hair blazing against her champagne wedding gown. She wasn't someone men crossed traffic to speak to like Dahlia. She wasn't thin nor heavy. If it weren't for her hair, she likely could have entered a crowded room and gone unnoticed. But her eyes were kind, her cheeks flushed with excitement and her happiness as palpable as Marco's. Marion was beautiful. And she loved Marco.

"He misses her every day," I finally answer.

"He does," Dahlia agrees. "Which is why you're the only one who can handle him, darling."

I toss the empty packaging into the recycling can. "Not the

only one." I roll my eyes. "You should see him around Captain Awesomeness."

"Excuse me?"

"Ryker," I clarify. "There's something odd about him, Dahlia." I scoot closer to her. "Haven't you noticed how people around here fall all over themselves to make him happy, even though they seem afraid of him?"

Dahlia gives it some thought. "I don't think afraid is the right word."

"Why not?" I ask.

Dahlia giggles. "Livvie, the guy is a walking piece of sculpted marble. He intimidates just by breathing."

"He doesn't intimidate Marco," I reply. "They have some kind of bromance going on." I deepen my light voice as much as I can manage. "Hello, *sir*. Let me flex my Herculean muscles so you can see how magnificent I am."

It's a pathetic attempt to mimic Ryker's voice, not that it discourages me from trying to imitate Marco. "*Olivia*. Stop your hard work and come bask in Ryker's splendor. Hurry up. He's flexing!"

Dahlia throws back her head, her laughter echoing like a chorus of bells. I hold out my hands. "I'm not exaggerating," I tell her. "Marco even refers to him as 'son.'"

Dahlia sighs and reaches for her iPad. "Darling, Marco has every right to praise him. Ryker is making the firm an outrageous amount of money. He's brilliant and a real shark in court." She smiles. "And don't get me started on that rock-hard ass of his. You could crack an oyster on that beauty."

"Thank you."

We jump at the sound of Ryker's throaty timbre. "Mr. I Can Shuck Oysters with my Butt Cheeks" arrived like a shadow.

I'm not sure if Dahlia is blushing, but I certainly am. She

practically falls off the desk in her haste to scramble away. "D-d-do you want a sandwich?" she asks him like a dumbass.

"*No.*"

"Okay, bye." She runs. Yes, *runs* down the length of the hall. Her admirers shoot out from their perspective offices and cubicles to get one last look.

Jane stops her so-called typing just to turn around and laugh at me. Nice. I thought girlfriend was on my side.

I whirl around and return to my computer screen, scrolling through the icons as if I have some life-altering memo to write and doing my best to ignore the piercing blue eyes searing a hole into my back. I click on my legal documents file and pretend to review the one that pops up.

"I've been offered a new case," Ryker says, his voice irritated.

I ignore him.

"It's high profile," he adds.

I start typing more information into the brief. Not that it needs it.

"You're going to help me with it."

My fingers slow to a stop over my keyboard. Anger dissolves what remains of my humiliation. I swivel my seat to face him, gripping the armrests to keep from hurtling a paperweight at him. "You have an army of associates and legal assistants at your disposal. Command one of them to help you."

Ryker squares his jaw. "I don't want an associate. I want a paralegal and admin who knows what the hell she's doing."

"You already have one," I remind him.

"Chelsea is barely competent on her best days and embarrassing on her worst. *I want you.*"

I stand hard enough to roll my chair away and shove my hands on my hips. "Well, you can't have me. Marco's in the middle of a huge case—"

"We spoke before he left." His gruff voice deepens. "He said if I need you, I could have you."

I count off five names, using my fingers. "Tara, Willow, Amy, Kimmi, Sue. They're all excellent. Pick one of them."

"*No.*" He clenches his teeth, his tone bordering on lethal. "*You're* the only one who can help me."

It takes all I have not to punch him in his perfect nose.

3

I spend the next two weeks seeing to Ryker's every need. Well, in between dashes to Marco's office to make sure he doesn't wear the same suit to court every day. I expect my time with Ryker to be tension filled and cutthroat at best. At first, it is. I only speak if spoken to or if there is an issue that needs his immediate attention. Things change when his client's case unfolds, and her needs take precedence.

Brielle is the wife of a New York aristocrat, Pence Chandler. She met him when she was seventeen and waitressing. As a broke high school drop-out, she was the perfect person for a predator like Pence to target. He wined and dined her. He also took her virginity against her will.

Anxiety-ridden and emotionally traumatized from decades of abuse, Brielle is painfully fragile and addicted to oxycodone. She's hard to calm and even harder to focus.

Ryker's patience with Brielle surprises me. He remains calm and gentle even when she falls into hysterics. Yet, it's not enough. Brielle is terrified of Ryker. He has to sit across the room when we meet while I sit beside her, holding her hand and serving as a buffer.

"Don't worry about taking notes," he told me before our first meeting. "We'll record our sessions and address her issues later. "Soothe her with your voice and praise any show of strength she demonstrates. Most importantly, never leave us alone. Every man Brielle has known has harmed her. To her, I'm just another potential abuser. I need her to trust me. It's the only way I can help her."

I lower a fresh cup of coffee on Ryker's desk. "Why are you helping her?" I ask.

I feel him watching me as I return to my seat. But as I settle, I realize the only thing on his mind is work. He scrolls through his computer, his focus intense.

We spend the morning discussing an incident with Brielle in which Pence locked her in a dog kennel for several days. Brielle can't brave through the session, so we're forced to end early.

Ryker reaches for the coffee as he flips through the file I composed earlier. The sleeves of his crisp white shirt are rolled and hug his muscular forearms. He ditched his tie around four o'clock. It lays over the armrest of his leather couch beside his jacket.

He furrows his thick brows. "She's a client."

I tug the hem of my olive tank dress, keeping my legs crossed although he can't see them beneath my new desk. That's right, my *new* desk. It wasn't enough to work directly with Ryker. I was moved *into* his office.

He reasoned that my cubical was on the opposite end of the building, creating challenges should he need me. I reasoned he was out of his damn mind. The first few days were claustrophobic, his commanding presence appearing to take up the entire room despite its large expanse.

Now, it's not so bad.

"You're a criminal defense attorney," I remind him. "This is a divorce case."

Ryker leans back, examining me closely. "The extent of the abuse Brielle has endured is more in line with my criminal law expertise. Another attorney will handle the divorce settlement, including compensation for her psychiatric and medical care."

I wrinkle my nose. "Pence will deny everything. He and his team will rally witnesses and paint Brielle as an unstable gold digger."

Ryker pushes the file away and takes a sip of his coffee. "I don't care. As long as Brielle keeps it together, I can prove the abuse."

"What is it?" he asks when I remain quiet. "You don't seem satisfied with my response."

I swivel in my chair, still puzzled. "This just isn't your typical case."

"No. It's not."

I stop moving. "Then why did you take it?"

"She needs protection," Ryker replies. "The legal army at Pence's disposal will eat Brielle alive without proper representation. With his reputation and that of his family's on the line, they'll stop at nothing to destroy her."

I almost don't say what I do. It comes out anyway. "The victims in your other cases needed protection, too."

His gaze locks on mine. "I know."

This is the first time Ryker has acknowledged that they were victims; those harmed by the men he's represented. It grants me a new perspective. Ryker isn't someone pretending to save a fallen hero. Nor is he taking these cases for the fame and fortune they guarantee.

He's an attorney. One who dutifully represents his clients, including someone as heartbreaking as Brielle.

I find myself smiling, recalling the kindness and compassion he's demonstrated to Brielle. Captain Awesomeness is human after all.

Ryker angles his chin, seemingly surprised that I'm capable of more than glowering and grumbling. His gaze softens, and for the briefest of moments, the corner of his mouth curves into a smirk.

I rest my chin on my hand. Hmmm, that dimple isn't so bad. It's cute. Sexy…

"I'm sorry. Am I interrupting something?" Chelsea, Ryker's admin and paralegal, rests against the doorframe, her tall, voluptuous body poised for a better view of her assets. Her finger twirls a long strand of hair. She laughs. "It seems that I am."

Ryker lifts a pen and scribbles his signature on a letter to opposing counsel. "We're working," he answers with all the warmth of an ice cube. "Is there something you want?"

Besides her legs wrapped around your waist? Probably not. The old Olivia, the one in college, would have replied as much. The new Olivia has the class and grace to keep her thoughts, however true, to herself.

I've never had a problem with Chelsea, a rarity considering the female staff has rallied to publicly stone her more than once. But I've also never associated with her in the past. That changed when I began working with Ryker.

It started out with a few bumps when we'd pass each other in the hall. Don't get me wrong, the first time, it seemed innocent enough, both of us distracted and appearing rushed. The second incident wasn't so innocent. She's bigger than me and the documents I was sorting through went flying. "Oops, sorry," she said, hurrying away and not bothering to help me.

There were also days I'd arrive at work with all my writing tools missing, paperwork out of numerical order, and Chelsea laughing as she runway strutted past the door. Petty? Yes. Worth flipping out over? Not yet.

Chelsea smiles impishly, her bright red lipstick giving her an unfair pouty mouth. "You've had a long day, Ryke. I thought you could use you a cup of java."

Ryker motions to the coffee on his desk with his pen. "Olivia already took care of me."

"I'll bet she did," Chelsea replies. She pushes away from the door and struts toward him, giving me a generous view of her curves as she bends over to place another cup of coffee on Ryker's desk. "Here. Have something hotter."

I didn't miss the tension in Ryker's jaw when she referred to him as "Ryke." It was too familiar. I wonder briefly if they've been intimate before deciding I'd rather not know. Chelsea is a walking version of Barbie. Me? At barely five feet tall with crazy rainbow hair, I'm more Skateboard Skipper.

"I don't need more coffee." Ryker's attention shifts to me. "What about you, Olivia?"

Well, doesn't that just that stick a bee in Chelsea's too-tight skirt? "Tea would be lovely, but I can make it myself."

Chelsea whips around. "Yes, *you* can," she interjects. Rage flares like fire around her. I do a double-take, confused by her anger and why she's marching toward me.

"Chelsea." Ryker's steely voice glues her in place.

She shudders once, twice, taking several gulps of air before composing herself. I half expect her to turn into a werewolf. "Yes, Ryke?" she asks, smiling sweetly.

"Address me as Mr. Scott," he snaps. "Don't interrupt us again."

It takes Chelsea a moment to move again. Who am I kidding? It takes *me* a moment to move again. My gaze bounces between them as the tension surges out of control. She seems seconds from, I don't know, screaming? Sprouting a tail? Instead, she squares her shoulders and leaves, her stilettos stabbing against the tile.

Office drama exists everywhere, and this firm has seen its share. But Chelsea's demeanor borders on dangerous. I almost expected her to attack.

I return to my work, debating if I should nail garlic to the crazy bitch's cubicle when an email catches my attention. Oh, no. "Ryker, the court clerk just reached out to me. Brielle made a formal request to dismiss her restraining order."

Ryker presses his palms against his desk and rises. "It's only been two days since the judge granted it!"

And it took an entire week of testimony to obtain it. Brielle had barely survived.

"Why would she drop it?" he says.

He knows why. Like me, he just doesn't want to admit it. I forward the email as I speak. "The clerk didn't mention a reason and apologizes for not calling you sooner. She was in a different hearing, and the attending clerk didn't think to make you aware." I slump into my seat as I finish reading. "The only reason a judge didn't hear Brielle's request today is because of the late hour. She's scheduled to go before Judge Ormond first thing in the morning."

Ryker's frown deepens as he reads the email. "Brielle did this without consulting me."

"I know." I shake my head. "What else do you think she's done without you?"

Anger seethes like a building twister along Ryker's features. "Call her, now. I'll phone the prosecutor's office to make sure she hasn't dropped the fucking criminal charges."

I call every number and contact we have. I can't find Brielle anywhere. After an hour of trying to locate her, and following Ryker's swearing match with opposing counsel, I leave for a much-needed cup of tea.

My hands pass along my hair. We've had a long day, and it's far from over. Yet I hope for more time, just for Brielle.

I enter our formal lounge and head toward the black and chrome kitchen. Once a month, the partners pay a caterer to serve the staff an elaborate lunch. It's one of the many perks of working at such a prestigious firm.

I turn on the Keurig and start a fresh cup of coffee for Ryker, before sorting through the tins of tea. I groan when a pair of stilettos stamp along the tile behind me. Once again, the unstable skank that is Chelsea graces me with her presence.

"Are you screwing him?" she asks.

She doesn't even wait for me to turn around. "I don't blame you," she adds. "He's a fine piece of ass."

A month or so ago, her comment would have been laughable. Not today. Brielle is in trouble and in possible danger. I'm scared for her and feeling protective of Ryker.

I cross my arms. Chelsea's viciousness is reminiscent of a serpent ready to strike. She's a woman who enjoys intimidating and hurting those who'll allow it. Being petite, I look younger than twenty-six. I smile often and rarely raise my voice. It's understandable why Chelsea perceives me as an easy target. But I'm not weak.

The sun will freeze before I take this psycho's shit.

"You're out of line," I tell her.

"Am I?" She pouts her lips. "You've only been here a year and a half. How is it you're the highest paid admin in the firm? Doing more than fetching coffee?"

"I'm doing a lot more," I agree. "I stay late every day. I work weekends and holidays when our attorneys need extra help. I take on tasks no one seems to have time for and organize events to reward the staff. I go above and beyond my duties, and I'm rewarded for it. For you to suggest I'm engaging in inappropriate behavior is offensive and ridiculous."

A wicked grin spreads across her face. She's enjoying herself. "I'm sure you've been rewarded. My boss is equipped to thank you in every way and in every position possible." She slithers her way to the counter and dips her finger into a leftover piece of cheesecake. Slowly, she flicks her tongue up and down, closing her eyes as she sucks the last bit of cream from the tip. "Mm. Good." She smiles without humor. "How good does Ryker taste?"

Professionalism has its limits and, when push comes to shove, you don't mess with a pixie.

I scoop a chunk of cake and smash it into her face, tangling my fingers into her hair to keep her in place. She whips from side to side, slapping at my arms. I snag another handful and add a second layer. As I reach for more, she breaks free in one furious lurch.

Chelsea wipes globs of cake from her eyes, the fury she demonstrated in Ryker's office returning in one foul sweep. "I'll have you fired for keeping him from me!"

Her response gives me pause. "What?"

She glances around as if someone else spoke. Nope, that bit of crazy was all you, Chels.

Chelsea glares, like I'm the lunatic here. "I said, I'll have you fired for this."

She towers over me, but I've had my share of smackdowns, and I'm not afraid to fight. I close the space between us. "Is that so? Who's doing the firing, Marco or Bill? Which senior partner has *your* back, Chelsea? You're lazy and inept. The only attention you've earned is from spreading your legs like a pair of wings!"

"*Get out.*"

The air stills, lodging painfully in my chest. Ryker stands in the doorway, his hands balled into fists. Aside from the time I ran into him, I've never seen him so furious.

"*Fine*," I snap, storming toward the door. "Good luck getting any work done with bleached bitch Barbie!"

He turns his gaze upward and swears. "Not *you*, Olivia."

"Huh?"

Ryker doesn't bother elaborating. He walks to my side, keeping his glare trained on Chelsea. "As of this moment, you're banned from the building," he tells her. "Take your purse and leave. You can return for your personal items with a security escort only."

Chelsea bursts into tears, composes herself, then starts crying all over again. When she speaks, there's no trace of sadness, only enough anger to burn.

She points to me, her hand shaking. "Olivia assaulted me. I can sue her. I can sue *you* and this whole damn firm."

Steel carries more warmth than what Ryker offers. "Try it. Your attorney won't stand a chance against us."

Chelsea's demeanor dissolves, whatever emotions she's feeling numbing her. She walks past us slowly, her steps unsure as if treading through rough terrain.

What. The. Hell?

"Chelsea?" Ryker calls. "Don't forget, we have surveillance of your actions from the first moment you stepped into this building." He motions to the ceiling where a security camera flashes a red light.

Chelsea takes off running. Ryker trails her. I rinse my hands quickly and alert security, hurrying after them. With just a few strokes of her keyboard, Chelsea can access a great deal of confidential information. We can't allow her to leave with anything damaging.

Security meets us in the hall just as my office phone rings. Ryker and I exchange glances. The line is secure. We know who it is. I race into the office and throw myself across the desk to answer it. "MacGregor and Santonelli."

Brielle's voice shakes, thick with tears. "O-Olivia?"

I press the button to speaker. "I'm here, Brielle. So is Ryker."

Ryker grips the edge of my desk. "Are you all right?" he asks.

"I-I'm fine," she stammers. "Everything's fine. Just fine."

The fear in her voice echoes with a ghost-like air. Ryker tightens his grip, his voice calm considering his anger. "You motioned to have the restraining order dropped without consulting me. Has Pence been in touch? Did he make you do this?"

"He didn't make me do anything. I-I-I wanted to."

If she were here, I'd hug her. "Why, Brielle?" I ask. "You're so close to being free of him."

Brielle doesn't cry that sad, soft way some women do. She cries like a child who is scared and hurt. "I don't want to lose him. He l-loves me, Olivia."

"*What*?"

I clasp Ryker's arm to calm him. He fixes on my hand and takes several controlled breaths. "Tell me what's happening," he adds more calmly.

"Pence is different. He's ch-changed."

I can barely understand the words coming out of her mouth. She sniffs, trying to collect herself enough to speak. "He's asked me to forgive him. He wants us to b-be together. Like a real family."

This is the same man who's choked her and forced her to have sex with other men as he beat her.

Ryker leans into the phone. "Brielle, listen to me. You're scared. I don't want you to be. The restraining order and all the steps you've taken will help you finally be safe and happy. Don't let him take that away from you."

Brielle's choking breaths clench my heart. But it's the low whisper I catch in the background that sends it racing. "Tell him, he works for you. That it's your decision. Not his."

Pence is there with her. I dig my nails into Ryker's skin. He can't hear him, but I can. "Pence is coaching her," I whisper. "I can hear him."

Ryker looks ready to break my desk in half. He motions to my cell phone. I snatch it off the desk along with Brielle's contact information.

"Where are you?" he asks Brielle.

The calmness in his voice is miraculous. I can barely dial. I rush out of the room and into the hall, whispering into the phone. "This is Olivia Finn at the law firm of MacGregor and Santonelli. One of our clients is in danger and being held against her will. I need patrols at the following addresses."

The screaming from my landline has me jetting back in. "*Help me*," Brielle pleads. "*Help me!*"

A gun blasts.

Then silence. Only silence.

"Hello? Hello? Ma'am?"

My cell phone slips from my grasp. I stare at the office phone, unable to answer the dispatcher.

Ryker swears, charging from the office like a storm.

4

Two weeks have passed since Brielle's murder. Her death was ruled a home invasion gone wrong. It was horrible and wrong. Worst of all, we couldn't prove Pence was involved. Ryker hadn't heard his voice, and all I had was my super-secret pixie hearing as evidence.

Pence's legal team had him out on bail within hours. With no victim, all pending charges against him were dropped. I was miserable, convinced life was so unfair... until pieces of Pence were discovered floating along the Hudson River.

No one knew who killed Pence, and not too many people seemed to care. Pence had made his share of enemies in life. What struck me was *how* he died, sliced in half from left shoulder to right hip, clean cut. The coroners and detectives were baffled as to what type of device could have made such a precision cut, especially once it was determined Pence was alive pre-cut.

I wish I could say he didn't deserve it.

I returned to my cubicle, to my Marco duties, and to Ryker barely doing more than nodding in my direction. I thought our time helping Brielle would bond us and that maybe we'd become friends. I was wrong. We've barely spoken.

When Friday arrives, I gather my courage and knock on his office door. "Yes?"

I open the door and smile. I hadn't shared his office for long, yet my gaze wanders to the empty space where my desk once stood. It seems so barren.

"Hey," I say.

Today Ryker is wearing a dark blue silk shirt with a silver tie. The jacket hangs from the open door of his closet. He shuts his laptop and offers me a curt nod. "Olivia."

"Hey," I say again. Well, isn't this going just peachy? "May I come in?"

He motions me to one of the leather chairs perched in front of his desk. "How can I help you?"

His throaty timbre makes me smile. I missed it and hadn't realized until now. "It's been a rough few weeks, hasn't it?" I ask.

A flicker of understanding dances along his strong features. Aside from that, and the breaths he takes, he doesn't react. My thumb grazes over the stack of mail I need to leave at the desk for the courier. "Ah, Dahlia and I are going to the Glen tonight. To celebrate the long weekend."

"That restricted dance club in the city?"

No. Any and all Fae are welcomed. Just not any humans. "Yes. But before then, we're having dinner in Hoboken at Leo's Grandevous. I was wondering if you'd like to join us for dinner."

"You want to have dinner with me."

It's more of a statement than a question. My toes curl, and I find myself blushing. "Dahlia will be there, too," I add quickly.

My blush deepens when he doesn't do more than look at me. Why is this so hard?

There's a knock on the door. I welcome it like a boxer following a brutal round.

"Come in, Judith," Ryker says.

His new assistant hurries in with a stack of folders, her steely gray hair tied into a tight bun. She lays out each folder in front of Ryker. I recognize a few motions and a letter to the superior court judge, along with a name I didn't need to see.

"Here is everything you asked for, Mr. Scott," Judith says. "I'll be at my desk should you need anything else." She smiles before hurrying out. "Nice to see you, Olivia."

I barely hear the door shut, the name on the documents making me see red. "That says Bryan Spackler."

Ryker threads his fingers together. "It does."

"He's the football player accused of raping that young fan in the bathroom." I stand slowly. Ryker watches me, exactly as he did when Brielle cried, while she relived everything that monster had done to her.

"Olivia—"

"How can you do this?" I demand. "You've seen firsthand how these men torment their victims. How can you go back to representing them?"

He stands and crosses his arm. "It's not so simple, Olivia."

A sense of betrayal burns a hole in my stomach. He knew Brielle. He saw how fragile she was and how nothing we did would ever erase the trauma she endured. Of all the cases Ryker could take, he took on another high-profile client with plenty of money to buy his freedom and his innocence.

"I'm sure it's not," I fire back. "How else will you make junior partner in the next year?"

A slap across his face would have been less damaging than my words. Every muscle in his body tenses as if clinging to life.

He leans forward, pressing his palms against his desk. "You have *no idea* what I'm doing."

"Yes, I do," I bite out. "Believe me, you're the right man for

the job." I barrel out of his office and down the long stretch of
cubicles and offices.

Asshole. Ryker Scott is a complete asshole.

Dahlia leads me past the long line of Fae waiting to gain
entrance into the Glen. Fae can differentiate each other as easily
as humans distinguish blondes from brunettes, no matter how
good the glamour.

The line extends around the block. All Fae will be allowed in
until the club reaches capacity. Humans will be asked to leave,
politely or not so politely, by the dragons in their human form at
the door.

Dahlia flings an arm around me. "Darling, I don't like you so
sad," she says.

I lean against her, allowing her exotic fragrance of jasmine
and juniper to soothe me. I barely ate at dinner. And if it hadn't
been for Dahlia's insistence, I would have walked back to our
apartment instead of taking the Path into the city.

A brisk walk later, and I am still in a hideous mood. "I know.
I just expected more from Ryker."

She kisses the top of my head. It earns us a few hoots and
howls from a band of passing sailors and a loud request to, "Do
it again, ba-*by*."

Dahlia ignores them. "You're being too hard on him, Livvie.
Did you honestly think he'd change everything about his practice? Only take cases for battered children and the elderly?" She
shakes her head. "The firm is legendary for their criminal
defense, and they gained that reputation by defending the worst
offenders with the biggest bank accounts."

"Bill and Marco don't."

"Bill and Marco paid their dues, building the firm from the

ground up. They've reached a point where they can pick and choose who they represent." She smiles softly. "Perhaps that's what Ryker is striving for."

"Maybe," I reply. "It's just hard to give him the benefit of the doubt with how easily he switched gears."

"You're assuming it's easy for him, darling. I don't know the man, but he leaves me with the impression he's different from the other associates trying to claw their way to the top."

Her voice trails when she catches the head bouncer's eye.

Frankie is in his signature black fatigues tonight, his spikey dark hair and brown eyes shiny beneath the overhanging lights and his New York accent as loud and bold as ever. "Next person in line," he barks.

Dahlia smiles. "Enough pouting, Livvie," she says. "Time to have fun."

Frankie's gaze travels the length of Dahlia's body when we approach. In a dress that resembles poured silver over butt and bosom, she's received a lot of attention tonight. None of it has mattered to her. Until now.

"Hey, Dahlia. Save me a dance later?"

Dahlia pushes up on her toes and nips his chin in true nymph fashion. "I'll save you more than that, baby."

Dahlia calls her friends "darling." Only Frankie has earned "baby" status. And Frankie very much knows it. If he were in his dragon form, smoke would puff from his snout in the shape of Dahlia's figure. A growl of anticipation vibrates deep in his throat. He sweeps his lips over hers before opening the velvet ropes and motioning us through.

"Nymph" equals easy access, anywhere, anytime.

"Hey, Liv," Frankie says as an afterthought.

I wave, laughing. "Hey, Frankie."

We disappear into the dark hall that leads into the club.

Frankie is my pal. To Dahlia, he's a lot more. "You're taking him home with you tonight. Aren't you?"

Dahlia tosses her long black braids behind her. "Of course. We have Monday off, why not take advantage of it?" She glances over her shoulder even though the door is shut. "Too much time has passed since my last night with him."

For a roomful of beings with sensitive hearing, the DJ is blasting Cardi B a little too loudly. I shout to be heard. "That's because you won't commit. Dahlia, Frankie would marry you if you'd let him."

She laughs. "Maybe one day I'll let him."

Lights flash and magical mist pours across the dance floor, allowing privacy to those desperate for touch. Fae aren't plentiful, and neither are establishments for us to gather. That's what makes the Glen fun. It doesn't just bring my kind together, it frees us. No glamour, no pretending. We discuss magic and the old realm, curse Death for destroying it and celebrate our survival.

With a shimmy and a shake, lavender and silver wings sprout from Dahlia's back. She stretches, relishing the feel of simply being herself. She winks at me, her glimmering lavender eyes and lips radiant.

A drunk mountain troll stumbles between us. She releases my hand, allowing him through before clasping my hand and guiding us through the gyrating swarm of bodies. "Let's have a drink, darling."

I squeeze her hand. Fae are affectionate beings. In the human world, we cage our need to caress, embrace, and make love. It's a way to keep our identities secret and another way to prevent Death from finding us.

Bill's broken glamour was a result of a stolen kiss. It revealed his form to a human and, worst of all, damaged his talisman. Our talismans remain the only way to hide from those who hunt us. Without them, it's a death warrant with our executioners often seconds from being collected.

A banshee sprints away from the bar and through the swarm of Fae. With all the grace of a swan, she leaps into the air and straddles the male who entered behind us. "David!" she screeches. "Sorry," she adds when we groan and cover our ears.

"David" loses his tiny accountant persona, morphing into a giant cyclops with a long blond mohawk. He laughs, catching the banshee when her legs break free of his widening waist.

She screeches. Again. The thought of *that voice* in the throes of passion makes me cringe. "David is going to need serious earplugs to get through the night," I mutter.

Dahlia giggles, her laughter like wind chimes in the soft breeze. "Perhaps. But it will be worth it, darling," she sings.

I'll bet.

The club smells of lust and desire. Elves, fairies, and dwarves make out on the dance floor. Along the bar, two garden gnomes are one drink shy from having sex. Their red pointy hats fall away as their tiny bodies roll down the length of the bar.

"Hey!" the giant behind the bar roars. "I'm trying to work here!"

Heat and need press against my back as the passion escalates around me. No one will go home alone tonight.

Except maybe me.

Dahlia blames my truant sex drive on my lack of wings and magic. I'm not certain. I've had sex. I just haven't had any of the good kind. Sometimes, it's felt nice. Sort of. But it's never anything like I think it's supposed to be. When Frankie spends the night with Dahlia, their cries and roars and scorched head-board leave me thinking I'm missing out on something phenomenal.

"Hey, Livvie." Andrew, an elf who charmed his way into my bed, inches toward me. "Want a drink?"

"She would love one," Dahlia answers for me. She nudges me in Andrew's direction, smiling as she steps back and beats her wings.

Like a seasoned ballerina, she pirouettes, soaring above me. She lands on the dance floor, moving to the beat the moment her feet touch.

I try to smile. Andrew is cute. Whiskey-colored waves of hair drape down to his shoulders, his pointed ears pushing through the thick strands. His amber eyes sparkle as he smiles, reminding me of his playful nature. As a third-year surgical resident at NYU, Andrew isn't pulling in the big bucks yet. But he always looks clean-cut and nice.

Dark jeans cover his long legs, and a tight blue Abercrombie and Fitch T-shirt hugs his lean athletic build. I ease away from his lips when he bends to kiss me and twirl in my flirty blue summer dress. "Look," I say. "We match."

He laughs, his attention falling to where the hem of my dress teases my knees. "I think you have better legs, gorgeous. Come on. Let's have a drink. We'll toast to us."

I hesitate. I don't want to lead him on. I also don't want to be rude. "All right," I agree.

Andrew orders me a blueberry martini. The giant swears, struggling to grasp the tiny glass without breaking the stem. He roars when he tries to pour the drink, and the gnomes almost tip over the glass. "Get a room, ya horny little bastards."

The giant just finishes pouring my drink when the gnomes roll back. Andrew snatches the glass and hands it to me, his reflexes no match for the overly amorous little folk.

"I haven't seen you in a while, pretty girl. What have you been up to?"

"I've been busy at the firm. What about you? How is your residency going?"

He kisses my cheek and nuzzles my neck, a strong indication

that his residency is the last thing on his mind. His smooth skin tickles and... that's about it. It pretty much sums up our last night together.

We talk for a while. Dahlia remains on the dance floor, stirring it up with a dwarf doing the lawn mower. Dwarves aren't known for their dance skills. Or grace. Dahlia's dance partner is no exception. He knocks over a group of leprechauns like bowling pins, earning him a magical zap. The dwarf, being of tough-skin, brushes off the spell and moves on to the "Robot." Dahlia laughs. She's flirting and having fun, until Frankie shows.

Frankie crosses the dance floor, evidently having given up his post at the door. His hands find Dahlia's waist and pull her away from the dwarf. Dahlia's lavender eyes and smile light up the dance floor. She flutters her sparkling lashes, inviting Frankie to kiss her. And does he ever.

Their hips sway, matching the rhythm of Rihanna's sexiest song. With each movement, their bodies commit to spending the night, vowing to please, to claim, to entice. I glance down at my empty glass. Dahlia shares more heat on the dance floor than I've ever experienced in the bedroom.

Andrew lifts my glass from my hand and places my glass on the bar, his attention sweeping from Dahlia to me. The intensity in his features promises to raise the temperature of bedrooms past. I'm not as certain and unsure whether I should try.

He gathers me to him, whispering low into my ear. "Dance with me, Olivia. Let's start our night off right."

I allow Andrew to guide me, cringing when the lawn gnomes pile into a set of glasses and send them crashing to the floor.

"Son of a banshee's whore!" the giant hollers.

Those gnomes, I envy them, as I do all the beings clutching each other around me. No one else exists except their partners, and nothing matters except pleasing and loving them.

Andrew stops a few bodies away from Dahlia and Frankie. I

love to dance. At home, there are days we lock up our apartment tight, and Dahlia enchants the living room to mimic a
mystical forest. She doesn't possess much more magic than that,
but it's enough to permit a little fun. I slap on fake wings and
prance around with my bestie, singing to music and spinning
with joy.

I don't share the same enthusiasm with Andrew, but I decide
to try, allowing him to pull me close.

He nibbles on my ear. It feels wet, although I'm certain it's
supposed to feel good. I groan, frustrated. There's something
wrong with me, and it's not due to the lack of wings or magic.

Andrew is cute, damn it, and the sex was...acceptable. Stars
know the elf tried. Passed out right after, bless his little heart. It
must be me. I'm clearly not giving in to my pixie nature. I mean,
look at Dahlia and Frankie. They have no issue surrendering to their
mystical halves. It amplifies their attraction and drives them to
please and explore.

Wings and magic deficient or not, I'm still a Fae.

I close my eyes and surrender my body to Andrew, mimic-
king the movements of my kind who know how to take and
receive pleasure.

I rock my waist, front, side, back, the perfect rhythm to show
Andrew that I need him. Front, side, back, again, and again, and
again, trying to make it feel natural and not so forced.

"*Jesus*," Andrew murmurs. My shoulders slump when something hard pushes into my belly. Andrew doesn't have to force
anything.

Andrew allows me to lead him, willing to let me do anything.
It doesn't feel right. *He* doesn't feel right. I close my eyes,
allowing my mind and body to seek someone I can surrender to.
I sort through men I find handsome, Colton Haynes, Tyler
Posey, and Chris Hemsworth. My delicate senses should
respond to one of these sexy icons. Instead, a male who has no

business occupying my thoughts shoves the others aside and makes his presence known.

"*Olivia*," his throaty timbre whispers.

The lean body in my grasp vanishes, replaced by hard muscle and a tall rigid frame. I dig my nails into his shoulders, surprised that he's here, but unwilling to let him go.

"Olivia," he whispers again. "*My Olivia.*"

That voice pulses lower, to my feminine regions and deeper into my core. It prods, begging access in while strong hands rake down my waist and seize my backside. I lift my face, disbelieving who is here.

My breath releases in shaky bursts. Ryker is with me. I reach up, smoothing his short dark hair, feeling the spiky softness roughen as my fingertips sweep down to touch the tiny hairs crawling along his jaw. I stop when I reach the indentation on his chin and circle it with my tongue. It's delicious, salty, sweet, the perfect taste of male.

Ryker fastens his gaze on mine, his blue irises firing with danger and desire. I should look away. But I can't. They're a beautiful peril I don't wish to escape.

His jaw tightens as does his hold, every bit of his flesh demanding to know my secrets.

I'll tell him anything for a chance to lay naked in his bed.

"Do you want me?" he rasps.

"Yes—"

His mouth cuts me off, his tongue forcing mine into submission. His hands, those amazingly large hands, clutch me, keeping our bodies cemented. He wants me. Ryker Scott *wants me*.

My neck arches as I come up for air, giving him space to play. He nibbles my chin, his teeth lightly searching my flesh. I moan, begging for more.

Lips, soft and hungry, explore my mouth while his hands

hunt me, pleading to my body to finish surrendering to his.

I fasten my arms around him, nipping his neck and stroking his ear with my tongue. He's challenging me to be aggressive, and I answer the call.

Before I'm ready, he abruptly breaks away. "I knew you wanted me," Andrew gasps.

I stagger away, sweeping the area. Ryker is gone. Only Andrew remains, his face flushed and his arousal clear.

He pants. "Let's go to my place," he says. "It's closer."

I blink back at him. *What* just happened? I cover my forehead, fighting the urge to pass out. Why was I thinking about Ryker? I hate Ryker. Don't I?

Andrew reaches for me, his lust clear. "Olivia, come on. We have all night. I'll drive you back home in the morning."

I drop my hand away as that strange fog I was under starts to lift. "Livvie," Andrew laughs. "What's wrong?"

Dahlia's scream freezes everything, cutting through Eminem's hard tirade.

I hurry to her, scared that she's hurt. Nothing prepares me for what I find.

Magic burns through the enchanted mist where Dahlia's talisman lies in pieces at her feet. The stone at the center is shattered, and the pearls from her necklace bounce free along the floor.

I look up in horror.

Frankie hauls her to him, his glowing predator eyes scanning the area for someone or some*thing*.

Another scream to my right. Then one behind a group of trolls. A fourth sounds near the DJ stand. It's then I see the cause.

A little gremlin materializes, his green body trembling yet his face determined as he reaches for a banshee and snatches her talisman.

A *pop* shoots in the air, followed by a furious roar. The giant bartender sobs, lifting his broken talisman away from the slick wood.

The flashing club lights explode in shards of raining glass, and the music grinds to a deafening halt. Scattered cries bounce from all directions, hidden and sharper by the sudden darkness.

My vision adjusts as Death declares its presence in an ensemble of ravenous howls.

Screams punch through the air. Each loss of a talisman is luring the Cù-Sìth closer.

Two more gremlins materialize, shattering talismans with growing urgency. They're common Fae. Why are they working with Death?

Someone shoves past me. Then another, and another. The crowd stampedes forward, trampling over each other to reach the exits.

I catch sight of Frankie as I'm pushed farther away. He removes his talisman and places it around Dahlia's neck.

Dahlia sobs into her hands. "No," she tells him. "I won't take it from you, baby."

Andrew wrenches me to him. "We have to leave, Oliva. We have to leave *now*."

I break away from him and force my way toward Dahlia, reaching out through the throng of running Fae. "Dahlia. *Dahlia!*"

Tears stream from her beautiful lavender eyes when she sees me. She shakes her head, her expression breaking. "Run, Livvie. *Run!*"

Andrew snags my waist and lugs me back. I struggle against him. No way I'm leaving my only family behind.

I jerk free from him and throw myself against the crowd. I'm almost to Dahlia when a small green hand reaches out, ripping the talisman from my neck.

5

I've faced the Cù-Sìth three times in my life. Once, when we crossed the Fae realm into Earth. The last time I saw my father. The next was at the train station in England. I was ten and actively searching for Platform 9 ¾. My brother Kaelen watched me as Mama instructed, laughing at my naiveté.

Mama paged through a tourist book she'd purchased. She loved photography, and this volume included bright, beautiful pictures. She was trying to decide whether we should continue along the countryside or head to Italy the next day.

My sisters loitered close to her, keeping a safe distance from the young men stepping off the train en route home. It was the first time I noticed how taken humans were with their beauty, and I wondered if there would come a time a boy would look at me with interest.

I skipped back and forth along the pavement, smiling at the way Mama's long red hair swayed in the breeze like bits of flame. She returned my smile each time. There were five us, but she always had a way of making us feel special.

I was still smiling when a vagrant hurried past me with his head down. My nose crinkled from his scent of old liquor and sweat, but also from the feeling that something was wrong. He dove at Mama like a falcon, wrenching the talisman from her neck and running too fast for someone so drunk.

It didn't seem real. None of it. Not my mother's paling skin when she grasped her bare collar. Not the echoing howls of the Cù-Sìth bounding down the tracks.

My mother stilled. The rise and fall of her shoulders her only movement. The veil the talisman provided was gone. She knew her time had come.

My sisters refused to accept her fate. They tried to haul Mama away. She yelled at them to be quiet and run, smacking at their hands, pleading with them to leave her.

They wouldn't listen to Mama and tried to protect her. When the hounds tackled Mama, my three sisters flung themselves on top of them, sobbing as the pack shredded her soul. Their shrieks of rage and sadness drew more attention than their talismans could muffle. It took mere seconds for the pack to sense them and turn on them.

My families' bodies vanished from human eyes following the first lethal bite. Except for a mist Death used to camouflage their presence and squelch their victims' cries, nothing had changed for the humans.

But I wasn't human.

I heard and saw it all. The last image was that of my eldest sister, Niamh, screaming when Cathasach dug his fangs into her soul and dragged her off to eat.

My brother hauled me behind where platform 9 ¾ should have been, clasping my mouth, but not my hazel eyes. They screamed my terror in the form of endless tears...

~

My third brush with Cù-Sìth was in Bill's office. Now, it's the fourth. As I gape at the broken chain that symbolizes my shattered veil, I realize it will be the last.

The fleet of haunting cries draws nearer. Thunder strikes, rattling down the club walls and vibrating my feet hard enough to knock my teeth together.

Like the other times, Cathasach returns. His vicious and familiar howls echoing above the chaos.

"Olivia!" Andrew calls for me. His handsome face twists in fear. He's fighting the throng of Fae trying to escape to reach me. His efforts cease when he catches sight of my bare neck. With a pained sigh, he turns, moving with the crowd fighting their way to the exit. He knows my life is over. As far as he's concerned, there's nothing left to do.

The dance floor empties out except for those of us without talismans. A fairy. The giant. A banshee. An elf. Me and Dahlia. And Frankie, who refused to abandon her.

Frankie speaks low into his earpiece. "Death is here. I need fire, and I need it now."

Dragon fire is the only thing capable of warding off Death. But it's temporary, and the number of hounds will certainly drain the flame.

Black and green smoke filters through the walls and vents in a rush, billowing out to form the giant, shaggy bodies of nine Cù-Sìth. Drool drips from their fangs over the cluster of tasty souls gathered before them.

The pack circles us, Cathasach at the lead, sniffing and growling as they decide who to eat first. They're patient, unlike last time. With nowhere for us to run, they have that luxury.

More swirls of green and white appear, whisking past us and out the exits. More of the pack arrives, prowling after those who tried to escape.

We inch back as they circle. Except for the banshee. She

shrieks, racing through an opening. The closest hound severs her neck in one bite. She never stood a chance.

Translucent hands reached up from her body only to be ripped by a second hound anxious for a taste. Her murder sets off a frenzy of excited howls. The fairy takes flight, reaching the elevated ceiling before two Cù-Sìth sandwich her in midair. The giant is next, followed by the elf. They jet in opposite directions.

So do five hounds.

Four tackle the roaring giant. The other one has fun with the elf. The blood-curdling rips of tearing muscle twists my stomach into a merciless knot. But it's their sorrowful and defeated sobs that puncture my heart.

Nine hounds have a taste. None are full.

Only Dahlia, Frankie, and I are left. But they can't see Frankie.

Frankie placed his talisman back around his neck. In refusing to take his necklace, Dahlia denied its power. It will only spare Frankie, and he's not going down without a fight.

He leads Dahlia to my side. "I love you," he whispers, causing her tears to run faster. I clutch Dahlia's hand, trembling. It's time for Frankie to fight. Backup has arrived.

Six dragons stalk forward, spreading out along the dance floor, fear and defiance etching deep lines into their faces. Frankie steps away from us, takes a breath, and transforms into his dormant form. Silver scales run the length of a Clydesdale-sized body, and fierce yellow eyes target the advancing hounds. With a flick of his spiked tail, Frankie curls his long reptilian body around us, the chain of his talisman tight against his throat.

One by one, the other dragons assume their mammoth and lethal counterparts. With a roar, Frankie unleashes a funnel of flame, catching the hounds that pounce.

The Cù-Sìth yelp, caught unprepared. They scamper back in

funnels of smoke, struggling to avoid Frankie's rapid bursts of flame.

Dahlia and I huddle against Frankie's belly when the other dragons shoot their fire, our bodies shaking violently as we try in vain to quiet our cries.

Speakers explode like bombs. Wires short-circuit in a wash of blinding sparks. A rafter snaps in half, crashing onto the bar. Bottles of liquor shatter, spilling the alcohol and igniting the bar in a sea of flames.

The Cù-Sìth dodge and veer, hunting and sorting through the chaos. The dragons strategically set off their flames. Alternating their streams and changing direction, making the hounds work to find them.

The dragons demand revenge for our kind. But the Cù-Sìth won't easily abandon their prey. They want more souls, and they aren't without friends.

The gremlins reappear, materializing in a series of *pops*. With shaking hands, they snatch the talismans of three dragons. The fight leaves us, and the war between dragons and Death begins.

All the hounds attack. Except for one.

Cathasach prowls toward us. Another gremlin appears, pointing wildly in Frankie's direction. Frankie snatches him up and swallows him whole, but not before Cathasach homes in on his location.

He bulldozes into Frankie, sending him spinning like a gargantuan top into the cinderblock wall. The wall caves in and another beam breaks from the ceiling, burying Frankie.

Frankie doesn't move after that. Either he's dead, or he will be. We're on our own.

Two more dragons meet their fate, their gurgled roars abruptly silenced in sickening bites. They don't matter to Cathasach. He lurks forward, his blood-red eyes catching like fire as he licks his jowls. With fangs that appear to smile and a devilish gaze that recognizes me, Cathasach bypasses Dahlia. He's chosen his meal. I'm next to die.

I scream and so does Dahlia when he tackles me. Air leaves my lungs in an agonizing rush. He pins me to the blistering dance floor, one paw at my throat, the other burying into my stomach. I choke out a cry, struggling to draw in air. He answers my efforts by pressing more of his weight.

Dahlia screams. All the remaining Cù-Sìth strike her at once, shoving her between them like a toy, their anticipation and arousal growing with Dahlia's increasing terror.

I twist beneath Cathasach's hold, swearing and out of my mind with fright. I'm scared. But I'm more scared for Dahlia.

"*No... no... Dahlia!*

Green smoke encloses Cathasach. The filthy hound with the shaggy green fur disappears, replaced by a naked male with iridescent jade hair falling like a matted curtain around my face. He reeks of sweat and murder, his glowing red eyes chilling my racing heart. Death can take many forms. Strange that I fear the man more than the beast.

I scream, flailing madly when Dahlia's wings are ripped from her body.

Cathasach looms over me, tightening his hold on my throat. Grimy nails scrape and tug, puncturing my skin. I expect unfathomable pain and a slow death. He's taking his time, writhing with pleasure as he claims my soul. But with every squeeze, his hold diminishes.

With a snarl and a hiss, the Alpha withdraws what remains of his hand. Something eats through his flesh, shriveling the muscle and charring the bone so brutally, the length of his arm disintegrates to ash.

Through my incredulity, I understand. *I* did this to him. *I* caused his pain. *I* have magic!

The realization snaps me from my shock and forces me into action. I dig my fingers into his face, piercing the meaty skin. Within me, something dormant rises, sizzling the tissue beneath my touch.

Cathasach lurches off me, the four scorched lines from my nails eating their way through his flesh.

6

Cathasach vanishes into a funnel of green smoke, transforming into his beast. He wobbles on three legs as my magic eats its way up his chest. The scratches I made expand, collapsing his right eye inward. A sprite pokes her head through the socket. She shimmies out, breaking free and leading two more with her.

Cathasach is bleeding out souls.

The escaping sprites entice another hound. She turns on Cathasach, biting his face. He retaliates with a snap of his jaws. Their bodies clash as they maul each other.

I ease away, whipping around when a dragon wails. He's out of fire, and two Cù-Sìth are on him. I sprint across the flaming dance floor, screaming with anger. With a leap, I soar onto a hound's back when he rakes his claws across the other dragon's stomach.

My nails push into his matted fur. It doesn't take much for his shoulder blade to dissolve into crumbles and for my fingers to seep farther in. Power surges through me. I can't control it and don't know how long it will last. But while it's here, I'm using all I can.

The hound flings me from his back. I land near another wounded dragon, crying out when my right arm snaps in half. The dragon crawls to me in his human form. He still has his talisman and therefore his veil and is likely less conspicuous in his human form. But his talisman remained in place, veiling him.

He presses his hand to his side, covering the bloody fang marks. "What did you do?" he gasps.

"I don't know," I reply, my voice hoarse with pain.

I look to where souls spill from the hound I attacked and the feeding frenzy that occurs among the Cù-Sìth. It's the distraction I think we need to escape, until I realize Cathasach's body has already begun to mend. With each soul he reclaims, his wicked body heals him. The slices in his face knit tight, and a new leg punches through the hole in his chest in a barrage of sickening crunches.

It won't be long before the hounds finish feasting. I need to hurry.

I force myself to my feet, biting back a shriek when my arm snaps into place. The urgency my body uses to heal me just about knocks me out. I shouldn't move right now. I just don't have a choice.

With my good hand, I snatch two talismans from the floor and toss them to a dragon. He's gutted, and his friend slumped beside him is unconscious and bleeding. The dragon releases his hold over his gaping wound and catches the talismans, welding the broken chains with a minute stream of flame. I drag my feet forward as the dragon places the talismans around himself and his friend. I don't offer him much. I only hope it's enough.

A mournful growl erupts from the corner of the room. Hot tears drip from my eyes. I know what's happening long before I dare look.

Frankie curls around Dahlia's mutilated form. What's left of her lovely wings lay like the remains of a broken spider web.

Anger spurs through me. My sweet Dahlia. My beautiful friend. I dive on top of the closest hound, straddling his back and tangling my fingers into his fur to keep from being tossed.

Ribbons of multi-colored flames shoot from all directions. Frankie and the other dragons release the fire they have left, sparing me from the advancing Cù-Sìth. The Glen was built to withstand dragon flames, but its design is reaching its limits.

Thick black smoke billows toward the ceiling fans and sections of the ceiling break apart. I ignore it and the burning in my lungs, using the searing effect of my hands to pierce through fur and bone. My grief and anger release through my touch, my body and soul hell-bent on hurting the writhing creature beneath me.

My hand reaches the hound's beating heart as I lurch forward. My fingertips barely graze it when the large beast collapses beneath me. I don't manage more than a breath when something solid strikes my side, sending me rolling across the dance floor and into the wall.

The wall feels cool against my cheek. A sharp contrast from my sweat-soaked back and the blistering heat rising around me. I don't want to move. But they're coming. They *won't stop* coming.

I tip onto my back and turn my head. Through strands of my hair, I see the pack closing in. They're all here save Cathasach. Pain radiates down my spine as I crane to watch the greedy Alpha devour the escaping souls from the hound I killed. My thighs seared large gashes into the creature's flesh, burning through it like cheap fabric. There's no smoke. No flame. Just crumbling specks of embers disintegrating the hound to ash.

The damage my skin inflicted came at the price of the rest of my body. I wheeze with every intake of air. My ribs are cracked, and my knee throbs with every beat of my racing heart. Something is wrong with my hip, and warm fluid is pouring from my shoulder. Blood seeps into my eyes, making it hard to keep them open. Still, I rise, staggering into a standing position and sobbing.

I swipe at my face with a trembling hand. Everything hurts. My body, so injured, struggles to heal me and is losing the fight. Each effort made to mend me is torture. Yet nothing compares to what Dahlia endured. She's gone. No longer will she brighten my world with her smile.

"Olivia!" Frankie hollers. He's bleeding from a deep gash across his human face. He remains standing, unlike his fallen friends.

His talisman dangles over his broad chest. I shake my head. He needs to be quiet and make an escape. My good hand will lash out, and my legs will kick. I'll fight to the end. But my stars, I've never felt so alone.

A breath, as warm as summer, whispers tight against my ear. From one terrifying thought to the next, I realize something else is here.

The sound of two blades clashing in battle halt the Cù-Sìth's advancing steps. Cathasach's blood-red eyes fire with rage. The pack growls and fixes on a spot near my feet. There's no warning. Everything happens at once.

With a snap like a wet sheet, a shadow of midnight blue appears. As quickly as it comes, it vanishes, unlike the decapitated head rolling toward me. I jolt, my mouth agape as souls burst through the neck of the dead Cù-Sìth like a dam. Another snap in the air. Another severed head. The translucent images of fleeing Fae whitening our burning surroundings.

The Cù-Sìth allow the souls to escape. Not one tries to eat or give chase. Their hackles rise, saliva dripping from their snarling gums.

My gaze darts in all directions. There's another monster in our midst, and it scares me more than the hounds.

The Cù-Sìth bark in frantic yips mixed with growls as another decapitated head falls with a wet splat. *It* scares them. If they fear it—if *it* can kill *them*… what's it going to do to me?

Cathasach vanishes in a funnel of green, slithering around his kin. He reappears in his human form directly in front of me. I barely register his presence when he yanks me to him by the front of my dress.

Blood swirls in his irises like liquid fire, his voice booming as he searches the air. "You want what's mine?" he spits. "Show yourself and take her!"

His matted hair whips me across the face when he turns abruptly. He drags me with him, shoving his hounds aside. My fingers dig into his forearm as the creature he challenged appears.

In a blur of azure and black, I catch a long stream of silver. Flames eating a nearby speaker reflect against the curved blade as it comes down on Cathasach. Cathasach veers back, dropping me and clasping the long gash across his throat.

I fall on my side. In a churn of black and dark shades of blue, a cloaked figure rises, one hand gripping a dagger, the other raised over his head, a giant scythe clenched tight in his fist.

A black hood hides his face, and pliable black armor covers his imposing form. He swings his scythe at a charging hound and digs his dagger into another hound that follows. Both strikes are lethal. Neither Cù-Sìth rises.

A scream rips through my throat. The Grim Reaper has arrived. He's fighting the Cù-Sìth for the right to claim my soul.

The Reaper charges the advancing hounds, twirling his scythe with lethal grace. I scramble away, my knees scraping along the beaten down floor.

Cathasach yanks me up by the hair. "He wants you," he rasps

in my ear. His long tongue flicks the blood streaming down my cheek. "Shall I tell him you're mine?"

I smash him in the ribs with my elbow, clawing at his face when he hunches. The searing sensation in my fingertips surges. I scratch him deeper. He backhands me, sending me spinning into the wall.

Deep green blood drips from the fresh gashes on Cathasach's face. The souls he devoured must have offered him some protection. But that protection is fading fast.

The Reaper races toward me, his heavy boots pounding against the dance floor, and his scythe lifting to strike. With a throaty growl, Cathasach leaves me, shooting in a green burst of smoke and colliding into the Reaper as a shaggy beast with hateful, vile eyes.

The force knocks the scythe from the Reaper's grip. They roll along the floor, the Reaper fisting Cathasach's matted green fur while the death hound snaps his jaws at the Reaper's throat.

With a grunt, the Reaper kicks Cathasach across the length of the room. The Reaper rolls toward his scythe, narrowly avoiding the jaws of another hound. He rises, spinning with his weapon and uses the momentum to split his attacker's neck.

A large shaggy skull rolls toward the incoming pack. More souls spill out, soaring toward the inferno the ceiling has become.

Four Cù-Sìth remain, including Cathasach. Through the crash and crumbling of the ceiling, their massive claws scrape against the floor. They circle the Reaper. Beneath his dark hood, the Reaper watches them. Slowly, he lifts his scythe. Instead of wielding it, he slams the point onto the floor, tracing a line into the concrete. "*Ardú!*" he roars. *Rise*.

The line fires electric blue. From it, ghostly elves with kilts and swords emerge. They charge the closest hounds as the

Reaper and Cathasach clash. With a swipe of his scythe, the Reaper guts Cathasach, sending Cathasach reeling back. The faint image of a dead Fae reaches out from Cathasach's gut. Not just any Fae. My mother... my... *mother*. I knew she dwelled within Cathasach as his prisoner. But to see her gaunt face, her traumatized and weeping features—to witness her suffering? It incites my nightmares and stalls what remains of my courage. Her hands extend, stretching through the breaks in Cathasach's skin, her dark eyes brimming with misery. *Olivia*, she mouths.

I barely feel Frankie's pulls to my arm. "Livvie!" he yells. "We have to get out of here."

I point in my mother's direction. Frankie doesn't understand. Adrenaline fights through my shock and exhaustion. Now is my chance to set Mama free. I have to take it.

I break free from Frankie and fling myself on top of Cathasach. He disappears in a cloud of green smoke, laughing. "Find me if you can, little pixie."

I chase Cathasach's smoky essence as he jets into the wall. My body slams against the cinderblock, barely catching the last few wisps of his green haze as he disappears. I pound at the wall. "*Come back here!*"

Fangs dig into my hair, cutting off my cries and hauling me back. I flail wildly, kicking and screaming as the hound drags me away. The Reaper's scythe flashes above my head. I scrunch my eyes closed as it comes down.

My head smacks against the floor as the harsh pull to my scalp eases. I push up on my arms, scuttling away from where the Reaper's scythe is embedded into the dance floor.

The Reaper is fighting two hounds. He catches one in the air when it leaps and stabs the hound through the heart. The other Cù-Sìth lunges at his back, ripping off the Grim Reaper's hood.

I expect a nightmarish monster hidden beneath the cloak, something hungry to eat me and eager to hurt me. I *don't* expect piercing blue eyes.

Nor do I expect Ryker.

7

The two ghostly elves Ryker commands to "rise" race to help him, their kilts fluttering with each pump of their brawny legs. They gut the hound who outed Ryker as the Grim Reaper, freeing a cluster of souls.

I laugh as Ryker struggles to his feet. He watches me, panting, sweat streaming from the crown of his cropped hair. He doesn't bother hiding anymore. He doesn't have to. I've seen what he really is.

He wrenches his scythe from the floor. I laugh again, briefly aware of my mounting hysteria as my crazed giggles morph into anguished sobs.

Ryker scrapes the point of the blade over what remains of the dance floor. Electric blue energy builds from the scratch.

"*Codladh,*" he orders. *Sleep.*

The warriors bow. They march to the line and dissolve into the light.

A flaming rafter falls with a crash, igniting a booth. The building is close to crumbling like a fiery deck of cards. I no longer care.

Dead Fae surround me. I lay on the floor where Dahlia had stood trembling. Tears well in my eyes. I ignore the pain radiating from my arm and into my skull and stroke a small piece of her wing. It's soft, silky, but cold. So cold.

The dragons are gone. I can't blame them. The Grim Reaper arrived to claim us.

The Cù-Sìth vanished into smoke. They feared the Reaper, too. Death can kill Death and send it to an insufferable hell. I glance at my palm and to my ash-coated nails. If so, what does that make me?

Ryker sheaths two daggers. Skulls top their hilts. He keeps his scythe close as he walks to me, his heavy boots crumbling the glowing embers at his feet.

He extends his leather gloved hand. "Come, Olivia."

My attention returns to the burning booth. Dahlia is dead. My dead mother pleaded with me to save her. And Ryker is the fucking Grim Reaper. You can say I've officially lost it.

Another rafter hurtles downward, followed by two more. The heat from the flames dries my eyes faster than the tears can form.

Ryker lifts me, tucking me against him. Something in me snaps. I thrash and punch at his chest. *"Don't touch me!"*

He shoves his face into mine, his rigid expression silencing me instantly. "I won't leave you to die!"

The scythe vanishes when he slams the base against the floor. In one move, he envelopes me in his cloak, pressing me hard against his chest.

Cold night air chills my heated body. It takes me a moment to make out my surroundings. A large dumpster with a warped metal lid rests against the graffiti-smeared wall. Clumps of dirty napkins roll along the soiled concrete. I'm in an alley with Ryker, his beating heart pounding between my breasts and his pronounced breathing causing my body to move with his.

Ryker slides me down his chest, releasing me. I hold my fractured arm, ready to bolt when the roar of multiple sirens scream past us.

Ryker surprises me by taking several steps back, giving me ample space. This man before me, with black armor and a cape that waves in the subtle breeze, isn't someone I know. Or thought I knew.

I stare at him. "You…" What? Lied to me about being a lawyer? Pretended *not* to be the Grim Reaper? "You're one of them," I say simply.

Ryker clenches his jaw. "I am *not* one of them, Olivia."

Something in the way he speaks my name shatters what remains of my trodden emotions. I grip my dangling arm tighter, seeking warmth and comfort to spare what remains of my sanity. "This isn't happening," I whisper.

Ryker says nothing. He just stands there, taking me in.

I'm not certain how long we wait in silence. There's a shift in the night, and a hidden presence emerges.

It begins with one. The soul of a fairy flutters from her perch on the fire escape. She circles Ryker cautiously, wringing her hands.

Ryker nods, his focus remaining trained on me. "Yes," he tells her.

The fairy jerks from side to side, motioning others forward. Two elves materialize through the walls. They exchange anxious glances and advance slowly, joining the fairy. Dozens of gnomes pop out from the dumpster, hope glimmering beneath their bruised expressions.

"*Jesus*." Frankie stands at the mouth of the alley, watching the growing number of souls gathering around Ryker. Fear and awe crease the deep lines ringing his eyes.

Frankie is scared, just as he was in the club. But he didn't run, not as far as he could have. Gray sweatpants cover his long legs and a blanket drapes over his shoulders.

Ryker speaks in that familiar quiet rumble. "I'm leaving Olivia in your care and trust that you'll see her safely home."

Frankie offers a stiff nod and extends his hand. "Let's go, Livvie."

Ryker fixes Frankie with a cold stare. For a moment, I think he'll kill him. "She'll need another talisman," Ryker tells him. "And she'll need one soon. Do I make myself clear?"

Frankie drops his gaze, balling his hands into fists. "I understand, man."

The entire alley is packed with wall to wall souls. I recognize a few who escaped from the Cù-Sìth's mangled forms. "They're going with you?" I ask.

Ryker bows his head. "I'm taking them to their resting place before Cathasach returns with more hounds or another form of Death latches onto their essences."

The souls quiver at Cathasach's name. Still, more appear. Two leprechaun children scurry forward and wrap their small arms around Ryker's legs. The rest move closer, packing tighter around Ryker, their faces pleading with him to hurry.

Ryker is their *savior*.

"But you're a lawyer," I add numbly, and rather stupidly.

His brow knits tight. "I still am, Olivia."

With a whip-like crack, and in a blaze of azure, Ryker rockets up and into the starry night, the translucent bodies of Fae shooting after him.

"This is messed up," Frankie says. He grabs my arm and leads me out of the alley. I follow robotically after him, torn between screaming and crying.

Frankie digs into the pocket of his sweatpants and pulls out a cell phone. "I'm near Second and 53rd. I have Olivia, she's… all right. I think." He gives me the once over, his bloodshot and strained brown eyes seeing more than just my injuries. "Bring me some wheels and a talisman from one of the fallen."

He disconnects and reaches into the other pocket for a pack of cigarettes. He told Dahlia he was going to quit. I don't remind him. I can't.

Frankie lights a cigarette with a puff of flame he spouts from his mouth. With a shaking hand, he raises the cigarette to his lips. "He called to me. Just now," he says, motioning to where Ryker had stood. "I heard him in my head, ordering me to come to him. I ignored his voice, thinking I was losing my mind, until the pull became too much. When I saw him, I thought he'd come for me." He takes a long drag. "In a way, I wish he had."

A Beamer squeals to a halt along the curb. The dragon bouncer who was gutted, slips out, shock riddling his youthful features. "Shit," he says.

Yes. That pretty much sums up my night.

He walks to us slowly. A thick bandage shows through his tight white T-shirt, and his dark skin carries a healthier tone. He's healing. As long as he wears his talisman, Death won't find him.

He's almost to us when he doubles back and wrenches open the passenger door. He rustles through the glove compartment and returns with a talisman. It's a plain gold circle with a small diamond at its base. He points to where the broken links were welded. "It's not much, but the veil will hold. It was Arnie's." He swallows hard. "He didn't make it."

Arnie was one of the bouncers who tried to protect me. My throat constricts as I struggle to speak. "How many dragons lost their lives?"

"Their lives? Or their souls?" Frankie asks bitterly. He tosses his cigarette butt on the sidewalk and mashes it with his foot.

With a sigh, he reaches for the spare talisman and places it around my neck. "Three. We lost three."

Tears blur my vision. "I'm sorry."

"You didn't call Death, Livvie. And you sure as hell didn't break those talismans." Frankie lights another cigarette and blows out a long puff of smoke. "You've got nothing to be sorry about."

I'm not so sure. Those dragons who died stayed and fought for me. I purse my lips, fighting back my tears.

Frankie's friend shakes his head. "The rest of us only made it because of you," he insists. "I—*we* saw what you did. How did you do it? Take on Death like that? You burned them like I would paper, except with no fire. I thought you were that pixie without magic."

I shudder from the cold and from his words. "I thought I was, too."

Frankie flicks his cigarette on the sidewalk and slips the blanket from his shoulders around me. He leads me to the Beamer, keeping his voice rough. "Olivia didn't know she had any magic, let alone the power to hurt Death. If she did…"

She wouldn't have let Dahlia die. I can't read thoughts. But I read his just fine. They mirror mine and poke at my heart.

Frankie's friend walks us to the car. "Keys are in the car," he says. "Mr. Sebastian says to keep it as long as you want."

My ribs burn as I lower myself into the cold leather seat. The dragon notices me struggle and reaches for my seatbelt. "Here. Lemme help," he offers.

I can wiggle the fingers of my right hand, but each movement sends jolts of pain through my fractured arm. "Thank you," I gasp.

He grips the door frame to shut it but doesn't quite make it. "Olivia… what are you, exactly?"

He waits for me to tell him something no-doubt

extraordinary. It's not what he gets. "I don't know," I answer, truthfully.

Frankie starts the car. "I'll tell you what she is," he says. "She's our hero."

Funny thing is, I don't feel like one.

8

Frankie peels the BMW away from the curb, making his way around the fire trucks, police cruisers, ambulances, and news vans swarming the area. New York earned its nickname as "the city that never sleeps" for a reason. Even in the predawn hours, large crowds gather for a peek of the action and for a chance to make it on national news.

The smoke billowing from the Glen stretches into the night. Firefighters won't discover bodies buried in the ashes, and police offers won't find club patrons to interview. Fae have a way of disappearing. We stay quiet and keep our secrets. We learn to hide in the open and not be found. Many of our kind even possess the power to alter memories.

Frankie drives in silence, swiping his face to keep the tears reddening his eyes from falling. It's only when we enter the Holland Tunnel that he finally speaks. "Mr. Sebastian is the Glen's owner. He's fixing it so it looks like the club caught fire as a result of bad wiring and a faulty sprinkler system."

"The Fae, who were there, will go along with any excuse."

Frankie keeps his focus ahead. "Yeah. The media will tell them exactly what they need to say if caught." He wipes his face again. "I'm going after the gremlins. Dante, the other dragon, thinks he recognized one of them."

I place my hand over my chest. It's the first time I notice my blue dress is shredded. Torn strips of lace barely keep my breasts covered. It shocks me, despite knowing how rough Cathasach handled me. I tug the blanket closer. "What are you going to do to the gremlin if you find him?" I ask.

"Pound the fuck out of him until he tells me why our own has turned against us." He punches the gas, passing a car on our right. "I need you to contact Bill. He needs to know what's up. This isn't good, Olivia. Whatever this is, it isn't good."

"All right," I stammer.

Bill is a respected and widely known gargoyle. While Fae don't have their own governing body, Bill is perceived as a leader among our kind. He helped Dahlia obtain her office manager job at the firm and, when I couldn't find a decent job with an English degree, Dahlia convinced him to hire me as an administrative assistant and paralegal.

"Give Olivia a chance, Bill," Dahlia begged him. "You'll love her, darling."

Dahlia always watched out for me. We met at the College of New Jersey when I was a sad little first-year student, and she was a junior and resident adviser. She recognized my loneliness and literally took me under her wings.

And now she's gone.

I cry all the way to Hoboken. Frankie lets me. He doesn't tell me to be strong or plead with me to stop. I'm grateful for it. Except he also doesn't say everything will be all right. I gather it's because it's a lie. Nothing will ever be the same.

Frankie pulls the car in front of my apartment building, a trendy brick-front complex filled with young singles taking advantage of everything Hoboken offers.

He hastily wipes away the tears smearing his cheeks. "I loved her, too, Livvie," he says. "Too bad I didn't tell her when it mattered."

I glance at my dirty hands. There's not just soot coating my nails. There's blood. "She knew, Frankie. If there was any doubt, you shredded it when you offered her your life."

He looks at me. "But she didn't take it, Liv."

I manage a small smile that doesn't quite last. "Only because she loved you, too."

He jerks his head away, cursing. There are times kindness hurts more. Frankie deserved the blow. He called me a hero. But he's the one who offered Dahlia his talisman.

Dawn breaks over the horizon as Frankie walks me up to my apartment. I fumble with the keypad on my door, hitting several random numbers before I remember the right combination.

Frankie cups my shoulder when I try to step inside. "We're going to find out who did this to Dahlia, you hear me? And when we do, he's going to pay."

He kisses my head like a parent would a small child. I thank him. At least, I try.

Frankie doesn't leave until I shut the door behind me. His heavy feet trod toward the elevator. It's only when I hear the door to the rear stairwell open and close that I move into the apartment.

The familiarity of the cool honey wood floors and the sense of home should bring me comfort. I barely feel my soles slap against the slick wood and half-heartedly glance around the small living space. Cream comfy couches are set around a barnyard-style coffee table, while the pink throw pillows and lavender window treatments make a firm declaration that females occupy this space. Well, two had, anyway.

I sniff as I roll back the barnyard-style door leading to my small bedroom. Stark white linens and bright floral pillows cover my full-sized bed. Its softness and promise of rest lures me to it. I ignore its pull and strip out of my clothes, tossing them in the bright yellow wastebasket and pad into my private bath.

I spend an hour showering and scrubbing my body clean of Death's impurities. Remnants of Cathasach's laugh haunts me with each pass of my sponge; so do Dahlia's screams. His pack tore her apart to eat her soul. If he took the largest piece of her, was she now caged within his gut, just like my mother?

Are my sisters there, too? And

my father? What of him?

I lean against the tile. Death. So much Death. Everyone I love is gone. My body shakes horribly when I step out from the shower, though the water was as hot as I could stand.

The wound on my head is sealed, my hip is better, but my ribs still ached. I pull on a nightie and wrap a thick cotton robe around me. Each task is torture. Somehow, I manage.

My hands still tremble when I phone Bill.

"Hello?" his sleepy voice answers.

"Dahlia's dead."

There's no more to say. I disconnect. A few minutes later, there's a knock on my door.

"It's us," Bill calls.

I open the heavy door to find Jane standing beside him. He must have summoned our little druid priestess and requested a transport via magic. I'd woken him from sleep, yet he still managed to dress neatly in a light blue polo and freshly pressed tan slacks. He even managed a pair of polished dress shoes.

He rubs his goatee, his expression worried and despondent. "We can't come in unless you invite us, Livvie," he reminds me.

My hands grip the collar of my robe. In my state, I forgot all about the protective wards. "My apologies. Please come in."

The threshold hums and Jane steps in, followed closely by Bill. Bill wraps an arm around me when I can't seem to move and leads me past our kitchen into the living room. His posture is leaden with grief. Mine isn't much better. Jane sits beside me, her beady eyes trained ahead.

"Tell us," Bill says.

And I do.

The story grows more unbelievable as I sort through each event. Sitting becomes too much for Bill, he paces along the small space, his heavy feet threatening to wear out the floral print area rug Dahlia selected. She liked flowers and bright colors. Like me, she was born on a bed of daffodils.

Bill pauses, tightening his jaw when I speak of the gremlins and how they stole our talismans and how Cathasach and his hounds arrived to maul us. But when I explain that I hurt Death, neither Bill nor Jane move.

I stretch out my hand, inspecting every streak and bruise along my arm. "You were right, Jane. I have magic. I just never expected this."

Their scrutinizing gazes make me squirm. Do I frighten them? I hope not. I need them. They're my only friends.

Relief sweeps over my aching muscles when Jane offers a gentle smile.

Bill isn't so reassuring. He closes the small space separating us and grips my shoulders, easing his hold when he sees me wince. His hands fall away. "Olivia, do you have any idea what this means?"

I stare at him. "Not really."

It's Jane who answers, smiling softly as a single tear slides down her cheek. "You're immune to Death, Livvie," she croaks. "You can save us all."

9

"No," I say. "That can't be right."

Bill stands over me. "I know it sounds impossible."

I nod. That's really all I can do.

Bill smooths his hand along his beard. "Earth's magic clashes with our own. It's weakened most of our power. But in some, it's altered it, morphing it into the unexpected."

"Do you mean like Jane becoming the Hydra?"

"Exactly," Bill agrees. "In Fae, Jane was simply a druid priestess." Jane clears her throat. "Forgive me, Jane. I meant the most powerful of druid priestess. But no one could command another form and maintain it, unless it's an ability they were born with."

Like gnomes when they assume the forms of toadstools, I infer.

"If Jane hadn't crossed with her pet snake," Bill continues. "She never would have become the Hydra."

Jane watches me as I stand. I mean to head into the kitchen to make tea. When you learn you're some kind of magical pariah, tea sounds like a good idea. I change my mind, wondering if we have alcohol in the house or possibly a sledge-hammer to beat my brains in. Yes. That will work.

I turn toward the large windows. Rays of brilliant sunlight

penetrating through the openings in the lavender curtains, casting a sting across my tired eyes. I grip the ends to seal out the light. Mostly, I end up holding them as I work through Bill's reasoning. "My wings were torn from me when I crossed."

"I know, Olivia," Bill replies quietly. He sighs. I'm not certain what I look like; however, I am sure "stable" is the last word that comes to mind.

"The world is believed to be in a delicate balance," he reminds me. "When you crossed, this realm took something sacred from you. As a pixie, your wings were your source of power and identity. I believe in exchange for that loss, Earth's magic granted you something more powerful."

"Then what did it do to Ryker?"

My back is to them. That doesn't mean I miss the stillness in the air that follows. *Just say it*, my mind insists.

They need to know. It's the right thing to do. I'm just struggling to believe it myself, and oddly enough, I feel like I'm betraying Ryker.

My words come out in a rush. "Ryker is the Grim Reaper. He was there. He saved me. He fought Cathasach and killed his hounds…"

Neither Bill nor Jane seem to take a breath until I finish my riveting tale of Ryker and his scary-as-hell scythe. The lethality he commanded was a combination of grace and raw power. I don't quite capture it in words. Nothing can. I try my best anyway.

Bill clenches his fists, cracking his knuckles. "He carried the souls to the Afterlife?" I nod. "You're sure of this?"

I rub my face, the motion making me dizzy. "As much as I can be. They, the souls, I mean, went to him willingly. They sought him and followed him… upward."

Bill whips out his phone, typing feverishly. "Jane, these circumstances necessitate you contacting the remaining

Ancients. They must be made aware." He pauses, his brows scrunching. "Did he try to feed from you or touch you in any way?"

I sink into the couch, no longer able to stand. "No, to the eating part. And while he didn't touch me, he did carry me out of the club." Looking back, we were mighty close. It's not something I dare mention now. Not with how stressed Bill appears. "Jane, if I'm immune to Death, how could Ryker touch me without disintegrating like the Cù-Sìth?"

Jane shakes her head, worry forming deep ridges into her wrinkled face. Bill slows his frantic texting to a stop. "This doesn't make sense. All forms of Death from Fae nourish and strengthen themselves by consuming souls. All of them. Otherwise, the magic of Earth's realm causes them insufferable anguish."

It explains why the Cù-Sìth are especially ravenous. They're warding off potential pain.

Bill kneels in front of me. "Olivia, I don't believe Ryker carried those souls into the Afterlife."

The gnawing feeling in my belly returns when I remember those little leprechaun children, clutching his legs and placing their souls in his care. "You think he tricked those souls into trusting him?" My voice quivers. I'm suddenly so cold. "Only to devour them?"

"I don't know," Bill admits. "But I'd be a fool to presume he's an ally just because he chose to save you. He's worked at the firm what? A year? In that time, he's managed to keep his true nature a secret from us. How is that even possible?"

"I don't know," I confess. "Do you think he knows what *we* are? Every Fae in the office wears a talisman. The magic should have kept us veiled from him."

"In theory, you're correct." Bill tucks his phone back into his pocket. "Except I find it odd that of all the places he could have worked, why my firm? The office has a modest number of Fae. If he can detect us through our veils, and he's looking for souls to feed his needs, there are larger corporations he could infiltrate that would provide a greater bounty."

"Lawyer," Jane croaks.

"That's a good point," I say. "Why would a Grim Reaper assume a human's existence? Ryker attended law school and actively practices. I always pictured Death as those dark entities that skulk in the shadows waiting to pounce."

"Most do," Bill agrees.

"Then what's up with Ryker?" I press.

"I wish I knew."

It's what Bill claims. Except the way he regards Jane tells me he's already labeled Ryker a threat, one that needs to be contained if not eliminated. I clutch one of the bright throw pillows against me. "There were a lot of souls, Bill. Too many to count at the time. They swarmed him from all directions. Even those hesitant to approach were won over by his mere presence."

Bill places his hand on my knee. "Olivia, I know you want to believe he's different. But may I remind you, Ryker is Death. Some forms hunt like the Cù-Sìth. Others entice their victims into their dark webs, trapping their prey before they can escape."

Bill has a point. Ryker is a predator. The way he attacked the Cù-Sìth and the viciousness behind each blow proves he's dangerous. I'm not naïve, nor am I stupid. What I can't understand is why he didn't attack me or leave me to die?

"Bill, I'd given up. I lay on the floor as the building burned. Call it shock or misery, but I was done." It's not an easy thing to admit, but it's something he and Jane need to hear. "Ryker could have left me and returned for my soul when I was no longer a threat."

Bill doesn't hesitate to answer. "Unless you're a threat in life and in death."

I stumble through my words, desperate to convince them. "He couldn't have eaten those souls, Bill. There were little ones, children." Bill regards me like I've lost it. Maybe he's right. "He told me he was different."

My face falls into the pillow. I know how pathetic I sound.

The judgmental silence that follows is more than I can bear. I don't want to be wrong about Ryker. I also don't want to play the fool.

After a long drawn out moment, Jane stands and shuffles to the door, her long black dress trailing behind her. "Come," she croaks to Bill in her rusty voice. "Much to be done."

You can say Jane is Fae's version of Yoda.

Bill waits before following. "Olivia, I don't know what's happening, but I find Ryker's presence and actions questionable. Until we know his true purpose, I want you to stay away from him. Do you hear me? Stay far away from Ryker Scott."

I stay awake the remainder of the day, ignoring my body's pleas for rest and the aches eating away at my bones. Rest leaves me to all those horrible thoughts, taunting me with questions I have no answers to and memories I can't stand to relive.

Bill promised to phone Dahlia's family. There won't be a funeral. Fae learned long ago to mourn in secret and in small numbers so as not to taunt Death. A large crowd of grief-stricken Fae works like dangling fresh meat before a hungry gator's face, as collective grief diminishes the effects of our talismans. Any version of Death could swarm the somber scene like a soul buffet. And graveyards? They're Death's chosen lairs. It's where they lurk until they catch a whiff of a soul, preying on each other when their hunger becomes too great. My kind stay far away from graveyards and cry for our dead alone.

I lay on the couch most of the day, staring at the TV with the volume turned up as loud as I can stand. It's a tactic to keep me distracted. At some point I make soup but don't eat it, choosing to play with the carrots and bits of rice floating to the surface.

When the sunlight fades, and my living room enshrouded in darkness, I embrace the inevitable and retire to my bed.

The air conditioning in the building has turned the brick complex into a virtual meat locker. I crawl beneath my thick white linens, clutching my floral pillows against me. I try not to think - thinking is bad - and succumb to a numbness that may permit some sleep.

Tension stiffens every bone, every muscle, every organ, turning my breathing into an arduous task. My eyelids droop, fighting my anxiety and losing.

It's as if I haven't been awake for more than a day. Once more, I'm alert, my heart rate accelerating and those awful tears burning.

A heavy hand travels the length of my spine, resting against my shoulder.

"Peace," a deep voice whispers in my ear. His warm breath tickles and stirs a shudder.

But no one is here.

"Peace," he murmurs, his lips teasing the ridge.

"There is no peace," I mutter. I try to pry open my eyes and escape the purgatory I'm in. I'm not asleep. I'm not awake. I'm in between, with only the voice and his fingertips drawing waves along my spine.

"Not now," the deep voice rumbles. "But there will be."

"I don't believe you." I bury my face in the pillow. I think that's what it is. "Death has found me too many times, robbing me of my peace," I mumble. Bitter tears breech through my fog only to vanish when I unexpectedly yawn. I fight to speak. "There is no peace. Not for me."

"Peace," the voice says, deepening to a thrum.

"Not... meant... to have it," I insist.

"You will. I swear it..."

I wake to the sound of my cell phone ringing. "*Are you all right?*" Bill growls when I answer.

It's still dark outside. I rub my eyes. "What time is it?"

Bill speaks with more fury than I could have ever imagined. "Midnight. Why haven't you called? I've been trying to reach you for two days!"

"You just left this morning," I say slowly, working through what he said.

"Olivia, that was Saturday. It's Monday night."

I jerk up so hard, I almost fall off the bed.

Bill continues, his voice lessening only slightly in severity. "I went to your home and pounded on your door. I even sent Fae to search for you. My fear was that the Cù-Sith had found you."

"I've been asleep." I push my crazy hair from my face and pause. My right hand and arm are back to full working order. "I'm so sorry, Bill. Between my injuries and everything that happened, my body likely shut down."

"Yes, yes, of course. My apologies." He clears his throat. "I don't want to lose you, too. Dahlia's death was a tragedy. It shouldn't have happened."

My fingers run through my borrowed talisman. "There's a lot that shouldn't have happened."

"I know, Olivia. Jane and I, along with the Ancients and a few others, are working to make it right." The shuffle of papers on the other line tells me Bill has been busy. "I'd like you to come to work tomorrow— Forgive me, I know it's a terrible request given everything you've endured. But it can't wait. The Ancients have tasked me with identifying the source behind the attacks and bringing the perpetrators to justice." He hesitates, tapping what sounds like a pen against a stack of papers. "I've arranged a private meeting on the 28th floor…with Ryker."

My fingers curl tightly against the phone. "Do think that's wise?"

"We have no choice. We need a better understanding of what we're facing. Jane will be in attendance for your safety, as well as the dragons. I promise, nothing will happen to you."

Bill wants to mean what he says. But he wasn't there. He didn't witness what I had. "Did you speak to Ryker?" I ask. "Directly, I mean?"

"Yes."

I take a breath. "What did he say… about everything?"

"Nothing. He agreed to attend the meeting, but only if I guaranteed your presence."

10

I step off the bus on Hudson Street, a block from the office building where I work, in head to toe pink. Yes, pink. This pixie needs brightness in her life, any way she can get it.

A few men repairing a large pothole whistle at me as I pass. When you work in Jersey City (or anywhere in the Tri-State area), you never know what adventure lurks around the bend. If the crazy guy masturbating two seats behind me was any indication of what my day is going to be like, my appointment with Death is a very, *very* bad idea.

My steps are quick, despite what waits for me. I want answers. I just don't want to die getting them. Will I welcome what Ryker has to say, or will his words throw me into a dark place I'll never wake from?

I cross the lobby, groaning. Good ol' security half-wit Ralph is on duty. He barely glances up from slopping down his greasy Taylor ham and cheese sandwich. "You're needed on the 28th, Alexandria," he mutters between licks of ketchup from his fingers.

Thanks, jackass. I've worked there for a year and a half and

am required to present my ID when entering the building. You'd
think he'd know my name, especially given my unique hair.

I step into the elevator to giggles and familiar voices.
Humans. I recognize them by their good cheer. The leprechaun
and she-elf who work in Archives aren't laughing. They hurry to
catch the elevator before it closes, pausing briefly when they see
me.

Fear and sorrow drown their typically pleasant demeanors.

A law intern held the doors open when he saw them
approach. The leprechaun enters first, offering me a sympa-
thetic smile. The elf squeezes in beside me and gently strokes
my arm. They heard about Dahlia. Word of Death spreads
quickly among the Fae.

They mean well, but their kindness chips away at my resolve.
I can't break down. There's too much that awaits, and I need my
wits.

I focus on the elevator numbers as they blink off one by one.
Don't cry. Don't cry. This is not the time.

I take a calming breath and at least four more. The idle
elevator chatter bothers me. Someone complains about a hang-
over, and a woman bemoans the barista who screwed up her
latte. I want to scream that there are worse things in life. By
some miracle, they're the first to pile out.

The elevator accelerates quickly; so does my heartbeat. As it
comes to an abrupt stop, my stomach lurches into my throat.
Like the first mournful blast of "Taps", the elevator *dings* open
and shuts behind me like a closing casket. I should run. These
are all bad signs. Still, I walk through the large open area and
toward the Fae folk sitting at the granite boardroom table, hoping
my shakes will lessen to manageable quivers.

The 28th floor was recently vacated by a computer software
company with more brain power than money to satisfy its

arrears. Jade-green marble tile spreads brilliantly along the expanse, catching the light from the bare wall of windows.

Unlike the 29th and 30th floors that MacGregor and Santonelli own, there are no offices or cubicles. There's not much of anything except the table and chairs at the end. The owners must want potential buyers to imagine the possibilities the mammoth space holds. All I can imagine is where my bleeding corpse will lie following a quick swing of Ryker's scythe.

I don't want to believe Ryker will kill me, just like I didn't want to believe he could go on representing murderous and iniquitous clients. But he helped free those I believed were guilty, and he'll likely do it again.

Well, after he dumps my body in Staten Island.

Bill waits at the center of the table. Jane sits to his left, her candy cane and ribbon wand steady in her hand. A gray-haired gentleman in a jet-black suit and tie sits to Bill's right, tapping his gold pinky ring impatiently against the table. *Dragon*, my pixie instincts tell me. Yet even if my Fae intuition failed to reveal his race, Frankie's presence proclaims it loud and clear.

Frankie stands behind pinky ring dude, flanked by six more dragons. I recognize two from Friday night's attack.

The tension heating the room gathers an edge the closer I step. I half expect to be knifed in the chest when I reach the table. Anger surges to the surface and screams for blood.

I adjust the purse strap on my shoulder. My lunch is tucked inside. I hope I live to eat it. "Miss Olivia Finn." Bill motions to the pinky ring dragon. "I'd like you to meet Mr. Sebastian."

"Hi."

Under other circumstances, I'd offer old snarl tooth my hand. And under other circumstances, perhaps Mr. Sebastian wouldn't meet me with a frown.

"There must be a mistake," he says. He scrutinizes me from

big, multi-colored hair, to floral pink mini dress, and all the way down to my hot pink pumps. "She's a damn rainbow."

"She's the real thing, Mr. Sebastian. I assure you," Frankie says, beating Bill to my defense, and possibly Jane's hex given the way her beady eyes glare at him.

Frankie is back in black camo clothes and boots. His brown eyes carry the grief of a wounded man, but his hard face discloses his need to avenge.

The elevator *dings* behind me. The doors part. Ryker steps through.

And I'm wrenched across the table.

My purse falls from my shoulder, spilling my container of soup, a hairbrush and wallet, and my emergency stock of tampons. Glorious. Nothing like a bout of extra humiliation on your death-day.

"My apologies," Bill mutters, lowering me to his side.

Everyone is on their feet except for Jane. My water bottle rolls along the length of the floor, stopping beneath Ryker's foot. His cold, piercing gaze locks on me as he bends to retrieve the bottle. I expect the black and azure armor and cape of his alter ego. Instead, a freshly pressed charcoal suit with a crisp white shirt and blue tie provide his only protection.

He walks with purpose toward us, like a tiger staking out his turf at mealtime. I shudder. Okay. Maybe he is here to kill me.

"That's far enough," Bill says when mere feet separate us.

Ryker stops, hints of annoyance sizzling his lethal stare. "If I wanted to kill you, you'd already be dead."

The bare face truth of his statement has me all but keeling over.

Bill leans forward, no trace of fear in his face or his voice. "Then what you do want?"

"Freedom," Ryker replies, his focus returning to me. "Something only Olivia can grant me."

He lifts his hand, offering me the water bottle. The plastic tip meets an invisible force. Sparks of red magic clash against it, sending streams of water and fragmented bits of warped plastic shooting across the room. The dragons vanish except for Frankie, who stays by Mr. Sebastian. They materialize along with three more dragons directly behind Ryker.

Ryker shakes out his hand from a deep crouch on the floor, anger and pain darkening his features. His gaze cuts to Jane. "Druid priestess?" he asks. Jane answers with a blink. "Impressive. Too bad your trap can't hold me."

A charred ring circles Ryker and fires a deep red. Bill and Jane obviously prepared before I arrived. "You caged him?" I ask.

Bill's focus doesn't waver. "We need to take precautions. I can't risk anything happening to you."

"I would *never* hurt her," Ryker growls.

The force in which Ryker responds strikes us all. Ryker was met with a strong offense and a show of collective force. He should be wary. The rest should demonstrate confidence in numbers and strength. That's not what happens. The rigid and guarded stances betray fear of what Ryker is and what he can do. Ryker's warning that he could kill us wasn't a mere threat. It's a statement of fact.

Ryker flexes his grip, appearing to rein in his temper. "I've been alone with Olivia in the past. I've had several opportunities to kill her—

"Nice," I say.

He frowns. Oh, like I'm the lunatic here.

"But I haven't," he bites out, ignoring the interruption. "Why would I harm her now?"

"Because she knows what you are." Bill's voice remains steady. "We all do."

Ryker's deadly tone reverberates across the floor. "You have *no idea* what I am."

The icy scratch of fingers dig their way up my arms. Cobras don't need to announce they're deadly for people to fear them. They slither along, aware of their power and intimidate by simply *being*. Ryker is the same way, the venom in his voice suggesting he's moments from striking.

My feelings fluctuate between reassuring him and running for my life. Jane remains neutral, giving no indication of what I should do. Bill and the dragons have me ready to sprint toward the stairwell. As predators, they recognize another foe, and like Ryker, their tightening postures indicate they're ready to fight.

Only Frankie keeps his cool. He walks around the table, his movements cautious yet imperturbable. "The night of the Cù-Sìth attack, he protected Olivia and entrusted me with taking her home."

Bill stays focused on Ryker. "Do you know what Olivia is?" he asks him.

Ryker grinds his teeth, muscling through the enchantment. Jane's binding spell harmed him, but it didn't disable him as she likely intended. "No," Ryker admits. "I'm guessing she's some subspecies of lawn gnome."

"I'm a *pixie*," I reply rather defensively.

The barest glimpse of a smirk curves the edges of Ryker's mouth. It was brief, but there.

Mr. Sebastian dissects him from head to foot. "You can't distinguish one Fae from another, yet you appear at a club designed specifically for our kind. Don't tell me it's mere coincidence two kinds of Death appeared that night."

Ryker stiffens and doesn't reply. Bill huffs, his patience wearing thin. "If you want us to trust you, you need to explain your presence."

Ryker doesn't move and gives nothing away. My life is an open book. His is a locked diary tightly wrapped in cellophane.

I hate the escalating tension. "Please, say something," I beg.

Ryker lowers his head, muttering a curse. When he looks up, the force of his presence bowls me over. "I heard you calling to me. Sometimes, your thoughts invade my own."

Doesn't that bring me more attention than I ever wanted or needed.

"You brought him onto my premises!" Mr. Sebastian's incredulous tone awakens the dragons' dormant forms. They abandon Ryker and close in on me, their eyes ablaze in yellow and orange light.

Frankie steps in front of me, shielding me with his body as Bill yanks me back. "Stand down," Frankie snarls. "She's one of us!"

"You sure 'bout dat, Frankie?" one of the dragons spits out. "You heard him. She called him to us!"

"I-I-I didn't!" I insist.

Jane clutches my hand and mumbles a spell. Frankie and Bill shove two dragons away from me. My shoulder blades fall back against the large windows as a dragon transforms into his dormant form. Purple and gray scales erupt from his skin, and his body expands four times its size. His snout widens ready to spill flame.

"Don't do it, Aaron," Frankie warns. "I'll kill you if you get anywhere near her."

A sharp snap slices the air. My body is wrenched from the floor, and I'm blinded in darkness. I release a startled breath to find myself halfway across the room and clutched against Ryker.

The long black cape of his kick-ass death suit cascades downward as he grips his scythe.

"I told you, I would never hurt Olivia," he rumbles, his arm tight around my waist. "And I'll be damned if I let anyone touch her."

11

Death does many things, like frighten, mesmerize, and entrap you, refusing to let go. Ryker, true to his nature, manages all at once and shockingly so. He also does a stellar job of making me blush.

Jane offers an approving nod, seemingly undisturbed by how easily Ryker tore through her binding spell. Bill's gaze cuts from her to us. "Dismiss your dragons, Sebastian."

The air surrounding Mr. Sebastian alters from irritated, to furious, to eerily calm. "Leave us," he says.

The dragons pile out in line formation. Well, once they free their buddy from the cocoon Jane wrapped him in. He shrugs loose from the webbing, perturbed and naked. His clothes lay in tatters on the floor, ripped to pieces from the abrupt trans-formation.

Tone butt cheeks see-saw up and down as the dragon and his friends march toward the elevator in obedient silence. Frankie stays behind. When he stepped up to defend me, he made it clear no one, not even his boss, would order him around.

Jane holds out a hand, gesturing for all to take their seats. Ryker releases me only once everyone settles. "I prefer to stand," he says.

"Me, too," I agree. That's a lie. My knees are rattling hard enough that everyone can hear. I just want to stand in solidarity with Ryker. Grim Reaper or not, he protected me.

Bill sits slowly, steepling his fingers as he leans forward. "You said Olivia summoned you. What did you mean by that?"

Ryker squares his jaw, remaining guarded. "There are times I can sense thoughts, provided they're strong enough. It's an ability that's sporadic at best." He waits and adds, "For some reason, I hear Olivia's thoughts more."

I cover my face, dreading the "thoughts" he might have latched onto.

Ryker examines me closely, his face heating though his tone maintains that vigilant edge. "In Fae, my senses alerted me when someone passed. It's how I knew I was needed. The body would call me to claim the soul. The night of the attack, Olivia called me to her."

"She called you?" Bill repeats slowly.

"Yes," Ryker answers. "Or at the very least, had strong thoughts of me."

He cocks his chin at the return of my blush. Did he have to be so, so… honest? And while we're at it, couldn't he have picked a better choice of words? Or maybe, lied about how the call was made?

The "strong thoughts" I had didn't initially pertain to life and death. They were about Ryker's body tight against mine. Had he felt me, too? Or did he experience just traces? I'm hoping for the latter and tried to spin it. "I was angry at you for taking that new case." *And imagining your hips grinding against me while your mouth worked me like you owned me.*

I obviously didn't add the last part. I wince anyway, hoping that much wasn't inferred by his superpowers.

He nods. "The feelings I sensed in you were forceful and dominant."

"I wouldn't go that far," I mutter.

He inspects me. So, does everyone else. Ryker continues slowly. "They magnified with your fear. It drove them to the surface."

My lips part as I gasp. "You knew I was in trouble."

"Yes. But the connection that drew me faded in and out. I couldn't place your exact location," Ryker explains. "It was only when I remembered where you were going that I was able to find you."

Ryker's attention returns to the others. Bill's wariness surprisingly lessens. "Did you know the Cù-Sìth would be there?" Bill asks.

"No. I can sense other forms of Death within a small radius. But I had no idea the danger Olivia was in until I arrived."

I can't believe it. Ryker charged to my rescue, knowing my life was in danger even after I'd spent a year being rude to him. That afternoon alone, I behaved especially harsh, refusing to show him even an ounce of respect despite witnessing his kindness.

The guilt makes me want to crawl beneath the table. Ryker came for me. He fought off the hounds. He risked his life. And every instinct I possess screams he'd do it again.

"Thank you," I say softly. "For searching me out and not abandoning me, even when you saw what I was up against." My hand reaches for his. All I manage is to brush his fist with my fingertips. I realize this is unexpected and bold on my part. He's not my lover, and I should hesitate to call Death my friend.

My fingers curl inward when he returns to analyze me like a

puzzle he can't figure out. "You told me you're not like the others. I think I believe you." I glance around, realizing I may not be alone. "Will you tell us what kind of Death you are?"

Ryker focuses on the hand that touched him. "I'm the Ankou."

Everyone freezes. We collectively stop breathing except for Ryker. His chest rises and falls in harsh movements, waiting for us to pass judgment.

It's Bill who finally speaks. "The King of Dead," he articulates slowly.

Ryker nods. It's all I can do not to place my head between my knees. My girl Jane is kind enough to materialize a chair behind me when my knees of steel give out. She materializes beside me in her own chair, her small feet dangling above the floor and her hand steadying me.

"Th-thanks," I stammer, gripping the armrest and trying to relax my breathing. Manic Monday just nose-dived into suckdom.

Bill drums his fingers against the table. He knows what the Ankou is. Still, he takes his time absorbing this knowledge before verbalizing it. "You died at the last hour, on the last day of the year?" Ryker nods. "And therefore, assigned the duty of carrying souls into the Afterlife."

"A year," Jane croaks.

Bill swipes at his face. "She's right. Your duty as the Ankou lasts only a year. A successor is said to replace you at the end of your term and carry your soul away as his first task. How is it possible you still remain?"

Ryker adjusts his grip on his scythe. "I died a hundred years ago in Fae, around the time Death began to hunt the living. Few died of natural causes during my months of service. By the end of the year, no souls remained for me to attend to."

"So, you had no one to replace you and no one to take you into the Afterlife," I finish for him.

Ryker's jaw tightens at the sound of my quivering voice. "I've been alone for a hundred years, Olivia, waiting for an opportunity to find my peace. When Death destroyed Fae, I was forced to enter this realm." He stops moving. "And here I remain."

Bill swears beneath his breath. Like me, he likely expected a few bombshells, not back-to-back missile airstrikes with a nuclear bomb drop for an encore. "Can another replace you?" he asks.

"The chance of a surrogate is almost impossible given how the Ankou is selected." Ryker shakes his head. "And if this realm has taught me anything, it's that the rules don't apply the same way they do in Fae." He sighs, appearing to look into the distance. "I've come to accept there will be no substitute."

I stare at my palms, unable to bear the heartbreak clouding Ryker's typically self-assured tone. I've spent my life mostly alone. Mostly. I had my father for a while, my sisters and mother a little longer. When my brother ditched me in college, I found Dahlia. But I always had *someone*. For a century, Ryker has walked alone.

"How do you eat?" Mr. Sebastian asks.

My head jerks up by the suspicion his voice carries and with morbid curiosity. Ryker is Death. How *does* he eat?

"I'd like to know as well," Bill agrees. He scratches the whiskers of his thickening goatee. "Earth's magic had a damaging effect on our forms of Death. They no longer hunt Fae for pleasure or sport, they *need* to consume our souls to soothe the agony that accompanies their hunger. As the Ankou, are you the exception?"

Everyone tenses, waiting for Ryker's response. I dig my nails into the arms of my chair, silently begging him to say he isn't capable of devouring souls like the wretched Cù-Sìth.

"I am not the exception," Ryker responds.

No one stirs. Ryker has a gift for rendering folks speechless and immobile. If it weren't for the mass of regret weighing tangibly against his shoulders, I would bolt from the room screaming.

"Jesus," Frankie mutters. He takes a step back, no longer excited to rush to his defense.

"How do you choose them?" I didn't realize I spoke aloud until every face in the room meets mine.

The rumble in Ryker's voice rocks the room. "Being a criminal defense attorney has its advantages. I meet all sorts of deserving souls to sate my hunger."

My jaw crashes down to my toes. "Holy *shit*. You're eating the clients!" He doesn't answer. I suppose his silence is answer enough.

I stand, pointing, remembering… *sliced in half, from left shoulder to right hip, clean cut.* "You killed Chandler—Brielle's husband—with your…" I swallowed hard as my widening eyes dart along the length of Ryker's long curved blade.

Bill surprises me by giving Ryker his back. He stares out the window. "The senator's son, the one accused of hurting that young child, he died shortly after his acquittal in a motor vehicle accident." His spine stiffens. "I must ask, were you the cause?"

Ryker trains his ice blue gaze on me. "Yes."

Why he picked me to look at when he answers is beyond me. I don't run as my mind insists I should. I don't cower, like my body urges. My heart takes precedent, and it's busy breaking. Ryker has no choice but to trudge through his existence. He eats souls. *Souls.* Not for pleasure. For him, there's no other choice. In his place, I would've gone mad.

"Chandler's soul will last me another few weeks," he admits.

"And then what?" Mr. Sebastian asks, his thick white brows furrowing tight with displeasure.

Ryker glares at him. Oh, look, Mr. Sebastian quickly recoils. "The others I've represented will meet me again in time. Until then, I find others through my interaction with the prosecutors office."

"You're taking out human criminals." Frankie lets out a long whistle. "That's how you eat."

"No. It's how I survive without pain," Ryker interjects, his throaty voice sharp. "I assure you; it comes at a price."

Jane angles her chin, understanding. Good for her. I can barely keep from falling over. Shock and compassion battle it out in my brain, with shock swinging hard to win. I wring my hands. There's something I need to know. Ryker's response will determine whether he is my friend or my enemy.

"The night Brielle was killed, you left the office." Ryker straightens. He already knows the question ready to tear from my lips. "Did you—She wasn't a bad person, just damaged. She didn't deserve…"

"I carried her soul into the Afterlife," he answers quietly. "I found her with the same innate trait passed to me when I became the Ankou. Chandler was hovering over her body, screaming at her and accusing her of making him kill her."

"Okay… Okay," I say. Ryker's eyes widen when I meet him with a grateful smile. "Thank you for showing her mercy."

"Why did you?" Mr. Sebastian asks. He surprises me by walking to Ryker's side, examining him with newfound curiosity all the while keeping his distance. "Humans have their own species of Death to transport them."

Ryker passes his scythe into his left hand and lowers it, so the handle hangs parallel to the floor. "You're not going to like what I have to say."

"Probably not," Bill agrees.

He waits, choosing his words carefully. "I've determined that Fae versions of Death will soon target human souls. Their mounting numbers, despite the small amount of Fae in the Tri-State area, lead me to believe they're evolving. I didn't want to chance them taking Brielle's soul, given how they swarmed the firm last month. Their lair is close to here. I just can't pinpoint the exact location."

Bill turns from the window. "You sensed their presence that day they came after me?"

"Yes, but for some reason, they can't always sense me, and I can't always distinguish between Fae and human." He jerks his chin in Bill's direction. "Like you mentioned, Earth's realm has affected our magic."

"Which explains why we didn't sense you, either," Bill reasons.

"Exactly," Ryker agrees.

Bill holds out a hand. "Just so we're clear, you're the Ankou. Who feeds off souls?" Ryker answers by not answering. "How did you come to us? It's no coincidence that you're here of all places, especially if you claim you can't differentiate Fae from humans."

"I'm here because of Olivia."

Well, isn't that a kick to the face I didn't need? "What?"

Ryker lowers his defenses. It's brief, but I see it as clearly as the sun beaming through the wall of windows. He replies as if the world doesn't exist, except for us. "I think you attract Death, Olivia. Every decision I've made since crossing into this realm— attending law school, working at this firm—have led me to you." The intensity in his blue eyes flares. "Except I'm not the only one. Whatever draws me, also lures Cathasach and the others."

I open and close my mouth several times. Of all the things he could have said, nothing disturbs me more. Except he has a point. All the times I've encountered Death can't be by chance. Could I have led them to my family... and Dahlia?

"Life," Jane croaks, her beady black irises brimming with sadness.

Bill stiffens. "By the stars," he gasps. "It must be so."

"What is it?" Ryker asks. When no one answers, the air around him crackles with mounting fury. "You're not the only one seeking answers, and I've more than complied!"

"You have." Bill looks to Jane. She blinks once, allowing Bill to continue, except he doesn't seem ready to explain. "What I'm about to share cannot leave this room. Olivia's very existence depends on it."

Ryker and the dragons cut their gazes toward me before bowing their heads in agreement. I fall as still as stone, not knowing what Bill will say and just as terrified.

Bill releases a long, hesitant breath, his gaze dulling as if he's committing an unpardonable sin. "Forgive me, Livvie," he says.

"Just say it," I tell him just as quietly.

He avoids looking at me as he explains. "Jane believes Olivia is immune to Death."

Ryker leans back on heels. "I concluded as much when I saw her effect on the Cù-Sìth. What I don't understand is how." He grinds his teeth when Bill says nothing more. "Just *tell me*."

Bill's anger and resentment matches Ryker's. "Just as you're Death, Olivia is Life. Your kind carries the darkness which silences every last breath and crumbles every stalk. She carries the light of every creature ever born, flower bloomed, air breathed." He faces me then. "Olivia is Life, it is the only perceivable explanation."

Ryker responds as if slapped. "How is this possible?"

"The same way it's possible you and the others exist," Bill answers. "This realm maintains a delicate balance. Olivia falls on one side of the scale."

And more than a dozen species of Death—monsters eager to harm me while I stand alone—wait on the other side. Tears leak down my cheeks. This isn't a burden I can bare or attention I desire. "Jane?" I ask.

She nods once, clutching my hand tighter. No Fae on Earth knows more than Jane. She wouldn't lie to me or dream up possibilities that weren't true. Jane is my friend. And the being who just predicted my doom.

"Strength," she croaks.

Jane wants me to be strong. I want her to take it all back. More tears fall. This can't be happening to me.

Heavy boots shuffle along the tile. Ryker kneels beside me and places my hand in his. "Olivia, look at me."

I shake my head, withdrawing my hand from Jane's to cover my eyes and soothe their growing sting. For some reason, I don't release Ryker. Perhaps I need to feel close to Death. It does remain my inevitable end.

"*Beag tuar ceatha*, please look at me."

I choke out a laugh through my tears. Ryker called me "little rainbow." It takes me a moment to meet his mesmerizing gaze.

Every line on his handsome face is as rigid as his jaw and stance. He breathes danger and destruction, yet despite his ire, he keeps his voice and gaze tender. "Don't be afraid," he murmurs. "I swear, I will protect you."

Bill marches to us, his steps quick, placing a shielding hand at my shoulder. "You barely know her. Why would you make her such a promise?"

Ryker stands to meet him. "If what you say is true, Olivia possesses the power to defeat Death."

"We know," Bill answers gruffly.

"But she doesn't know how to use that power," Ryker answers just as harshly. "*I do*. I can teach her to fight and destroy every form of Death that threatens the Fae." His focus returns to me. "In doing so, she can free the entombed souls."

"And what do you ask for in exchange?" Bill demands, his voice vibrating with distrust. "Death doesn't bargain without receiving something in return."

The coldness in Ryker's stare solidifies into an icy tundra. "If by some miracle we can pull this off and defeat Death, I want Olivia to kill me. She alone can help me find my peace."

12

I slump to the floor. In my defense, I don't lose consciousness. And I only drool a tiny bit. Thankfully, good ol' Jane is there to help a sister out. She materializes a paper bag I can breathe into. Within seconds... okay, not really. Less than ten minutes later, I'm feeling more positive about the whole "freeing the damned souls from the murderous Reapers and killing the hot guy who helps" pitch. Okay. Maybe not.

Ryker falls to one knee beside me. I use the opportunity to smack him in the shoulder with the paper bag. "Are you out of your mind?"

He frowns as if appalled by my rudeness. Like, I'm the unreasonable one here. "It's a fair request," he counters.

"No. It's not." I resume my bag breathing, glaring and muttering obscenities deep within my paper protection.

Ryker bows his head. "Olivia, there's nothing for me here. Everything I held sacred was lost to me long ago."

"Death has nothing to live for," Jane croaks.

Ryker doesn't respond. Yet, the sadness dimming his imposing stance corroborates Jane's reasoning. He stands, lifting his scythe. "My true form died long ago, but my soul remains in this vessel, impatient to ascend into the Afterlife. You can help me take that step."

Frankie swears like the true New Yorker he is. He reaches for his smokes but thinks better of it. "What if doesn't work? Say Olivia touches you and destroys your Ankou form. How do you know you won't be stuck here?"

"I don't. My hope is that the Reapers charged with carrying human souls will help me on. I've met my share. There are a few who are willing."

"That's assuming you and Olivia succeed in conquering Death," Bill says. He sighs wearily. "I believe Olivia and the power she's unearthed are this realm's gift to us—the chance at freedom from those who hunt us. But I also recognize her vulnerability and your numbers. It's very possible you won't succeed."

Every face in the room reflects Bill's misgivings. "I'm not a fool," Ryker says. "There is much Death and only two of us. But I'm a worthy opponent. The others know as much. With the proper tutelage, I hope to make Olivia just as formidable." He motions to me. "If Olivia truly is Life, she's stronger. Look at the Life that inhabits this realm. It gives her power. I can teach her to fight, and I can teach her to win. In time, she may be unstoppable."

I suck on that bag like there's candy sitting at the bottom. Me? Unstoppable? Clearly, they hadn't seen me trip over the throw rug this morning.

A thought occurs to me, and I lower my paper bag. "Don't you mean there are four of us? Those you summoned from the dance floor, could they help us as well?" My mind clings to the possibility that maybe we're not so alone.

"Who?" Mr. Sebastian spits out. I almost forgot about Captain Cheery Pants.

Ryker is long done answering questions. His resentment

strikes a match over each syllable. "Dugan and Phillip are the spirits of Scottish warriors assigned to serve me as the Ankou. They draw their strength from mine. Their presence leaches my power. I only summon them when desperate."

No wonder he was drained following the fight. I crumble the bag and throw it to the side. "You've spoken to Earth's Reapers?" He nods. "I hope you realize how creepy that sounds," I add. "What did you do, discuss your end over a few beers?"

Ryker arches a brow. I think he finds me as hilarious as Mr. Sebastian. "We encounter each other from time to time. Earth's Reapers aren't afforded an Afterlife. Many sympathize with my quest. Very few have accepted their fate."

"You seriously trust these demented freaks?" I throw out a hand. "No offense."

He's ready to slice my head off. I just know it. His voice lowers to a whisper. I wouldn't call it a friendly whisper. "If it means my peace, it's a chance I'm willing to take."

Frankie crosses his arms, like Ryker, he's just a wall of muscle. "Why can't they kill you? Why make Olivia do it? This little pixie doesn't have it in her, man."

Frankie's right. The Cù-Sìth are one thing. They've hurt me and those I love. Ryker hasn't done anything.

"Don't you think I've tried?" Ryker asks. "Earth's Reapers are not like Fae's. They don't cause death; they only see to those who succumb to it. And our forms of Death will devour what remains of my soul if given the chance."

"This isn't right," Bill says. He's returned to staring out across the Hudson. "Your request is not just. What makes you think Olivia will ever agree to this madness?"

"It's not madness. It's a fair exchange. We free all the trapped souls. And she frees me of this wretched existence. I know you can see it, Bill. Let Olivia see it, too."

No one speaks, their minds grinding to a halt as loudly as mine. How has my life come to this?

Ryker kneels beside me, his voice quiet. "What are you thinking, *beag tuar ceatha*?"

"Don't call me that," I say, pushing away the strands of my technicolored hair. The motion doesn't help much. Full and thick, my hair falls around my face as I lower my chin and tuck my legs beneath me. "You can't refer to me as 'little rainbow' in one breath, then beg me to murder you in the next. It's not right." *And it makes me sad.*

Ryker places his hand gently on my shoulder. "This isn't murder, Olivia. It's mercy. It's what I offered Brielle, and what I beg of you now."

I hate the despair in his voice. For someone who looks strong and youthful, he seems so weak and exhausted. The speck of vulnerability doesn't last. For his sake, I hope I'm the only one who notices. "Ryker, I don't know if I can do this, any of it."

My voice thickens with each word. I don't want Ryker hurt. I also don't want to be the cause of his pain. This is the same man who tended to the souls swarming the alley. They sought his help, and he gave it to them, ignoring the injuries he endured following his brawl with *soul eaters* and saving me. Before that, he helped Brielle achieve the peace that had eluded her for so long. Peace, I note, that has eluded him even longer.

A century without family, or anyone he can call a friend. I don't know how he's managed.

"You can. Have faith." His gaze searches mine. "I'll help you through this. But then you must help me, Olivia, as only you can."

I look at him and take in everything he offers. This is my chance to help him, my family, and Dahlia, the opportunity to fight back just as I've always wanted. I have the tools and a master willing to teach me how to use them. I just don't care for the price.

Something in me stirs. He senses it and helps me up from the floor. "I can't guarantee the outcome," he says. "But I promise to do everything in my power to keep you safe and to teach you to survive in my absence. If matters unravel beyond repair, and should I perish before you can help me, disappear. Do you hear me? Find the strongest talisman and hide. In time, even without me, you'll find a way to avenge the Fae."

I'm not sure I believe him, even as our gazes weld like melting steel. Can I do this? The Ankou before me insists I can. But what if he's wrong?

Ryker lifts my hand and brushes my knuckles with his soft lips. "Will you help, little rainbow? Will you help me have my peace?"

Everyone waits for me to respond. I stand, unable to breathe, merely gaping at the way his warm breath teases my skin. I suppose those around me expect something profound, words that will rouse them into applause and cheers.

I don't have it in me so, I simply speak the truth. "If this is what you truly want, I'll do it for you. But you must do something more for me."

He squares his shoulders, his hard exterior forming a protective aura around him. "What is it?"

"I want to be the one to kill Cathasach. When he's dead, I want you to guide the souls of my family into the Afterlife…"

13

The dragons return. One of them, the naked one, resumes his reptilian form and gulps down the contents of my spilled soup, including the container and lid. It must have been tasty.

Frankie helps me retrieve the items that spilled from my purse, sans the tampons. Statement of fact: New York boyz avoid feminine products at all costs. I suppose it makes them go blind or grow hair on their palms.

Ryker, Bill, and Mr. Sebastian speak quietly. Jane interjects occasionally in one-word protests. They discuss my training, while it seems laughable, and my safety, which very much isn't.

"The best way to hide is out in the open," Ryker reasons. "Olivia should resume her duties here, preferably in the morning. I'll work with her in the afternoons, evenings, and weekends in my apartment."

"I'll contribute to the costs of training Olivia," Mr. Sebastian offers. "If it means ridding us of these damn hell hounds, I'll give you every last penny I have."

"I'll assure the firm keeps you and Olivia on salary," Bill adds. He's troubled. I can see it, only because I know him so well, just like I can see him doing his best to hide it from the others. "The Ancients have expressed their desire to help."

"What about Marco?"

They look at me when I speak. Considering I'm Life and all, they forget I'm waiting mere feet from them. I don't know if I should excuse it for worry, fear, or something else entirely. Regardless, I don't like it.

"I'll tell Marco you're working on a special case," Bill says, answering Ryker as if he asked. "And that Olivia will be assisting you. Jane, will you help facilitate his understanding?"

I blink back at Bill. He looks away, reaching for his phone.

Jane keeps her attention on Ryker. "Don't hurt her," she croaks.

Ryker holds firm to his scythe. "I'll keep her safe. My home is warded and secure—"

"Not what I mean." It's the last thing Jane says. She shuffles toward the elevator, the hem of her long black dress dragging against the tile.

Frankie passes me my hairbrush. I'm not certain how long he held it before I finally notice. "You sure you want to do this, Livvie?" he asks.

"No," I answer. "I only know that I have to make a choice." It hurts to say her name and hurts me more to say it to Frankie. "I don't want what happened to Dahlia to happen to anyone else. For that, I can't run."

We bow our heads. It's not a silent tribute or anything we plan. It just happens, a brief moment to remember a sweet soul. Frankie takes my hands and squeezes them; he keeps his chin lowered and so do I. "If I can help in any way, Livvie, call me. I've got you. I swear I'll do whatever it takes."

My hands fall when he releases them, feeling heavy. Frankie crosses the room, the other dragons shadowing him. They step into the elevator with him. He keeps his attention ahead. The others give him space, even Mr. Sebastian, who positions himself at the very front. They're not a single force. Not anymore.

As the doors shut, Frankie finally meets my gaze, anger and grief solidifying his already firm posture.

I miss him the moment he's gone. I'm left with Bill and Ryker. Bill sighs. "When do you think she can start?"

Again, it's as if I'm not there. "I don't know," I reply, bewildered by how he's acting. "Whenever Ryker thinks it's best, I imagine."

"I suppose you're correct," Bill says. "Please, call me if you need me. I'll be on my way."

Bill walks to the elevator, not exactly rushing, yet also not exactly overjoyed to stay. I watch him with my mouth agape and uncertain what changed between us.

The elevator dings, and Bill steps inside. Unlike Frankie, he doesn't meet my face. Instead, he looks past me, to the wall of windows where Ryker stands.

Ryker scrutinizes Bill. It's like I missed something between them, or maybe us. I almost ask Ryker about it, except it doesn't feel right. Ryker saved my life, but Bill is my friend. At least, it's what I think he still is.

Ryker eases to my side. "Let me take you to lunch. We can discuss the details of your training and set goals. If you feel you're ready, we can start as early as tomorrow."

I glance at my bright fuchsia shoes. Savior of the Fae. That's me. "The sooner we start, the better?"

Ryker takes in my shaky visage. His behemoth form towers over me. I peg him at least a foot and a half taller. My petite stature usually makes me the smallest person in the room. Next to him, and guessing what lies ahead, I feel minuscule, a cricket waiting for a careless foot to stomp its life out.

The coldness in his arctic eyes dim. "This is a lot for you to take in."

"Mm," I agree.

"If I could, I'd give you more time to absorb it all and come to terms with your destiny."

"My destiny?" It starts off as a question yet, it's not exactly how it ends. It's more of a statement of fact. I just can't wrap my mind around it. Not yet.

"Cathasach is aware of you, Olivia. He'll actively hunt you. It's only a matter of time."

"He's right, Olivia," Bill says. "There's not much time."

I startle at Bill's voice. I didn't even notice him return. Ryker frowns, appearing equally bothered.

"We should head upstairs," Bill says. "There's much to be done."

I follow behind him slowly. Bill seems more like himself, now, except the sudden shift in his demeanor is unsettling.

I step into the elevator with my gargoyle in glamour boss and the Grim Reaper Ankou. No, this doesn't sound crazy or anything.

My focus travels up, and I freeze. The curve of Ryker's scythe dangles just above my head. One slice. That's all it will take to split my head open and spill the contents of my brain in tiny chunks— I cough nervously, putting an abrupt halt to my thoughts. "Shouldn't you..."

Midnight blue smoke churns from the staff, encasing Ryker. The elevator *dings* open and the doors part, revealing Ryker in full *GQ* mode, his mojo of death powerful enough to sharpen the collar of his dress shirt.

We step out with his hand resting against the small of my back. His solid and warm touch straightens my spine enough to hang a flag from. Another blush. At this point, what's one more?

I turn around to catch Bill's stare burning a hole through Ryker's hand and into my back. He looks forward when he sees me. We're going to have to have a talk. Now just isn't the time.

"Aren't you worried about the cameras?" I mutter to Ryker.

He almost smiles. "Death isn't visible on film."

Oddly enough, that makes sense.

Helen, the receptionist, widens her eyes and flashes a phony smile. Like Bill, she notices Ryker leading me forward. "Good morning, Mr. Scott. A little late this morning, aren't we, Olivia?"

Bill's typically smooth voice is as jagged as shattered flint. "Morning meeting, Helen. We were all in attendance."

"Yes, Mr. MacGregor. Good morning, sir." Helen was so captivated by Ryker's display of affection, she hadn't noticed Bill. Her attention returns to the stack of papers on her desk, collating them quickly as she rushes to assume the role of a dili- gent worker. Her acting skills are shoddy at best, and even with Bill here, she can't seem to keep her eyes off us.

I pushed a strand of pink hair behind my ear. "Feeling protective?" Sexy feels aside, it's the best way to describe how he holds me.

"Excuse me?" Ryker catches himself and immediately drops his hand. "Forgive me. Perhaps I am."

The sense of security his touch provided abandons me like a passing breeze. I didn't realize the safety I felt until it left me. Without thinking, I clutch his arm. A mound of hard muscle greets me beneath his tailored suit. Death is a walking mass of stacked stone! If this is how he'll expect my training to go, I'd better up my protein intake.

I squeeze again. Damn. Heat builds along my hand and between my breasts. He can't be real. No one is this—

"Is something wrong?" he asks when I give yet another heartfelt squeeze.

"No. I just think we should censor our behavior in the office."

"Is that why you're squeezing my arm like a loaf of bread?" Ryker mutters, nodding to a junior associate as he passes.

Oh, no. Not a loaf of bread, big boy. I rip my hand off him. If I were any smoother, I'd slide across the tile. "Rumors spread quickly," I say as if I hadn't just fondled him. "I don't want to give anyone the wrong impression of us."

Ryker's voice stiffens, and his face flushes slightly. "Of course. It won't happen again."

I groan and cover my face, wishing my legs were longer so I could kick my own ass.

I start to apologize when Ryker turns rather abruptly into his office. Bill stomps forward to walk beside me instead of shadowing. We continue down the row of offices and cubicles. I glance over my shoulder, wishing I hadn't embarrassed him... and perhaps for different circumstances where I could welcome his touch.

"Don't get attached, Olivia," Bill rumbles. "He is Death, and that is his fate. It doesn't have to be yours."

My focus stays ahead, mortification cooling the effects of Ryker's contact. "I know, Bill. But he's as human as the rest of us."

"No, he's not, Olivia." He stops in front of my cubicle. "If you are to become everything we hope you are capable of, you must never forget what Ryker is or what his nature compels him to do. Do you understand me?"

Bill had assumed a fatherly role from the moment we met, and he learned of my past. I briefly questioned his behavior earlier. Now, all I see is the man who took me under his Gargoyle wing. Like a good father, he's watching out for me, his family, and taking his role seriously. "I understand, Bill."

His voice softens, and his forlorn deportment returns. "We lost our dear Dahlia and countless others that night, and we will lose many more before this madness reaches an end. I don't want you among the fallen, Olivia." He shakes his head, the weight of his worries encapsulating him at once. "Consider Ryker's actions and intent every time you're with him. You care deeply, it's one of your many redeeming qualities. But this situation doesn't call for your kindness or compassion. It demands your wit and strength. Think with your head and guard your heart at all costs."

Bill is speaking as someone who wasn't there that night and who didn't see the side of Ryker I had experienced. That doesn't mean I should ignore his warning or that I somehow know Ryker better than anyone.

"All right, Bill. I'll be careful." I adjust my purse closer against me, dreading my next question. "What will you tell everyone about Dahlia?"

Traces of guilt spread along Bill's smooth skin. "An email went out last night informing the staff that Dahlia gave her notice and took a job out of state. The explanation while simple, is believable, and allows few questions."

"I suppose you're right." I drop my heavy bag on my desk with a thud, wishing there was a better way to say goodbye.

Bill's hand finds my shoulder. "Dahlia deserves justice and honor, just as the others lost to us. You possess the power to achieve both. I only wish I could offer you, and her, more."

"Me, too."

"Olivia!" Marco hollers loud enough to rattle the windows of his office. "Where the hell—"

"Your briefcase is in your closet," I call out.

"I meant—"

"And your iPad is inside the rear pocket," I remind him. "But—"

"I charged it on Friday before I left and powered it down to conserve the battery. Do you remember your password?" I ask.

"Of course, I do. I'm not a moron!" he yells. There's a brief pause, followed by more yelling. "Damn it. Did you change my password?"

"No, Marco." I sigh. "Give me a second. I'll be right in."

"*Fine.* But you better bring coffee!"

I pinch the bridge of my nose. Doesn't Marco realize I have briefs to type and souls to free? "Are you sure Marco will be okay without me, Bill? I just caught him up to speed from my last stint with Ryker."

"Ryker's PA and mine will take over your duties. Jane will also help as needed. Won't you, Jane?"

Jane shuffles into her cubicle, steaming cup of coffee in hand. "What?" she squawks.

"I said you'll help Marco if he needs it," Bill repeats a little louder.

"I don't want the Crypt Keeper's mother helping me!" Marco barks. "What I want is a damn cup of coffee. Hell's bells, isn't she dead yet?"

I dive across the partition separating our cubicles when Jane reaches for her candy-cane wand. It doesn't matter how fast I move. Jane, bless her osteoporosis backside, is faster.

"*Dhíoghail dom*," she spits, her beady black irises gleaming with hate.

Avenge me. Holy stars, she just whacked Marco with the evil eye.

Time slows, except for us. The papers I scatter in my haste remain suspended, the edges barely beginning to flutter. Bill and I exchange glances, panic spreading across our features like a bad rash.

Not Jane. She sips her coffee as if the gamut of her curse isn't intensifying into the mini tornado at the tip of her wand. With an angry boom of thunder, the diminutive twister swirls away from the wand and ransacks its way into Marco's office.

Bill mutters a few swears and chases after it, his legs

pumping fast. The tornado beats him to Marco, banging into the massive desk and scattering everything on it.

Marco's paperweight, briefcase, iPad, and a few pens fall on the floor with a crash, morphing into tarantulas the size of their former counterparts. Let me tell you, an iPad turned arachnid is one f 'ing huge spider.

Marco screams, his caterpillar-thick eyebrows shooting up his receding hairline. His howls, in retrospect, don't compare to the shrieks that follow when the tornado swallows his desk and spits out Harry Potter's Aragog.

"Jane, stop it!" I yell, lunging for her wand. She jerks her hand away, still sipping and still very much keeping her wand from me.

Marco's ear-splitting cries pound against my sensitive ears. The mammoth spider spreads her fangs, nailing Marco in the face with a thick stream of web. Bill roars, exploding into his gargoyle form. He grips the spider's two front legs, barely keeping the pinchers from stabbing Marco's flailing body.

The other versions of Jane's creepy crawlies scuttle around Bill and swarm Marco's rotund form. The smallest one, bright yellow and likely a former highlighter, leaps into the air, latching onto one of Marco's eyebrows, trying to eat it.

I whirl back, horrified. "*Jane*, stop it!"

She takes another sip of coffee. I swing my leg over the divider and land sprawled across her desk, trying futilely to filch her wand. "You're going to kill Marco!"

"Yup," she croaks, scooting away on her office chair with a sudden rush of her power.

"Grath the wanth!" Bill roars at me, his forked tongue shooting through his fangs like a streamer. He snaps off one of the arachnid legs, but seven angry ones still remain, hell-bent on reaching poor Marco.

"I'm trying!" I yell back.

I kick off my shoes and jet after Jane. She zig-zags along the rows of cubicles, giggling like a possessed kid on a Big Wheel instead of an old druid priestess on a very modern office chair. She speeds up when she sees me coming, her black veil flapping behind her like a kite.

"Jane, get back here, now!"

The one superpower I possess being a pixie is my innate ability to prance. Sure, it's not much to brag about, but it helps now. My legs propel me off the floor and onto a desk. I catapult over a service guy frozen in the middle of towing away our broken copier, the hem of my skirt skimming his bald head.

Ryker glances up from his paperwork as I land. By no small miracle, I manage to clutch the back of Jane's chair. She drags me along, not slowing down. I pull my body up and wrench the candy-cane wand from her grip. The chair dwindles to a stop, back where we started.

I stand, panting as I lift the over-accessorized little stick above my head and away from Jane. I may be short, but I have enough height to foil Jane.

"Harumph," she snaps.

Just because I have the wand doesn't mean I let my guard down. For a little old lady, Jane packs quite the sucker punch. "Jane, I'll give you your wand back if you promise to expunge the curse. You know how Marco is. He didn't mean to insult you."

She responds with a defiant tilt of her sharp chin and an arthritic middle finger in Marco's direction.

A dismembered spider leg slaps against the glass. Bill broke off two more in our absence and squashed three smaller spiders with his gargantuan foot. One creeps out of the office and scrambles beneath Jane's desk.

"Oliviath!" Bill roars, motioning to where poor Marco lays mummified in the corner.

Jane notices and resumes her hellish giggles.

"Jane," I tell her. "That's not funny?"

"What happened?" Ryker asks. He stalks down the hall, taking in the frozen atmosphere and its occupants. His widening stare homes in on the chaos that is Marco's office.

Ryker's arrival momentarily distracts me, and Jane takes full advantage. She leaps into the air and out of her orthopedic shoes, reaching for her wand.

I hold tight, and so does she. The wand shakes at jack-hammer speed. I think Jane's wand is reacting to her power. We discover too late it's reacting to mine. The wand tumbles between us and spins, the heart and ribbon end stopping and aiming at Marco's office. The overhead lights illuminate in blinding capacity, far exceeding their wattage and buzzing as if ready to explode.

Except the only thing that explodes are the spiders. All of them.

Like the sound of rupturing balloons, they detonate.

I expect blood, guts, and innards—whatever makes up ginormous arachnoids. Instead, petals of roses, pansies, lilacs, lilies, and daisies smack against the fishbowl office and shoot through the open door like cannon fodder, knocking Jane and me on our asses.

"Shit," she crows when I push up on my elbows.

Ryker remains a stone wall, watching the floral surplus spill from the office. I suppose nothing really "wows" the Grim Reaper.

Bill wades through waist-deep flowers, growling. The virtual garden does little to hide his super-sized male parts as he rustles into the hall. Thank the stars his new talisman holds strong, dangling from a gold chain an inch below his collarbone. He prowls toward Jane, flapping his wings to relieve them of the mounds of buttercups adorning the arches.

"Janeth," he hisses. "Thith ith no wayth for anth Ancienth tooth behaveth."

"What?" Jane croaks.

I'm learning Jane's hearing is selective at best.

Flowers cascade down my dress as I stand. "He says, 'this is no way for an Ancient to behave.'" I frown at her. "And he's right."

She raises her thin brows at me.

"Jane," I say. "Don't you blame me for this. I'm not the one who sent tarantulas to kill Marco."

She smirks.

I gasp at her cheekiness. "I have no idea how this happened. You clean this mess up this instant!"

"Spoilsport," she quips. She holds out her hand. "Wand."

I mutter something, too, it's just not worth repeating. "She wants us to find her wand."

"Mm. Mm. Miff. Moff!" Marco is hollering beneath layers of blossoms and webbing.

Bill rolls his large almond eyes. "I'llth gothe freeth himth."

Ryker crouches beside me as I crawl along the sea of blooms. "Did you ever do anything like this before?"

My hands search blindly beneath about twenty pounds of flowers. I sneeze when a stigma pushes up my nose. "No. But I've never dared to touch Jane's wand before."

"Trigger," Jane croaks, returning to her cubicle.

Ryker gives it some thought. "She's right. Your contact with Cathasach could have triggered your power and possibly more."

"That's fantastic," I add. I'd gone from no magic to killing death hounds and converting spiders into petal popping piñatas.

The fun doesn't seem to end. My eyes widen when I find Jane's wand beneath an extra thick mound of flowers.

I lift it, victoriously…and double the florals overtaking the office. The force knocks us backward. Ryker yanks the vibrating wand from my grasp and tosses it to Jane. She catches it as if the wicked thing couldn't wait to return to her liver-spotted grip.

"Goth damth ith!" Bill roars over Jane's devilish giggles.

Ryker rests his head on a bed of rose petals and shifts his gaze my way, spitting out a leaf so he can speak. "We shouldn't delay your training. If Cathasach has triggered your magic, you must learn to master it before it takes control…"

14

It took Jane an hour to clean up her mess. She had to alter the fucker's (aka Marco's) memory, re-grow his eyebrow, and return his furniture and office supplies back to pre-arachnid glory. It should have taken her less time, but the little dickens was having too much fun.

Ryker waits near my desk. He's not hovering, per se, yet I'm innately aware of his presence. I'm not certain when that sense of his presence began. Maybe it was always there, and I was too blind to see it.

"Are you almost ready?" he asks.

"Just a moment, please." I type quickly and work just as fast. I have to manage my workload, take care of Marco, and support the less-experienced staff. Right now, my super organization skills and resourcefulness just aren't happening. Stars, I can practically feel every breath Ryker takes.

I type and retype the email to Bill's secretary and the two new hires. I try to be specific on what Marco needs for his next few hearings and how to handle his moods. Between the three of them, I'm hoping they'll keep him satisfied or, at the very least, non-homicidal.

"Olivia!"

"Second drawer on your left, Marco!" I yell back.

"You don't even know—" He slides the drawer open. "*Fine.* But that's not where I want it!"

I don't miss a beat, speaking calmly. "Then put it where you want it, but don't forget to tell me where." I snatch the giant coffee an intern brought and hurry into Marco's office. Ryker follows. He doesn't make a sound, except here I am, feeling him again. "I have your coffee and a few documents that require your signature."

He skims the letter at the top of the pile. "Who the hell is Diamond? And why do I have to pay her this ridiculous amount?"

I clear my throat. This will be fun. "Her name is pronounced Dee-ah-mund and—"

"Is this a joke, Olivia?" He leans forward, his new eyebrow giving an extra angry twitch. "Have I *ever* left you with the impression that I like jokes?"

I continue, unaffected, and hoping to heaven and back Jane didn't give that eyebrow a life of its own. "She's a new hire, with a great deal of experience, and it's only three-grand more a year than what you paid Chelsea."

"Why should I pay Ruby—"

"Diamond," I correct, emphasizing the correct pronunciation.

Oh, stars, and doesn't that piss Marco off. "With a name like that she belongs on a pole with clear heels, Olivia. Not in my office!"

"Marco," I say, forcing a patient smile. "How can I say this? We need quality workers—"

"Not strippers," he mocks.

So much for patience. I ram my hands on my hips. "Marco, I am sick of the skanks that occupy space here looking to snag an attorney instead of focusing on their jobs. By paying a little more, for better quality, production will increase, and you'll make it up in profit."

Maybe it's me, but the new brow seems extra fuzzier and extra moodier. Or maybe it's just Marco. "Why do I put up with you?" he snarls.

"Because I take care of you and I know what I'm doing." I point to the paper. "Date and initial here."

He glares. I sigh. "Marco, I have a lot on my plate. Diamond starts tomorrow. I'd like you to be nice to her."

He grips his pen, ready to chomp it in half. "Are you saying I'm not nice?"

"Yes. I am." I totally go Jersey and lift a hand. "Marco, this case I'm helping Ryker with will be tough to get through. I'm not sure how available I'll be. I want you to be patient..."

"I'm patient!"

"...with everyone who's covering for me. They're here to help you."

His upper lip curls. Well, isn't this going just smoothly? I slap my hand over my forehead. "For pity's sake, Marco!"

Ryker edges around me, closing the distance between him and Marco. He doesn't loom nor touch him, but he's close, his deep rumbling voice soft. "I recognize this is a difficult time for you, sir. I appreciate your willingness to allow Olivia to assist me. She's irreplaceable to you, and you fear losing her. I know this. Take comfort in knowing she'll back to you soon. And, in her absence, allow the staff to help and work with you."

Marco's scowl softens with each passing word. "Very well, son," he says. He finishes signing the form and signs the next few documents without question. "Just be sure I get her back in one piece."

"Yes, sir." Ryker rights himself and motions toward the door. "Shall we, Olivia?"

I blink back at them. "Ah, yeah. Bye, Marco."

Marco doesn't glance up. Everyone else does as we pass. The associate who always fixated on Dahlia abandons his office when he sees us. "Hey, Ryker—I mean, Mr. Scott."

It occurs to me that aside from the partners, I'm the only one who called Ryker by his first name. Bob, the associate, leans casually against the door. "Heard you have a big case. What's it about?"

"Murder," Ryker replies.

Bob blows out a breath. "Damn, man. You get all the good cases. I'd love to sink my teeth into a murder case. Hey, do you need any help?"

"Olivia is helping me."

His greed is sleazy enough to make me want to shower. "Is she?"

I lift my chin. "I'm capable of more than just making coffee," I remind him.

His grin broadens. "I bet you are."

Ryker steps closer to me. "I hope you're not implying something other than Olivia's professional skills. It won't sit well with me or the partners."

Bob keeps his attention on me. Had he caught the barest trace of Ryker's lethal stare, that stupid smile would slide right off his face. "Not at all. But if you change your mind—"

"I won't. Olivia is the only one I need."

Bob does a double-take when Ryker steps toward him, stunned by Ryker's tightening stance and balled fists. Bob knows he crossed a dangerous line. "Ah, yeah," he says, coughing into his shoulder. "Sorry to hear about Dahlia quitting, Olivia. She was sweet."

Sweet piece of ass that I never got to bite is probably what he really means. *Idiot.* I'm two seconds from punching him in his super-sized Adam's apple.

"Let's go, Olivia," Ryker rumbles, keeping Bob in his sights as we continue down the hall.

I'm glad Ryker can see past Bob's phony persona. I've never liked Bob, yet his behavior tugs at my heart. It's a reminder that Dahlia is no longer around for him to flirt with. She's gone, and suffering, just like my family.

I take several deep breaths when we enter the elevator, trying to will away my tears. Moving on without Dahlia is excruciating. How am I going to focus my magic and train with barely more than a day to mourn? I need more time than this...

My throat tightens, and my breathing grows frantic, despite my efforts to slow it. I start hyperventilating, pining to see my friend's sweet face and missing the gentle way she took care of everyone.

Dahlia is gone. Just like everyone I loved before her.

Ryker narrows in, close enough for his body heat to stroke against the length of my arm. His presence, so warm, contrasts the cool soothing air filling my lungs and slows my rapid breathing. Each intake of air is like ice to my throbbing wounds, and every beat of my heart is like a heavy stone lifting from the rubble that buries me.

Tears drizzle down my cheeks as I lower my lashes and choke back a cry from the reprieve.

A deep thrum murmurs in my ear. *Peace*, it whispers.

I jerk away, reaching for the banister to steady me. Ryker stretches out his hand, trying to catch me. My gaze travels from his hand, up his arm, to that dimple, unable to go farther. "D-did you just do something to me?"

Ryker withdraws his hand and straightens, turning his body dead center toward the door.

"Did you?" I repeat quietly.

"The Ankou is tasked with many things," he says. "He doesn't exist simply to care for those who died."

"He doesn't?" I question.

He straightens further. "I'm sorry," I add. "I don't mean to disrespect you or sound naive. It's just that all I know about Death is shrouded in darkness."

"Ryker?" I ask. "Tell me what else the Ankou does."

Ryker looks over his shoulder, his features a mixture of strength and sadness. "He comforts those in mourning."

The elevator *dings* and the doors part. He steps out, pausing as if uncertain if I'll follow. I force myself forward, still stunned and not fast enough.

Ryker's arm whips out, preventing the doors from ramming me. I step past him and into the foyer, my gaze cemented with his.

"Olivia," he rasps. "The Ankou also aids with revenge. Trust in me, and Cathasach will pay for every life he stole from you."

That voice carries more potent energy and fury in its rumble than a thousand storms. It's captivating. There's no escape from it *or him*. I should fight. Instead, everything about Ryker engulfs me, and I just let it happen.

Ryker isn't a man.

Or beast.

Or anything so simply defined.

He represents the ultimate end. And he's exactly who I need. His ice-blue eyes are chains of silver, binding me to him. Or maybe I'm holding him. Neither of us moves. Neither of us turns away.

I realize I'm in trouble. A pixie playing with red-hot Death.

"Mr. Scott, your limo is waiting." It's not enough for Ralph the security guard to yell across the foyer. He waves like a tween at a One Direction reunion, big smile and all.

I wait for him to throw his panties next until I realize how fixated Ryker remains. "Trust me," he murmurs.

"I will," I promise.

Ralph jogs up to us, out of breath from the distance he cleared from the main doors to the elevators. "Is everything all right, sir? Do you need help carrying your briefcase?"

"No. Perhaps you should offer Olivia assistance with her purse."

Ralph wrenches my purse from my grasp. Ryker eases away from me like it pains him. "We should go, there's much to do."

Ryker doesn't move until I do. The limo driver hops out and hurries to open the door. Ralph beats him to it. I pause before entering, my voice surprisingly steady considering the near breakdown I almost had and my exchange with Ryker.

Something happened between Ryker and me, although I'm not certain what it is. My hand rests on the doorframe as I address the driver. "Mr. Santonelli needs to be in court by eight thirty every morning for an important case. Make sure you're here by eight and please call upstairs the moment you arrive."

"Sure thing, Olivia." He winks at me. "Wouldn't want to make the big boss mad."

Ryker's steely exterior "encourages" the driver to return to his seat. I don't even get a chance to thank him. I slip inside and shimmy to the far side. Ryker doesn't close in, giving me ample space.

I fold my hands on my lap, speaking only when we reach the next block. "You came to me the other night, didn't you? You were there, in my room with me when I cried."

Ryker stares out the window as we roll to a stop. A homeless woman shuffles by, pushing her shopping cart. "A part of me was with you," he admits. "As I mentioned, I hear and sense thoughts at times. Most are muddled at best."

"Except mine."

The woman pauses as she reaches the window. She can't see in, but she tilts her head as if she can.

Traffic opens up, and the limo accelerates. I turn to watch the woman, who can't seem to look away. "Your thoughts tend to be clearer," Ryker agrees. "They're especially more pronounced when your emotions reach their peak. In the hours that followed the attack at the Glen, your feelings shoved your thoughts to the surface. I felt everything, your pain, your sorrow, your guilt. Except it wasn't until you gave in to your exhaustion that I was able to reach you."

The woman with her shopping cart is barely visible now. But I know she's there and watching. I turn away, not only because I think I understand why she's so captivated, but because of what Ryker tells me. "You helped me mourn," I guess.

He rests his elbow against the window ledge and cups his chin with his thumb and forefinger. "Yes."

My eyes want to well with tears, but I don't let them. "And you helped soothe me."

He nods.

"Did you touch me? I felt a strong hand…"

He turns his attention to where the rows of buildings on Hudson Street pass in a blur. "Not in the physical sense. My power primarily invades the mind to help those struggling with loss. The touch you sensed was likely your mind's interpretation of comfort."

I felt his heavy palm and his long fingers press against me, just as they had when we entered the firm. I should have recognized his caress, warm, hard, and capturing me with a small part of himself. Still, I believe him. My pixie nature makes me naturally affectionate. Dahlia and I constantly held hands and hugged like little girls. These actions were strange to some. To us, it felt natural, like a bond all sisters should share. So, of course, that night I sought the contact of another to soothe me. I just didn't realize it was Ryker.

I scoot closer to him, examining the way his broad shoulders and build appear to take up so much room. A thought occurs to me, one that makes me gasp with sudden understanding.

"You help Marco grieve, don't you?" I ask. "That's why he relaxes around you. You soothe the daily agony he endures from losing his wife."

Ryker waits to answer. He seems hesitant to betray Marco. "Mr. Santonelli hurts a great deal," he admits. "When I met him, all his thoughts revolved around joining her."

My lips part. "He was suicidal." I thought he was, which is why I practically coddle him.

"Very much so," he agrees. "Now, he wishes for cancer or an ailment he can't possibly heal from. Aside from you, I sense his thoughts the most. There are times the man begs for death."

"Except when he's with you," I presume.

"Or you," Ryker clarifies. He lowers his hand at the sight of my small smile. "You've been good for him, Olivia. You help him focus on his responsibilities, and you're a reminder that he still has a purpose."

I slide along the seat, shortening what remains of the space between us, our legs almost touching. "This is why he feels so close to you, and why he calls you 'son.'"

"I understand him," he responds. He watches my knee hit his leg when the driver careens over a pothole. "I know what it feels like to be alone."

My hand clutches my chest, the drop in his casual tone making me sad. Ryker's duties as the Ankou demand a great deal from him and give nothing in return.

I slip my hand into the crook of his arm. He raises an eyebrow, staring at my hand as it rests against him. I should pull away. I don't, feeling that need for touch kick in, and offer a gentle squeeze instead.

"Thank you," I say softly. "For helping me, and Marco."

Bill's warning to keep my distance chastises me the entire

drive. I wonder if he somehow warned Ryker, too. If so, we both ignore him, holding our positions until the limo angles up to a curve.

"We're here," he murmurs.

I grin. "Okay. Let's see what you've got, o' bringer of doom."

Although his jaw clenches at the insult, the subtle twitch in his lips gives away his amusement. What can I say? I'm damn hilarious.

Ryker lowers his head, avoiding direct eye contact with me when the driver opens the door. I spin a little, taking in the small row homes across the street and the large brick building behind me.

"Are we in the Heights?" Jersey City's Heights, to be exact. "You're not far from the office."

"Yes," he replies, keeping close to me.

We walk toward a large converted warehouse, six stories tall with freshly laid brick. Ryker leads me beneath a curved archway that opens to a partially hidden old-world garden. Wrought iron chairs and tables are spread around the perimeter to give a park-like setting while large clay pots of overflowing impatiens offer bursts of color. I peek into the large fountain at the center where small carp flutter and splash.

"This was originally a housing complex for the wealthy," Ryker explains before I can hit him with my many questions. "Following the Great Depression, it was converted into a cannery." He points to the side. "A two-story office composed mostly of sheetrock and rusty metal took up this area. The owners tore it down and expanded the garden." He motions to the left. "This side was the original building constructed in the late eighteen-hundreds. The right was added about two years ago to wrap around and enclose the area."

"It's beautiful." My heels tap against the rust-colored concrete, stained to give it a classic bucolic feel. I pause and sweep my shoe over it. The texture holds a rough grain, likely capable of withstanding even the toughest winters. "How long have you lived here?"

"Almost three years. The left side needed extensive renovation to the original woodwork and ceilings, but the owners knew if they took the time, it would attract the right buyers."

We walk across the courtyard and to another archway draped with a curtain of small leaf ivy. He pauses, allowing the workers carrying buckets of paint to pass before leading me into the beautiful Italian tiled foyer.

Blue and yellow floral patterns greet our feet and create a pathway to an antique steel elevator with the crisscrossing gates. Ryker unhooks one side, and we stepped inside.

"This is nice," I say. "Classy."

He smirks. "I like what they've done," he agrees.

"I mean you. Talking." I grin. "I never knew you could spit out so many words at one time, counselor."

One side of his mouth curves upward, not quite a smile, but I'm gaining ground. With luck, I'll see a few teeth by the end of the week.

He leans back on his heels. "Perhaps I would have said more if you hadn't ripped my head off every time I glanced in your direction."

My cheeks warm. "I don't know what you mean." I frown at his growing smirk. "But you probably deserved it anyway."

The elevator crawls upward, squeaking to a halt when we reach the top floor. He yanks the gates open and waits for me to pass him. A large steel door rests a few steps away, reinforced with square sheets of copper, bronze, and brown metal, adding a touch of artistry to what could have otherwise been a boring door. He mutters something before unlocking it and slides the door to the side.

My eyes tear from the amount of sunshine pooling into the

room and setting the honey wood floors ablaze. Ryker doesn't own an apartment on the sixth floor. He owns the whole damn floor.

"Come in," he says.

My vision begins to adjust to the brightness after what must be several not-so-sexy blinking moments on my part. I'm glad; this sight is worth seeing.

Leaves of different shapes and sizes were carefully etched into the soaring white tiered ceiling, forming a swirling pattern of foliage. "The owners weren't aware of the workmanship until they removed the fabricated ceiling," Ryker explains.

I wrench my head to take it in the majesty. "Do all the floors have…this?" I ask.

"The ceiling on the floor below sprawls upward of eighteen feet. But it isn't as detailed."

"You poor sap," I say, thoughtfully, scoring me another smirk.

"I'll recover given the price was far less."

"You bought the floor below?" I ask. The wall of windows before me already provides a million-dollar view of the Hudson River. Ryker probably shelled out a lot more than that for each floor.

"The firm pays me well," Ryker adds, his tone intensifying in severity. "And I need the space."

His tone suggests I should shut my mouth. The flicker of shame dulling his features makes me press. I drop my giant pink purse on the floor and inch closer. "Why?"

He tightens his jaw. "For privacy."

My instincts warn I've pushed enough. I don't heed them. I can't. If we're going to trust each other, we have to know each other. "What do you need privacy for?"

His hands curl into tight fists. "You don't want to know."

"Probably not," I agree. I wait, watching Ryker's intensity sharpen into a blade that viciously stabs the air in front of me.

After what feels like an eternity, I press a little more. "Just tell me," I say, quietly.

His face meets mine in true "Prince of the Dead, I pick my teeth with a scythe mode." I hold my ground, trying to quiet the terrified side of me informing me I'm seconds from losing my breakfast, shrieking, and possibly bleeding.

"For when I eat, Olivia," he replies. "I need privacy, so no one hears me devouring souls."

15

"Oh."

"Oh?" Ryker stares at me like I flashed my pathetic boobage. "Is that all you have to say?"

"Well, no." I think about it. "Is it painful?"

"Do you really want to know?" he hisses, advancing closer. "Do you want to know how it feels to consume a *living spirit*?"

The regret and shame coating his words like tar keep me in place. Death can't live, not really. But he can be tortured. "I want to know more about you." I take his hand and squeeze it. "We need to trust each other, right?"

Bill warned me against lowering my guard and opening my heart. I heard him loud and clear. Except here I go, drawing closer and touching Ryker. I suppose if I can lure Death, maybe Death can lure me just as strongly.

My chest constricts with each passing heartbeat. For a moment, I feel that same pure and wretched fear that has haunted me for so long. It doesn't last, although part of me assumes it should.

Ryker's broad shoulders tense like a panther before he pounces on his meal. I don't like being afraid. Fear is a creature easily fed and riled. I breathe in and out and squeeze tighter. This same hand I hold, warm and powerful, raised me from the floor when fear left me too crippled to act. And this same rough voice pledged to keep me safe.

Maybe I'm a fool. Maybe my actions will lead to my ultimate end. If so, I'm the fool who's not letting go.

Ryker's impermeable force tames as my hand disappears in his grip. His voice, conversely, lowers and remains prickly. "I don't want to discuss what I am any further."

I manage a small smile. "Okay."

A knee to the nuts would have earned me the same reaction.

"*Okay*?" he asks, perplexity smoothing the hard lines of his features.

My smile widens. Bewilderment doesn't quite suit Captain Awesomeness. Rage? Sure. Aggression? Absolutely. But confusion? Nope. This male is very sure of himself and his actions. At least when it pertains to everything but me.

I release him and sashay into the kitchen, smoothing my hand along the sand and white quartz counter in the state-of-the-art chrome kitchen. "What's for lunch?"

"*What*?"

The cabinets are darker than the floor, giving the kitchen its own turn in the spotlight while managing to blend in with the extra-large loft. My brow puckers when I peek into his empty fridge. "You said you were going to feed me."

"I just told you I feast on souls," he fires back.

I open the freezer. It's clean and sadly just as empty. "Oh, I heard you."

"This is all you have to say?"

"You're the one who says he doesn't want to talk about it." I shut the fridge and find him standing beside me. "Did you change your mind? If so, I'm all ears."

"*No*." He watches me carefully. "There's something wrong with you."

"Says the guy who munches on souls like Cheerios." And, well, doesn't that earn me the glower of Death? I try not to grin. Okay, King of the Dead aside Ryker is…different. I shrug, attempting to shake off my growing interest. "Where's your food? I know you nibble on more than just people."

"I don't frighten you." It's not really a question.

"Oh, sure you do," I answered truthfully.

"It doesn't seem that way."

I hold out a hand. "Trust me, I've almost peed myself at least twice." I pause. "That was probably TMI, wasn't it?"

He reaches out to touch me, pulling back before his fingers can brush my arm. I angle my chin and try to gauge his reaction. His attempt to caress me isn't a belligerent move by any means. I sense his discretion and hesitation when he reached out, just as easily as I sense the growing strain between us.

He edges away, bothered by his response. I don't like the distance between us, though it's only a few feet, just like I don't like the escalating tension.

"Would you prefer I shake in my cute shoes, Mr. Scott?" I ask.

He opens his mouth to say something and closes it again, muttering what sounds like Irish swears.

I lean against the counter. Oh. It's cool. "Look, there's probably a lot about you that'll eventually earn me a trip to the nuthouse."

"*Perhaps*," he growls.

I place my hand firmly on my hip. "Did you just *growl* at me?" He doesn't answer. I sigh. "Ryker, don't be so cranky. If you don't want to talk about yourself, that's fine, for now. Eventually, though, you will because you have to."

"And why is that?"

My temper relaxes. "Because there's no one else to tell."

He regards me for a long time. "That doesn't mean I'll be forthcoming with my condition."

"Probably not," I agree. "But no worries." I move forward and tip my head up, so he has to look at me. "I hev veys ov makin' you tawk."

Evidently, the Grim Reaper isn't a fan of my humor. I guess I'll have to try harder. "What's your problem?" Or not.

He straightens. "My *problem*?"

I shove my nose into his. Well, not really. He does tower over me and all. "You saved my petite yet firm ass, you rise up to defend me, you demonstrate kindness and compassion, yet you're all pissy that I'm not cowering in terror."

"It's not that I want you to fear me. That's the last thing I want."

"Then what is it?"

He grinds his teeth. "I *expect* you to be afraid."

"Why?" I shrug. "I mean, besides the obvious."

Ryker looks ready to snap me into a straitjacket himself. He holds out his hands. "You know what I am, and what I'm capable of unleashing. Yet you skitter around my lair asking about lunch."

"I didn't skitter—" I shoot back. "Wait, did you just call your apartment your *lair*? Who do you think you are? Batman?"

His glower vanishes, liquefied by hints of sadness. "What I'm trying to say is, any rational person would be more wary of me."

My humor dissolves. "Maybe I'm not so rational."

He stills as I walk past him and toward the giant windows with the rambling view of the Hudson. A group of twenty-some-things speed by in a boat, laughing, enjoying life. My stars, I envy them. "Maybe all the times I've faced Death has affected my judgment," I reason aloud. The boat circles around, joined by another. "I'll admit, you do scare me, probably more than I dare to admit. But what scares me more is going after every version of Death. This task, mission, fiasco, whatever you want to call it, shouldn't have been shoved onto me. Except that it was." I glance over my shoulder. "I believe you when you say you want to help me. Maybe it's what helps me be less afraid. Am I wrong to trust that you won't hurt me?"

Redwoods have to be more pliable than this guy. "No," he replies, stiffly.

I beam at him. "Then stop trying to scare me and give me something to eat."

We walk to a bistro two blocks from his loft and sit in the outside patio. Considering the warm day, few gnats or pesky insects interrupt our meal. I wonder if they, like most living creatures, fear Ryker.

I munch on the kale, strawberry, and feta cheese salad he recommended and do my best not to lick the plate. *Yum.* I point to the last hunk of cheese with my fork. "This is perfection. How did I not hear of this place before?"

"I'm sure you have your pick of places in Hoboken." He smears a slice of sourdough bread with the olive and oil paste. "If you enjoyed this, your entrée will be much to your liking."

"You're a fan of good food."

"I am," he agrees.

"Then why don't you have any food in your kitchen?"

He lowers his slice of bread onto his plate. "My free time is better spent perfecting my fighting skills. It's easier for me to order from the many restaurants in the area than to take the time to prepare and clean." He shrugs. "Besides, why bother? It's just me."

I stop chewing, swallowing what remains in my mouth. "You work?" He nods. "Then you work out?" He watches me. "But nothing else?"

His silence is response enough.

"May I take your plate, sir?"

The waitress licks her lips, liking what she sees in my companion. But when Ryker lifts his head to acknowledge her, she shrinks away from him despite his polite tone. "Yes, thank you."

She lifts his plate carefully to avoid touching him, remaining equally fearful and captivated by him. She's pretty. Really pretty. And she bugs me. Her leering is obvious, and so is my presence. Sweetheart, I'm sitting right here.

Ryker doesn't give off a "let's have sex standing up" vibe like most who match him in looks would. At least not on purpose. What is prominent is his edge, sharp enough to sever throats with mild effort. Danger and unrest seep from his pores, battling with and against his allure. I sense it, and so does our waitress.

Her long red hair bounces behind her, and her hips demonstrate a high interest in straddling him. Ryker doesn't follow her flouncing and voluptuous hips as she disappears into the restaurant. His attention politely remains on me. "What would you like to do when we're done with our meal?"

I lean in close, my eyes cutting from side to side as if I'm afraid anyone passing might hear our secrets. "Grocery shopping."

"Excuse me?"

"If I'm going to spend days upon weeks with you, I'll need snacks and lots to eat." I waggle my brows. "You'd be surprised how much a pixie can eat."

Something, possibly the start of a phantom smile, twitches the edges of his lips. I grin and wink. Sooner or later, I'm going to draw a real smile from the Bringer of Doom.

The waitress returns with my marinated shrimp and octopus inked couscous. Mango chunks and avocado slices poke between the black mounds. My mouth waters. "Hello, baby," I rasp.

Ryker waits for the waitress to leave before slicing into his red snapper stuffed to the literal gills with shitake mushrooms. "Olivia, there's much we need to discuss with regard to the Cù-Sìth and your training."

I pop a shrimp into my mouth. *Oh, yeah.* This dude can pick a restaurant. "We can discuss it while we shop. I'll just need a few things for dinner."

"We could order in—"

"I'm thinking pasta," I say. "Do you like Italian?"

"Do you like interrupting me?" he counters.

I reach for another shrimp. "You probably aren't used to that. Are you, big guy? So, do you?"

"Do I what?"

"Like Italian?" I repeat.

The corner of his mouth curves ever so slightly. I'm getting closer.

"Are you planning to cook for me?"

"Darn tootin' I am." I eye his snapper. "Aren't you going to share? It's kind of stingy not to share."

He moves his plate closer, and I swear I almost hear a chuckle. Almost. I lift a portion of my meal with my fork and spoon, careful to include every delectable ingredient and drop it onto his bread plate. I then go to town on the piece of snapper he slices for me. "Don't forget to include a little risotto," I remind him. "I love risotto. Oh! Are those capers?"

"Olivia?"

I lower my fork, knowing who called to me even before I peer over the patio's small stone wall. Andrew waits frozen, the group of young men and women with him quieting as they take in his pallor. The young woman at his side tugs on his arm. "Are you all right?" she asks him.

"I'm fine," he answers. "Why don't you go? I'll catch up with you at the hospital."

"But..." she begins, her attention drifting to me.

By the way her arm winds around him, she's more familiar with Andrew than the others. Despite her touch and beauty, Andrew's attention remains solely on me.

Their friends encourage the woman along. Slowly, she relinquishes her hold. Andrew, although seemingly oblivious to anyone but me, waits until the group disappears around the corner before bounding over the small wall with elfish grace.

Although quick in action, he appears hesitant to approach, his stride more cautious than purposeful. Regret, and possibly more, haunts and blanches his youthful features and makes him appear older despite the bright green T-shirt and jeans he wears. He swallows hard and kneels beside me, taking my hands within his. "It really is you," he tells me.

I try to smile. My unease makes it difficult. His touch, while warm, doesn't comfort me, nor does it grant me the courage to speak. Andrew is a reminder of that horrible night. Vivid memories strike me like physical blows and shove away the cheer I found in Ryker's presence.

Andrew's thumb strokes the inside of my palm. "I thought you were dead," he says, gripping my hands tighter. "There was talk that you made it out of the club—that you survived. I didn't believe it. I *heard* the hounds and knew they were coming for you."

My eyes prick with the first sting of tears.

He smiles and cups my face with his hands. "How did you do it, beautiful?"

I recoil from his touch and his term of endearment. The legs of Ryker's chair scrape against the slab foundation and Ryker prowls to my side, his protective aura enclosing me. It's only then the emotions twisting my belly lessen.

Andrew drops his hands and stands. I stand, too.

Ryker doesn't greet Andrew with kindness or warmth. He doesn't know Andrew, and while Andrew doesn't pose a threat to me, my reaction to Andrew's caress alerts Ryker that I don't want him touching me.

"Who's this?" Andrew asks, his voice no longer gentle.

Andrew's irate demeanor gives me pause. I don't belong to Andrew, and he interrupted my lunch with Ryker.

"This is my friend, Ryker. Ryker, this is Andrew." I press my hand against Ryker's arm to halt his advance, while the other motions to my talisman. "Ryker rescued me from the hounds. He secured another talisman for me that veiled me from Death." Andrew examines Ryker. I'll give him this, if he's afraid, he's not showing it. "How did you manage that?" he asks Ryker. "What do you do, walk around with spare talismans shoved in your pockets, friend?"

"I'm not your friend," Ryker replies, his throaty timbre clipped. "And if you were Olivia's, you wouldn't have abandoned her."

"I did *not* abandon her!" Andrew hisses.

But he had.

Andrew stands his ground, his suspicion of Ryker escalating. "Where did you come from? I don't remember seeing you that night."

I answer for him. "He charged in following the arrival of the Cù-Sìth."

The mention of the death hounds by their true name makes

Andrew tense. Or perhaps it's knowing Ryker barreled into the club when everyone else retreated. Either way, Andrew doesn't challenge him further. It's just as well. One way or another, Andrew would lose to Ryker.

"Ryker saved me from Death," I repeat. "I would have died if it wasn't for him."

Andrew thaws his icy stance as the hurt trembling my voice works its way along my features. "I didn't abandon you, Olivia. I only left because there was nothing more I could do."

I think back to how willingly Frankie offered Dahlia his talisman. Except Andrew isn't Frankie, I'm not Dahlia, and we never shared what they did. "I know."

Andrew reaches for me, his aggression long gone. "Livvie," he says.

I edge away from him and angle my body toward Ryker.

Ryker's heavy palm immediately finds the curve of my back, giving me an additional boost so I may finish speaking. "It's okay, Andrew. I understand your reasons for leaving." I'm being honest, and although there's more to say, I don't bother. Andrew never promised me forever or pretended to be more than he was. He wanted to live. I can't fault him for it.

I offer him a weak smile. "Good luck with your residency. I know you'll make a wonderful surgeon."

He nods, knowing this is our goodbye. "See you around, Liv." He crosses the patio, this time taking the time to unlatch the metal gate leading to the sidewalk.

Ryker remains trained on Andrew, watching him walk in the direction his friends had disappeared. Andrew whips out his cell phone, ready, I presume, to move on with his life and on to the next willing female.

Ryker frowns when he catches me watching him. I smile, really smile. "You asked me why I'm not as afraid of you as I should be," I remind him. I motion to Andrew, who vanishes around the corner without another glance back. "It's because unlike Andrew, you would never leave me alone and vulnerable, would you?"

Ryker's ice-blue eyes spark with a fire that cements me in place. "No. I would die for you, Olivia."

16

"Are you good with a whip?"

I push up on my elbows from where I lay plastered on the wood floor and glower at Ryker. In his black basketball shorts and a tight sleeveless T-shirt, he isn't exactly the Grim Reaper personified. In fact, all his ensemble does is provide a better glimpse at those boulders I once mistakenly referred to simply as "muscles."

"Is this a serious question?"

He deepens his already hard scowl. "You have limber wrists. It's a fair question."

"I own fifteen pairs of shoes in varying shades of pink. What do you think?" I rub my rump. He spent this morning's session trying to teach me to shoot a gun in his fifth-floor apartment. I was doing amazingly well until he added bullets. He warned me the kickback could knock me on my ass. I just didn't realize he meant literally.

Ryker drags a hand through his short-buzzed hair and paces the room. He stops in front of the reinforced steel and cinderblock wall he uses as a gun range. Too bad my bullets never became one with the target, an eight-foot-tall outline of an ogre. I didn't even hit the paper! I cross my arms. Where did the big ol' bullet go?

Ryker wonders the same thing. He lifts the edge of the target and drops it when something catches his attention on the far side of the room.

"Oh, no. Did I hit the window?" I ask when he moves toward it.

He nods, walking as his frown deepens. "I don't know if this is the right course of action for you. Your aim is atrocious, you take too long to fall into a proper stance, and you're obviously scared of the blast, even with the silencer." He peers out the window. "You also killed a pigeon."

I scramble to the window where my bullet created a perfect hole. Gray and white plumage scatters along the ledge. Something, maybe a foot, curls tight in the corner. I cover my eyes. My tears flowing from one breath to the next. I've never killed anything, not even a bug.

Ryker stiffens beside me. "Are you crying?" My rapid sniffling answers his question. As does the pathetic whimpering that follows. He pauses. "It was a clean death," he offers.

"Is that supposed to make me feel better?" By now, I'm bawling. Great, some seeker of death I am.

Ryker is so quiet he practically disappears. I'm sure he made a run for it until he taps my shoulder in true "there, there" fashion. "It was an accident, Olivia. I'm certain his spirit recognizes as much and has forgiven you."

I drop my hands and glare. "You really know how to lay on the sympathy, you know that? Give up lawyering and death. Writing for Hallmark is clearly your calling."

He crosses his massive arms over his equally massive chest. "What would you prefer I say?"

I wipe my eyes. "You can start by explaining why I'm

learning to shoot in the first place. Just yesterday you told me that bullets and ammo have no effect on Reapers."

"They don't," he agrees. "But your energy does."

"My what?"

"Your magic," he clarifies. "It's what you used that night against the Cù-Sìth. You can manipulate it to extend past you."

"I can?"

"Yes," he replies like it's obvious.

I wipe my eyes with my stretchy T-shirt. "This would have been good info to share yesterday, rather than the hours we spent reviewing Evil Reapers of Doom 101."

"Study will be just as valuable to you as your ability to engage in combat." He sighs when I stare blankly back at him. "Come with me."

He walks, well, not really. Ryker doesn't "walk" anywhere. Truer to his nature, he *stalks* across the room to where several gym mats are pressed against the wall. He sits, inviting me to join him. I more or less shimmy to his side, crisscrossing my legs and wiping the last of my tears.

"The power you possess rests at your fingertips," he tells me.

"Right." I flex and straighten my fingers. "That's how I cause the most damage."

"But it's not limited to your hands alone. You can release it from within you and send it into your opponent."

I tilt my head, trying to wrap my mind around what he tells me. "Will it come back?"

He shakes his head. "Consider it a breath that leaves you. That same breath doesn't return, yet it doesn't stop you from breathing. However—"

"There's always a 'however,' isn't there?" I ask, making a face.

"Yes. Just as there's always a student determined to interrupt the class." He ignores my scowl at the dig. "Your magic, while permanent, will weaken you if overused or overstressed, just like your body. One of the many things I'll help you with is building your stamina. But that will take time. For now, we'll work on releasing and managing your power."

Ryker leans forward and slams his hand against the honey wood floor. The head of his scythe protrudes. He clasps it tight and tosses it in the air. In one smooth move, he stands and catches it mid-staff. "My power to kill comes from within me. I transfer it into my weapons and make them more lethal. If I didn't, it would just be a staff with a curved blade at the end.

"Capable of gutting pigs in a single bound."

The edges of his lips curve into another "almost" smile. "Agreed. But it's my will that sharpens the blade, strengthens the cut, and assures the kill with little effort." He halts his almost smile. "It's become second nature for me, more like blinking than a task. With time, I hope it will become the same for you."

My fingers braid through my hair. "When you went after Brielle's husband, it was one clean cut, from his shoulder to his hip. Wasn't it?"

"It was." He taps the end of the scythe against the floor, returning it to the area between dimensions where he stores it.

Not too long ago, I was shopping for another pair of pink pumps to add to my growing collection. Now, here I am sitting with one of the most feared creatures in existence discussing slicing and dicing.

Ryker resumes his seat beside me, waiting for me to speak. "Olivia," he says when I remain quiet.

I shake my head. "I know the type of man Brielle's husband was. You don't owe me an explanation."

He rests his head against the cinderblock wall, pondering his retort. "You're wrong. It seems I owe you more."

"Ryker, this isn't the time to spare my feelings." My face meets his. "And please don't apologize for being honest. I prefer truth to lies no matter the circumstance, especially now." For all

I'm trying to be tough; I wiggle my toes nervously. "I won't survive otherwise. You know I won't."

"Does this mean that you trust me?"

It's more a final acknowledgment than a question. I smile. "Would I be here with you if I didn't?"

"I suppose not."

I release my hair, allowing myself a moment to take him in. The morning was rushed, filled with instruction, quick exchanges, and loads of information. There was little opportunity for small talk. Despite it all, and murdered pigeon aside, the time spent with him was nice.

Ryker stares back at me, swallowing hard. I watch, briefly mesmerized by how his Adam's apple slides along his throat. I wonder how many women have taken a bite. My body heats at the thought, and my reason mentally slaps me across the face.

Ryker lifts his head from the wall, his icy gaze dropping from my eyes to fix on my mouth. Again, he swallows hard. Again, I watch him watch me.

My gentle heartbeat morphs into one dull thud against my sternum, painful and magnificent all at once. My mind tries to suppress the throb, interjecting with logic I have no desire to hear. It screams at me anyway. *Don't go there, Olivia. This isn't a true man or a true Fae. He is the ultimate end, dangerous and terminal.*

You forgot sexy, my forlorn womanly parts purr.

Something else, maybe my sanity, rushes forward and kicks me in the virtual shins. *Don't toy with Death*, it insists when my body draws closer to his. *Someone alive can't be with someone who's dead.*

The last statement is the slamming door I need to halt my lascivious desires. I jerk away from Ryker as if struck. "You think I can transfer my anti-death ray into the bullets?" I ask.

Ryker stills. I grimace when he swallows yet again. Damn

that tempting little Adam's apple. He clears his throat. "It's a theory. One I hope you will eventually master. But I fear it won't be soon enough based on this morning's display. You're too preoccupied with learning the bare basics of shooting. Focusing your magic on the bullet as it leaves the chamber and maintaining it until it strikes your opponent is a skill that will take time."

My fingers find a new section of hair to braid. "Then why did we waste the whole morning? I could have swung by the firm. Seriously, if sending my mojo into the bullet is so hard, why even bother?"

"I needed to gauge where we could start. If your shooting ability was less…"

"Laughable?" I guess.

He smirks. Smirks look damn good on him.

He can eat you; my sanity reminds me with an annoying jab.

"Awkward may be a better term," Ryker replies. He leans and rests his elbows against his legs. "If you could shoot and release your magic into the bullet, you could fire from a greater distance and avoid engaging the Reapers directly."

I release my hair, understanding. "You don't want me touching them."

"If you can avoid it, no," he admits.

"Why?"

"At close range, they can knock you down hard enough to lose consciousness, leaving you vulnerable. Any direct attempt to kill you should fail, but it won't stop them from harming you in other ways."

His "other ways" remark chills me to my bones. I hadn't thought about the more creative things the Reapers could do to me and with good reason.

Ryker squares his jaw. "I won't let them hurt you."

"If you can avoid it. But what if you can't?" My hair falls around my face. "And what if they hurt you, too?"

"It's the chance we have to take, Olivia."

The tension spreads along his shoulders and down his arms. "There are many of them and only two of us. Bill, the dragons, and Jane may be our allies, but they don't possess the power to defeat Death like we do. They must keep their veils and hide just to stand a chance. In the end, it will come down to us, and us alone."

I stare at my hands. "I just hope we're enough."

"I do, too."

A light rain drizzles against the window, transforming into a full summer shower before I speak again. "You mentioned a whip. Why that of all things?"

"Give me your hand," he says.

I do without question. It surprises Ryker, and I suppose me, too.

He holds my wrist palm side up and taps the center. "Your power releases here, but it generates from your center or possibly your heart. From what I can interpret, your magic grows in viciousness when you're angry."

"That sounds about right," I agree. Fear may have fueled my actions, yet it was my fury that compelled me to fight back.

Ryker continues, his voice wary as if listening in on my thoughts. "Your 'death ray,' as you call it, can extend to any part of your body, your legs, your feet, even your teeth if you're desperate enough. If I'm right, you can extend it several lengths beyond your body just as I do with my scythe."

"If I'm holding something."

"Correct," he says.

"Which is why you want me to try out a whip," I reason.

"Exactly."

He crosses the room and slips behind the spiraling metal

stairs that lead up to his residence. A large wooden sea trunk straight off the set of *The Pirates of the Caribbean* rests against the wall. He fumbles through it, removing several sheathed swords, a clear case of daggers packed in foam inserts, and what appears to be a set of tongs with vicious teeth levitating within a crystal case. I hear a hum. I think it's some sort of electrical device within the building until I realize it's coming from the tongs.

"Um, what's that?" I ask, pointing to the scary thing as it continues to sing.

Ryker carefully lowers it to the floor beside him. "Egg extractor."

This time, I'm the one swallowing hard. "You don't mean chicken eggs, do you?"

"No."

My ovaries find someplace to hide (somewhere between my twisting bowels and left kidney), and my legs can't close tight enough. "Remember what I said about telling me the truth, the whole truth, and nothing but the truth," I ask.

"Yes?"

"I take it back," I say, shuddering.

Ryker resumes his search until he finds a black braided whip at the base of the trunk. He casts it aside and carefully returns the weapons. I start to relax until he lifts the humming tongs and places his lips close to the case. "Quiet, Vanessa," he whis- pers. "It's not time."

"Vanessa" immediately silences her song, apparently disappointed there are no eggs to extract. This time, my ovaries lurch in the direction of my throat.

Ryker prowls back to the center of the room, holding tight to the whip's handle and allowing the rest to dangle at his side. In my mind, whips are long, like the one Indiana Jones uses to leap from one crumbling Mayan ruin to the next. The one Ryker carries is only about five feet in length.

"This is a snake whip," he explains.

"To whip snakes?"

His frown tells me no. "Never mind," I mutter.

"Watch me carefully. When I'm done, you may try it." He whirls his wrist, keeping the black braided end spiraling beside him. He then turns to face the outline of the ogre we used to practice shooting.

Several feet remain between Ryker and his target. With a quick snap of his wrist, the whip extends out. A thin stream of azure light fires from its tip, the projecting magic slicing the paper from one corner to the next in a perfect line.

My jaw lands somewhere near my ovaries.

He jerks the tail back and smoothly resumes the spinning motion, stalking back to me like his perfect performance was as easy as skipping rope. "Now, you try."

I stare blankly between him and the target. The stupid sections of paper are practically laughing at me.

"Olivia, *try.*"

"I'm not sure I can even cut that straight a line with scissors." "I'm not asking you to use scissors. Nor am I asking the impossible. The beauty of this weapon is that even in a child's hands, it can make a tremendous impact."

"You let little kids play with this shit?" All humor is lost on Captain Awesomeness. I throw my hands in the air. "You know, just because you're Death and all doesn't mean you have to take everything so seriously."

"Just *try it,*" he says more sternly. "We'll start slow. Focus your killing energy into your hand and send it into the whip like an electric current running through a power line."

He places the handle in my palm, rolling his eyes when I drop it. "Olivia, it's not going to hurt you."

Ryker slaps it back into my hand, refusing to release it until he's certain it's secure within my grasp. "Think back to the night you were attacked," he tells me. "Focus on the anger that surged through your veins and the energy you felt when you touched Cathasach."

"I don't know if I can," I confess. "I'm still not sure how I pulled it off."

He analyzes me, something about me catching his attention. "The energy you sensed, was it cold, or something altogether different?"

I think back to the sensation as it left my fingertips and tore into Cathasach's flesh. "Mm. No. It was more like a burning heat. But it wasn't painful."

"Then concentrate on that burn and how it felt. Build it within you and push it out through your hand and out the length of the leather."

"Just so you know, this is some freaky conversation we have going on. What's next? Ball gags and ass-less chaps?" I laugh. He doesn't. "*Fine*," I grumble.

I tighten my grip. My hand grows warmer. I can't be sure if it's due to how hard I'm clenching this thing or if it's all due to Ryker's crazy sexy body heat.

I close my eyes and envision my "wattage" building from my heart and shooting outward. "Is anything happening?" I ask through clenched teeth.

When he doesn't respond, I open my eyes to find Ryker rubbing the light stubble edging his jaw. At this rate, he's going to rub that dimple right off his face.

"What's holding you back?" he asks. "You're not even trying."

"I am so trying."

He shakes his head. "Your efforts are pitiable at best."

"Don't be such a hard-ass," I snap.

I clench my hand tighter when he frowns. "And don't look at me that way when I accuse you of being a hard-ass. You've had years, and bodies, and loads of practice. I had one experience." I hold out a finger. "One. I was terrified, and angry, and watching Fae folk die around me. For you to say I'm not trying is bull—"

Like the strike of a match, something fires within me. The burn, the one I attempted to describe, flares when those horrible memories of the Glen resurface.

Pink light—that's right, *pink*—floods from my hand and into the handle.

"More," Ryker says. "Feel it and let it fuel you."

I scrunch my face, sensing the flame start to die.

"Olivia, *do not* allow it to fade."

I swear and grit my teeth, struggling to reignite it.

"*Olivia.*"

"I'm trying!"

The light vanishes as if snuffed. It's all I can do not to throw the ridiculous thing across the room. I clasp my free hand over my face, trying not to scream. "Sorry," I say. "I'm doing exactly what you tell me to do. But it's like something is missing…"

Ryker's arm slips around my waist, crossing over my belly and latching tight to the opposite side. He pulls me against him and those damn fine baby-makin' hips of his. My eyes widen to frisbees. It's bad enough to feel his stiff, *rigid* body against me, but then my butt cheeks develop a mind of their own, clenching and unclenching, seeking out his nether regions.

"Um, Ryker?"

"Shhh," Ryker whispers low in my ear, his chest vibrating against my back. "You described your magic like a burn. Can you feel it? Is it hard?"

"Ah…"

"*Good,*" he rumbles. "As it grows, allow the heat to travel through your core."

"Oh, it's traveling," I mumble, my pelvic floor aching.

He lowers his chin, curving into me. "This is what I want,

what I seek. Build that heat and allow it to encase every part of you."

My eyes roll into the back of my head. "You don't know what you're asking," I stammer.

"Yes, I do," he rasps. His free hand smooths over my knuckles, maintaining my hold over the handle of the whip.

The now familiar spark takes life, smoldering rapidly.

Blinding fuchsia light skids along the whip, extending past the tip and swerving in serpentine motions across the floor. The sudden sizzle has nothing to do with my rage and everything to do with Ryker's body closing in.

"More," he begs me. "Give me *more*."

The heat within me sputters, rising mercilessly between my breasts and tightening the tips. I arch my back and gasp, my eyelashes fluttering.

Ryker's hold magnifies. "Don't fight it," he pleads. "Allow the release and let it consume you."

Dear. Lord.

A groan breaks free from my throat. Something primal and hungry detonates, gifting my female parts with more hum than Vanessa.

Ryker's breathy voice brushes against my flesh. "Just like that. Don't stop."

My thighs quiver, batting against him. Without warning, my power rocks through me like a horny rhino who caught view of a nice ass to ram. Sharp pain launches from my belly, burrowing its way south.

I wrench away from Ryker, stumbling backward and landing on my ass.

I'm not happy. I'm not sated. I am *mortified*.

It takes me a full minute to pry my fingers free from my scorching face.

Ryker kneels by the abandoned whip, nodding approvingly

as the leather smokes with bright pink energy. The entire floor smells of burnt wood. Swirls and patterns brand the floor and far wall. Under Ryker's "tutelage" I could have burned the whole damn building down.

"This is excellent, Olivia," he says. "Well, done." He does a double take when he catches sight of my pathetic and panting self. "Are you all right? Your face is flushed."

No, I'm not all right. I think I had an orgasm. "Fine, fine. Just fine. A little hot, nothing more."

He doesn't believe me. There's a shock. He offers me a hand to help me to my feet. Being the slick gal, I am, I lurch upward and almost ass-plant again.

Ryker eyes me like the psycho I no doubt resemble. "Are you certain you're all right?"

"Yup." I salute him. That's how we cool chicks roll.

He watches me dust off, which is ridiculous. Even with the burn marks, I can probably serve an eight-course meal across this meticulous floor.

I clear my throat. "Okay. What's next?"

Ryker lifts the whip and holds it out to me. My magic, while evidently strong enough to singe wood and concrete, left the leather unaffected. "Take it," he says. "Now that you're more familiar with how to rile your power, practice maneuvering the whip. I'll lead you from behind—"

I yank the whip from his grasp. "Nope. Not necessary. I got it."

I flick my wrist.

And take out Ryker's eye.

With a jump and a scream, I watch it plop on the floor.

17

"I'm, like, so sorry!"

"It's *fine*."

"If it's so 'fine,' why are you growling at me?"

Ryker holds tight to his bleeding face, glaring at me with the one good eye he has left after squaring off with my whip of doom.

I race around the kitchen, searching for a dishtowel. I finally find an unopened pack and rip open the plastic packaging with my teeth.

Blood is seeping through his thick fingers. Like he has a hole in his skull. Which, thanks to me, he does!

I run water over the towel and hurry to where he sits on the barstool, his body curled. "Move your hand," I say, my voice trembling.

"No."

"What do you mean, 'no?'" My voice is no longer trembling. "Move your hand now."

"You won't like what you see," he replies.

"I already don't like what I see." I grind my teeth when he

just sits there. "You are, like, the most stubborn Grim Reaper, ever."

"You take out my eye, and now you're insulting me?" he asks.

"It's because I took out your eye that I should see. Now, move your hand."

"I said, *no*," he growls yet again.

I shove my face into his, livid. "Move it, or I'll move it for you!"

One side of his mouth lifts into a mini smirk. "I'd like to see you try, Tinkerbell."

I stiffen. "Did you really just go there?" The mini smirk widens.

Like the strike of a cobra, my hand grips his wrist and yanks. Twice. And once more. I throw my body weight into pulling his arm down, and all I manage to do is slide my feet across the wood floor.

Damn slippery floor.

A barrage of deep rumbles follows a light choking sound. My jaw pops open. "Are you laughing at me?"

Ryker's shoulders shake. "No," he says.

"You are so laughing at me!"

"I don't mean to." He clears his throat. "I just find you…"

I scowl, at least, I pretend to. My spaghetti arms are pathetic at best. Still, I cross them and lift my chin defiantly. "You find me what? Intimidating, strong, imposing?"

"Sweet," he offers and drops his bloody hand.

I take it back. He shouldn't have shown me, and I shouldn't have asked.

My arms fall at my sides, and lights dance in my vision like it's prom night. A gash, as thick as two of my fingers, cuts through Ryker's forehead down to where his eye is supposed to be, to his jaw, exposing bone. Shit. *That's bone!* His eyelid dangles in two pieces, the ends flapping open when he breathes.

I swallow enough bile to punch through my belly like an *Alien* lovechild.

"It's not that bad," he says, watching me sway from side to side. "The bleeding has subsided."

"Wha-wha." I try to control my breathing. "Wh-why does it look like that?" I ask, pointing. "The viper whip—"

"Snake whip," he corrects.

"Whatever. It couldn't have done all—" I wave my crazy hands around his face, "—this! You need stitches!"

"No," he says calmly. "I don't."

"And a doctor."

He shakes his head.

"And plastic surgery!" I don't also mention a glass eye. I grab my purse and pull at his arm. "Mother of elves and hobbits, maybe Jane can help." I take another glance and cringe. "But I think it's going to cost you."

Ryker reaches for my hand, instantly steadying me. "I believe this is a good thing."

"I believe you're nuts."

He laughs again, proving that he's actually capable of smiling. He has such a nice smile. Too bad his gaping wound and oozing vessels detract from what's otherwise a dashing grin. "Olivia, the power you transferred continues to burn me—"

"Oh my God!"

He holds out a hand. "Again, this is a good thing. If your residual power can do all this—" he motions to his mangled face, "—you truly are Life and the perfect weapon to mark an end to the Cù-Sìth."

I should be twirling with joy at the news. But I can't. It came at the price of Ryker's perfect face. I ruined him when his only intent was to guide me. Guilt digs into me like a knife, deep into my gut, twisting once, twice. I want to cry with how bad I feel. Most of all, I want to help him.

I drop my purse and reach for his face, gently stroking around his mutilated skin.

Ryker's muscles press against his shirt, stiffening the moment I touch him.

Slowly, almost imperceivably, he leans into my hand.

I cradle his face, obscuring his injuries and permitting only a view of his profile. "I'm sorry," I whisper, breathless with guilt. "I'm so sorry."

I kiss his cheek and rest my forehead against him, keeping one hand over the damaged tissue. My other hand cups his shoulder. I ruined him. Even if Ryker heals, an ugly scar will permanently mar his visage.

"I'm so sorry," I say again, fixing on his former self. Ryker was beautiful, *flawless*—from the rugged firmness of his jaw, to the trace of stubble crawling from the sideburns of his buzzed hair, to his regal nose. And don't get me started on the captivating coldness of his ice-blue eyes.

I wrecked him. My throat tightens and sours. I'm seconds from releasing tears that won't easily stop.

"This feels…nice," he rumbles. I'm sure I misheard. "What does?"

"You. Touching me."

"I like to touch." I smile against his cheek when I realize how I sound. "I've always been affectionate." I lean in closer. "So, if you don't mind, I'd rather not stop."

"I don't mind." He pauses as if debating whether to continue. "No one touches me."

That can't be right. "Ever?"

"No."

I've seen others withdraw in his presence. But I was certain eventually someone would have the gumption to cozy up to him. I mean, the waitress from yesterday was obviously attracted to him. With a little time and some effort from Ryker, she would do more than stroke his face.

My body sinks against his. "Nah."

"Nah?" he asks. It's like he can't believe such a sound would come out of my mouth.

"You heard me," I say. "I find it hard to believe you don't get touched all over the place." I blush. "Well, you know what I mean."

There's a palpable, almost audible pause, and then Ryker curls his arm around my back, his palm trailing up to rest between my shoulder blades. "Humans and Fae alike have kept their distance from me for over a century. Their instincts warn them I can take their souls."

I'm ready to cry, this time for him. Ryker is more alone than I ever could have guessed. In a hundred years, no one has allowed his caress let alone warmed his bed.

I sweep my lips over his cheek, relishing the warmth emanating from his skin. "I get that you don't exactly ooze kittens riding merrily on prancing ponies. But that tramp really wanted you."

He adjusts his hold to pull me closer. The warmth between us increases. I almost forget how to breathe. "Are you speaking of Chelsea, my former secretary?"

"No."

"Christen from the mailroom?" he guesses.

"No…"

"Abigail from payroll?"

Seriously? "I was talking about our waitress from the other day. Jiminy Cricket, Ryker, do you keep the mounting list of hoes on your iPad?"

His chest vibrates against me as he chuckles. "These women—"

"Airhead sluts from the planet Spank Me are a better choice of words," I mutter.

He pauses. I don't have to look at him to know he's smirking. "Regardless of how you describe them, they all have one thing in common."

"They want to rock you like a hurricane?"

"No. They fear me."

I quiet. Understanding to a point. "Chelsea wasn't afraid of you," I remind him. "I mean, she was, and she wasn't."

"Chelsea is different," he says, remembering.

"That she is."

"You don't understand," he says. "Despite the boldness Chelsea demonstrated in your presence, she was terrified of being alone with me. She'd enter my office only if the shades were open, and even then, she'd leave the door ajar."

"I didn't really see that side," I say. "I mostly had a good look at her inner psycho."

"Chelsea isn't psychotic, Olivia. She carries a darkness, one she likely keeps well hidden, except in my presence. The darkness I carry stirs hers awake and entices her closer."

"Ah. She wants to be Mrs. Grim Reaper of Death," I deduce.

"No," he says. "She wants to embrace her darkness. She likes it. It gives her a false sense of power. What she doesn't recognize is, as much as her soul craves it, her body can't handle it. When we started working together, Chelsea began to perceive you as a threat, someone depriving her of what she feels she deserves. It was too much for her, and she fell apart. Had I known what it would do to her and how quickly, I would have requested her termination sooner."

I think on it, and I think a little more. "Why isn't your new secretary afraid of you?"

"Judith doesn't carry the same fear most do. She's a widow and childless. She isn't afraid to die." He shrugs. "Unlike many, she's prepared herself for it."

"Does it bother you that almost everyone is afraid of you?" I ask.

"No. It's better this way."

I smile against his cheek, smiling wider when his body temperature rises. "I don't believe you. If you enjoy my touch, you'll enjoy another's."

Mr. Awesome doesn't quite have an answer for that. Instead, he says, "Tell me something about you."

Mm. I'm practically glued to him. "What do you want to know?"

"Bill told me the Cù-Sìth robbed you of your family, except for your brother."

"That's right," I say, no longer smiling. "My brother, Kellen, is five years older than me. Although he never did well in school, he was ludicrously smart. He gathered what remained of our family fortune and used it to help us survive until I was old enough to attend college." My free hand circles Ryker's waist, helping me seek the comfort I need when I think of my one remaining family member. "He helped me move in on the first day of orientation, hugged me goodbye, and I never saw him again."

"What happened to him?"

"I don't know. He never called, and he changed his phone number. When Thanksgiving break rolled around, I took an Uber to Pluckemin to find our home sold and empty. Dahlia's family came for me, and we spent every break searching for him. He covered his tracks well and obviously didn't want to be found. When my sophomore year began, I stopped looking."

"He left you? All alone to fend for yourself?"

"I thought so at first. Until I looked at my bank statements and saw I had enough money to pay my tuition and room and board for the entirety of my college career."

"But it wasn't enough."

"No," I admit. "I wanted my brother back. Kellen was broken, Ryker, damaged emotionally and I suppose beyond repair. Still, he was a part of me."

My head falls against Ryker's shoulder. It should be ridiculous for us to hold each other like this, especially after the damage I inflicted. But, like I said, I seek and give affection, and, when I really think about it, Life and Death go hand and hand. They belong together. It makes sense for us to be this close.

"As the only boy, Kellen was closest to my father and assumed the role of patriarch when my father died," I explain. "Kellen acclimated to this realm surprisingly well and helped make our transition easier. He had a way of making us laugh until it hurt and was always quick to smile and make friends. But watching the Cù-Sìth devour our mother and sisters sent Kellen spiraling into that darkness he fought against for so long. He didn't speak much after that, to me, or to anyone. He isolated himself from everyone and went from being popular to that strange young man everyone stayed away from."

"I see."

Yeah, maybe he does. Without thinking, I skim his skin with my fingers. Gentle warmth pours from the tips as I guide them along his cheek. Smooth softness and heat tantalize me with each stroke, and so does something more.

I jerk back, my eyes flying open when I see his face.

"What's wrong?" he asks.

A thin coat of ash smears his face. "We have to go to the bathroom."

"Excuse me?"

I grip his hands. He doesn't fight me and allows me to lead him down the hall. "Is it this way?" I ask.

"Yes. The next door on your left."

My sneakers squeak against the cold emerald tile. I shove

Ryker in front of the oval mirror. He stills at the sight of his reflection and tries to wipe the soot from his face.

I turn on the faucets full blast. "Here. Use water."

Ryker jumps when I drench his shirt. He shoots me a reproachful glare and adjusts the stream. "Hurry up," I insist.

He cups the water in his hands and splashes his face. The ash washes away, revealing fresh, unmarred skin and—score—a brand-new eye. I don't know what happened, I'm just thrilled that it did.

"Yes!" I toss him a towel and dance around the small space, waving my arms in the air. "Oh, yes, baby, yes!"

Ryker wipes his face, eyeing me up and down. "Your dance skills are atrocious."

"I'm flossing," I say.

"How can that possibly benefit your gums?"

Evidently, he's not feeling my sexy self. "It's just the name of the dance," I explain moving my arms and hips faster. "Besides, these aren't my real moves."

"They're not? Good."

I ignore the dig. "This is my impromptu, 'Yay, you're not scarred for life' dance."

"That's nice," he says, having nothing better. He tosses the towel into the hamper and steps into the hall.

"Where are you going?" I ask. "You're going to miss my split." He glances over his shoulder. "I'm certain your flexibility is most impressive, and I'm confident it will aid in your training. Let's return to the Bat Cave and put it to good use."

My hands drop. "We're not doing the whip thing again, are we?"

He frowns. "You need the practice."

"Did you enjoy losing an eye?"

"No," he growls. "Which is why *you need* the practice."

Three hours later, we abandon the "how to torture" lair and return upstairs. I burned lines into his once lovely floor and into his less than lovely cinderblock walls. My aim remains hideous, yet my transfer of energy has improved. I stagger all the way up the curved staircase, using the banister to haul my wobbly body.

I fall dramatically when I reach the top floor and attempt to crawl. "Food...must...have...food."

Ryker steps over me. I can hear the laughter in his voice. "Does this mean you're not cooking for me?"

"I cooked last night." I roll onto my back and drape my limp arm over my eyes. "How about we order in? Does that super awesome bistro deliver?"

"It does." He fumbles through a drawer and a few cabinets before the magical sound of filtered water fills my ears. "Come to the couch."

"No. It's too damn far." I'm not exaggerating. It's a big-ass space.

"We really must work on your stamina."

I wiggle my arms. At least I try to. They weigh more than I remember. Maybe Ryker is holding them down with his Death mojo. "With all the typing and passing out coffee I do, you'd think my guns would be more menacing." I wiggle them again. Big mistake. "Ouch."

"I wouldn't call them guns."

"No need to be insulting, oh Bringer of Doom."

"They're more like slingshots," he adds.

Now he's just being mean. "That's not true."

"You're right. Slingshots are tougher. Perhaps those plastic paddle balls are more accurate. Are you familiar with them? They're given out at fairs to children."

"Settle down, Death. You think you're funny, but you're not."
Okay, that didn't sound weird or anything.

He fumbles with what sounds like several sheets of paper.
"Would you care to join me on the couch, Thumbelina? Or
would you prefer I carry you?"

My thighs and arms want us carried. My pride doesn't appreciate his Disney humor and tells my limbs to take a dive into the
nearest rose bush. While my legs did little more than stand, they
ache like hell.

I stagger from the floor across the loft and flop onto the
burnt-orange couch. Before another witty and spellbinding
remark can spew from my mouth, I down the glass of water
Ryker poured me. Water good.

I peer over his arm and read the menu, contemplating what
will best rejuvenate my spirit and silence my screaming thighs.
"Let's start with the calamari. You strike me as a fried squid kind
of fellow. Oh, and tell them to include extra lime and that
yummy garlic sauce. I'll have the marinated rabbit and wild rice,
and the beet and goat cheese salad. For dessert, I'll pop in the
blackberry pie we bought yesterday. Their selection sounds a
little too frou-frou."

"Says the woman who prances," he mumbles.

He chuckles when I nudge his arm. He waves me away like a
gnat and continues to skim through the menu.

I'm stretching my leg over my head when he finishes placing
the order. "Why am I so sore?" I bemoan.

"You've roused a great deal of dormant magic in a very short
amount of time. You also stress and tense your body with every
release. As your confidence grows, you'll use your power more
efficiently, and it will become second nature." He watches me
point my toe north. "Would you like me to help you?"

Yes, I would, big boy. Somehow, I keep my mouth shut and my tongue from lolling. I like Ryker. *Really* like him. And more than my sanity insists I should.

The time we spend holding each other is sweet and wonderfully easy. I want more, but I shouldn't go there. Embraces can easily lead to intimacy neither of us may be ready for. My first attempt to stir my magic proved as much.

I try to smile and barely manage. I wish our situation allowed us to be more than what we are. "No, thank you," I finally reply. "I'll manage."

Ryker returns his attention to the menu, despite already placing our order. "Very well."

I lower my leg, knowing I offended him, searching for something to say. As I think about it, I place my hand on his knee. He looks from my hand to my face. No words come, only silence and my desire to draw closer. My fingers squeeze as the sun abruptly fades and shrouds the loft in sudden darkness.

Thunder booms, making me jolt. Ryker rises, his attention toward the row of windows. "The weather called for sun all day," I stammer.

Ryker's features harden. He steps closer toward the windows. "Although it has been threatening to storm," I add rather hurriedly.

Another crash of thunder echoes in the distance. I rush to Ryker's side. Black clouds bleed from the left and right, the biggest surge of clouds coming at us dead center from the direction of the city.

Ryker presses his hand against my belly, urging me away from the windows. "It's Cathasach," he bites out. "He's hunting you."

18

I move several steps back when Ryker's hand slips away. He stands in front of me, facing the window and what's coming head on. Me, I'm scanning the room for someplace to hide. Another boom of thunder sounds. This one is louder, closer.

Ryker reaches for me. I don't realize I'm trembling until he grasps my elbow and steadies me. "He can't unearth you here, Olivia. My wards are strong, and your talisman will keep you veiled."

My instincts say otherwise and urge me to flee. "He's closing in," I stammer.

Ryker's expression darkens. He knows I'm right. "He may have sensed you through the magic you created, but my wards are designed to disorient. You won't be easy to track."

"Just here, or everywhere?" I catch my reflection in the glass as the sky morphs into night. My eyes are wild.

Ryker's face splits with hesitancy and frustration. "Your magic carries a unique feel and scent. In using it against him, he's familiar with it. Should you use it outside my wards, he'll latch on to your aroma and find you—with or without the veil of your talisman. Until you learn to master your power, never use it outside my home."

"I won't," I promise. He drops his hand away from my shoulder. Almost immediately, my body resumes the horrible shuddering. I scoff at my shaking hands. "I'm the one begging to kill him. How can I pull it off when I'm this scared?"

Ryker's throaty timbre remains a force onto itself. "You want to survive. You want to avenge. That's how. Remember that when your fear threatens to overtake you."

I nod. He's right. "Okay… I—"

Something hard crashes against the window. I jump, biting back a scream. Large scarred paws covered in white fur slap against the glass, the jagged claws scraping lines of azure mist into the magical defenses. The hound's head pops up, sniffing in the direction of the river.

"Ryker?"

"It's all right," Ryker replies, his voice a low whisper. "He's only searching."

The hound's head whips in our direction, his eyes locking on me.

"*Ryker.*"

Ryker shoots out his hand, his scythe at the ready in his grip. "Steady, Olivia."

The death hound peels back his lips from his razor-sharp fangs. Drool streams down his filthy mouth when he snarls. He can already taste my flesh.

The hound rakes his claws along the glass, trying to force his way in.

Blood drains from my face, and my stomach gives a nauseating lurch. I cover my mouth; certain I'll be sick.

The hound tips back his head, his maw stretching. The howl he releases rattles the row of windows and alerts his pack.

Hundreds of his kin respond in a chorus of famished yelps. They want me, and now they know where I am.

"Ryker, they're coming."

"I know," he says.

My knees buckle, and I collapse, terror clenching my throat. We can't fight an army of Cù-Sìth!

The hound's red eyes flare, seeing right through me to where my heart barrels against my ribcage. He's readying to crash through the window and kill me. There's doubt in my mind. Instead, the massive beast pushes away from the glass and soars toward the sky, merging with the advancing cluster of dark clouds drawing nearer.

Through the inky blackness, I make out the blurred outlines of the Cù-Sìth, the largest of all in the lead. *Cathasach.*

His fangs snap in anticipation, inciting his pack as they advance with blinding speed.

Furious howls slice at my ears. I can't move, fear reducing me to a frightened rabbit, cowering in a glen.

I barely catch sight of Ryker prowling forward. He slams the base of his scythe to the floor. *"Chosaint di!"*

Protect her.

Ryker is reinforcing his wards.

Mounds of matted beasts collide into the wall of glass, piling forward until the entire view is blocked with writhing bodies. Some jerk their heads, confused as to where to go. Still more shove the weaker away, the pain from their impact feeding their fury. They turn on each other, clawing and biting into their kin and snaking their heavy forms through the heap.

My hairs stand on end as the hounds divide into smaller, brawling groups until the disorientation of Ryker's ward scatters them in wayward directions.

Ryker pants, streams of sweat gliding down his temples. The

boost to the wards drained him. Still, his concern remains on me. "Don't be afraid."

I take in how much keeping them back must have cost him. "Are you all right?"

"I'm *fine*," he says. "I'm more concerned about you." He frowns. "You're shaking."

I'm sure he expected more from me. I glance down, trying to compose myself. "They almost found me. If your defenses are so formidable, how did they manage?"

"They know you're close, Olivia. They just don't know where." He frowns when I don't appear convinced. "The first hound couldn't sense you," he reminds me.

"Then why the need for that?" I motion to his scythe. "And for the extra magic?"

With a snap of his wrist, his scythe vanishes. "I needed to strengthen the wards. I suspected there were many, but not this many."

The tip of my tongue glides along the back of my teeth. I don't want to articulate what I've guessed all along. It comes out anyway. It needs to. "We're not enough. Are we?"

Ryker lowers himself on the floor beside me and slips his arm around my shoulders. "We don't need to be many, *beag tuar ceatha*. We only need to fight smart." He jerks his chin in the direction of the window. "Did you see them? They're nothing more than mindless beasts."

"Mindless beasts with fangs and claws plenty capable of killing me."

"Only if given the chance. I don't plan to give them that chance. Do you?"

"That's not the plan." I look up at him. "How will we kill them without a direct standoff?"

Ryker rubs his jaw, giving my question the time it deserves. "Cathasach is pivotal to their power and strength.

So long as an Alph leads them, they're impossible to annihilate. We must figure out a way to face him alone. If we can
kill him, we'll have a small window of time when the others
become mortal and before another Alpha takes his place."

I regard him as if he's nuts since, well, right now he sounds it.
"There were more than a hundred, Ryker. Mortal or not, we can't
kill that many alone."

"You're right," he agrees. "We'll need our allies to help us. In
their mortal form, the Cù-Sìth are easier to kill. Dragon fire
alone can eliminate them."

Hope straightens my spine. "Okay. Let's say we manage to
kill Cathasach. How long do we have until the others battle it
out for top dog?"

Ryker doesn't answer.

"A week?" I guess.

Silence.

"A day?" I press.

Still nothing.

"Don't tell me we have less than a day to kill a hundred death
hounds!"

"We may have an hour," he tells me.

"*May* have an hour? You're telling me we could potentially
have less than that?" That's when hope waves buh-bye.

I stand and pace, ready to give up my Death Seeker crown.
Ryker leans back on his palms. "Olivia, the fall of an Alpha is a
good thing."

"Yeah. For a full five minutes."

"Have you ever watched nature shows?" he asks. "Those
involving wolves?"

My steps halt. "Sure," I say, wondering where he's going with
this. "I like wolves."

"Then you've seen how an Alpha earns his place. It's a

vicious brawl, often to the death. Chaos reigns, as does confu- sion. Those who fight must stay focused to survive."

"And those watching are distracted," I say.

"Precisely."

He rises and leads me back to the couch. Thunder announces its presence in the distance as rain speckles gently against the glass. I sit rather clumsily. My muscles throb. Yet my pain is secondary to my lingering fear. "How do you do it?"

"Do what?" he asks.

"Keep all this faith going?" I lean into him, tucking my legs beneath me.

"I have to," he says. "You remain my only means to find my peace."

I shrink away. "Please don't."

Ryker stays with his back against the couch, his stance relaxed considering what he alluded to. "Olivia, I'm tired of walking this earth less than a Fae, and even less of a man. Regardless of what you see, I'm barely more than a shell, the soul housed within minuscule at best."

Tears blur my vision. I blink them away, allowing them to roll down my cheeks. "But I like what I see." I wrap my arms around his. "And I like who you are."

Ryker lowers his head. "I don't."

"Why don't you?" I ask.

He glares at me. "How can you ask such a question?"

Ryker is all sorts of scary when he glares. Except, here I am, offering a smile. "I want to know. You're a good person. I never realized since I was too busy judging you, but you are."

"I'm the Scottish version of the Grim Reaper," he says slowly, as if I hadn't picked up on that little tidbit before.

I nod. "Yeah, you are."

"I eat souls."

I point. "Only the bad ones," I remind him.

"I am *Death*."

I shrug with one shoulder. "We all have our things."

He narrows his icy baby blues. "There's something wrong with you."

I sigh. "You've mentioned that." I adjust my weight and lean my head against his shoulder, curling my arms tighter around his. Part of me is afraid to let him go. The other part seeks comfort only he can provide.

I remain very much terrified beyond reason. Especially given Ryker's lowdown on what happens when we kill Cathasach. The Alpha's death isn't the end to the Cù-Sìth. It's a small opportunity we can use to our advantage, *if* we can kill Cathasach in the first place.

The weight of everything that could go wrong threatens to crack my skull. I don't want to focus on our ever-mounting troubles, nor do I want to think about me. So, I ask Ryker maybe something I shouldn't. "Did your family cross through?"

I don't just welcome the distraction Ryker's saga will grant me. I want to know more about him. This dude is willing to die for me—and I don't even know his favorite color! I need to know him more and take in what remains of his soul.

The light rain sprinkling the window drums a little harder. I wait patiently for him to answer, allowing the beat of the gentle sound to ease my stress. It takes Ryker a long time. It doesn't matter. He's worth the wait.

"I don't know," he says finally. "Everything was lost to me when I became the Ankou. If any of my clan still lives, I'm likely nothing more than a distant memory."

"How did you die?" Well, aren't I just on a roll?

"Do you really want to know?" he asks.

"Yes. But you don't have to tell me."

His response comes without hesitation. Maybe he needed to tell me as much as I needed to hear it. "I was hunting alone. I didn't need the game," he says, remembering. "I needed a distraction."

"From your womanly woes?" I guess. I smile when his upper arm tenses against my cheek. "You did, didn't you?"

"How did you know?" he asks.

"It's always about womanly woes. We have that effect." I snuggle closer, his body generously warming my chilled skin. "You were saying?"

He chuckles. It doesn't last, his humor quickly fading. "I came upon another form of Death prowling through my land. He was on his way to claim an aging and sickly leprechaun. I didn't realize what he was. I merely envied the beautiful stallion he rode despite my fine steed." He breathes deeply. "In my youth and arrogance, I challenged him to a hunt."

I groan. This wasn't good. "What were the terms?"

He pauses, and I can picture him mentally kicking himself. "The first to return to the spot where we met with a white stag would win. The winner could have anything of his choosing."

"You wanted his horse," I guess.

"Yes. And he wanted my soul. He agreed, and I believed him the fool for it. I knew my land and knew where herds of white stags gathered. I returned to our meeting point less than half an hour later with the largest and grandest buck I'd ever killed. He was a beautiful creature, his pelt was so white, it glowed."

Not so beautiful Ryker wanted to spare him. I don't remind him. It's clear how much he regrets what he did in his tone. "Death was already there waiting, wasn't he?"

"Yes. Perched on a mound of white stags."

"Oh," I say.

Ryker stares up at his magnificent ceiling. I doubt he really sees it. "I was fated to marry a woman I didn't love or want to bed. Before that day, I thought my future was a fate worse than death. What a fool I was, Olivia."

I sit up and gently turn his face toward mine. "You didn't make the right choice, Ryker. That doesn't mean you deserved what happened." I search his stone-cold face. It reveals nothing, just the barest glimpse of his torment. "You need to forgive yourself. It's clear you haven't."

"I wish I could. I left my family without a male heir to continue our legacy, and an innocent maiden without a groom."

"Did you try to approach them while you still remained in Fae?" Thunder cries out in the distance, flickering the lights. My grip tightens around him.

Ryker tries to smile. "It's not the Cù-Sìth," he assures me. "It's just a storm triggered by their massive presence and magic." His small smile weakens. "There are rules I must follow as the Ankou. Most are ingrained within me. Some I've discovered accidentally. When the first year of the sentence came and went without reprieve, I sought out my mother. I wanted to hear her voice and apologize for leaving her the way I did. The moment I approached her, her heart began to slow. She didn't see me, and I was several yards away, yet I almost killed her."

"Whoa."

"My actions were foolish," he says. "I should have known better. But my loneliness was more than I could bear. I just...*longed* to feel normal."

"Did you ever manage to feel like yourself?"

"No." His sullen features keep me in place. "I've been lost since I gambled with Death. When I crossed into earth's realm, I wandered for decades, trying to find a place in this world to exist. I studied cultures and people, folklore and magic, religion and what most held as truth. A few years ago, something in me stirred, leading me in a direction I questioned more than once. I attended law school, initially dismissing my desire as a need to acclimate better among humans."

"Did you like it?"

He angles his chin. "Like what?"

"Law school at Harvard?" I grin when the edges of his lips curve.

"Nowhere in this world will you find a larger group of arrogant, bloodthirsty sharks than at Harvard." He smirks. "I fit right in."

Something slams into the door, rattling the metal. We leap to our feet, our bodies rigid. "What was that?" I ask.

Again, something strikes. This time harder.

Ryker's fists clench, and he practically growls. "It can't be," he says.

The door shakes again. "What can't be?"

"Ryker?"

"*Ryker?*"

"My wards are failing," he says.

"*What?*"

He shoots me a hard stare. "The hounds should not have returned this soon unless…"

He doesn't have to finish his thought. "Unless there are too many for the wards to shield us against," I answer for him.

Ryker cracks his wrist. A dagger with a skull at its hilt appears in his palm. "Take this."

"What is it?"

"My dagger of death."

I gape at the giant black thing with a blade the size of my head. "Dagger of death? Is this a joke?"

He clenches his teeth as something slams into the door. "*Just take it.*"

Ryker prowls toward the door, catching the scythe that appears from thin air. With a snap of his free hand, another dagger manifests in his grip. I pad behind him, clutching my weapon against my heart and trying to call forth my power. "Can't you just teleport us out?"

"No. If only a few have found their way through, we might be able to kill them before they alert the others. It will give me time to reinforce the wards."

"What happens if we can't kill them?"

Ryker ignores my question. "Don't engage them directly," he orders. "Point the dagger and extend your power through the tip."

"It's not as long as the whip," I choke out.

His voice lowers. "It doesn't have to be. Slash, point, and jab, as far away as you can. Your magic will do the rest."

The next bang makes me jump. My breath catches. We're in serious trouble.

"Stay behind me," Ryker mashes out. "If something happens to me, or if I'm taken, shut the door. The wards should hold long enough for you to phone Jane. She'll pull you somewhere safe."

I nod until I realize what he's saying. "What? *No*. I'm not leaving you!"

"*Olivia*."

Another crash.

My voice lowers, and I scowl, feeling the fire within me catch and intensify. My hands surge with pink magic, and so does my blade. "If you think I'll cower while the Cù-Sìth make you their bitch, you're out of your scythe-wielding mind."

"You are insufferable!"

"And you sell seashells by the seashore," I fire back. "*Dagger* of *death*? Really? Is that the best you can do?"

"Bite your tongue and *focus*."

The next jolt against the heavy metal is the loudest of all. The wards around the frame hum, sending streams of azure light to crawl along the walls and ceiling like thickening branches. Ryker clasps the handle with the hand holding the dagger. "On the count of three. Ready?"

"Yes." My hand clutches the hilt, my entire body sizzling with magic. I wouldn't let these monsters take Ryker. No way.

"One." His grip tightens.

"Two."

He bends his knees.

"*Three.*"

Ryker flings the door open, his scythe raised, his battle cry riling mine.

I grit my teeth and scream, ramming my blade forward.

Hot pink energy shoots from the tip and across the hall, spewing like a busted hydrant and showering the steel elevator in bright light.

The teenager in a backward baseball cap standing in front of us, his arms filled with boxes of take-out, shrieks with the force of a thousand pre-pubescent boys. He drops the contents of the box and staggers backward.

Ryker and I lower our weapons and withdraw our collective power, my face on fire as a wet spot spreads along the groin of the delivery boy's jeans. I reach out a hand, stumbling over an apology.

Delivery Boy doesn't want to hear it.

With crazy hormonal speed, he bolts. Ryker and I stick our heads out, watching the poor bastard jetting toward the emergency exit and screaming as if pursued by Vanessa.

My hand clasps over my mouth as I look wide-eyed up at Ryker.

"My wards did hold," he mutters. He glances down at me and then back in the direction where the delivery boy disappeared. "I'll call in a tip."

"Make it good one," I mumble.

19

We ate the food. It wasn't as pretty following the tumble to the floor, but the containers held it tight, and the yummy flavor remained.

I'm munching on my last piece of pie when Ryker appears from his bedroom with his cell phone pressed against his ear.

"Yes. Thank you. And please extend our apologies to the young man." He disconnects and takes a seat on the barstool beside me.

I lower my fork. "Did you tell the kid's boss that we mistook him for the evil leader of the hounds of death, who we deemed ready to rip our souls from our bodies, and that perhaps next time, the kid should knock politely instead of rudely banging on the door with his foot?"

"No. I told him that it was a prank meant for a friend we were expecting."

"That works, too," I agree. I sip on my wine. The alcohol, and the humiliation of the experience, heats my cheeks. "He accused us of snorting cocaine, didn't he?"

Ryker rubs his eyes. "To wake us from our heroin stupor," he adds.

"Heroin stupor?" I question. At Ryker's nod, I take another sip. "We make quite the pair, don't we?"

He fills his wineglass. "That we do." He swirls the red liquid against the glass, watching the legs form. "You need to start listening better," he says.

I quirk a brow. "What do you think I spent the day doing?"

He shakes his head. "I mean when it comes to your safety. The expectation is that you are the one who will save the Fae. That won't happen if you die."

All right. Now I'm annoyed. "Are you worried about the future of Fae, or are you more concerned with your own hide?" I lean forward. "That maybe I won't last long enough to grant you that peace you so desperately seek?"

Rage sharpens the angles in Ryker's face. I hit a nerve. So, had he. I'm trying. Can't he see how overwhelmed and terrified I am?

"Your existence is more valuable than mine," he grinds out. "I'm just another form of Death. You are Life, and the only chance the Fae have to survive."

"How can you think so little of yourself? Or tell me your existence doesn't matter? It matters to me."

When he doesn't say anything, I'm ready to beat him over the head with a wine bottle. "All right. You know everything. What happens if what remains of your soul gets gobbled up by Cathasach? You think you have it bad now, what's it going to be like trapped inside of him with all those miserable souls you, as the Ankou, are helpless to save?"

He points to himself. "If I fall at the hands of the Cù-Sìth, I'm one loss out of thousands. If you're killed, especially by Cathasach, the consequences are catastrophic. Death becomes unstoppable."

"Don't you think I know that? The thought has raked

through my mind a thousand times over. I'm not naïve, Ryker. Stop treating me as if I am."

"Then why don't your actions reflect the importance of your survival?" he demands.

I push away from the raised counter and stomp toward his bedroom. I'm not certain where I'm headed. I'm just too livid to keep still. When I'm almost to the hall, I whirl around and storm back to him. "I didn't sign up for this. Any of it. You pretend to know what I'm going through, but you have no fucking idea!" My eyes sting with growing ire. "You may be lonely but being alone means having no one to answer to. I now answer to every last Fae, the living *and* the dead. I don't need to be reminded of what happens if I fail."

Ryker looms over me. "Until you start heeding my orders, I will remind you of it and more. I told you to call out to Jane, that she would protect you and stow you somewhere safe. Instead of obeying, you took out your anger on me. We thought Death was at my door, and all you did was argue. Just as you're doing now."

I throw my hands in the air. "I don't want to be stowed. Not if it means losing you!"

"Why?"

Is he really this thick? "Because I care about you. Why can't you understand that? I'm not letting you die just to save my own ass."

He lifts his chin. "You need to accept that it may come to that."

I point at him, aiming for the dimple. "No. *You* need to stop whining about how expendable you are and shut the hell up."

The air between us thickens enough to pound nails through. I just royally pissed off a guy who carries a scythe and knows how to use it. And I could give a fairy's flat ass. Life can be hard. Suck it, Death.

Our gazes drill into each other for what feels like ages. My stomach roils, churning my dinner painfully. It had tasted so good. Except nothing tastes good now.

This was Day One of training. The results were adequate at best. How will Day Two, or Three go? Will I even see the following week?

Cathasach is gaming for me, and nothing will distract him and his pack from the hunt. He wants to devour me and make me suffer. And here I stand at odds with the one being who can help me fight him.

Ryker's seething glare eases away when a tear moistens my hot cheeks. He sighs. "I don't want to fight with you, Olivia."

"I don't want to fight with you, either." More tears trickle to my chin. "I know what I have to do. Just as I know you're the only one who can teach me the right way to do it." My heart begs him to listen when all he does is look at me. "I'm not trying to be difficult, and I promise to work on it. But you need to work on not being such a martyr. I don't see you as expend- able, so, stop acting like you are, and we'll both be better   for it."

Ryker closes in. He watches my tears slide like tiny rivers before cupping my face in his hands. His thumbs swipe my cheeks, the gentle contact soothing me and my misery. "I don't mean to act as a martyr. My objective is to find peace, not substitute it for a different form of hell. I can only accomplish my task with your help. But even if you couldn't grant me eternal rest, I would sacrifice myself to keep you safe."

That's not what I want to hear. "*Why*?"

"Because I care for you as well, Olivia. More than you realize or desire."

Time stops as if slammed into a wall. My mind insists that Ryker is only attracted to me because he's another form of Death, that what he feels isn't what I think it is. Even if it is, it's not right. Never have two beings been more opposite or fated to end so disastrously. "You shouldn't," I tell him, my voice thick with sadness.

His deep gaze searches mine for an eternity. Finally, he lowers his hands from my face. "Very well," he says.

Ryker gives me his back and walks toward the spiraling metal staircase that leads to the Bat Cave. "Come. There is one more thing I need to teach you before we end our day."

I hurry to catch up to him, slowing only when I begin my descent down the tricky steps. "Are you angry with me?" I ask.

"No." He walks to the center of the room and turns to face me, his expression weary. "I know you prefer to not entertain thoughts of my death—"

"You've got that right," I mutter.

I expect him to grow irate for cutting him off. Instead, the side of his mouth curves into a smirk. "You can't deny the possibility exists."

For either of us, I don't add.

He frowns as if my thoughts had reached his. Slowly, he relaxes his eyebrows. "I want to leave Dugan and Phillip in your care should I fail you."

"Um," I look around, whispering low if they can hear us. "Isn't that against the rules?"

"I don't see how. They are in my charge."

I blink back him. "I'm not the Ankou," I remind him.

"True, but you're forgetting there won't be another Ankou to take my place."

"Why?" I ask.

There he goes again, giving thought to what he should tell me and what he should leave out. "One of two things will happen should Cathasach claim my soul. Either they will enter their eternal peace, which I doubt. Or they will be trapped along with me, which is more likely."

"Why won't Doogie and Phil—"

"Dugan and Phillip," he interrupts, his smirk returning.

"Yeah, yeah," I say, batting my hands. "What I'm trying to say is, why wouldn't they be allowed into the Afterlife?"

"The penance for the sins they committed is servitude to the Ankou."

"They've served every Ankou that ever was?" I ask. Ryker nods. "Wow. They must've been quite the bad boys." His edgy posture makes it clear I shouldn't delve into the nature of their sins.

"I appreciate what you're trying to do," I add. "But I don't want to be responsible for your buddies."

Ryker takes several steps back and shoots out his arm, his scythe appearing almost instantly. I don't even flinch, which troubles me. It seems I'm getting a little too used to his neck-slicing weapon of choice.

Ryker holds his scythe at his side, parallel to the floor. It's the first time I realize that the battered handle has runes etched in varying patterns. I recognize some: protection, wrath, strength. Obviously, I don't have time to analyze more, not with the seriousness Ryker pegs me with.

"My warriors may not be pure of heart, but they are my charge and have been loyal to me for more than a century. I prefer to leave them to aid and protect you rather than risk their imprisonment within the Cù-Sìth." He passes me his scythe. "Take it."

"Um, why?"

He shakes his head as if annoyed. Still, I recognize a hint of humor. "Must you question everything I ask?"

I grin. "It seems to me you don't like being questioned. In fact, you kind of strike me as a 'do as I command, or I'll kill you' kind of guy." I hold out my hand. "Then again, it's just a guess."

Granite carries more warmth than this guy. "I know, I know," I tell him. "I'm *insufferable*."

Ryker ignores me and drops his scythe into my outstretched hands. I drop it, point down, into his already abused floor.

Ryker pinches the bridge of his nose. Hands down, I'm like, his bestest student, ever. "This thing is heavier than I thought," I offer apologetically.

"I can see as much," he mutters. "Remind me to begin our weight training regimen tomorrow. Now, trace a line into the floor with the point—"

He cringes at the horrid scratching noise the blade makes as I create my line. Well, it's not exactly a line, more like a zig-zag with the occasional swerve.

"I said *trace*. Not dig a hole en route to China."

"Sorry. This thing weighs a ton."

Ryker clenches his jaw, muttering through his teeth. I notice he does that a lot in my presence. "Force your power through the tip of the base and command them to rise," he says. "*Ardú.*"

"In the future, that would be great info to start with." I examine my pathetic line that resembles more of a beak than anything I recall in geometry. "Should I go back and try again?"

Ryker squeezes his eyes shut. This guy is all sorts of crazy about me. "Please don't," he snaps. "The floor is not your enemy. Keep going, and, for once, do as I ask."

"I do the stuff you ask." He looks at me. "Mostly," I mumble, thinking back.

I take a breath and will my power through the scythe and into the line. This time, it's not as hard to call it forward, but it is more draining. "*Ardú,*" I call out.

My scratch flares pink and not much more.

"Louder," Ryker insists.

"*Ardú!*"

"It's a command. Not a request," Ryker instructs. "Compel them to rise."

My shoulders droop. "I don't like ordering people around. It's rude and just not in me."

The big bad smirk returns. "Pretend it's me, on a Monday, lying across your desk, requesting you massage my feet."

"*Ardú,* damn it!"

The semi line ignites with pink light. Doogie and Phil rise, swords out, their scowls trained on me. Ryker walks around them to stand by my side. "Dugan, Phillip, this is Olivia. You're aware we will help her face the Cù-Sìth. Should I perish, your loyalty will pass to her."

Doogie's scowl deepens. Phil flips me off. My guess is Phil is the bigger sinner of the two. Well, isn't dealing with dead Scottish warriors just a laugh a minute?

Ryker's lethal glare shifts to Phil. "Phillip, this is not appropriate behavior in the presence of a lady." Phil tucks his sword into the sheath at his side and adds a second finger. Ryker takes a step forward. "This isn't a request, Phillip. Either pledge your loyalty to Olivia in my absence or spend damnation swimming in the bowels of the Cù-Sìth."

Ryker has a gift for painting quite the visual. Doogie, although his ghostly form darkens with annoyance, he places his hand over his heart and bows.

For now, this appears good enough for Ryker. "Good. Tell them to sleep."

"*Codladh,*" I say, demonstrating what I hope is respect in my voice.

Doogie disappears into my fading pink line. Phil places his hand over his heart and bows. It's not as deep, and more curt than Doogie. Still, I try to smile, thinking he's on board... Until he gives me his back, bends over, and lifts his kilt as he vanishes into the floor.

The theory that Scots don't wear anything beneath that kilt? It's true, folks.

Ryker rubs his chin. "They were…hesitant."

"And hairy," I add. "Especially Phil. The ghoul needs a serious ass wax."

"The added hair had its benefits in the Scottish Highlands during the winter months," Ryker reasons.

I bark out a laugh, noting Death does have a sense of humor.

My smile remains on my return home. "What else do you have planned, besides my obvious need to bulk up?" I ask Ryker.

His lips twitch. "Bulk isn't necessary. You just need enough strength to wield any weapon at your disposal and feed it with your power."

"If you're expecting me to swing that scythe of yours, I'll need some toning."

He pokes me in the arm. "If this is the extent of your strength, you're right."

I rub my arm defensively, not that it'd hurt. "Believe it or not, I'm tougher than I look."

His blue eyes tame. "I know," he says.

Ryker walks me to my door. I punch the keypad and wait for the wards to allow me in. I grip the handle only to hesitate. "Thank you for today. I know it wasn't easy, and that we fought more than once, but I appreciate your help."

"You're welcome, Olivia."

I expect him to go all Obi-Wan Kenobi on me and say something meaningful and somewhat riddled. In the end, Ryker remains Ryker, allowing his quiet disposition to ooze mystery for him. "Goodnight, Olivia."

"Goodnight, Ryker. I'll see you in the morning."

I step into the foyer. No, the day wasn't perfect, but we ended on a good note. My smile fades as the door quietly shuts behind me, and the protective wards close me in.

Once more, I'm alone. Or so I believe until I see farther in.

The lamp in our tiny living room is the only light on, shadowing the dark, unmoving forms waiting for me.

My muscles twitch painfully. I know who's here despite their hidden faces and silence. I should have sensed the familiarity of their presence. Mostly, I should have sensed their grief.

Ryker's company had dulled my mourning. Perhaps that's why I was able to function. Now that he's gone, my sadness returns with an unfathomable charge.

Each step I take intensifies the harsh pangs to my chest. I'm not ready to see them. Not yet. Not when guilt still reigns within me and beats me with blow after blow.

The short walk past the kitchen is the longest I've ever taken. I anticipated they'd come. It shouldn't surprise me like it does. Maybe I expected them later. No. That's not true. Maybe I secretly wished I didn't have to face them at all. Except here they are, and I won't run.

Dahlia's parents, her brother, and sister wait in our small living room, their willowy frames taking up the dimly lit and cramped area where they stand.

I'm not sure what to say, especially when they don't seem up to speaking. Dahlia's brother and sister nod to me, tears streaking their faces as they lead their mother past me.

Dahlia's mother stares blindly ahead, her elegant frame curled inward and her perfect face a phantom of what was once so wonderfully animated.

I've lost parents and siblings. She lost her child. I don't have to be a mother to know there's no worse pain.

"We came for her things," her younger brother croaks. He might have said more, but those few words are enough to break the sobs loose from him and his sister. Their mother doesn't flinch, maintaining her vacant expression.

I reach out to Dahlia's mother, my throat constricting. Her children lead her quickly away when she sways, and her thin form threatens to buckle. They disappear before they reach the door in a wave of somber magic that exposes their pain.

That pain drives into my heart like a stake. They were so kind to me when my brother left. They invited me to every holi- day, every family gathering, everything that meant anything to them. Now, it seems goodbye has come. They lost their Dahlia. Maybe they blame me, or perhaps I remind them too much of her. Whatever the reason doesn't matter. I won't see them again. I'm sure of it.

"They say you're the one who can save us."

I whip around. In my grief and need to comfort her family, I forgot the one member who remains.

Dahlia's father towers over me, his heartbroken expression begging me to answer. "Is it true?" he asks.

"I'm told that I am." My response is lame and lacks the confi- dence I think he yearns for. While I'm starting to accept what I am, I still don't believe I'm the best or strongest for the task.

"That's not good enough," he says, his normal tenor unusu- ally hollow. "You have to *know* who and what you are. For us, and for our Dahlia."

He brushes past me without another word, his form disinte- grating until it vanishes in the hall.

For a long time, my body refuses to move and barely breathes. When I finally push myself forward, I find myself wandering around my apartment.

Dahlia's family left the drapes and communal furnishings. I knew what to expect before I opened her bedroom door, yet it still didn't lessen the blow. Gone was the canopy white bed, the lavender and seafoam bedding, and pretty curtains tucked just so. The teal chairs that pointed toward her window were absent as well as her desk, chair, and laptop.

The room, while clean, lay empty of anything that made it Dahlia, another harsh reminder my friend will never return. I shut the door. As soon as I can, I'll move out. While I can afford the apartment alone, it's just not the same without her. Her room can never be an office, or a spare bedroom. It will always be Dahlia's space, the place we munched on popcorn while mulling over where to shop, what to cook, or what movie to see. The teal chairs…that's where she first told me she loved Frankie and that one day they would have a family of their own.

Frankie wished he told Dahlia he loved her sooner. He never knew Dahlia had wished for so much more.

I pour myself a glass of iced tea, the last from the batch I made the last time we cooked. As I finish the glass, I stare at Dahlia's closed bedroom door, promising myself I would no longer open it.

After showering, I slip into bed, the pain in my chest stirring as I curl into the sheets. Ryker helped me deal with my pain. In his presence, the hole in my heart filled and made living without Dahlia possible. But he isn't here now. And I really want him to be.

I reach for my cell phone and hit his number.

"What's wrong?" he asks.

"Nothing." *I just need to hear your voice.*

I crawl farther beneath the covers and sweep my damp hair over the pillow. "What are your plans for tomorrow? Are we covering all medieval weaponry or only that ball thingy with the spikes?"

He chuckles. "I prefer you master your whip before we move forward. We'll begin with a small run—"

"A run?" I interrupt. "As in, running?"

"You may prance if it's more to your liking."

He's making fun of me. I grin, welcoming the distraction. "Only if you prance with me."

"Death doesn't prance."

"Does it boogie?" I muse.

"No."

"How about shimmy?" I offer. "Surely Death shimmies?"

"Olivia, we need to build your stamina. That means running—"

"Or prancing," I remind him.

"And weight training as we discussed."

"You're going to make me lift heavy objects that make me go *umph*, aren't you?" I guess.

"Yes," he agrees. "And plenty of them."

We continue our banter between discussions of whip training and basic beheading techniques. Seriously, that's what he calls them. Our talk lasts an hour. When I disconnect, my eyes are heavy with sleep. My thoughts, though, immediately return to Dahlia.

The way her father regarded me when he asked me to avenge his daughter haunts me. I don't know if I can save her. Without Ryker, I'm not sure I can save myself. A hundred Cù- Sìth with bear-sized bodies and snapping jaws and a psycho Alpha egging them on, that's what awaits me.

The reminder chills me. I burrow deeper in my bed. As I close my eyes, the memory of Dahlia's smiling face causes them to burn.

My body shudders. I don't want to cry, yet there's that impending sob twisting my heart. I clench my jaw and try to beat it back, knowing I'm moments from losing it.

I gasp when a heavy hand falls upon my shoulder, cooling my mounting hysteria. "*Peace*," a throaty voice whispers.

Tears trickle in zigzags along my face, and still I manage to smile. My hand reaches up to cup my shoulder. I can't feel his rough knuckles beneath my fingers, but I know my protector is here. He sensed my grief and appeared to comfort me.

I squeeze my shoulder. "Hi, Ryker."

I sense that pause. He has the habit of taking one when he ponders how to respond. "Sleep, Olivia," he says. "I am with you."

He is, allowing me to surrender to darkness.

20

The summer abandoned us like a bitter lover, leaving the brisk September air to contend with. I adjust my thick scarf as I hurry from the bus. I haven't returned to the firm in several weeks. Although Ryker and I leave the impression we still work here, our training has intensified, and there's little time to do much else.

I rarely check in on Marco, and that's a very bad thing. Without Ryker or me, Marco has become more monster than man. I advise the staff when I can, and conference call with him when he's close to losing it and firing everyone in sight. But as much as I care for him, and the poor bastards left to deal with him, I can't ignore my life and death commitments.

I've learned a tremendous amount in a short span of time, and my stamina is slowly increasing. Still, it's neither fast nor impressive enough for the Ancients' liking. They're worried the Cù-Sìth will continue to multiply, and as Ryker predicted, they fear the hounds will evolve and target the human populace.

Ryker waits for me outside the elevators in a crisp black suit pressed sharp enough to skewer steaks. He doesn't appear pleased. I loosen the buttons of my light blue pea coat. "What's wrong?"

"There's been a new development," he says. "We're needed on the 28th floor."

"That's fantastic news, seeing how our last meeting there almost resulted in a roomful of dead dragons," I mutter. I examine Ryker's scowl. "It involves dead dragons?"

He presses the "up" button. "It involves Sebastian," he says. "He and his family are marked for death."

I'm sure I misheard. "Is that possible?"

"Apparently, it is."

The doors part and we step inside. A few workers anxious to start their day run to catch it. At the sight of Ryker's oh-so-friendly face, they stop short and stumble into each other.

The woman hovering behind the small group looks ready to bolt. "We'll take the next one," she stammers.

I elbow Ryker lightly the moment the doors shut. "We need to work on your warm and cuddly side." I sense a smirk in the making, but it doesn't quite manifest. "Maybe we should get you a puppy."

"No."

"Kitten?" I suggest.

"*No.*"

"How about—"

"If you say parakeet, I'll add another mile to your run," he grinds out.

I snap my mouth shut. As it is, I can barely prance the two miles we're doing. Ryker assured me our runs would become easier and more enjoyable. So far, it's a "hell, no" on both counts. I hate our early morning sprints around Jersey City and have tripped more than once. And don't get me started on all the seasoned joggers I've flipped off who easily pass me. Those who don't flat out laugh at me mutter stupendous remarks like, "No pain, no gain," and "Holy shit, she looks ready to die."

My silence earns me that smirk and lifts the tension in the elevator. I smile, grateful for the comfortable air between us I've come to expect.

The elevator doors part. Ryker allows me through, catching up to me in two strides. We walk side by side, the 28th floor morphing with every step we take.

Grass sprouts beneath our feet, replacing the tile floor. Roots push out from the base of the support beams and bark encapsulates their lengths, turning them into trees that branch out and canopy the ceiling with lush green and gold foliage. Fairy lanterns fall from the twisted branches, adding more light from their small chambers than should be feasible.

It's beautiful. I want to sink into the thick grass and take it all in. But like my well-being, it's only temporary, a make-believe moment that won't last.

The granite boardroom table at the end of the glen that Jane created is replaced with an outrageously large redwood stump. Beautifully ornate chairs crafted from tree roots and entwined with ivy and small white flowers surround the perimeter. I pause when two pairs of small, fluorescent bluebirds flutter in front of Ryker and me.

"No, thank you," he says. He places his hand on my lower back when I don't reply. "They're offering to take your coat."

"Oh." I place my purse on the, well, *forest floor* and unbutton my coat. My cashmere coat falls from my shoulders. The two birds closest to Ryker catch it before it hits the ground and disappear with it behind a stand of thick trees. Another bird clips the end of my scarf and swoops around me, sweeping it gently from my neck and fluttering away with it.

The remaining bird zigzags around my large purse expectantly. "No, thank you, little one," I say. "I'd like to keep it with me."

The bird doesn't seem to mind and chirps merrily away to find his peeps. "Wow," I say. "That was some serious Cinderella-gets-prepped-for-the-ball action."

"It's because you weren't raised in Fae," Ryker replies. "Come, Olivia. They're waiting."

The old 28th floor was mammoth. Jane's version is colossal. Mr. Sebastian waits a short distance away at the new conference table along with Bill, about ten dragons, and Jane, who is perched on top of the giant stump with her candy-cane wand in her wrinkled hands.

I grin, speaking through my teeth. "They must have paid her well to enchant our surroundings."

"It seems that way," Ryker agrees.

Jane wiggles her feet, showing off the rubies encrusting her orthopedic shoes. I try not to laugh. Good for the little Hydra.

Ryker's voice turns more serious. "I imagine this is the Ancients' new headquarters."

"No one mentioned this before?" I ask, almost stopping.

"The Ancients don't trust me," he mutters. "They're very careful not to divulge anything." He pauses. "And if we continue seeing each other as much as we have, they won't trust you, either."

Ryker and I have grown close over these last few months, training as much as we have. Some moments are exceptionally hard. My frustration with my haphazard magic often leaves me miserable and doubting my ability to do anything. Still, he remains patient and encouraging, all the while pushing me and challenging me to do more.

The times when it's just us, quietly sharing a meal, or when I'm trying to make him less-scary and Reaper-like, are my favorite moments with him. More than once, I've wanted to kiss him. And more than once, my sanity warned against it.

It's just as well. Ryker keeps a professional distance, even when I stir a sexy smile from his lips.

I shrug. "Oh, well."

He stops out of earshot. "It doesn't trouble you that the Ancients consider you in league with me?"

I angle my chin, surprised by his remark. "Why would it? Ryker, we're doing everything for the Fae. If it's not enough, that's their problem, not ours. Besides, I'm already bending over. Don't need the ol' hair pulled, too."

Ah, there's that smirk I adore.

I try to suppress one myself as we continue forward. Based on Bill's solidifying expression, I should have tried harder. He offers a stiff nod and motions us to sit. "Thank you for taking the time out of your training to join us," he says, not meaning a word of it.

Ryker pulls out my chair. I pause before sitting. Bill's tone actually hurts, as does his emphasis on the word "training." Without meaning to, I lower my gaze like a reprimanded child. I catch myself and raise my chin, hurt turning to anger. I haven't lured Ryker to bed. In truth, I've squashed each moment of weakness and want. I won't apologize for our friendship, nor will I distance myself from Ryker in Bill's presence just because I feel a tang of guilt. "No problem, Bill." I smile at Ryker. "What can we help you with?"

My response does nothing to loosen Bill's rigid stance. Annoyance flickers in his face and further tenses his features.

Jane levitates from her position on the table and takes a seat to my left. I turn from Bill and focus on my favorite druid priestess. "Hey, Jane. Nice shoes, girl."

Jane pats my hand hello and looks to Bill as Ryker sits to my right. Her black, beady eyes shimmer, scrutinizing Bill. This time, Bill's in the hot seat looking rather uncomfortable.

"Forgive me, Olivia," Bill adds, quietly.

I'm not certain he means it. Jane, although temperamental and a little on the whack-job side, is a revered Ancient. I take Bill's apology more for show and respect for Jane, not for me. It hurts me a little more. We were friends. I don't know if we are anymore. I want to take him aside to talk to him, except now is not the time. Mr. Sebastian sits directly across from me. Fae can live a long time by human standards. Dragons especially can walk the earth for thousands of years. I'm not sure Mr. Sebastian has many years left. He's aged about twenty years since I last
saw him.

Deep grooves cut into wrinkles I hadn't previously noticed, and his white hair sticks out in crazed tufts. He coughs to clear his throat. Again, and again, and again, more like an ailing man than one who was once so smug.

"I need your help," he spits out.

He motions to a dragon with short blond hair, his hand quivering and jerky. The dragon leans forward, sliding several pictures across the smooth surface. I'm still gaping at the hot mess Sebastian has become when Blond Boy points to the first photo.

A peace sign minus its circle and smeared in red covers a large white door.

I crinkle my brow. "What is that?"

"The symbol for Death," Ryker answers.

Mr. Sebastian nods, what remains of his composure crumbling. He's shaking hard enough to bang his pinky ring against the table. Blond Boy peers at him briefly and points to the next picture. "They used blood from the bodies to draw it."

"Blood from the bodies?" I ask. My voice trails as he points to the next row of pictures. Racks of giant ribs litter a sprawling lawn. I make out a leg shoved into one cavity and part of a face draped over a headless torso.

More pictures follow, all with varying images of dismembered and mutilated parts. I lower my hands away from my mouth and stare ahead, unable to take the carnage. Ryker can fill me in later. This is a Death show. My people are known for skipping through fields of daisies and skinny dipping in secluded ponds, not this shit.

"They're dragons in their true form," Blond Boy explains. "The hounds killed them. The only reason they didn't get the kid was because his friend had invited him to a Yankees game that night."

"What kid?" Ryker scans each photo as he waits for an answer. No one seems ready to talk.

"What kid?" Ryker repeats not so politely.

"My son," Mr. Sebastian replies. His anger momentarily eases his quivers, not that it lasts. "They're after my boy."

I squeeze Ryker's hand, not realizing I'd reached for him until then. "How do you know?"

Sebastian laughs in the crazed, high-pitched laughter of a terrified individual. It freaks me out and sends a chill barreling down my spine. The dragons in the room exchange nervous glances, knowing full well their boss is on the edge of the cliff and ready to jump.

"Mr. Sebastian," I say slowly. "How exactly do you know?"

He stands abruptly, slapping his palms on the table. "Cathasach told me himself!"

He's yelling, his shoulders shaking violently. He drops his head and tries to reel in his hysteria. "The gremlins are working with them," he stammers. "They brought the Cù-Sìth to my home and ripped our talismans from our necks. Cathasach forced me to watch as his pack murdered my staff and security detail. I saw them tear my people apart."

The forest surrounding us grows eerily quiet. The birds stop singing, and the gentle breeze vanishes. It's as if everyone and everything fears the Cù-Sìth will hear them.

My knuckles ache with how hard I'm clenching Ryker's hand. It doesn't seem to bother him. He strokes me gently, offering reassurance I don't feel then.

Sweat and tears pour from Mr. Sebastian's face, beading against the table. He waves off a handkerchief Blond Boy offers, meeting my face dead on. "Cathasach threatened to take my son if I don't lead him to the Ancients. I have ten days before they return."

I don't hesitate to speak, not when there's an Ancient right smack in front of me. "What happens if they claim an Ancient's soul?"

Bill glances at Jane, his expression sad. Jane barely blinks, remaining calm. "They will see through her eyes and our magic," Bill explains. "Our talismans and veils will mean nothing." He sighs. "They will also leech her power and take it as their own."

It's all rainbows and pixie dust up in this bitch.

Bill's attention fixes on me. "You have to stop them, Olivia."

Ryker releases my hand. "She's not ready. We need more time."

This pleases Bill as much as you think. "How long?"

Ryker balls his hands into fists. He doesn't want to make them aware that my first day of Save the World Camp was surprisingly spellbinding and accelerated compared to those that followed. It will take years to master my power. I've barely had more than a few weeks.

Ryker's had a hundred years.

And the Cù-Sìth have had since the dawn of existence.

"I don't know when Olivia's training will be complete," Ryker says. He switches gears, trying to keep the attention off me. "Do you know where the Cù-Sìth are hiding?"

Bill quirks his jaw. He doesn't miss the abrupt change in subject. "The packs are scattered. We've learned of some locations, but not all."

"What about Cathasach?" Ryker presses.

"His lair remains a mystery," Bill replies, addressing Ryker as if I'm no longer an option.

Ryker gives it some thought. I'm just not thrilled with where those thoughts lead. "Leave the hounds for me to hunt," he says. "I'll kill as many as I can and buy us time until we can locate Cathasach."

I straighten. "What if this is what the hounds are counting on to trap you?"

"We can't simply sit around, Olivia," he grinds out.

Great, now he's mad at me. I cross my arms. "Fine. Then I'll hunt with you."

"You need to focus on your training," he bites out, ignoring my protest to round on Bill. "Use every source available to find Cathasach. We have to end this before they claim an Ancient."

"*What about my son?*" Mr. Sebastian demands.

His roars bring us to our feet. My hand instinctively buries deep within my purse, reaching for the handle of my whip.

Jane alone remains sitting, her hold over her wand the only indication she's ready to throw down.

Mr. Sebastian's eyes flare from human brown to perilous dragon yellow. He slaps his hands over his eyes, rubbing them hard. As he drops them away, every groove, angle, and wrinkle expose his desperation. "Please, Olivia. Help my Stevie. He's all I have left."

I speak without thinking, unable to stand the misery

plaguing his very existence. "All right," I agree. "I'll do whatever it takes to keep him safe."

"*Olivia*," Bill and Ryker snarl.

Well, isn't this a wondrous way for them to bond?

Ryker inches closer, his foreboding presence jabbing me with a tangible poke. "You cannot take this responsibility on your own. You haven't mastered enough of your power to protect yourself, much less a soul marked for death."

"Ryker, he's a kid," I point out. "I can't turn my back on a child."

"You're not ready," Ryker reminds me.

"Not ready" is an understatement. Mercifully, he keeps the extent of my inadequacies to himself. Still, that doesn't mean I'm inept or that I can't help.

"Little Stevie needs me," I tell him.

"We need you more." Bill advances in Sebastian's direction. "My apologies, Walter. We can't risk Olivia's safety to guard one soul."

The dragons gather around Sebastian when his skin deepens to a vicious purple. "You promised to help me!"

"No," Bill snaps, his own teeth showing. "I only agreed to meet with you and gauge Olivia's readiness. I never promised anything."

Bill sighs, attempting to reel in the patience he's most known for. "I know you lost a great deal when you crossed over."

"You know nothing!" Mr. Sebastian hollers. "My wife, my father—" he yanks the pictures from the table and throws them at Bill, "—my *family* slaughtered like game by that son of a whore!"

The dragons yank him back when he lunges at Bill. Bill doesn't react, his calm replacing his anger. Me, I can't stop my heart from racing. A Dragon vs. Gargoyle showdown is like two

Jersey girls fighting, not something you want to be anywhere near.

Ryker clasps my arm and tries to angle me behind him. I ease away. As much as I don't like Mr. Sebastian, I feel and empathize with his pain.

"I'll protect your son," I assure him. "I swear I will."

Ryker glares at me, his kickass Ankou super suit clinging to his form. The edges of his cape flutter from the restless breeze sweeping through the trees. "Olivia, Cathasach wants you dead. Your capture is catastrophically more disastrous than the fall of an Ancient."

"Tell me about it," I agree.

Ryker seethes, as in practically singes a hole into the ground where he stands. He hasn't been this miffed at me in ages. I must be doing something right.

"Do you also know that in taking on the role as this boy's protector, you'll announce your presence to Cathasach and his entire pack?" Ryker snarls. "That death mark is ingrained to find Sebastian and any member of his family anywhere."

"Only if the kid stays with his father," I reply. "A death mark only extends to other family members if they're within the threshold of the home at the time of its placement. Little Stevie was at the ball game the night of the attack."

I cross my arms when Ryker's brows join tight enough to hold a pencil and configure fractions. He probably thought I wouldn't remember that speck of Cù-Sìth trivia. Game on, Death. I'm smarter than I look. "And before you say anything, if Stevie and Mr. Sebastian remain apart, without speaking and without seeing each other, Cathasach can't extend the mark through their father and son blood bond."

I don't exactly add neener, neener, neener, but it's implied.

Bill speaks up. "Stopping them from communicating and contacting each other may not be enough. If their thoughts for each other are strong, that may be enough to lead the hounds to you."

"You're wrong, Bill," Sebastian insists. "As Olivia said, Stevie wasn't home when the hounds arrived. He was nowhere near my home and hasn't returned since. He is immune to the full power of the death mark."

"You're making assumptions," Bill replies. "I'm not," Sebastian adds. "You know I'm not."

Bill's voice remains flat. "It's not a chance we're willing to take."

Ryker, like Bill, won't budge. I move closer to him. "Stevie is an innocent little kid, Ryker. Enough innocents have perished. I'm not adding another to the mounting list."

"No," he growls. "I refuse to allow *anything* to happen to you."

Funny how a potentially swoon-worthy moment can be tainted by a direct order to cease and desist. "Ryker, may I have a word with you, Bill, and Jane alone?" I smile through gritted teeth. I confess, it's not one of my cuter grins.

The forest and dragons disappear, leaving Bill, Jane, Ryker, and I on a hilltop with a sea of stars blinking above us. Fireflies the size of my palm with flickering pastel lights spin around us, carrying trays of coffee and donuts.

Wow. Jane *is* good.

The fireflies veer my way with enough enthusiasm to shame a band of Girl Scouts. "No, thank you," I say, though the Boston creams look scrumptious.

Bill stops his pacing long enough to lift a cup of coffee from the passing tray. He takes a sip only after a firefly tips a little silver pitcher filled with cream into his cup and another firefly stirs. Okay. Things are getting weird now. "Olivia," he says. "The Ankou has a point. Taking Sebastian's son under your protection will only make it easier for Cathasach to find you."

I touch Ryker's arm, not really loving how Bill continues to refer to Ryker as the "Ankou." He has a name and like it or not, Ryker is one of us. "Ryker," I say. "Between your power and Jane's, you can amass a disorientation ward strong enough to an keep the hounds away and buy us more time. You heard Sebastian; his son wasn't home when the death mark was created. All we need is to find a place to hide little Stevie where you and Jane can set up the wards."

Ryker shakes his head. "It's not so simple, Olivia. My magic clashes with the living Fae's power. My wards will cancel out Jane's, and hers mine."

"Seriously? The wards in your home worked well when…"

My voice trails at Ryker's warning stare. He doesn't want me to mention our near miss with the Cù-Sìth at his place. Bill lowers his mug carefully. Ryker continues as if uninterrupted. "The wards in my home work well because I've spent years building and reinforcing them." He motions around. "Jane's magic comes easily to her because it doesn't require the power protection wards do. We don't have time to build the wards Sebastian needs to shield his son."

"Can we reinforce one in another home? It's my under-standing Sebastian owns several residences."

Ryker rubs his eyes. "If Cathasach found him once, he'll find him again. The boy isn't safe anywhere, and neither is anyone who's with him."

In the silence that follows, Bill accepts another cup of coffee. "Someone led the gremlins to Walter Sebastian's house and ordered them to steal their talismans," he says.

I understand what Bill means. The gremlins aren't working alone. "There's another Fae involved," I agree. "A strong one."

Bill tightens his grip on his coffee. "Yes," he says. "Gremlins are infamous for causing mischief. They'll hide keys or fill mailboxes with shaving cream. But the silliness they engage in is never meant to harm. Look at them now; they're robbing Fae of their protection and watching them die. What's the point? What's in it for them? World domination if they succeed? No. These are simple Fae with no more cunning or malice than a small child. Whoever else is involved is working directly with Cathasach."

Ryker grinds his teeth. "Have your sources found any of the gremlins?"

"Frankie found one who was at the club the night of the attack." Bill sighs. "He disappeared the moment Frankie kicked down his door. According to Sebastian, he's one of several gremlins who materialized at his home."

Jane polishes off her donut. "Decision," she crows.

I lift my purse. "She wants us to make a decision. I've already made mine," I remind them.

Ryker looks to Bill. "We told you, we don't like your decision."

"No, we don't," Bill agrees.

They chose a great time to be BFFs. I adjust the position of my whip and meet their faces. "I'm not letting that little boy die. Mr. Sebastian has experienced enough loss. We all have." I poke Ryker in the chest when he tries to argue. "Ryker, I don't like the idea of you hunting the Cù-Sìth without me, and yet you'll do it regardless of what I say."

"That's different," he says.

I ram my fists on my hips. It's hard to pull off tough-as-hell in pastels, but I do my darndest. "No, it's not. You're risking yourself to help the Ancients and the Fae. I'm trying to save a young dragon and buy the Ancients more time." My brows knit tighter the longer he glares. "You can't stop me." My eyes cut to Bill. "And neither can you. So, work with me to help this little boy or don't. Either way, I'm not hiding in the Bat Cave while Cathasach is out there hunting yet another innocent soul, and Ryker is fighting the Cù-Sìth alone."

I lift a blueberry donut from a passing tray and take a big bite. I chew slowly, waiting for the furious Grim Reaper and grumpy gargoyle to speak. Jane joins me by taking a cruller. She licks her lips. "Glen Cove," she says.

Bill snatches a glazed donut. "Fine, if that's what you wish." He waves the donut at me. "You will take the child to my beach house on Long Island. Jane warded it years ago, but it will need the extra protection. Jane, will you—" She nods and polishes off her second breakfast, allowing Bill to finish divulging his plan. "Your location will only be known to us, and us alone. In the meantime, we'll use every resource to find Cathasach."

"Reinforcing the wards will take time," Ryker adds. At Jane's nod, Ryker addresses me. "You and the boy will have to stay in my residence until we can move you. With the aggressive tactics Cathasach is using, we can't keep you in one place for long." To Bill, he says, "Tell the Ancients to go into hiding. Except for you, allow no one to know their whereabouts."

"Won't hide," Jane says, lifting her chin so a firefly can wipe her face with a moist towel.

Worry replaces Bill's frustration. "She won't leave Olivia to save herself. She's sworn to protect her even if it means her soul."

I hurry to Jane's side and clutch her delicate and elderly hands. "Jane, you can't—"

My words lodge in my throat. "You can't die, Livvie," she croaks. "You're the one." She squeezes my hands. It's all I can do not to cry. "It's time," she says.

The beautiful open field falls away as we return to the forest on the 28th floor. Mr. Sebastian leaps to his feet when he sees me wiping my eyes. Bill holds out a hand. "Surrender the boy to our care, Walter," he tells him. "Olivia will watch over him."

Tears fall in large drops against Sebastian's cheeks. He calls in the direction of a large stand of trees. "Frankie, bring Stevie out."

Frankie steps through the trees, glancing from side to side, ever watchful. Lack of sleep mars his strong face, yet he offers me a small grin. "Hey, Liv," he tells me.

I try to return his smile. Jane's pledge makes it hard. It's not easy to hear your friends are willing to die so you can live. "Hi, Frankie." I glance around him, half-expecting Mr. Sebastian's son to be glued to Frankie's tall legs.

Frankie shoots me a look I can't quite interpret before glancing over his shoulder. "Come on, kid. They're waiting for you." With the exception of the breeze rustling through the leaves, all is quiet.

Frankie raises his voice. "Kid, *come on!*"

Little Stevie steps out from a section of trees, texting away, the barbed leather dog collar around his neck one loop shy of choking him to death. He dressed up to meet Life. A gray T-shirt with two reindeer doing 69 hangs over his thin frame and past the crotch of his frayed jeans. He pauses long enough to scratch his ass before resuming his texting.

"This is Stevie, my son," Mr. Sebastian announces. "Stevie, meet Olivia. She's agreed to watch over you and assure your safety."

Stevie glances up. Chocolate-brown eyes coaled with black liner look up at me. He raises his fist, causing the rows of his spikey hair to bounce. "Hey. I go by Anthrax."

At least, I think that's what he said. The piercings lining his bottom lip make him hard to understand. Ryker and Bill train their glares on me.

Some days, it doesn't pay to be a hero.

21

"Where do you want these?" Stevie asks.

I glance up from my laptop to see the neat stacks of paper lining Ryker's dining room table. "With the depositions going to the Superior Court."

"Here?" Stevie points.

"No, those are copies of the criminal charges in Marco's new murder case. That's a separate matter."

Stevie wanders to the other side. "Oh. The ones going to the judge."

"Exactly." I smile approvingly when he coordinates them to the right case. Piercings, obsession with roadkill, and his bizarre taste in T-shirts aside, Stevie is a good kid. The first few days at Ryker's were hard on him. He was cut off from his friends, his father, and his home. When I started assigning him projects to help me with Marco's workload, Stevie came out of his slump and became quite the chatterbox.

Stevie returns to the copier behind me and sorts through the assignments topped with sticky notes. "Are you going to practice today, Livvie?"

I stop scrolling. I was training in the Bat Cave without Ryker, just as he wanted. My progress had dwindled and, at times, ground to a halt. I'm not sure if it's from the lack of Ryker or his instruction. What I know is, I can't focus without him here. I'm scared to death for him. He's out there all alone, hunting hounds and here I am, losing control over my magic. There are moments when I can't even raise a spark. I'm going backward in ability, and I don't know how to fix it.

"Liv?" Stevie asks.

I clear my throat. "Yes. As soon as I finish with this disposition, we'll head downstairs."

Stevie flicks through the stacks of paper. "Can I run them down to the firm? It will be good to get out."

For both of us, I agree. *Even in this weather*. "It's not safe, Stevie," I say. "I'm sorry."

The wind has picked up since the morning. Waves splash against the dock, and the current has increased in velocity. The raging river is so loud, Stevie can hear it through the dense glass, despite that his hearing isn't as acute as mine.

"I know you're right," Stevie mutters. "I'm just starting to feel trapped." He punches a few buttons on the copier. The machine buzzes and sorts several stacks before he speaks again. "Hey, Liv. Can I take a picture of you?"

I continue typing. "What for?"

"When I get out of here, I want to show my friends what you look like."

My heart warms. I'm touched the little dragon considers me a friend. "Sure, Stevie."

He comes around me and lifts his phone, snapping a few selfies of us. I resume my typing when he stands. "Cool," he says. "Hey. Would you mind if I tell them we're doing it?"

My fingers freeze over the keyboard, and bile stews in my belly. *Ew*. "Absolutely not," I say.

"How come?"

"It's inappropriate and illegal." I shudder as my nausea worsens. "Not to mention, it's creepy! Why would you want anyone to think we…" Good stars. I can't even say the words.

"Cuz you're cute. Plus, it's the best excuse for being away."

"Stevie, I don't want to go to prison. Please think of something else. Tell them you went to rock star camp or something."

"*Rock star camp?*"

"Or something," I say again. "I don't care what you make up so long as it doesn't involve me and underage debauchery."

He chuckles. "'Kay. It's just as well. None of my friends would believe I banged a girl as hot as you. I'm just a skinny kid who—"

"Who needs to make copies," I finish for him. "Seriously, Stevie. No more. You're wiggin' me out."

"I'm almost sixteen…"

I cover my ears. "La, la, la. I'm not listening."

I shove Stevie's twisted hormonal thoughts out of my head. It's easy seeing how every thought always returns to Ryker. I've barely seen him since Stevie and I moved in four days ago. Ryker isn't technically alive and doesn't need to sleep. That doesn't mean he can't experience exhaustion.

Bill's leads have located several Cù-Sìth packs, and they're finding more each day. Ryker, true to his word, is taking on as many as he can. He hasn't told me how many. But I've seen him return for weapons, reeking of wrath and death.

The rare times he returns to rest, he locks himself in his bedroom and won't allow me in.

"Hey, Liv?"

Stevie pulls me from my thoughts. "Yes?"

"If something happens to my dad, you know, if the hounds get him, will you tell me?"

He keeps his back to me. Still, I can sense the tension beneath his *Bo-Peep Makes Out with Werewolf* T-shirt and along his lanky shoulders. "I'll always be honest with you, Stevie. I'm just hoping I won't have to be honest about that."

"Yeah. Me, too."

He shuffles through the legal folders, his focus faltering, and his movements more robotic.

Poor kid has really had it rough. I offer him a small smile. "Let's go workout downstairs," I say. "We'll start on the treadmill, and then you can help me with target practice."

"Yeah?" he asks. At my nod, he stacks the paperwork in his hands and sets it on the copier. "Can I run in my jeans? I have sneakers on."

I stand and tug my tank top over my leggings. "You can try. If it doesn't work, just come back up and change."

"Cool." He follows me down the winding metal staircase, frowning at the sea chest shoved against the wall. The force of the egg extractor's hum is rattling it against the floor. "Whoa. Vanessa's sure in a mood."

"That she is," I mutter, giving Vanessa ample space. I hurry across the room and to the treadmills Ryker ordered. Vanessa and I will never be BFFs, and that's fine with me.

"Do you want to try for four miles this time?" Stevie asks.

I shake my head. "No, I'm still struggling with three—"

Something heavy crashes upstairs, rumbling the ceiling. We jerk our heads up and back away. "Did the flat screen fall over or something?" Stevie asks.

I snag his wrist, pulling him farther away, my gaze fixed on the ceiling. "That wasn't the flat screen, Stevie…"

The lights flicker. Roars belt from all sides like cannon fodder. We whip around, our mounting panic making us bump into each other. "Liv, what's happening?"

I race toward my whip lying on the mat. The air ripples in and snaps above me. Ryker falls *through* the ceiling and lands in front of me, bleeding and unmoving, his armor torn to shreds.

"*Shit!*" Stevie yells.

The roars increase, echoing from all directions. The hounds are circling the building and closing in. I snatch my whip from the floor and fall to Ryker's side. Stevie stumbles beside me.

"Is he dead?" Stevie asks. His voice cracks, and his eyes search frantically, trying to pinpoint the direction of the roars.

"I don't know." I grasp Ryker's shoulder, my hands trembling. "Help me move him onto his back."

A howl - *Cathasach's* howl - thunders along the path of the windows. Something large and heavy hits the reinforced wall. Again, again, and again it strikes, each blow harder and faster.

"The Cù-Sìth are here," Stevie chokes, his skin blanching. "They're gonna kill me."

The wall cracks at the center. Then on the side. Then in the corner. More blows follow, peppering the floor with chunks of concrete.

Stevie is right. They're coming.

And I'm the only chance we have.

Ryker moans, barely breathing. I rise with my whip, fear slamming my heart hideously against my sternum. It hurts but doesn't compare to the anger burning its way through my veins.

My magic fires, sweeping through the length of my whip.

I charge to the wall, raising my whip over my head. "*Linn a chosaint!*" I scream, bringing the whip down. *Protect us.*

The force of my magic barrels down the braided leather. With a sharp hiss, the tip strikes the floor, releasing the magnitude of my power. The wood planks explode in a sea of angry pink light, tearing across the length in a wave that collides against the crumbling barrier.

My power detonates against the wall, its rebounding energy sends me soaring backward. I ram into the opposite wall, the impact cracking a vertebra in my neck. I should feel pain as I fall forward and bounce off the floor. I should feel the burn from the harsh speed at which my breath leaves my lungs. I should feel *something*.

Nothing comes. My nerves tingle faintly, and everything goes numb.

Time moves in sluggish bursts. I know I should get up. When I try, my limp arms slap uselessly against the floor. I'm somewhere near Vanessa. I can hear her angry protests, yet I can't seem to move.

"Livvie, *Livvie!*" Stevie hollers, his sound muffled.

I make out bits of pink light spreading along the loft and swirling back to me. My magic strikes me hard enough to jerk my head. It should hurt. Instead, its warmth encases me, and everything grows clearer.

I blink several times and sit up, confused how the cloud paralyzing my senses lifted so easily. The hounds are gone. The apartment is eerily quiet. I'm not hurt. I should be. But I'm not.

Tired, all I feel is tired.

Stevie's shakes me, his eyes wild. "You okay?"

I stand, slowly, feeling weightless. "I think so."

The pink light from my magic dwindles into tiny sparkles that float away as I return to Ryker's side. His breathing remains shallow and labored, and blood pools on the floor. Stevie helps me to roll him onto his back. I know Ryker is injured, and I expect a lot of damage. Still, it doesn't spare my heart when I see the suffering he's endured.

Dark crimson smears his face, and claw marks rake his chest in deep grooves, exposing rows of mangled muscle and tissue.

For a moment, all I can do is stare. Ryker bleeds because of me. Because he wants to keep me safe. This isn't right. It can't be.

"Livvie?"

Stevie is scared and needs reassurance. I have none to offer. I remove my shirt, leaving only my sports bra in place.

I used the soft lavender cotton to wipe Ryker's face. His nose is mashed in, and he's barely recognizable. My tears fall with each gentle stroke to his face, my sorrow worsening when I sweep over his dimple, and those full lips don't smirk.

"What happened?" I finally ask.

Stevie wipes his eyes. I think he's crying, too. "To him? I don't know. But you saved us."

I barely understand his words. "No."

"Yeah, you did, Olivia. That pink power of yours shut up the Cù-Sìth the moment it hit. It knocked you on your ass and everything, but it also beat them away. When I ran to the window, those asshats were gone." He waits. "It also healed you pretty damn fast."

I finish wiping Ryker's face and curl against him. His skin is so cold, and his breathing is barely visible. "I wasn't hurt, Stevie."

"Yeah, you were, Liv." Stevie removes his shirt and passes it to me when he notices my hands futilely trying to cover the large bite mark on Ryker's thigh. I ball the shirt and press it against his oozing leg. "You broke your neck when you hit the wall. I heard it snap. 'Cept your power somehow healed you."

"I just wish I could heal him."

"You...can't." Ryker stirs beneath me, his voice mere pants. "Not...like...before..."

Stevie and I gape at Ryker like a pair of idiots. "Death, you're like, still *alive*?" Stevie asks.

Ryker doesn't answer, but his tightening brows tell me he doesn't appreciate the way Stevie addressed him.

"Just call him Ryker," I interject.

"What did he mean when he said you helped him before?" Stevie asks.

I lean into Ryker. "I accidentally hurt him once with my magic. But since I caused the injury, I was able to withdraw that power and allow him to heal faster." I hold Ryker closer. "This time, I'm not the cause. I can't help him now."

"But he looks better than he did before he crash-landed," Stevie points out. "I mean, *damn*, I thought he was toast."

"It's only because he's the Ankou," I explain. "He's going to need more time. Here, help me get him upstairs."

It's only because Stevie is stronger than he looks, and Ryker somewhat helps, that we're able to wrench Ryker to his feet. Vanessa doesn't seem to appreciate us hauling Ryker up the stairs like we do and professes her displeasure in a series of alternating hums and hisses.

"Oh, shut up," I snap. "We're doing the best we can."

The wooden sea chest rattles and slides across the floor. Stevie glances down when the chest smacks against the bottom of the metal staircase. "We're almost to the top," I tell her. "You don't have to be so moody.

"I wouldn't piss off the egg extractor if I were you, Liv," Stevie says. "Bitch could do some serious damage to our future babies."

I groan. "Stevie, please stop talking about us having sex. It's ridiculous and disturbing."

A choking sound follows. I jerk around. Ryker has Stevie in a stranglehold.

"Ryker," I say. "What are you doing?" His head lolls from side to side, and he doesn't respond. Still, Stevie is turning blue. "Ryker!"

"Hmmm?"

"You're choking Stevie."

"Who?"   he   moans.

"Stevie!"

"Wha?"

"*Stevie!*"

Ryker's hold on Stevie relaxes enough for Stevie to slip away and plop on the floor. Ryker slumps, and we almost fall over.

I adjust my hold over Ryker. "He's just a kid," I whisper in Ryker's ear. "Don't take anything he says too seriously."

Ryker staggers forward. I can't be sure if he heard me. He seems so out of it. "Are you all right, Stevie?"

Stevie coughs a few times, his eyes wide as he clutches his throat. "Are you like, doing it with Death?"

My face burns as I lead Ryker to his room. "No, Stevie."

"Are you sure?" Stevie chuckles and coughs. "Your boyfriend seems a little jealous."

I try to ease Ryker onto his bed. I manage to get him halfway down when he slips from my grasp and collapses.

A deep-blue mist cocoons his form. It evaporates along with his armor, unveiling the extent of his injuries across his bare flesh.

Even as hurt as he is, Ryker is beautiful. I gape at his granite-smooth ass. Dahlia was right. You can crack oysters on that bad boy. I want to curl into bed with him, keep his body warm with mine until his bruises fade and his cuts are nothing more than faint scars. Would he welcome me beside him, or would he become angry that I saw him this way?

I lift the thick blanket on the foot of his king-sized bed and cover him with it, debating more than once whether to slip into bed with him. Even with all his strength and power, Ryker looks so vulnerable. I want to comfort him and offer kind words he may not be willing to hear and be the first person he sees when he wakes.

"You sure Life and Death aren't going at it?" Stevie calls from the living room.

"We're just friends," I say, barely above a whisper. I take another long look at him. "Just friends."

~

Ryker shudders, and I add another blanket. I've spent the day cleaning and bandaging his wounds and preparing dinner. He's awake now, his face tight with pain and exhaustion. I sit beside him and stroke his soft hair. "What happened?"

Ryker slides his hand over mine. His show of affection stalls my heartbeat. I've missed him. It wasn't easy having him away.

"There were too many," he admits. "This time, they were ready for me."

"Cathasach?"

"No. He arrived after his Beta and hounds became better acquainted with me."

He's trying to make a joke. I'm not laughing. I crawl beneath the outermost cover, careful to keep the bedding between us like a barrier. He's naked below the layers. In tending to his wounds, dressing him was the last thing on my mind.

Being clothed appears to be the last thing on his mind, too.

He watches me as if debating whether to draw closer. I really want him to, especially now.

The desire to touch and soothe him overwhelms. I don't just want to be close to Ryker. I *need* to be.

"You were outnumbered," I restate quietly.

"Yes."

Traces of older cuts line his face. This attack wasn't the only battle he fought today. "Where were you earlier?"

"I found another pack near an old cemetery in Brooklyn."

I look around, struggling to word how I feel and how much his actions are killing me. The right words don't follow, no matter how much I want them to. "Ryker, I don't like this."

"I killed five there, Olivia." His face tightens, and he takes a moment to catch his breath. "It may not seem like much, but it adds to my other kills. There are twenty-six fewer Cù-Sìth to harm you."

He's making it all about me when it's really about him and

all the harm and danger he's facing. I gather the bedding closer
to him, beating down the emotions he stirs with his throaty
timbre. Ryker wants to protect me, and in many ways, he seems
obliged. Is it because I'm the path to his eternal peace? Or is
there something else from me he wants?

"Ryker, the deaths of these hounds come with a hefty price."
My hand grips the fabric tightly. I want to scream from all the
guilt and sadness. "Look at you. You spent the day being
pummeled and were almost captured. What were you thinking,
continuing to fight the way you did?"

He edges closer, despite the pain his movements inflict. "My
belief was that the hounds wouldn't expect another attack in the
same day. I was wrong. They knew I'd come for them. They just
didn't know where I'd attack."

I thought he'd elaborate. His explanation doesn't fit how
troubled he seems. I try to search his mind and find a way into
his thoughts, just as he does with me. Nothing comes, but I can't
let this go. "What aren't you telling me?"

"I tell you all you need to know, Olivia."

The muscles along my neck stiffen. "You're keeping things
from me." He doesn't answer. It both hurts and angers me.
"Ryker, just tell me."

"It will only upset you."

"Because it involves me directly," I guess. His silence hits me
harder than anything he can possibly say. "I have a right to know."

He frowns as an angry lump filled with tears builds in my
throat. "I'm not trying to upset you."

"It's too late for that," I bite out.

He swears and shoves the blankets down, his anger resur-
facing and sharpening his chiseled features. I think it's directed
at me until he tells me something that chills me down to my
bones. "Cathasach has claimed you as his. He told me in

explicit detail what he plans to do to you before he takes your soul."

My eyes widen as his steel. "Please don't tell me what he said," I say, my words coming out rushed. Cathasach is an evil and twisted monster. I suppose I should have guessed as much, but sometimes, those dark corners of your mind are too dark, and you just shouldn't go there.

"I don't plan to," he says gruffly. "Nor will I allow him to have you."

Unless you can't stop him because you're already dead.

The bedding now lies beneath Ryker's arms, exposing the pattern of bruises and scratches painting his muscular chest. He sweeps my rainbow hair away from my face. His bandaged fingers catch some of the strands despite the care he uses. It doesn't bother me. My touch may offer him comfort, but I need his then. "*Beag tuar ceatha*," he murmurs. "I don't want you to be afraid."

It's strange given what I just learned, but right now, I'm more afraid of losing Ryker than anything Cathasach can subject me to. "If you mean that, you'll stop hunting the hounds without me."

He pulls his hand away when I reach for it. "No. It's not an option."

His withdrawal leaves me cold. I push forward, although I know he wants me to leave. "Why did you go after the Beta, Ryker? He's the number two guy for a reason."

He bristles at my tone. "You're angry with me."

I wasn't aware how tight my jaw is until I attempt to relax my voice. "I am. This whole seek-and-destroy mission you've engaged in is more suicidal than strategic. You don't want me hurt; I get that and appreciate it more than you'll ever know. But I won't stay quiet about how much it hurts me to watch you suffer."

"Olivia, we'll soon face Cathasach. There's no choice, not with how quickly the Cù-Sìth are multiplying. In killing his Beta, chaos will erupt within the pack. These hounds are blood-thirsty and tired of Cathasach's reign. Many will seek the position of Beta with the goal of becoming Alpha. I'm not a fool. Nor am I suicidal. I'm trying to use the disruption to our advantage—"

He grimaces and curls inward, his features slow to relax. I inch closer, but my proximity further tightens his features. "I'm sorry. Am I making it worse by being so close?"

"No. Your presence helps me more than you realize." His head sags into the pillow. "Just let me do what I have to."

"No."

He pops his head up. "*Olivia.*"

"Ryker, your strategy isn't working. I almost lost you." I smooth the bandage covering his arm. "Like you said, they were ready for you, and they will be again." My gaze drags along every injury his position allows. How did you even escape?"

"Dugan and Phillip helped me back to the loft."

My eyebrows lift. "That was them dropping you off upstairs?"

"Yes. Their energy was draining mine, and I needed them to return to their rest." He swallows hard. "I tried to materialize into my room so you wouldn't see me. I couldn't manage and landed on the floor below. I wasn't aware that the hounds had followed me back until they tried to break through my wards."

"They tracked your magic and sensed it inside." Like it or not, I'm getting to know these stupid dogs.

He nods. "In my weakened state, and in their high numbers, the disorientation spell failed." The edges of his mouth curves. "Until you strengthened it. You followed your instincts, and it worked."

I stroke his arm. "I'm surprised my magic didn't clash with yours."

"So am I." He's almost smiling. "Perhaps our powers can complement each other."

"Perhaps." My fingers caress him gently. "Why didn't you want me to see you?"

"Hmmm?"

I lift my fingers away from his arm and trace the line of stubble on his jaw. "You said you tried to land in your room and away from me. I need to know when you're hurt so I can help." I frown when he turns away from my touch. "Ryker, why are you hiding from me?"

"I need to eat," he growls.

I tilt my head. "The lasagna is almost ready…"

Darkness encapsulates Ryker like a closing casket. I freeze, not daring to move.

"Olivia," he rasps. His eyes glaze with need. His voice rough as if starved. His words stabbing the space between us. "I don't need food. I *need* a *soul*."

22

In the days that pass, Ryker's hunger worsens. He bows his back viciously enough to crack his spine. I shut the bedroom door, trying to muffle his growls. That's right, *growls*. Ryker is more creature than man, the curse of being the Grim Reaper taking its toll and raiding his body.

Stevie glances up from his failed attempts to play a video game, clutching the controller against his *Baby Sheep Ate My Dingo* T-shirt.

I sit on my hands to keep him from seeing how bad they are trembling. He tugs off his earbuds, the music blasting as the pieces bounce along the couch.

"Has he picked out, you know, his food?" Stevie asks.

I stare at the flat screen where Stevie's armed forces are being slaughtered. "Yes. He just needs to gather enough strength to find him."

"Him? It's definitely a him?" Stevie shudders. "It's not me, is it? You'd tell me if it was, right?"

I pat his knee with my quivering palm. "No. It's not you. You have nothing to be afraid of."

We startle when Ryker pounds against the wall. His knuckles

are already shredded. I don't know how many more blows he can endure before the skin tears from the bone.

I clear my throat and try to steady my voice. "Stevie, don't worry. Ryker isn't going to hurt you." More wall beating ensues, shaking a black and white photo of a city landscape above the flat screen. "But just in case, I want you to stay away from him."

Stevie jumps when the photo falls and the glass shatters. His head whips in the direction of the door as if Ryker will tear through. Slowly, he returns his attention back to me. "You got it, Liv. No problem."

He tosses the remote. *Game Over* flashes on the screen. Nice. Real nice.

"Why can't he just go?" Stevie asks. "Shit. He's been losing it for days."

"He's still weak from his fight with hounds. Materializing from the apartment, finding his food, and bringing it back here takes energy—"

"*Here?*" Stevie asks, his face aghast. "Ryker is going to eat *here?*"

I bury my face in my hands. I don't like this situation any better than Stevie. It scares me. I'm barely eating, much less sleeping, images of Ryker standing over my bed keeping me up at night.

"Stevie, with the amount of Death lurking around, Ryker has to return here to eat. It's the only safe place for him. If he doesn't, the Cù-Sìth or something else will find him at his most vulnerable." I stand, debating whether to share the rest.

"What's wrong?" he asks. "You look, I don't know, *guilty.*"

"It's nothing," I mumble. I take in the Hudson, trying to calm. Darkness claims the river save for the distant city lights and the full moon trickling their glow against the waves. There are no boats, and the current seems oddly restless. I wonder if it can sense Ryker's pain…and maybe mine.

Stevie leans forward, rubbing his hands together as if trying to warm them. "Liv, you told me you'd be straight with me. If you have something to say. Just say it, babe."

I slump onto the couch and cover my face when Ryker snarls. I mean to sit carefully, except my rattling knees aren't having it. "Ryker waited too long to eat. He's in pain as a result and unable to heal. If that's not bad enough, his pain is intensi- fying his hunger. Do you understand?"

"Oh, yeah," Stevie says, his pale face losing an extra shade of color. "Death is getting whacked from all directions, and we'll be seriously screwed in the eye sockets if he doesn't get some soon." Thanks for the visual. "Ah, yes," I say. "Something like that." I cover my ears when Ryker releases a vicious bellow. I don't know how much more he can take.

"Why do you look so bummed. Livvie?" Stevie asks. "I get that you're scared, but why are you all, guilty like?"

I don't want to admit what I do. For now, though, Stevie and I only have each other. "I think Ryker waited to eat because of me."

"Huh? Why would he wait, knowing how much it's going to hurt?" Stevie asks. He rubs his hands more frantically. "You said he's been the Ankou for like, a century. He must have known this would happen if he didn't keep on top of his eating habits."

I stare at the hall leading to Ryker's bedroom. The door has begun to rattle from his snarls. "We were spending a lot of time together, Stevie," I say, remembering when we were getting to know each other and when he wasn't so scary. "We trained here, we worked at the office. We were always together. Always."

Stevie keeps his head in the direction of the hall where our bedrooms and Ryker's office are located. "I thought you moved in when I did. How was it he was always with you..." His gaze travels back to me. "Oh, I get it. You and him *are* together."

"It's not like that," I explain. "As the Ankou, his power allows him to assist others with their mourning. Dahlia's death triggered a lot of repressed memories. Ryker would appear in my room at night to comfort me and allow me to sleep."

"So, he was always with you."

I nod. "Yeah. He was."

What sounds like a car smashes into the bedroom door, splintering the frame. We jump to our feet. Silence overtakes the small hall and creeps into the living room. I run to the bedroom, my feet heavy as if encased with cement and the door appearing to move farther away.

I crash into the door. It won't give. I pound it on it, "Ryker, *Ryker!*" I twist the knob and shoulder the door. "Stevie, help me. I have to get in there."

We ram our bodies against the door. It takes three solid tries for the door to swing open.

We stumble in. Sheets from the bed and bloodied bandages litter the floor. I scan the suite and charge into the bathroom.

Ryker is gone.

I step back into the bedroom, my movements slow and unsteady. A strange scent thickens the room in a coat of black dust, swirling into the air and filling it with dread and sorrow.

"D-do you feel that?" Stevie stammers.

"Yes." I barely speak above a gasp, my arms begging to wrap around me and protect me from the circling misery.

Stevie backs out of the room, snagging my hand and taking me with him. "What is it?"

"It's death," I answer. "It's mixing with the remains of Ryker's torment."

He shivers. "How do you know that, Livvie?"

"I can feel him." I can. I'm just not sure how.

Below us, something heavy hits and rolls in opposite directions. I glance at Stevie. The smeared eyeliner rimming his light brown eyes clashes against his skin as his pallor worsens.

"Ryker's back," I rasp, my vacant voice widening his eyes.

"Th-that was quick."

Stevie doesn't quite finish speaking when my fingertips slip from his. I hurry toward the curved metal steps, stopping at the top at Stevie's quaking voice. "Livvie, I don't think you should, you know, *watch*."

I remain in place, wondering if he's right. "I just want to make sure he's okay."

Stevie follows. He's afraid to be alone, not that he's dying to see what Ryker is up to.

My bare feet touch the cool metal, barely making enough sound to matter but managing to rack me with chills just fine. I grip the railing, steadying myself before taking that next step. Down and around I go, pausing briefly when the ceiling still obstructs the floor below.

The way the staircase curves, my next few steps will offer a direct view. I take a breath, build my courage, and continue forward.

Ryker lays sprawled on his belly, his restored armor in place. The hood of his cape cloaks his face in darkness. I'm not certain if the hood fell that way or if it's an attempt to mask his shame. I'm not even sure if he knows I'm here. But I am. And nothing on Fae or Earth could prepare me for what I see.

The scythe lays discarded to his right. Blood stains the blade crimson and drips onto the polished wood like the soft fall of rain. I damaged the floor with my magic and weapons more times than I could count. Yet, in my eyes, the tiny red droplets mar the floor beyond repair.

Except it's not the blood, the scythe, or Ryker's body my gaze locks onto.

It's his meal, the translucent form of a forty-year-old man.

I recognize the man from the news. He's Don Fleycher, Washington D.C.'s infamous serial killer, still dressed in his prison-issued coveralls. Don spent decades murdering runaway teens he lured back to his home with the promise of food, money, and salvation. Seventeen bodies. That's how many were found buried in his backyard. Most were young girls, the youngest barely twelve. Girls likely escaping their own night- mares before Don showed them the true meaning of hell.

I can't imagine the pain he inflicted. But I see his.

What remains of his hair bats against his shoulders as he crawls away, sobbing. "No. Don't hurt me. *No!*" Vaporous saliva pools from his mouth and drizzles against his beard. "Please, man. *Please*. I don't want to die!"

He doesn't know he's already dead.

Ryker snatches his ankle and hauls him back. Don tries to dig his nails into the floor. His fingers ghost over the surface. He scratches the air wildly, his cries morphing into high-pitched squeals. "Help me! Jesus Christ, *help me!*"

The staircase rattles with how fast Stevie races back upstairs, his feet pounding the floor above until his bedroom door slams shut and his sound system blasts at full volume. He doesn't want to hear the screams.

Neither do I.

Ryker's grip fastens on Don's thigh, and he yanks him to him. Lustful growls thick with want and anticipation barrel from Ryker's chest. He rolls Don onto his back and drives his knee into his gut, keeping him in place. With his left hand, he clutches Don's throat, squeezing it tight and silencing his shrieks.

Don writhes, smacking Ryker's arm with his hands that flutter through, unable to suppress his wretched blubbering and chokes. His gaze begs Ryker for mercy.

If Ryker hesitates, I don't see it. He lifts his right hand. A ribbon of azure mist entwines the length like a deadly serpent. He strikes, puncturing through Don's chest and into his heart.

Don buckles, a pained gasp of air leaving his lungs.

His eyeballs cave inward.

His tongue lolls.

His teeth fall away like pebbles, deep into his throat.

With each licentious breath from Ryker, Don shrivels inward, the muscles of his arms sinking and tapering against brittle and snapping bones.

I squeeze the railing to keep me upright. This is Ryker. The real him. Who he will always be.

I didn't recognize his torment before. Not like I do now. It takes me seeing how he survives, how he *eats,* to fully understand what he is.

Maybe now I can find the courage to grant him mercy.

In a way, I can't wait. No one deserves to live like this.

Ryker shudders, moaning as the last of Don Fleycher vanishes. Ashes to ashes, dust to dust, is bullshit. There's no dust. No anything. Just the Grim Reaper hovering over what once had been.

"God."

Ryker gradually straightens. He hadn't noticed me. He does now that I've spoken. He lifts his hood slowly and drops it behind him, meeting me with pitch-black eyes that scream of murder.

23

Stevie watches me, perched on the large boulder outside Bill's beach house in Glen Cove. My magic shoots through the whip, the tip striking each rock he places along the sand with a loud *boom*. One by one the large rocks explode, falling like hail against the mini-waves as if they can't wait to feel the Atlantic's cool sting.

I don't hit each one on the first try. But I'm getting closer.

Ocean water softly soaks the pebbled beach. Stevie slides from the boulder when I polish off the last one. "Cool. You want to try smaller ones this time?"

I yank my whip back and spin it at my side, just like Ryker first demonstrated. The flicks of my wrist are now second nature, exactly as he intended.

It just sucks he's not here to see it.

It's been four days since I've seen or spoken with Ryker. The morning after I watched him eat, he told me Stevie and I were moving to Glen Cove. That was it. Still shaken from what I saw, I didn't argue. I should have. Now, it's too late.

Too late to call.

Too late to text.

Too late to say I'm sorry.

Ryker thinks he disgusts me.

He's wrong.

"You miss him, don't you?"

"Huh?" I ask.

Stevie picks up a flat rock and tosses it into the ocean. It skips twice before the water swallows it. "Ryker," he says. "You miss him. I can tell."

He's right. Life misses Death.

"I think we need time apart." I shrug. "It happens even amongst the best of friends."

I never imagined I'd be so honest with a fifteen-year-old boy, except, for now, Stevie and I only have each other.

The dim sun crawls along the horizon, warning our fun in the overcast October sky has drawn to a close. Jane's wards don't extend onto the beach after sunset. We need to hurry if we intend to stay safe. "It's late. Let's head inside."

Stevie throws another rock. This time, it skips four times. "We still have a good five minutes, but if you're not up to it, it's okay."

He knows my mind is elsewhere and doesn't push. I try to smile. "I think it's enough for today, Stevie.'"

He pinches his face. "I wish you'd do me one and call me by my nickname."

"Anthrax?" I ask.

He grins. "It sounds sexy when you say it."

"In that case, let's get back to the house, *Stevie*."

I laugh when he mumbles a curse, and I back up, winking before sprinting toward the house. It's my way of challenging him to a race. He bolts, fighting to catch up. I increase my speed and prance over the row of boulders, the sudden burst of energy making me quick and graceful.

One day I might stand a chance at winning. Not today. Dragon's blood does race through Stevie's veins. The little dickens beats me to the back steps of the brick terrace.

Stevie grins, proud of himself. "Since I won, again, I say we take Mamacita out for a spin tomorrow. We can use the portable ward we use forrunning."

Mamacita is Bill's shiny red '57 Chevy Convertible Street Rod. He told us that the house was ours, but the garage was "off limits." Of course, that's the first place Stevie rummaged through, fully expecting to find boxes of vintage porn.

I wish he found porn. It beats his obsession with Mamacita.

I cock my head. "Nice try. But let's go with no, never. I want to live."

Stevie's been eyeing up Mamacita since first pulling off the protective cover and unveiling sex, power, and crazy-speed on four asphalt burning wheels. He gaped at the shiny red minx (complete with custom plates!) for five full minutes before daring to touch her smooth and perfect body.

I've never cared much for cars. But *damn*, I don't blame Stevie for his preoccupation with Mamacita. Every night after dinner, he sits in the front seat, itching to open the garage door and start it. He finally found the keys. Sadly enough, I hop in beside him, imagining what it would feel like to hear her sweet engine purr.

"Come on, Liv. You know you want to."

"I know no such thing." I laugh. "Besides, I'm not sure how good the portable ward will work. Jane designed it to keep us hidden on our runs. It's not meant to hide anything at break-neck speed. Not to mention, if we took Mamacita out, you don't have to worry about the Cù-Sìth finding us, Bill will kill us himself."

"Liv, Bill doesn't have to know." He waggles his brows, making me giggle.

I stop laughing when the gray sky darkens to black.

Stevie loses his grin, and we hurry up the steps. The last trickle of sunlight dissolves as I shut the door. We breathe a sigh of relief when the reinforced wards hum and enclose us in their protection.

Stevie tosses his jacket over the couch. "Can we have the steaks tonight?"

"That sounds like a good idea," I reply. "They've been marinating since last night so they should be perfect." I clip my whip to my belt and wash the grime from my hands at the kitchen sink. Since leaving Jersey City, I always keep my weapon with me. I even sleep with it tucked under my pillow. While it's not the same as having Ryker with me, it offers a sense of security in his absence.

Stevie rummages through the industrial-sized fridge. "Can I have the beer that's in here?"

"Nope." I flip on the range hood. Mamacita may get me hot, but this six-burner stove is a close second.

"There's a whole case of Heineys in here," Stevie bemoans. "Bill won't miss one."

I slice the portobello mushrooms while garlic and olive oil heat. Stevie stands in front of the fridge with the door open, continuing to argue. I let him. If this is all he has to complain about, it's a big improvement.

I toss in the onions I diced earlier. Bill must entertain a great deal. The terrace, like the kitchen and rest of the house, is massive. I think his home is the biggest house on the block. I want to say he earned everything the right way. Except, I don't know who to trust anymore.

"Do you want a salad with dinner, or do you prefer steamed spinach?" I ask.

"You're not listening to me, are you?"

I set a cutting board and a knife on the center island. "I am, but that doesn't change my mind about the beer."

"You know what your problem is?" Stevie asks. "No," I reply. "But I'm sure you can't wait to tell me."

He chuckles. "You're Life and all, but you don't enjoy it."

I stir the garlic and onions as I allow Stevie's words to sink in. "I did once, as much as I could considering my past." My thoughts wander to Ryker's request of me to kill him. "Given what's happened, enjoying life to its fullest is a luxury I can no longer afford."

Stevie bustles about, setting the table, very much unaware of how the conversation affects me. "Wait and see, Liv. I'll make a delinquent out of you yet."

Smart kid or not, Stevie is a fifteen-year-old boy, not *girl*. If Stevie were a "Stephanie," I'd pour my heart out, demand comfort food, and have her channel surf for the most gut- wrenching chick flick she could find. Still, Stevie has a good heart, and I can't stop my smile. "Yeah, yeah. So, do you want salad or not?"

Stevie reaches for a mushroom and pops one in his mouth. "I'll take a salad, but no raw onions." He quiets, blushing a little. "The onions make me sneeze and, I, uh, don't want to start a fire."

I whip around. "You're releasing flame?"

He shrugs, his cheeks fully pink as he pulls the salad greens from the fridge. He places them on the opposite counter as if they're made of glass. "I still can't maintain a stream, but I'm getting close. I've been practicing in the shower."

I squeal and throw my arms around him. "Stevie. That's awesome, your first fire!"

He returns my embrace, genuinely happy. "I know, right? I thought something was wrong with me. Most dragons start to smoke when they hit puberty. I only started just this past summer. Two years, that's how long it's taken me."

I jump up and down, clapping. "Look at you go. Maybe you

can practice firing after our morning run. The wards should block your magic from humans like they do mine."

Stevie beams. "Okay. Yeah. I hadn't thought to practice anywhere except the shower."

It's great to see Stevie happy. The ten days Cathasach gave his father to surrender the Ancients are up in two.

Our wide grins fade when something wet splatters against the front of the house.

I turn off the stove and place the pan away from the burner, hoping I misheard—

Splat.

Stevie's mouth opens and closes several times. "Liv, what was that?" he spits out.

"I…"

More sounds follow. All dense. All moist.

Something hard rams the door.

Iniquity falls over me like pouring blood. I unsnap my whip.

More objects strike the door. I strain to hear. Whatever hit sounded…*sticky.*

I swallow hard, fearing the worst and knowing it's come.

"Stevie, grab a knife." More beats follow, growing louder. *Shit.* I glance over my shoulder. "Stevie, grab all the knives."

Stevie stuffs every knife from the butcher block into the back pockets of his worn jeans. I grip the handle of my whip, the braided leather falling to my side. I don't bother twirling it. There's no need yet. I do, however, accept the cleaver Stevie offers. "I bet it's just a bunch of stupid kids throwing eggs. I'd do it," he reasons. "I mean, it's almost Halloween and everything."

The goose bumps racing up my arms inform me that no, they're not eggs, there are no kids, and that Stevie is very much mistaken.

A spark builds within me and fires my whip bright pink. "It's not kids, Stevie. Send the text."

"*The* text?"

"Yes," I whisper. "It's time."

Stevie clutches two knives in one hand. His free hand taps our emergency number, the one that alerts Bill and the Ancients. "There's gotta be a mistake—a misunderstanding or something. Liv. There's still two days left."

"Cathasach is neither honorable nor righteous, Stevie. He's evil," I remind him. "*He's here.*"

"Ryker?" Stevie asks.

Acid burns its way into my throat. "No, Stevie. Cathasach."

"H-how do you know?"

The next few words make me want to cry. "I can feel him," I admit.

We step carefully across the tile floor. Cathasach's presence is vile. I sense him within me, my belly churning in painful bursts of fear that urge me to run and hide.

I can't hide. Not now, not ever. Not when Stevie is counting on me to protect him.

We slip into the hall that leads to the foyer. Stevie snags the portable ward dangling from the hook we leave it on. Jane gifted it to us to keep us hidden when we left the premises. We were on our own, and she didn't want us confined to the house.

Stevie places the silver chain around his neck. Smart boy. He knows we may have to bolt.

His trembling worsens with each step. "How did Cathasach figure out we were here?"

The sweat drenching my palm slickens the handle of my whip. "The same way he knew how to find your father," I reply. "Someone betrayed us."

Bam.

Bam.

Bam.

The strikes grow louder and more impatient.

"Little pixie. Little pixie. Come play with me," Cathasach coos, his voice garbled and thick with lust.

Stevie gasps. "Oh, *fuck me*."

I stop by the door leading to the basement and garage, gathering my courage. Adrenaline tears its way through my bloodstream, causing me to shake. If I were a fawn, I'd be tearing through the forest right now.

A thought occurs to me, and I motion back to the hook. "You may get your chance to drive," I say.

Stevie's eyes fly open. "Jane's wards aren't going to hold?"

"No," I admit. "Cathasach will find a way in." He has something up his sleeve. I can sense it in his arrogance. I just don't know what it is yet.

Cathasach calls to me again, his tone disturbingly aroused. "Come play with me, little pixie. I want to play with you."

My stomach roils, and I almost hurl. Stevie stretches his hand and snags the keys to Mamacita, his fingertips quaking. "You're coming with me, right, Liv?"

"I don't know," I tell him.

"Little pixie. I want to touch you. *Let me touch you*." He's growling, his voice wet with thirst for me. "I already feel you against me."

Furious tears brim Stevie's soft brown eyes. They're exactly what I need to shove my fear aside and build my growing anger. "I promised to keep you safe, Stevie, and I will. No matter what, you're making it out of here alive."

"What about you?" he asks.

"Don't worry about me."

"Liv, I-I-I can't leave you."

"You can and you will," I snap.

Stevie knows I'm not fooling around. He nods hesitantly and stiffens his posture.

"Little pixie—"

"For shit's sake, you smelly mutt, I'm coming!"

Okay. That gives everyone, including me, some serious pause. The air stills, and Stevie's mouth pops open.

I speak quickly, keeping my voice quiet. "I don't think Cathasach knows you're here. Let's keep it that way, okay?"

"Okay," Stevie whispers.

Something hits the foyer window as we round the corner. I recognize it as a heart.

A dragon's heart.

The large organ splatters against the glass, bright red blood smearing an ugly line as it slides down and topples over the ledge. I drop my cleaver and slap my hand over Stevie's mouth. His breath hitches. He knows what it is.

Stevie is taller than me by a good five inches. It doesn't matter. Right now, my will and strength are enough to silence him. His legs buckle, and we collapse, the knives in his hands falling against the marble floor.

"Don't scream. Don't cry," I urge. "We can't let him know you're here."

His mouth is hot against my palm, and his face reddens with stress and lack of breath. "I'm taking my hand away," I whisper. "But you have to keep it together. It's the only way we'll make it out of here alive—"

"*Olivia.*" Cathasach moans my name as if releasing his seed. "Please touch me…"

I bite back a furious scream.

Stevie is breathing fast, the dampness from his mouth drenching my hand. Eyeliner smears his face from the sweat pouring down his face. "Stevie," I say. "Promise me you'll stay quiet."

He nods with several violent shakes of his head. I'm not sure he's capable of keeping his promise. I drop my hand anyway. I *have* to get him out of here.

"I-it's my father," Stevie says, almost retching. "That was my dad's heart."

"We don't know that," I tell him firmly. "Are

you sure?" he asks.

Splat.

Splat.

Two more body parts smack against the window.

This time, a pair of kidneys.

We watch them slink down the glass. "*Livvie*," Stevie cries.

"He can't be positive you're here," I remind him. "He only knows that I am. This is a mind fuck, Stevie. He wants to hurt me and throw me off my game. To do so, he'll use someone I care about." I almost can't say their names. "Bill, Jane, or Ryker."

"What if it's Frankie?" Stevie presses. "You told me he dated your friend."

Terror nails me like a punch. I squash it down, willing myself to keep it together. "Whoever it is, I'm done with Cathasach toying with us." I stand, gripping my whip and the cleaver. "Stay out of sight. If the wards don't hold, get to Mamacita."

"Liv?"

I glance down. Stars, he looks so young. "Yes, Stevie?"

He swallows hard. "Is now a bad time to tell you I've never driven a car?"

I laugh a little too psychotically. "Yeah. It kind of is, Stevie."

"Livvie, I-I'm sorry."

"It's okay, little guy." I wipe away a tear with the back of my hand. Stevie is a good kid. He deserves to live. I'm going to give him that chance if it kills me.

But not before I take out Cathasach.

I clear my throat and square my shoulders. "Just do the best you can. I'll create a distraction so you can escape."

I don't wait for Stevie to agree. The rows of intestines splattering the glass and the kneecap that follows make it clear it's time to act. I stomp forward, motioning to Stevie to wait around the corner and by the basement door.

With one finger, I unlatch my talisman and shove it into the pocket of my leggings. Stevie gasps. But there's no point in hiding. Cathasach knows I'm here. He senses me just as I sense him.

I throw the front door open. Cathasach waits on the lawn in his human form. Grotesque matted green hair lies in clumps across his broad shoulders, and his red eyes burn with sin. Six hounds flank him. They snarl when they see me. I snarl right back.

Cathasach laughs, greeting me with a blood-smeared grin. He swings a decapitated head in his hand like a purse. I recognize him as the dragon who took Stevie to the baseball game.

Another fallen Fae. Another reason for Cathasach to die.

"I missed you, little pixie," Cathasach coos, ignoring my anger. "Are you ready to touch me?" His gaze sears red as his hand glides down his stomach to palm his erection.

Disgust and hatred rile my power, engulfing my body in bright pink light. My magic is no longer something I simply have. It's a living, breathing entity ready to sink her teeth.

The cleaver leaves my hand in a ball of pink, growing as it spins and striking a white hound. The white beast detonates with enough force to burn the closest hounds.

Including Cathasach.

Souls erupt like shrapnel, scattering in translucent streams that take to the skies. More Cù-Sìth arrive, eager to feed. My pink fire spreads, burning through the hounds and releasing more souls.

"Run," I scream without thinking. "*Run!*"

An elderly man walking his dog, and completely oblivious to the mayhem on the lawn, scowls. "I'm moving as fast as I can, lady," he yells. "Roger's gotta pee."

Cathasach roars, his entire left side aflame. He morphs into his beast and jets toward the door. I crouch and spin my whip, ready to strike.

I never get the chance.

A large green hound tackles Cathasach, resolute on taking his injured Alpha down. The hound yelps as my magic catches his fur. It singes him and spreads along his broad chest. He releases Cathasach, rolling along the grass to squelch the flames. Two more hounds appear and gang up on Cathasach, forcing him to the ground as the magic burning him begins to dwindle.

Cathasach lost two limbs and is bleeding souls. One of the hounds on top of him goes for his throat, and still, his rage pokes at me through the wards. The wards won't hold, and the hounds won't beat him. Cathasach is too strong.

"Livvie," Stevie urges. "The text. It never went through."

The increasing howls rattle the house. More Cù-Sìth are headed toward us, their outlines cutting into the blackening and azure sky. Azure—*Ryker*. I need Ryker.

The Cù-Sìth slam against the house, shaking the walls and foundation as they search for weaknesses in the ward. I clutch my whip against my chest, remembering who first held it and how I felt when he passed it to me. "Ryker!" I yell.

"His name is Roger!" the old man with the dog hollers from down the street.

Five hounds charge the front door. My body rekindles with pink light. I lift my whip, slashing across the wards.

I mean to reinforce the wards. Instead, my whip penetrates through the protection and strikes across three Cù-Sìth. They roar in agony, their faces splitting open as they burn in glorious pink.

A cluster of sprites clamber through the stretching and burning tissue. More beasts appear. I lift my whip, striking left and right. I think we have an edge and that I can hold them back.

The Cù-Sìth prove me wrong.

Chunks of ceiling fall in startling blasts. The Cù-Sìth are ripping the roof apart. Jowls and snapping fangs shove their way through the cracks, keen to gnaw on flesh.

Stevie scrambles to my side with every knife in his arsenal. I fling each one he passes me through the doorway. The first nails a random hound, engulfing him and another in flame. The other hounds disperse, dodging out of harm's way to chase after the shrieking and fleeing spirits.

Transparent apparitions blur the atmosphere. The faster ones shoot outward and away. The slower ones are torn to shreds, unable to escape. Glass shatters upstairs, and snarls berate us from every direction, overwhelming my senses and causing me to lose focus.

Stevie yells to be heard over the pandemonium bombarding Bill's home. "Olivia, your whip is cutting through Jane's defenses!"

He's right. Somehow, I weakened the ward.

A hound races past the door. I fling another knife and miss. They're baiting me. We can't just stand here.

Stevie reels. "*Liv!*" He points to the stairs and the advancing hounds. I throw a knife, and another, killing two as three more appear. Glass explodes in the kitchen. They're in. Time to run.

I shove Stevie ahead of me. "Mamacita?" he calls over his shoulder.

Hounds surround us at each end of the hall, their lips peeling back to expose their razor-sharp fangs.

"Oh, *hell* yeah," I reply.

We stumble through the basement door. I cling to the knob, scrunching my face as I call upon my magic. "*Sruthán.*"

Burn.

The knob illuminates in pink, the light spreading along the wood as a large paw punches through the wood.

Claws rake my arm. I scream, tumbling down the stairs and crashing into Stevie. He struggles to his feet, hauling me up and stuffing me into Mamacita.

Blood pours from my right arm, pooling on the leather seat. Stevie's entire body is shaking so hard, he can't slip the key into the ignition.

I get it together enough to hit the garage door opener clipped to the visor. The garage squeaks open, drawing the attention of the hounds circling the house.

Cold night air slams into our faces as Stevie finally shoves the key into the ignition. "Hang on!" he yells.

Mamacita roars to life and jerks forward.

And stops.

Jerks   forward.

And stops.

Jerks forward and…stops.

The Cù-Sìth form a wall in front of us, slamming their snouts and bodies against the dwindling wards.

What's left of the wards crack and splinter. They're almost through, and all we're doing is lunging and jolting.

Screw this.

I unbuckle my seat belt and stand, clinging to the rim of the windshield. "Stevie, listen to me." He swears instead, his panicked expression taking in the mounting cluster of death hounds. "Stevie!"

He glances up, sweat pouring down his body. "Ease off the clutch and push on the gas."

"That's what I did."

I take a breath. "Try again, this time, not so forcefully."

"I'm trying, Livvie," he says, his focus whipping from me to the hounds.

"Stevie, I need you to say calm," says the bleeding woman beside him, whose beating heart is seconds from imploding.

The hounds are ravenous, howling, snapping their jaws, and pieces of the wards are crashing against the foundation like breaking glass. My arm is on fire, and I think I'm losing too much blood. Still, an air of calm washes over me.

I know what's coming, and I know exactly what to do. I focus my power, and the car fires pink.

"Stevie," I say. "We're not alone."

Stevie looks behind him and jumps. Jane, my little druid priestess, sits in the back seat, her little feet dangling from the edge and her candy-cane-striped wand tight in her hand. She lifts her chin and takes in the rabid pack seconds from smashing through.

"*Fuck*," she croaks.

And then she smiles.

Stevie eases off the clutch.

And Mamacita shoots out of the garage like the road bitch she is.

I'm thrown back into the seat. We power through the hounds, bowling them over as my magic sets them ablaze. Stevie grinds the clutch until we reach full "eat my ass" speed.

The hounds we ram detonate like bombs, igniting the closest ones, but not the ones in the sky. They circle the house, searching and confused by the explosions.

It won't take long for them to notice our escape. We need more help.

Help arrives in the form of a little old man.

I yell at Stevie to stop when I see him. The tires burn nasty rubber, and the engine whines with how hard Stevie slams on the brakes. I topple into the dash and then lurch backward, my injured arm smacking hard into the seat.

The old man abandons the sidewalk, dragging his dog with him, just to yell at me. "What the heck's wrong with you, girl? This is a family neighborhood!"

I ignore his accusations of being "on the crack" and wink at Jane. "Pucker up, girlfriend."

There's no hesitation. Jane drags the little old man to her, her tongue shooting into his mouth and lapping it like a thirsty pup.

My guess is, it's been a while since the old man got some lovin'. He drops the leash, crushing Jane against his bony chest.

"Oh, *gawd*." Stevie gags over the moaning and slurping.

I cover my mouth. Yeah. It's kind of hard to watch.

The man grabs Jane's dangling breasts like they're defibrillator paddles and he needs to resuscitate. Jane reaches around him, her arthritic fingers massaging the old coot's sagging ass through a good inch of polyester.

Stevie gags some more and throws up over the side of Mamacita. I drum my fingers impatiently. The death hounds stop circling and sniff the air, trying to catch traces of my magic.

I straighten. "Jane, that's enough."

She ignores me and reaches for the safety pin holding up the old guy's pants. Jane, in addition to being loose-skinned and persnickety, is evidently horny as hell.

Lightning crashes in the distance, and roars accompany the thunder. Cathasach, now whole, stalks out from a smaller cluster of Cù-Sìth, freezing in place as his glowing red gaze fixes on me.

With a howl and another roll of thunder, he calls the entire pack.

"Jane, they're coming." I shake her shoulder. "Jane!"

Her liver-spotted hands stop their exploration of the man's deep south. I love Jane and am thrilled to pieces she got some. That said, *ew*.

Stevie slams on the accelerator, propelling us forward. The man gives chase, his plaid pants down to his ankles, his little dog barking after him, and his male parts dangling to his knees.

"Jesus *Christ*," Stevie spits out.

We careen over the corner as my little priestess's head splits in half and five slithering snake heads pour out.

The tails remain attached to Jane's torso, her tiny legs bouncing with every pothole Stevie runs over. The snakes writhe, thickening and lengthening, their forked tongues flicking with anticipation of their coiling bodies ready to strike.

"Will the ward keep us hidden?" Stevie asks. He hasn't noticed the snakes yet and continues to gag.

"No," I reply, glancing around. "Nothing is working."

My magic sparks in and out, blinking the car from fuchsia

back to red. Jolts of pain shoot down my arm in wicked pulls. Overusing my magic is keeping me from healing, and my body's need to heal is draining my magic.

I withdraw the power surrounding Mamacita, hoping to hang on to my reserves. Ominous clouds roll in from the west and east, cresting and descending on us in a monstrous wave.

"Give me the knives!"

Stevie drops the knives that remain beside me, his awkward movements causing the car to swerve. One of the snakes slinks between the seats and into the front, sliding across Stevie's lap.

Stevie doesn't take it well. "*AHHHHHH!*"

He loses control of Mamacita, and we bounce off a guardrail. I land on top of him and wrench the steering wheel, moving us back to the center of the road.

"Stevie, it's just Jane," I insist.

He yells some more when the snake circles his neck and licks his ear. By some miracle, he keeps the car on the road as the pack falls upon us.

I fling the knives at random. There's no strategy, I'm merely trying to keep us alive. My weakening magic burns the Cù-Sìth. Fire catches on their materializing bodies, singeing their fur but failing to fully ignite them.

I wasted too much energy at the house, and now we're paying for it. The hounds advance, reaching for Stevie and me.

With a chorus of hisses that chill my spine, Jane's snakes attack. They spit poison and fire, blinding and burning the hounds with the might of Jane's Ancient magic. They retaliate, biting the serpents' heads and tearing them from their bodies.

Bitches don't know when you sever a Hydra's head, two more grow in its place.

The snakes double, quadruple, octuple, shooting more hissing heads from their sliced necks. They protect Stevie as I beat back the circling hounds with my whip.

Poor Stevie races along the desolate highway, his skin blanched with fear, but his mind determined to survive.

Too bad only Death remains in sight.

The muscles of my injured arm scream as I lash out against the hounds. My fingers clenching the windshield grow numb and slick. I'm almost done, and I'm losing strength fast when Cathasach lands on the hood of the car.

His long, matted hair streams behind his human form as he rises from a deep crouch, his fiery eyes flashing and beckoning me forward.

"Oh, *come on*," I say.

I crack my whip in his direction, screaming and forcing my remaining power across its length. To my horror, the pink light fades before reaching the tip.

Cathasach snatches the end and yanks me to him, my body smacking hard against his chest. He clutches me tighter, baring his teeth inches from my face. I thrash, trying to break free and calling magic that no longer comes.

"Get off her," Stevie yells. "Jane. *Jane help!*"

Jane *can't.* The hounds pile on Mamacita at once, smothering Jane and the snakes.

Cathasach's tongue circles my mouth in grotesque licks. I jerk my head from side to side, but there's no escaping him.

The air snaps with azure light and Ryker appears, battered and bruised from battle. He wrenches Cathasach by his hair and drives a dagger deep into his throat. Cathasach laughs, choking on his spewing blood. He shoves me away, and I fall off the side of the racing car.

My skull crunches, and sound explodes in my ears as the world spins. Asphalt pummels and rakes my body. I roll to a stop, briefly aware of the darkness suffocating me when bloody fangs wrap around my throat.

25

I sit up with a jolt, disoriented and terrified, my throat so dry I can't scream.

"Liv, *Livvie*. It's okay. You're safe!"

I gape at Stevie with feral eyes, my breathing ragged and pained. I'm in Ryker's apartment, back in the guestroom I slept in.

Stevie claims I'm safe. Tell that to the rest of me. I clutch bed linens as if they can protect me from the next attack. The next strike. The next attack of Cathasach.

My vision gradually adjusts to the darkness. The only light dwindles in from the window, offering a gentle glow in an otherwise gloomy room. I release the balled clump of sheets carefully, my fingers throbbing from how hard I've held by bleak protection.

My muddled thoughts spin. I can't decipher whether the assault from the Cù-Sìth was a horrid dream or a very real nightmare. As I inch toward the bed, every aching muscle demanding attention proves no dream is this physically traumatic.

I cough a few times, letting my bewilderment and reality

battle it out. The coughs turn into chokes that hurt and make me grimace.

Stevie passes me a glass of ice water. "Here, Livvie. Take a drink."

I sip the cool liquid between coughs, giving my battered nerves time to settle. I finish the water and take the next glass Stevie fills, still confused about what happened and still very much in pain.

The cold water offers only a small reprieve. Heat rages over my skin and sweat plasters my rainbow locks to my face. I scratch at my neck, feeling itchy, only to pause when I find it bandaged.

"Can I take this off?" My voice is raspy and indiscernible.

Somehow, Stevie understands. He glances over his shoulder. If my lungs had any strength left, I'd gasp.

Ryker sits in a cushioned leather chair near the foot of the bed. The sleeves of his black dress shirt are rolled to his forearms, and neat dark slacks cover his legs. Had he a pen and a legal pad, he'd resemble the man I once knew only as an attorney.

For flicker in time, I wish that's all he was, a young associate on his way to making junior partner. Except an attorney couldn't have saved me from creatures who want me dead, nor from myself. Soul eating aside, Ryker is the best man I know. The awareness brims my eyes with tears.

"You saved me, again," I say. "Didn't you?"

Ryker keeps his head lowered and his muscular forearms over his thighs. He doesn't answer and won't look at me.

I can't be sure I don't deserve it.

"Can I help Liv take off that bandage?" Stevie asks. At Ryker's nod, Stevie stands and tugs at the tape fixed to my throat.

I pull away when it feels like my skin is tearing away. "It's all right, Stevie. I'll take care of it."

I peel off the dressing, blatantly slow. The tape has adhered to the tiny hairs and is refusing to give them up without a fight. It's my first clue that I was out a long time.

Stevie takes the wads of bandages when I finally finish.

"Thank you," I whisper. My fingers smooth over the rough surface where the puncture wounds have scabbed over. They still hurt. The wounds *still* hurt as if fresh.

My hands travel to my face. My throat wasn't the only part of me brutalized. Bandages cover almost every inch of me. I unroll the gauze wrapped around my head, gaping at the amount of dark blood staining it. "How long have I been out?"

Stevie plays with the spikes on his dog collar, taking his time to answer. "Four days." He glances behind him. "Ryker let go of Cathasach when he threw you off the car. Jane's snakes wrapped around me, and she transported me out." He scoffs. "She would've done it sooner, but she can only transport one being at a time. The farther she goes, the more it drains her. And we needed to go pretty damn far for the hounds not to find us."

"She also expended a lot of energy as the Hydra," I add quietly.

"Yeah. Those things were all over her. She barely got free enough to help me." He shrugs as if trying not to think too much about the incident. I can't blame him. "She took us to Flushing where Bill and Dad were waiting. Jane called them when she realized we were in trouble."

A small black snake slithers beneath the crack in the door. It inches up Stevie's leg and around his waist. He smiles, watching it climb and allowing it to coil around his shoulders. I recognize it as one of Jane's.

"Hey, girl," Stevie says when she flicks her tongue. He strokes her head with his finger. "This is Daisy. She hung out after Jane morphed back. Jane says she likes me and that I can keep her.

She's just a baby, and I think she got scared when the fight broke out."

"That's understandable," I mutter.

Stevie's smile fades. "Liv, even with our talismans, they could see me and Jane. How is that possible? And how did they get through Jane's wards like they did? Are they evolving?"

I pull another bandage from my shoulder. "I think they are."

"No," Ryker says. "Not this fast."

My head angles in Ryker's direction. It's the first time he's spoken, and he still won't look at me. I crumple the bandage and add it to the growing pile beside me. I don't want him angry with me, and I hate the tension between us. That doesn't mean I'm not to blame for our troubles.

I embarrassed him by watching him eat. I realize it now. When he approached me the next day, instead of speaking to him—instead of telling him I don't think less of him—I didn't speak at all. I let him believe he's the monster he claims to be.

Ryker feeds on souls. I knew that before accepting this gig. Seeing it shouldn't have changed my opinion of the man who's been kind, faithful, and a friend, a man who suffers and begs me for mercy.

I rub my face, wanting to slap myself instead of merely dabbing away the tear that releases. "Stevie, can you give us a minute?"

Stevie pets the snake circling his arm, oblivious to my girly emotions. "Only if you promise Jane will never hook-up in front of me again. Seriously, Liv, that was some messed up shit. I mean, the old guy's balls bounced to his toes."

"It kept us alive," I offer in way of an apology. I don't remind him that ball bouncing or not, I'd do it again.

I pour water from the pitcher and refill my glass, taking my time to give Stevie a chance to leave. As the door shuts behind him, I return the pitcher and glass to the nightstand and slip my legs from beneath the covers.

My spine stiffens when I realize I'm wearing one of my skimpy nighties. I purchased a slew of these silky things to help me feel sexy and to incite the desire I always seemed to lack.

They never did work. Nothing I tried work.

Looking at the male waiting for me, I realize only one thing ever had.

I scan the room. There's nothing more I need than to abandon the confines of my sweat-soaked sheets and dark environment. Still, I don't dare expose myself further, though, in a way, I'm ready to.

Bruises and scrapes form odd patterns along my legs and arms. Four days. That's how long I was unconscious. I suppose if my body weren't occupied healing my crushed skull, my lesser injuries would have mended by now.

My focus gradually falls on the footboard. Whoever dressed me left the matching robe draped over the edge. I stand and place the robe around me. My legs are wobbly, and I'm light- headed. I try not to show it and sit at the foot of the bed.

I cross my legs, ignoring the pain, and reach for Ryker's hands, which pains me for reasons that have nothing to do with my injuries.

"Hi," I say.

Ryker tenses as my hands slide over his. Slowly, he turns his palms, allowing me to link our fingers. My hands practically disappear within his and yet within a grip that can easily kill me, all I sense is kindness.

His tenderness should ease my worry and the tension between us. Knowing what I need to say, all it offers, is a moment of reprieve. "I'm sorry about the other day." My tone is barely above a whisper, my throat aching with more than thirst.

Ryker sighs. He releases me and walks to the window, his full attention on the Hudson and far away from me. "You almost died," he says. "Why would you apologize for such a thing?"

"That's not what I'm talking about."

He turns and cocks his head, his brows drawn tight.

I meander to his side, stopping just a few feet in front of him. "I'm talking about watching you eat. I shouldn't have, and just left you in peace."

"Peace," he states, his tone flat.

His features are more stone than flesh. I'm saying all the wrong things. But I need to make things right. "I was worried about you and wanted to make sure you were safe."

"Did you enjoy it?"

His comment takes me aback. But if he means to frighten me or shove this conversation aside, it's not happening.

"No," I admit. "Just like I know you didn't, either."

"Really?" His large form stiffens further. "Don't lie to me, Olivia. You saw how much I wanted that meal just as I saw your disgust when I finished."

"It wasn't disgust." It was pity for how he exists, but I won't admit it. "You were hungry," I say. "I saw how much you were hurting. I know it was necessary."

He laughs without humor. "It's not so simple, Olivia. I not only craved that meal, I relished every morsel, down to the last."

"I would have, too, if I were hungry," I reply, sticking to my guns. His ice-blue gaze turns dangerously cold. He didn't like the comparison. "You need souls like I need food."

"Does your food beg you not to kill it or *scream* when you ingest it?"

Something in me snaps. Ryker is furious—furious for what he is, how he lives, and how I saw him. But none of it is his fault. He never asked to become the Ankou. He was a foolish young man, like all young men are, and he paid an unimaginable price. I glare at him through impending tears. "Don't you dare berate yourself." I close the distance between us. "You once told me you only find deserving souls to feast from, and you're right. They deserve what happens to them, and Don Fleycher was no exception." His scowl sharpens when I name his victim. It doesn't stop me from gripping his arm. "You derive pleasure from eating. I get it, and it makes total sense. It also makes sense why it haunts you. I'm just sorry that it does. My stars, Ryker, I'm *so* sorry."

Ryker works his jaw, struggling to speak in the silence that followed. "You speak of peace." He waits for my nod. "The only peace I'll find is when you grant me mine."

"Don't do this," I plead.

"Don't do what?" he growls, looming over me. "Did you think I changed my mind? Seeing me feast through your eyes only solidified my decision." His expression shatters. "I want to die, Olivia. I want to end this madness. Kill the monster I've become, and I shall find my peace."

Ryker's anguish tears at my soul. I bury my face in my hands and sob. He stands there, watching me and letting me cry.

After what seems like forever, his strong arms find my waist, and he gathers me to him. Ryker bows his head and whispers in my hair, "Save your tears, *beag tuar ceatha*. If I mean anything to you, you'll stay true to your word."

As the grief spills into his voice, I realize I hadn't cried alone.

26

It takes me a long time to move after Ryker leaves. He endures and bleeds guilt every time he takes a breath, and because of it, he's asking me to be a real friend and end his pain. Seeing how he exists, I'd want the same.

I don't know when it will happen, but it will. I owe him as much.

I shower and make my bed with fresh linens, moving as fast as I can so I can get back to Ryker.

My steps are quick as I pass Stevie's room. He's singing, rather badly, to something too loud and too volatile for his own good. Still, he's enjoying himself as only Stevie can.

The quiet motor from the treadmill beckons me to the lower level. I'm wearing a white cashmere sweater and dark jeans accessorized with knee-high pink boots. My bruised body begged for sweats. I didn't oblige. I need to feel more like myself, and myself demands a little pink and a touch of style.

The heels of my boots *clink* and *clank* against the metal staircase. Ryker speeds along in basketball shorts and a gray T-shirt, his back to me. I don't have to tell him I'm here. He knew from the moment I reached the first step.

He slows the treadmill and bounces off before I'm halfway across the room, grabbing a towel from the rack to wipe his face. As he nears me, he lowers the towel, pausing to take me in. "Going out?"

I laugh despite the strain thickening the air between us. "I thought I'd go dancing, meet a cute guy, and bring him back here. You don't mind, do you?"

His scowl informs me he very much does mind and that someone will die if I do.

Alrighty then. I cross my arms. "We need to talk about what happened at the beach house." Anything is better than talks of him dying and me killing him.

"You almost *died*."

I kick at the floor with my boot. "I know," I reply. "Believe me, I wasn't trying to."

"What happened to Jane's wards?" he asks. "She worked night and day to reinforce them."

"I weakened them," I reply, recalling how they shattered like glass.

Ryker tosses his towel aside. "How exactly? You're *Life*—"

"So, I've heard," I mutter.

The edges of his mouth curve, and I swear I almost prance around the room in victory. "Your magic shouldn't have clashed with hers," he tells me.

"I know. Somehow, it did," I reply. "I tried fighting the hounds while we were still in the house." I explain about the knife throwing and how I shot my power through the door.

Ryker's brows tighten further. "Olivia, that shouldn't have affected the wards."

"Yet, it did," I say. "The harder I fought, the quicker the wards came down. The force was unbelievable. It brought Bill's place down like a kick to a pile of empty boxes." Images of the hounds tearing through the roof punch through my thoughts. "Nothing worked as it should."

Ryker places his hand on my lower back and leads me to the stack of exercise mats. My body warms from the reassurance of his touch, but I can't enjoy it. Everything we counted on to protect and shield us failed. Something went very wrong.

And I'm not the only one who sees it.

I look to Ryker's impenetrable stance. "We were betrayed, again," I say. I don't sound as distressed as I should feel. It should scare me, except I'm not as naïve as I used to be.

Ryker sits, waiting for me to join him before he continues. "I think it's Bill."

I shake my head. "It can't be."

Ryker squares his gaze on me. "It was his home, Olivia. His wards initiated by a priestess he sought independently of Jane. He knew them better than anyone."

"Jane's magic is powerful," I argue. "It would have offered additional protection."

"Not necessarily," he adds gruffly. "Jane only reinforced what was already in place."

He waits, allowing me to take in his theory. I never pegged Bill for a bad guy. And in many ways, I still can't. As angry and distrustful as he is of Ryker, I'm not certain I can take that final leap. "Maybe the other priestess, I don't know, sucked—or wasn't as powerful," I offer. The look Ryker shoots me informs me I'm the dumbest being to ever don pink boots.

"He knew you were there alone with Stevie."

"You and Jane did, too," I point out.

He tilts his head ever so slightly. "Are you saying it was one of us?"

"No, no, of course not, I just... Ryker, it *can't* be Bill. I know him. He's practically family." I stand, needing to pace, only to sit again. My hands chill, and I clutch them to my chest. "He wouldn't do that to me."

"Olivia," Ryker says gently. "You're no longer a pixie without magic. You're a threat to him and anyone in his station among the Fae."

"Bill doesn't care about his place among the Fae. He leads our people because we respect his wisdom and strength. It's why his connection to the Ancients has solidified."

Ryker passes a hand over his face. "That day Cathasach invaded Bill's office may have something to do with it."

"How so?" I ask.

"You told me Bill was bitten. Perhaps it helped Cathasach locate and somehow mark Bill."

"Is that even possible?" I ask.

Ryker rubs his jaw, passing a thumb over his dimple several times before speaking. "I don't know. Those who are bitten by the Cù-Sìth don't live to tell their secrets." His voice hardens. "Your magic burned the hound that tried to tear your throat out. He managed a small taste before your power ignited him. I seized the moment and brought you here."

I wondered what happened, not that I bothered asking. I was just grateful to be alive.

Again, Ryker had arrived to help. I place my hand on his thigh and squeeze. "Thank you. I don't think I tell you that enough. But please understand that your friendship means the world to me."

He dips his chin, barely acknowledging my words. "I've wondered that in acquiring a taste of Bill, Cathasach could compel him to do his bidding."

My hand slips from his leg. "I understand where you're going with this, and your suspicions of Bill. But I can't believe he'd hurt me or betray our kind. He's counting on me to save us."

"Or so he claims," Ryker adds.

"Ryker…no."

"Olivia, my theory is questionable, but I have no other explanation. Do you?"

I groan and push back my hair. Ryker has a point; only he, Bill, and Jane knew where we were. We didn't even tell Stevie. We just brought him to Glen Cove. "What about Stevie's electronic devices?" I ask. "His phone? His iPad? Could the gremlins or whatever is working with Cathasach track him using his portable devices?"

"Both your devices and Stevie's were new and untraceable."

"Oh," I say quietly. "Wait. And who provided us with these untraceable devices?"

"Bill," Ryker answers, curtly.

"Figures," I mutter.

We sit quietly. I don't realize my hand has returned to Ryker's thigh until I catch the way he fixes on me touching him. I should move my hand away. Instead, I offer another squeeze. I've missed him. It feels good to have him beside me.

Ryker watches me. "I heard you call to me and yell my name. The pack anticipated my arrival and surrounded the area long before I arrived." He releases a long breath. "My apologies for not reaching you sooner."

My brows pucker. "You still made it, Ryker. I'm not sitting here because of Stevie, or Jane, and I'm especially not here because of me. You rescued me in the nick of time, *again*. Seriously, at this rate, you need to start charging." I flick the edges of his shorts. "You're missing out on some big bucks, counselor."

He smirks. "I doubt you can afford my services."

"Maybe I can find another way to thank you," I offer without thinking.

Our smiles fade, and those startling irises weld me to him. I don't know exactly what happens. I just know I want him.

Ryker is no longer a friend. He's a lover whose body needs to press hard against me as I writhe beneath and beg for his pleasure.

My hand tightens over his leg. I lean forward, eager for his mouth, his taste. His eyes widen as I close in…and lower as he bends and circles my waist possessively. My tongue grazes the top of his lip. We've never touched like this before…

"Hey!" Stevie calls, making us jump. He skips down the stairs, gradually slowing to a stop when he spots us in our pre-coitus position.

I jerk my hands from Ryker as if burned. Stevie gapes as Ryker's arms leisurely slip from my waist. "Awk-*ward*," Stevie sings.

Vanessa launches into a frenzy, humming loud enough to bounce and clatter the sea chest she's stuffed in. I'm really starting to resent that utensil from hell.

Stevie's focus dances between us. He holds out my phone. "Bill just texted you. Something about finding Cathasach's lair."

27

The heels of my pink boots dig into the forest ground of the 28th floor. Bark and pine needles kick up with how hard I pace. Ryker didn't bother with a nice suit. Azure armor covers every inch of his hulking form.

"This sucks serious Vanessa-wanting eggs," I mutter.

Bill glances up from the giant table where he and Ryker analyze a large-scale map of Harsimus, a six-acre cemetery in Jersey City. "Who?" he asks.

I cringe. "Never mind."

"You're certain Cathasach is here?" Ryker asks.

"That's what our sources tell us," Bill answers. He traces his finger along the map. "The grounds are immense. I'm not quite sure how to pinpoint his location."

"If I'm close enough, I'll find him," Ryker replies, his raspy timbre stiff.

"Very well," Bill says, his voice weary. "The Ancients and Fae in league with us agree; we fight in a week's time." His soft brown eyes sweep over me. "I hope that will give you enough time to heal."

"It will," I assure him. It's what I say. I don't want him to know it will likely take longer than that.

Frankie walks around the wide tree trunk table and offers me a seat. I take it only to appear calmer in Stevie's presence. The Ancients stowed Mr. Sebastian in protective hiding the night before Cathasach was to come for him. So far, Sebastian and Stevie remain safe. It won't last. The clock is ticking, and poor Stevie knows it.

Jane shuffles along the ground, her long black dress trailing behind her, collecting dry leaves and debris. When she reaches me, her magic levitates her and gently places her in the seat beside me. She seems to have aged since the last time I saw her. It makes me sad. "Are you tired?" I ask. She nods. "Becoming the Hydra wore you out. Didn't it, Jane?"

She offers me a small wrinkly smile and pats my leg. It's her way of telling me not to worry. I will and always would. Jane is that rare kind of friend I never expected to make, and I cherish her more than I'm able to put into words.

To demonstrate that her druidness still kicks ass, Jane's minions of birds and fireflies appear in a rush, carrying trays of hors d' oeuvres. Stevie snags an entire tray of pigs in a blanket to wolf down. I take several prawns set in tiny shot glasses filled with cocktail sauce.

The calories do me a great deal of good. I've never healed this slowly. I understand my skull was crushed and my brain damaged, but everything hurts more than it should.

Ryker thinks my residual magic kept me alive. Any other Fae, even one as strong as Bill, wouldn't have survived the blows. Ryker also claims I was lucky to land the way I did, and that next time, a strike like that would kill me.

"Why are we attacking on Halloween?" I ask after swallowing my weight in mini quiches. I accept a cloth napkin from a passing butterfly, ignoring that the perky creature is the size of my leg. "Forget that it sounds cliché, it's the creepiest night of the year. Can't we wait until Thanksgiving? Or maybe Easter? Give me bunnies and Peeps. I'm tired of death hounds and festering Alphas."

Humor is wasted on the Dead and apparently everyone else.

Ryker shakes his head. "Death gathers on nights when Earth's magic is at is strongest. Halloween falls on one of those nights. If we're to annihilate the Cù-Sìth, we need them all in one place."

The quiche and shrimp do a few backflips in my stomach. "Death gathers on that night; that means other forms of it can join the Cù-Sìth."

The tension building in Ryker's shoulders does nothing to soothe me. Neither does what follows. "Most forms of Death avoid each other, as they're competing for the same food."

"But it's possible," I say. "On Halloween."

"Yes," he answers.

Stevie swears and reaches for a passing platter of mini pizzas. Good for him. My stomach recommends we never eat again.

Frankie swears, too. "With so many goddamn hounds, how will you ever get Cathasach alone?"

Ryker fiddles with the hilt of his dagger. "In the hours before, I'll cage several hounds and secure them at different locations. Once our allies are in position, my warriors and I will kill them."

Frankie shoots out a hand. "Wait a minute. You're going to bait Cathasach using other souls?" Ryker allows his closed mouth to answer for him. Smoke trails from Frankie's nose. "*Fuck that!*"

Bill glances up from marking something on the map. "Frankie, calm down."

"Don't tell me to calm down," Frankie snaps. "These poor

Fae have suffered long and hard, and now you're saying we get to watch them be re-eaten? That's the best you've got?"

Ryker rounds on him. "They're prisoners. That won't change so long as long as the Cù-Sìth reign."

Frankie flinches yet holds his ground. "What if Dahlia's there?" He looks at me. "What if she's one of those released just so those assholes can devour her again?"

I understand his pain. "Frankie, I saw my mother's face protrude from the body of a Cù-Sìth the night Dahlia died." His lips part. "I felt her fear and pain when the creature forced her back inside. I can't tell you what it did to me and how helpless I felt. What I can tell you is no matter what I felt, those souls feel more. This is our chance to end their torment. We have to take it."

Frankie lowers his head. "Sorry, I just…" He clears his throat, allowing the last of his smoke to stream from his lips. "Never mind. Just tell me what you want me to do, and I'll do it."

The suffering Frankie feels spills over his face, as does his determination. Frankie won't abandon us. "Thank you," I tell him quietly.

Ryker returns his attention to the map. "As soon as I find Cathasach, Olivia and I will attack."

Frankie circles the table, eyeing the large territory that makes up the cemetery. "How many Cù-Sìth are we looking at?"

Ryker gives it some, though. "Between my kills and Olivia's, roughly seventy."

Bill swipes his head with a heavy hand. I didn't realize how much he's sweating until streams of his perspiration soak into his hair. "There could be more?" he asks. Ryker nods. "Well, let's hope for less."

Bill returns to the map, not that he really sees it anymore. "Jane and the Ancients will take point here, here, here, and there," he says, pointing to each mark he made. "At your signal, they'll remove their talismans, drawing the hounds away from you and giving you time to kill Cathasach. As soon as he's dead, and the hounds become mortal, our allies will attack."

"How many Fae have agreed to join us?" Ryker asks.

Misery clouds Bill's features. "In addition to Frankie and two other dragons, we have three gargoyles, including myself."

"*And?*" I ask.

"A nymph and two leprechauns have also come forth," Bill adds.

I'm not trying to be a Debbie Downer, but you have to be fucking kidding me.

By some miracle, I manage to keep my mouth shut. Frankie doesn't.

"Are you shitting me?" Frankie says. "Every Fae out there has lost friends and family to these mutts. Why aren't they stepping up? This isn't just for the Fae; Earth is at stake if we don't stop them."

"Fear reigns more than vengeance," Bill says. Sweat drips down his forehead. "But there's time. With luck, and the right words, more will come forward."

Nine Fae, four Ancients, and us. I try not to hurl. Even if we kill Cathasach, we don't have the numbers to take down an army of death hounds.

"The Ancients are powerful and lethal," Bill reminds us. "But we must preserve them at all costs." He narrows his gaze at Jane. "If Olivia and Ryker fail to kill Cathasach, the Ancients are to return their talismans to their necks and materialize to safety. Isn't that right, Jane?"

Jane purses her lips, her way of saying she isn't agreeing to anything, won't materialize anywhere, and that the Cù-Sìth can kiss her sagging yet smackable ass.

My hand clasps her bony shoulder. "What if the talismans

don't work?" Everyone looks at me as if slapped. "I'm serious. They didn't work last time."

A little possum jumps on the table and starts pouring shots of scotch. Either Jane summoned him, or the little guy guessed the bottles of chilled champagne with strawberries won't cut it.

Bill takes a shot and plops into the throne-like chair. "I have no answers. For the time being, they're working, and the Ancients will reinforce them before battle."

He takes a sip of scotch, followed by another. I think it's too strong until he pours the whole thing down his throat. "I hope we're enough. Dear stars, we need to be."

Bill resembles nothing short of death warmed over. Perspiration saturates his face, and his dark skin acquires a gray tone. The stress has taken its toll on his glamour and dulled his beauty. This isn't the Bill I know, the one with quiet confidence and the grace of a king. This is a desperate male.

I don't want to admit that Ryker is right and that Bill, this male I've admired since the day we met, could betray me. I also don't have the luxury of being blind or naive. Too many lives are at stake.

Ryker edges his way to me. "Are we all in agreement?" he asks. Everyone nods except for Bill. He holds his scotch and stares in the direction of the trees where Stevie first appeared. Ryker notices. "Very well," he says, looking at Bill as he speaks. "If you'll excuse us, Olivia needs to rest and prepare."

Like a gentleman, Ryker pulls the chair out for me.

Stevie shoves the last pizza into his mouth, still chewing as he reaches for a tray of crab cakes hefted by a flock of emerald birds. "Can I take this with us?" he asks. "I'm still kinda hungry." At Jane's grin, he snatches the tray and hurries to catch us. "Can we watch *The Avengers* tonight? I'm in the mood for some fantasy. Reality is too scary, man."

"Sure," I say.

"Olivia," Bill says, calling to me.

"Yes, Bill?"

"I'm very sorry," he says.

I freeze. "About what?" I ask.

I think he's ready to tell me something important. Instead, he says, "About everything, child."

And then he's gone.

Those who remain mutter quietly among themselves, making plans to recruit family or send them abroad to England for safekeeping. I'm blinking at the empty space where Bill sat.

Jane waves her candy-cane wand, and Stevie dematerializes. I look up at Ryker when he places his arm around me, my heart breaking. His expression gives nothing away.

The air snaps, darkness cloaks me, and we return to Ryker's loft.

I'm not sure if Bill caught my expression, the one that begged him to stay true to me and the Fae. I hope he did. I hope I'm wrong and he left to recruit as many fighters as he can.

Stevie sits on the couch and perches the tray of crab cakes on his lap as he fumbles with the remote. "All right. We're good," he says. "It's still early. I think we can make it through *Civil War* if we start now."

I move toward the couch, my thoughts still on Bill, when Ryker's scythe springs into his hand. He slams it down with enough force to jolt me.

I stumble back, stunned. Ryker cuts a line into the floor, firing it with bright blue light. "*Ardú!*" he roars.

Dugan and Phillip leap from the expanding light and rush Stevie. Stevie leaps to his feet, spilling the tray of food on his lap. He lunges toward me. "Olivia!'

Dugan and Phillip overpower him. I grab my whip and charge. Ryker wrenches me back by the waist and rips the whip from my grasp. I kick out, screaming for Stevie as the

Scottish warriors drag him toward the blazing blue light. *"No. No!"*

Stevie jerks and writhes, smoke spewing from his mouth between terrified screams. "Olivia, help me. *Help me!"*

Stevie is sobbing, hysterical. I'm not that much better. Dugan and Phillip bow to Ryker and disappear with Stevie.

I kick back hard, slamming my heel into Ryker's shins and breaking his hold.

My knees slam against the floor as I fall against the fading blue light. I swear, over and over, again, slapping at the line as the last spark of magic dissipates and seals my only way to Stevie.

I stumble to my feet and reel on Ryker. *"What did you do to him?"*

Ryker straightens. "It's not what you think."

"What did you do?"

I throw myself at Ryker, determined to shove him from my sight. All I manage is to do is knock myself backward. "I trusted you," I yell. *"Tell me where he is!"*

Ryker meets me square in the face, his features pained, although I hadn't hurt him. "He's safe, Olivia, hidden between realms where he'll sleep. In a week's time, he'll awake on Jane's doorstep."

My chest rises and falls, the sting of betrayal spreading across my eyes. "Why? What's the point?"

"We can't wait for you to fully heal, Olivia. We don't have the time. As you saw, Bill can't be trusted." He pauses. "At dawn, we will face Cathasach in his domain. There, you will challenge him to the death."

28

I don't move for a long time, choosing instead to fume on the couch. Ryker set Bill up, formulating a plan he never intended to execute, all the while gathering information for our benefit. Or so he claims.

Ryker's manipulation and cunning infuriates me. It wasn't just directed at Bill.

My attention travels to the chunks of broken crab cakes littering the floor. The sight makes me sad, knowing who dropped them and where he now waits alone.

"When did you come up with this genius plan?" I mutter.

Ryker doesn't miss the unpleasantness in my voice. He leans back in the loveseat across from me. He changed into a black silk shirt and dark slacks. I suppose he was trying to appear less Ankou-ish and therefore less like an asshole. He didn't succeed.

Stevie wasn't gently escorted off the premises. He was snatched, without a warning, without an explanation, and without a choice.

Fury is my friend now, and we have dinner plans. I am *livid*. And I'm scared. More unsettling, I'm ill-prepared for what awaits.

"I formed a plan following a close examination of the map and my discussion with Bill."

"You made a decision without consulting me?" I ask. "Wow, that's so unlike you."

"Olivia, you're angry."

"No shit." I stand. "Why didn't you just tell me and Stevie your super awesome plan? He's just a kid, Ryker. I know you're like, a million, but he's just a kid."

Ryker squares his jaw. "The less Stevie knows, the more he's protected. I suspect Bill had a hand in every misfortune we've encountered. But I can't be certain he's acted alone. Had I discussed the matter with you, we would have wasted time, time neither we nor Stevie have."

"You *scared* him," I repeat. "Don't you hear what I'm saying? He's a child, and you frightened him."

Ryker bows his head, clasping his hands together. "My intention was to move him someplace safe, not to frighten him. There, between realms, he's at peace." He looks up. "I swear he's protected and no longer scared."

"You swear?" I bite out.

"Yes."

"I think you should know, your promises don't mean much right now."

His wounded expression is the last thing I catch as I stomp into the kitchen. Ryker ordered pizza for Stevie while I was in that stupid coma. I slap a few slices onto a cookie sheet and throw it in the oven.

I bought Ryker that cookie sheet, insisting he needed real things to call his own. I also bought him nice hand soap, the kind with olive oil and scented with mint. He needed things around here to make him someone, not just the Ankou.

My fingers tap along the controls. I wonder briefly if this is the last meal I'll have. Those thoughts don't last. Mostly, I wonder if I was foolish to forget that no matter all the pretty soaps and items I bought him, Ryker's been the Ankou for far longer.

I press my palms against the cool quartz counter and release a long breath. Ryker wraps a pair of very muscular and very hesitant arms around me. I turn and circle his waist with my slender arms, the same arms he trained to fight Cathasach. Death is all Ryker has known in the last century, and I've run out of time to teach him more.

"I'm sorry," Ryker whispers. "I wasn't fair to you or the boy."

My face falls against his chest. Maybe he did learn something after all. "If we pull Plan Crazy off and live, you can't continue to make all the decisions. You're no longer flying solo. We're partners, and I need to have a say."

Ryker smooths my hair. "You're correct in reminding me. For all that your presence has impacted my world, I still behave as if I walk it alone."

"You're not alone. I'm here." Well, at least for the moment.

Ryker tightens his hold. He knows what went unsaid. "Where is Stevie exactly?" I ask, my tone softening. "Please tell me there's Netflix."

"It's a space in time where those who mourn remember the good while living. It's not a permanent place, especially for the living. But it will hide him well until he appears at Jane's home."

I wish we could hide there with him. Except heroes don't hide, and it's time to come out swinging.

My attention travels to the wall of windows where only darkness awaits. "Tell me the plan."

"In an hour's time, we will leave and hunt the hounds. Dugan, Phillip, and I can trap them between realms but only for a time before they break free. When we've secured enough, we will release them from different points and behead them before they can fully escape."

"Holding them between realms will weaken you." I sigh when he doesn't respond. "So will summoning Doogie and Phil to fight."

"Trapping hounds isn't ideal," Ryker admits. "It's a waste of energy. But it's the only way to bait the Cù-Sìth and challenge Cathasach. Given what's happening, I see no other way."

"How exactly will I challenge Cathasach?"

Ryker releases me slowly and walks toward the windows, keeping his back to me. I don't have to examine his features to know how he feels. I can sense his anger and disgust. "Cathasach wants you," he says. "At my word, remove your talisman and call him to you as you would me."

I have dirty thoughts when it comes to Ryker. There, I said it. When I think of Cathasach, all I think is dirty. "Ah, come again?"

Ryker's spine stiffens. "You need to entice him, Olivia. You have to want him, if for nothing else to destroy him."

"I don't know if I can," I admit. Cathasach wants to torture me in ways I can't bear to think about. If he traps me, he'll fulfill his desires before killing me. It could take hours, even months if we fail.

Ryker returns to my side. "Olivia, calling him will lure him from the pack. It's the only way to take him alone."

Although I'm not exactly thrilled to pieces, he's right. "You'll be there with me?" I ask.

My voice is oddly clear despite how scared I feel. Ryker clasps my shoulders gently. "I promise you won't be alone." The pledge in his tone forces me to meet his face. "We will strike as one, quickly and without mercy."

"You'll be weak," I remind.

"It doesn't matter. By dawn's pure light, he won't be as potent. The moment he's dead, summon Jane."

I know where he's headed. "So, she and the Ancients can kill the remaining hounds."

"Exactly," he replies.

I struggle with my next question. "What if we can't kill him?"

"I'll get you to safety."

I lift my chin and square my jaw. "Not if you're already dead."

The air snaps, and the darkness enveloping me lifts, unveiling the sky. The moon shines dully against a canvas of black and gray. Night carries a scent that invades deep into blankets of moss littering the forests and every crevice along long, lonely city streets. This place is no different. Night reigns, and I smell it everywhere.

Frigid air strokes like a cold, invasive touch against my skin as Ryker lowers me to the frozen earth. My feet feel out of place in the cemetery. So, does the rest of me. I've never given much thought to where the dead lie buried. I've never had to. Fae don't have the luxury to mourn. Now that I'm here, it's clear I don't belong.

The warmth and comfort lingering from being so close to Ryker is stolen with each breath I take. I move for the sake of moving but can't keep my footing on the uneven ground. He clasps my shoulder, steadying me.

Worry deepens his frown. "Are you all right?"

"I'm fine," I reply. I take a step back and almost trip over a grave marker.

I edge away and hug my body tight. The thin seafoam jacket I'm wearing isn't equipped for October in Jersey. The biting cold practically laughs at it. It's just the one thing I own that provides a layer of protection and allows me to move well in a fight.

The familiar sense of fear pokes at my chest, tormenting my lungs. I'm scared. I don't like the plan. And then there's that pesky desire to live and not die a horrible, demented death.

Ryker assured me that Dugan and Phil will see to my escape should he "perish." *Perish.* There's a word. Gutted like a pig and gnawed to pieces as I watch, screaming, seems more apropos. It's what had happened to Dahlia...and my family...and those poor Fae from the club. Yet, here I stand, knock, knock, knockin' on Heaven's door.

I search my surroundings, gathering my nerve and squelching the itch to bolt. Shadows claim and rule Harsimus Cemetery like an invincible king. I expected to find long sweeping hills blanketed by meticulously kept acreage. Instead, towering monuments and tombstones weathered by storms and time stretch out like an ancient village.

A crumbling mausoleum overlooks the cemetery at the top of a hill. Cracked cement steps lead to a partially demolished door, and old trees with crooked branches creak and sway, reaching for, yet not quite touching, the archaic roof.

The hollow cries of hooting owls bounce along the marble gravestones, adding to the spook factor since that's the kind of shit owls pull in graveyards.

I'm vaguely aware of Ryker watching me when he lifts his arm and brings forth his scythe. His trademark weapon appears within his grip, the half-moon casting a shallow glow against the blade as he punctures the earth and releases his warriors.

"*Ardú,*" he commands.

His gaze briefly cuts my way as his men rise and bow. He knows I'm scared out of my mind. Instead of psyching me up and readying me to fight until my last crumbling body part, he and his buds make quick work of luring the first hound.

"Death calls," Ryker rumbles, his deep voice forceful.

Death answers Death within moments. Rustling stirs near an unkempt plot of shrubbery and trees, slow, at first, like the sound of a dry crumpling leaf, then louder and more distressed.

A hound pokes her lucid head through the dense vegetation.

The thick thorn brambles sweep through her misty body as she prowls forward and materializes into her corporeal form.

At first, I'm not certain she sees us. Her eyes are so dull, I almost mistake her for being blind. When she growls in challenge and skulks directly toward Ryker, there's no question she knows we're here. She didn't like being summoned and especially hates us disturbing her turf.

Her lips peel back, and a hideous howl rumbles through her freakishly large chest. I step back and tighten my grasp over my whip. She's the largest female we've come across, matching Cathasach in bulk and length.

Ryker widens the distance between us, luring the hound away from me. Dugan and Phillip shadow her, their steps silent. She draws closer to Ryker. She's almost to him, fixated on him even as he dissolves into the darkness.

Ryker bends his knees, his hands out, ready to strike. The hound bristles, her growls hideous and her hackles rising. She's ready, too.

Saliva streams from her jowls. That split second when predators pause before they attack arrives. Except she's no longer looking at Ryker. Her head whips, and her sights lock on me.

My talisman is firmly in place. She shouldn't be able to sense me. Yet, she does. In four quick strides, she's on me.

I don't think. I react. My first strike is strong. Glorious pink power races through the length of my whip, severing her head and freeing a flock of souls. Her body buckles and implodes, falling into crispy chunks.

The hound was big for a reason, stuffed to the gills with dead Fae. Souls spill from her remains, shrieking and sobbing as they tear free and into the cold night air. Their numbers and cries are too much to bear and too loud to ignore. A pack of Cù- Sìth rushes us from all sides, and there's nothing we can do to stop them.

The soul of a banshee shoves her face into mine, swatting at my shoulders and ignoring the way her translucent hands pass through me. Her mouth opens and closes several times. She tries to speak, but only whimpers and indiscernible words flow.

I attempt to hold her. All I feel is a faint sense of what once was. "You have to flee," I urge. "Death is coming for you."

My words only incite her horror. She screams louder, choking on her sobs, pleading through vacant eyes for me to save her.

I back away, trying to create some space to fight. The banshee follows, desperate for me to listen to her. Ryker and his warriors are outnumbered, and more hounds are bounding toward us. They leap over markers and from rooftops, crazed from all the souls soaring through the graveyard.

A Cù-Sìth charges the banshee. I see him coming through her transparent image, but I'm not fast enough. He barrels over me, pinning me as he devours her. She shrieks in pain, flailing and reaching for me.

"Get off her!" I scream. "*Let her go, you bastard!*"

Ryker wrenches the beast off me and disappears into the earth in a wash of azure light.

I scramble to my feet. "Ryker?"

He and the warriors are gone. I cling to the talisman around my neck, my knees knocking as the remaining Cù-Sìth circle and sniff the air, searching. The souls are gone, once more consumed. Unlike the female who attacked, they don't see me, yet.

The circle they form around me tightens, and their impatient growls grow more pronounced. They know there's more to eat and draw closer with each pass.

A green hound's tail brushes against my waist. The action freezes him in place. He knows Life remains. He bites the empty air in front of him, then to the left, narrowly missing my arm.

Fear sparks my magic. A slow burn catches where his heavy tail strikes my belly. He wags his tail faster, his excitement building.

My power is calling him to me and betraying my position. I try to summon it back. As much as I want these bitches to burn, I can't release more souls. The hounds are everywhere. Despite having their fill, they want more.

They want *me*.

I cringe when the hounds lap the air close to my face and take a breath. As air fills my lungs, I withdraw my power.

The hound's ears twitch. He glances around, appearing confused.

A thickly matted female prowls toward me, swallowing the remains of an elderly gnome. Another hound, the color of dry seaweed, follows, scanning the area just to my left.

"Ryker?" I call, barely above a whisper.

Azure light flashes beneath the approaching hounds and the one closest to me. Arms reach through, wrenching the immense beasts downward. Ryker and the warriors struggle to trap the hounds. Thanks to my ineptness, we have more bait than we bargained for and a whole lot of noise.

A second female appears, prowling in my direction, her steps quickening the closer she nears.

My talisman is failing me. The female stops suddenly, appearing to pinpoint my location. She jets forward, her thick paws barely grazing the ground.

Mere feet remain between us. I startle when Dugan and Phil drag her into the earth by her hindquarters. Another Cù-Sìth notices me and attacks.

Ryker's leather-gloved hands push through the hard ground in a flash of dark blue light. He pulls at the hound's fur until he latches on to the scruff of her neck and yanks her down.

Ryker and his warriors are fighting hard and smart,

surprising the hounds by appearing in different points. I can't stand here. I need to be ready. Surely, all the turmoil has alerted Cathasach.

My gaze homes in on my whip, lying near an abandoned shovel. I lunge for it and snag the handle. Phillip's face punctures through the ground, his features twisted with anger. Evidently, I haven't wowed him with my awesomeness.

I start to apologize when his eyes fly open, his full attention zipping behind me.

Something hard strikes my skull as I whip around, the blow sending me soaring. I land on my side several yards away. I catch flickers of Phil leaping upward and explosions of azure light.

Ryker is yelling for me. I barely hear him over the wash of hot fluid flooding my ear.

What seems like an army of Cù-Sìth howl and charge, catapulting through the dilapidated grounds as if beckoned. I push up on my hands, trying to get to my feet. Again, something strikes me, this time in the face.

Speckles of light flicker in my line of vision, and blood pours from my nose. I roll away, trying to distance myself from my attacker. I don't make it far.

Thick fingers tangle into my hair and yank my head back, the force craning my neck and threatening to break it.

"*Olivia!*"

My vision abruptly clears when Ryker calls to me. I can't think the way my head spins, that doesn't mean I don't react.

My body takes over, responding with force. I shoot my arm out, connecting with muscle and releasing bursts of my magic. My legs join the action, kicking into bone. I'm angry, furious, and every part of me reacts in turn.

Clanking metal rings out as Dugan and Phillip swing their swords, and I fight for my life. Roars ricochet from all directions.

Through it all, I hear Ryker, his furious baritone swearing as he fights his way to me.

My mind remains clouded. Still, I feel his desperation. I can't allow us to perish. I kick and jerk, breaking free. My knees crash onto a path of rocks. I crawl forward, managing a few feet when my attacker hauls me back by my waist and hair.

My magic powers outward, the pink color radiating and clashing into Ryker's vicious azure light. He and his warriors are battling it out with the encroaching hounds. Except they're not enough.

I scream, using my strength and magic against the strong arms wrenching me farther away from Ryker. A fist strikes the side of my head, jostling any cognizant thought but driving my will to survive.

I buckle, trying to break free, my body electrified and sizzling with power. It's not until I feel it explode from me that I realize it has no effect against my captor.

Shock claims my form. I'm not fighting Death. I'm fighting someone who is very much alive.

Rage replaces all emotion. Alive or dead, this male is my enemy. And I'm not done fighting.

My heel connects to a shin. Fire singes my cheeks as my captor roars and releases his flame. The burn to my flesh makes me lash out harder. I won't die. Not like this and not by his hands.

Another blow punches my head, dulling the escalating chaos surrounding me: the swing of Ryker's scythe, the grunts of his warriors, the howling of souls, and the barks of the feasting Cù-Sìth.

"I'll kill you," my attacker's familiar voice spits behind me. "I'll fucking kill you myself!"

Walter Sebastian wrenches my hair back and grips my throat, subduing me. He drags me up the crumbling steps of the mausoleum. My arms fall to my side as he squeezes my wind-pipe, and something pops.

My breath leaves me, and the world gently fades away. Shadows creep around my eyes like tendrils from a web that crisscross and thicken. The last thing I remember is the sun rising and the entire pack of Cù-Sìth swarming Ryker.

29

I wake to the sound of slurping. Never a good sign. I scramble away blindly and smack into a wall of dirt.

My hands slap my hair away from my face. Pebbles and bits of mud pepper my scalp. I swat at the crumbling debris as if it could hurt me, my heart accelerating faster than I'm prepared for.

The confusion takes a moment to clear. Dirt can't hurt me. It's not a threat. Cathasach standing mere feet from where I lay? He's a different story.

He rises in his human form, abandoning the dead dragon at his feet. Two other hounds circle the remains, searching for a bite despite Cathasach having stripped him clean of his soul.

The dragon isn't Walter Sebastian. Pity. If ever someone deserved to suffer a Cù-Sìth death, it's that bastard.

Cathasach's eyes fire red. I reach for my talisman out of instinct. My fingertips graze over my filthy jacket and not much more. My talisman is gone. It doesn't matter. It's clear I'm done hiding.

A wrought iron gate held closed with a chain and padlock is

the only thing separating me from Cathasach. I'm not stupid enough to think it offers any protection. I'm also not stupid enough to believe I stand a chance against him the way things are.

Cathasach widens his arms and grasps the bars, exposing the length of his naked form. "You're awake, little pixie," he murmurs, rocking his hips. "I've been waiting for you."

I avert my gaze, taking in my surroundings. Wall-to-wall packed earth makes up the underground labyrinth. Boulders and tree roots poke through the ceiling. I'm deep beneath the surface and very far from a way out.

There's no way I'm still in Harsimus. This place feels different. "Where am I?" I rasp, my throat achingly raw.

Cathasach smiles through crooked and slimy teeth. "Does it matter? You're with me."

My eyes sting. Cathasach laughs, his speech garbled. "Your tears won't spare you, my pet. I have much planned for us."

His arousal disgusts me. I can sense it. I can taste it, its vise tugging on my tattered and blood-stained clothes with lecherous hands.

"Little pixie," he coos. I don't have to see him to know he's stroking himself. His vile moans tell me more than I want to know.

My fingers dig into the moist earth, burrowing until they clench a few small pebbles.

"Do you want me?" Cathasach asks, his growls commanding me to answer. He laughs between grunts, his voice drawing closer. "Doesn't matter. I'll have you any way I want."

His transparent silhouette trails through the gate, his eyes blood red, and his smile lustful.

"*Dom a chosaint*," I grind out. *Protect me*.

Power burns its way from the center of my chest and into my hands. I fling the pebbles clutched in my grip. The small stones and crumbling soil connect with Cathasach as his translucent body solidifies. He roars, bounding back through the bars in a conduit of green smoke and slamming into his lurking hounds.

My crude bullets spray their fur and scald them with pink magic strong enough to tunnel through their thick and matted coats. Cathasach and his hounds are fast, but I caught them unprepared.

I lift handfuls of dirt and pitch them in rapid succession. There's no grace, my movements more akin to a toddler throwing a fit. Still, it's effective. With each toss, I inflict more damage, widening the holes eating through dense hides and bone. I don't stop, continuing to fling fistfuls of soil, pebbles, anything within my reach.

My attack causes a frenzy among the Cù-Sìth. Those lingering close by charge the hounds caught in my onslaught, guzzling down the escaping souls.

It's madness. Cathasach roars, drawing energy from the injured to seal his wounds and lock in the souls tearing through the damaged muscle. He doesn't care that his actions will kill off the afflicted hounds. He's greedy and selfish, wanting only to keep himself sated and regenerate the parts of his body damaged by my magic.

I back into a pocket of dirt in the corner, watching the hounds turn on each other and struggling to catch my breath. I'm terrified and hurt, and I'm alone. At best, I'm on borrowed time.

That doesn't mean I'm done fighting.

With a chorus of malicious howls, the hounds shoot upward in streams of white and green mist, clambering after the fleeing spirits. Only Cathasach briefly hangs back. His vicious gaze meets mine. In it, I see his pledge to punish me and make me scream.

It takes all my strength to lift my hand and extend my

middle finger.

He sees it and smiles. *Smiles*. No, he's not done with me yet.

It's only after Cathasach jets away to join the hunt that I allow my tears to escape. They fall in streams. I let them. Alone, I don't have to pretend to be brave. I can cower like I deserve to.

My self-pity doesn't last. I mean it when I say I'm not done fighting. I cover my mouth, coughing through my last choked sob only to coat my mouth with dirt. I spit out as much as I can. Every inch of me is filthy and caked with blood.

I drag my hands down my jeans, jumping when a little green hand pokes through the wall and offers me a handkerchief. The tiny green hand waves it when all I do is gape. It's a gremlin, and possibly the same one who stole my talisman at the club. I take a chance and lift it from his grasp.

"Thank you," I say.

He pokes his large and balding head through the wall, blinking at me with large eyes before pushing his skeletal body the remainder of the way. His small frame remains bare except for the little brown pants he's wearing. I wipe my face and wait for him to speak.

My lingering tears are enough to loosen some of the blood and dirt coating my face. I smear the handkerchief with all sorts of gross body fluids. Still, I don't need a mirror to know there's plenty more left.

Walter Sebastian struck me hard, not bothering to hold back because I'm a female or half his size. He wants me to die and made a damn good attempt.

"No," the little gremlin says. "He just wants his boy to live."

The little gremlin read my mind. It's a rare trait among their kind, but one they're known for.

"All this was about keeping Stevie alive?" I rest my head against the cavern wall and shake my head. "Sebastian betrayed us all for his son."

"Stevie is a good boy," the gremlin insists.

"I know he is. He's my friend," I reply. "That doesn't make him more deserving than anyone else. Look at how many died in his place."

The gremlin's sad, dark eyes glimmer. "My clan and I never wanted to hurt anyone."

Anger heats my cold cheeks. "Except that you did. You robbed the Fae at the club *and* the dragons who worked for Sebastian of their protection."

"No. We didn't, miss," he insists earnestly.

I gasp. "I saw you. You were there, grabbing as many talismans as you could. You ignored the screaming and the crying, and left, *fucking left,* when the hounds arrived to kill them—"

My words lodge in my throat as the shame wrinkling his features slumps his bony shoulders. "You're bound to serve Walter Sebastian, aren't you?" I say slowly.

It's illegal to enslave lesser Fae. The law was passed centuries ago.

The little gremlin glances around before speaking quietly. "The law was passed, yes, miss. But some of the higher classes—dragons, gargoyles, and fairies with royal blood—refuse to relinquish their hold." He swallows hard. "The few of us who are left cannot speak or rise against our masters. The magic that binds us is too strong, and we are not enough."

Given the tufts of gray hair sprouting from his thin arms, he must have been bound to Sebastian's family for centuries. And here I thought I couldn't hate the prick more.

I lean in and reach for the gremlin's little hands. He stares down, keeping his fingers clenched into fists as if unsure how to return the gesture. When he looks up at me, he seems close to tears.

"I can free you and anyone Sebastian has bound," I promise,

"but I need you to alert my friends and tell them where I am. Will you do that for me?"

"It's impossible," he whimpers. "I'm bound to him and must remain close."

I slowly withdraw my hands. "Sebastian is here?"

"Yes." The gremlin looks around again as if fearing he might be heard. "If Cathasach fails to take you alive, my master is to kill you and hand over your corpse."

I swallow, feeling sick. "I'm surprised Cathasach didn't already try."

"To take you?" the gremlin asks. "Oh, yes, miss. He tried while you slept."

My head jerks up. "What?"

"He sought you while you lay sleeping. Your magic protected you like a shield. Death couldn't approach you."

Okay. That's new. Too bad I haven't mastered that little skill awake.

I rub my head, sore from Sebastian pummeling me. "What's your name?" I ask when it's clear he's done speaking.

"Tobias."

I smile faintly. "I'm Olivia."

He nods. "I know. Everyone knows. You're the one who can save us."

"Not without help," I admit.

"But you're *Life*," Tobias insists.

My small smile fades. "Life alone isn't enough."

The ceiling above us trembles and dirt rains down. Tobias wrinkles his brow, focusing hard. Gremlins can see through earth. It's how they hunted in Fae for rabbits and rodents. Tobias is old, though, and appears to struggle. "The Alpha is hurt," he says. He squints. "A challenge was made and accepted."

"The Beta challenged Cathasach?"

"No. It's a younger hound eager to take his place." He blinks several times, straining to see. "They're all circling, watching, waiting. Another appears ready as well. If they harm Cathasach enough, the Beta will use it to his advantage and attack." He rubs his eyes, now red and swollen. "None of them will be enough to defeat Cathasach."

No. But they're enough to keep him occupied.

Tobias latches on to my thoughts and leaps away in fear, disappearing when I reach for him. I scramble to my feet and search my enclosure, calling to him. "Please, don't leave me, Tobias. I'm not going to hurt you."

He doesn't appear.

"Please, Tobias," I beg. "If you can't tell my friends my whereabouts, at least help me show them where I am."

Tobias reappears with an audible pop. "But Death will come."

I meet him with a hard stare. "I'm counting on it."

Tobias works fast, drawing the outline of Cathasach's lair into the dirt with a sharp rock. I was dragged all the way to Calvary Cemetery in Queens. We're far from Jersey, but not too far from Ryker's reach. At least, that's what I'm counting on.

I'm also hoping I'm not too far for Jane to hear me, too. She came to Bill's home when I was in trouble, except she knew where I was, and her magic encompassed the dwelling, allowing her to sense the attack. That's not the case now. Ryker remains my speck of hope.

My eyes carefully scan each section Tobias draws, focusing on the entries leading into the lair and what resembles an open arena. Every pathway continues to the arena if staying toward the right on the way in; and leads out if keeping left. One wrong turn and you can spend a lifetime down here.

The area where I'm being held leads directly to the arena. There are no other passages or dead ends in this section. Good. I won't get lost. Bad because there's nowhere to hide. I pause when it occurs to me it shouldn't matter. I'm done hiding.

I rub my hands and bounce in place, trying to shake off my excess energy before returning my full attention to the drawing. The way in seems simple enough. I ingrain the outline into my memory, allowing my emotions to take over as I do so.

My thoughts shift to Ryker, investing fully in him and our time together. I focus on the way my hands always disappeared within his grasp, how his body tightened when we held each other, and how his ice-blue gaze softened when I stirred his "almost" smiles. I take every moment of him in, allowing the last to linger and claim me.

His hands branded me as his, and his luscious mouth hovered over mine, ready to taste. The image fills my mind, ignoring the chamber's raw temperature and warming my body. An impish smile spreads along my face as I wonder how it would feel to tug on that bottom lip with my teeth. *Come here, and I'll kiss more than just your lips, big boy.*

Tobias glances up from his work, looking hopeful. I clear my throat, but not my blush. "Not you, Tobias."

"Oh," he says, sounding disappointed.

"How long has Cathasach been controlling Sebastian?" I ask. I'm not just trying to distract him from my wanton thoughts. I'm trying to gather more information.

Tobias resumes his work, his tone sad as he scratches the perimeter of the lair into the dirt. "Since he crossed into Earth's realm. Death was close when my mistress opened the portal."

"He allowed his *wife* to open the portal?" I ask.

"Her talisman had more power."

Sure, it did.

Tobias blinks back at me. He heard my thoughts, not that he mentions it. "Death arrived with us. The Alpha killed the mistress and the grand master. He was going for the boy when Mr. Sebastian struck a bargain."

"Sebastian was who brought Cathasach through from Fae?" It takes all I have not to scream when Tobias nods. "And three of his hounds following the bargain," he adds.

My pulse continues to throb, and my thoughts remain on Ryker. I'm hoping he's picking up this newfound knowledge and can use it to our advantage. "What was the bargain?" I ask.

Tobias circles his drawing, scrutinizing it closely but also appearing hesitant to answer.

"Tobias, you have to tell me. It's the only way I can help the Fae who remain, including your clan."

Tobias's voice quivers. He doesn't glance up from his work. "My master will feed me and my clan to the Cù-Sìth if I tell you."

"He'll do it anyway if it's what Cathasach wants. Look at what Sebastian did to his own dragons." Tobias lifts his chin.

"Please," I urge. "Tell me what he bargained."

"My master promised the Alpha unlimited souls in exchange for his life and that of his son's."

My mouth falls open as tears dribble down Tobias's long nose. "The club wasn't the first attack, was it?"

Tobias shakes his head. "The master has been sending us out for years. It started with elderly Fae living alone and wee ones left unattended. As the hounds grew in numbers, we trav- eled to small Fae villages in Europe and beyond."

Sebastian isn't a mere Fae. He's a hired killer. No wonder there are so many hounds. He's been feeding and allowing the Cù-Sìth to breed.

"Sebastian wasn't marked for death by Death, was he?"

294   CECY ROBSON

"No. The night we were sent to the club, the smoke was enchanted. It dulled your senses and made it easier to take your talismans." He paused. "All the talismans worn by the dragons save two were given to them by the master—"

Paws thunder above us, releasing more dirt from the ceiling. Tobias squints in the direction of the ceiling. "The Beta attacks." Despite the urgency, I cling to his last admission. "You said those talismans weren't fully equipped to protect the dragons," I remind him.

"No," Tobias replies. "They were strong enough to not arouse suspicion but weak enough for the hounds to sense and track them."

Which is why the dragons never stood a chance. My spine stiffens. Everything finally makes sense. Frankie gave me one of the fallen dragon's talismans. It's why I can't stay hidden and how Cathasach found me at Bill's.

"Do the talismans Sebastian gave the dragons interfere with magic?" I ask.

Tobias thinks about it. "No. But the collar young Stevie wears blocks fresh magic."

I pace, unable to keep still. My borrowed talisman might have led the Cù-Sìth to us, but it was Stevie's collar that brought down Jane's wards. Her magic at Bill's was new and fresh to the dwelling. Damn it. We were safer in Ryker's loft.

I push away my thick hair and swear. Sebastian made the hunt easier for Cathasach. Another thought occurs to me. Stevie's flame…that's why it took so long to manifest. The collar was suppressing the fresh magic within the young dragon.

My boy, Stevie, must be housing an inferno.

"Why did Sebastian want to dull Stevie's magic?"

"The boy has his mother's power." Tobias shrugs. "It's rumored he'll be the strongest dragon in history. Oh, and something about him harnessing the power to freeze as well as burn."

Stevie is a fire and ice dragon? If Cathasach found out, he'd eat Stevie whole...or use him as a weapon against the Fae.

I hurtle myself at the iron gates. I'm not strong, but neither is the compact soil the gate is fixed to. I fall to my knees, digging with my hands, grunting and cursing as I scoop dirt away.

Enough is enough. I'm out of here.

Something pops in the air, and the gate jars. Tobias stands on the other side, holding the chain and padlock in his hands. He drops both on the ground and opens the gate, allowing me through.

He sniffs, tears glistening his dark eyes. "I'm going to die for everything I told you," he says as a way of an explanation. "The master will know. He always knows."

Something hard strikes above us. A large boulder breaks through the ceiling and falls to our far left. "The Alpha lives," Tobias says. "Now the fight for the new Beta begins."

I look to the narrow passageway that leads to the arena and then back at Tobias. It's time. I only hope I won't stand alone.

My throat tightens. I don't want to cry. I want to be strong for me and the poor little gremlin who helped me. I clutch his shoulders. "Thank you, Tobias," I say quietly. "Look, chances are I may not make it—"

"No," he agrees. "You'll be ripped apart and devoured by the Alpha once he finishes filling you with his undead seed."

"I'm going to stop you right there, kid." I shake my head, not that it clears his shudder-inducing visuals. "As I was saying, I may not make it. But if I do, I swear you and your clan will have your freedom. Just stay alive, okay?"

Tobias isn't what one might call a motivational speaker in the making. "But, Miss, the Alpha's testes are the size of cantaloupes."

Two things: I'm never eating fruit again, *and* I'm getting the hell out of here.

I reach for the padlock and chain and wind the links around my hand.

Tobias clasps my wrist and digs in his heels when I start forward. "Wait. What are you doing?"

I set my jaw. "It's my turn to challenge Cathasach."

30

For all that I initially hurry forward, my steps slow the closer I draw to the arena. The clamor of snapping jaws and growls reverberate around the claustrophobic space, a barefaced reminder of what lies ahead. Regardless, I gather my courage and push forward, determined to smack evil across the face.

The path up to the arena is similar to a large hole, narrowing as I near its end. There's no light source to guide my way, and even with my heightened vision, it's difficult to see. I trip over protruding rocks more than once, banging my already bruised legs and rattling my chain.

The noise I make is thankfully no match for the increasing roars and whines of the battling Cù-Sìth. Those fighting want to win, and those watching are hungry for a chance to strike.

I crouch low, falling to a crawl when the hole narrows and inclines more drastically. I poke my head out at the top. "Ryker," I whisper. "I'm ready. I hope you are, too."

He doesn't answer, and I can't be sure he heard me. Maybe it's better. I'm truly not ready. Life is supposed to be a bitch. I'm not. I just want to live and for my kind to survive.

I finish scurrying out of the stupid hole and army crawl

along the ground. The entire Cù-Sìth pack is assembled, circling the fighting hounds restlessly just a few yards away. They're anxious for their brethren to die and claim their souls. The larger hounds push the smaller pups aside, eager to fill their bellies.

My fingers pass along the chain as I try to gauge the number of Cù-Sìth present. Although they're moving fast and it makes it hard to count, I guestimate there are at least a hundred, not the seventy or so Ryker believed. Stars above, they multiply quickly. The smaller, younger hounds make up at least a third of the pack.

They all need to go. It's only a matter of time before they wipe out the Fae.

I tighten my grip around the chain, wrestling with how best to strike as I scan the environment. What I originally interpreted as an arena is more like two acres of elevated space. The floor is mostly soil mixed with clay, and the walls are stone and etched with markings. I look closer, realizing I'm in a large burial chamber, possibly occult based on the symbols engraved into the walls.

Wonderful. So much for hallowed grounds.

Near the far corner where the exit lies, Cathasach feasts in his beast form. His mutilated body is regenerating slowly following his showdown. He isn't whole yet, and, Alpha or not, he's seriously wounded. This is my chance. There won't be another.

I rise and march forward, ready to kick ass. "Cathasach," I call.

No one so much as blinks my way. The pack is so enthralled by the fighting hounds and the promise of more food they don't notice Life coming right at them.

"Cathasach!" I call louder.

Again. Nada.

Seriously?

I pause, wondering if I can just sneak the hell out of here. I then realize that's part of the problem.

Ryker told me in order to challenge Cathasach and call him to me, I have to *want* him here. But I don't actually want him here. I don't want to fight him. I don't want to hurt or bleed. I don't want to die. What I want is to get out of this damn crypt and lock myself in a room with access to comfort food and Netflix.

Except food and Netflix wasn't what I yearned for all those years I cried for my family. They weren't what I needed when I watched my sweet Dahlia mauled. It didn't matter that Dahlia was kind or generous, or the friend I depended on when I found myself alone. The Cù-Sìth took what they wanted from her and every Fae with a family, with friends. The victims deserve better. They deserve vengeance.

"Then *fight*," Ryker whispers tightly.

I whip around, expecting him directly behind me. But only beetles scamper along the soil where he should stand. That doesn't stop the smile curving my lips. I can't see or sense, but he's here. Ryker *is* here.

Hope stirs my courage *and* my magic.

"*Gortaítear*," I chant. *Hurt*.

"*Fulaing*."   *Suffer*.

"*Sruthán!*" *Burn*!

My power shoots through my arm hard enough to rattle me. I hurtle the padlock into the air in a swirl of angry pink that grows in size and intensity. It lands in the middle of a cluster of hounds with a *thump*.

A hundred sets of drooling fangs and snarling jowls jerk my way and…nothing happens. My stomach drops down to my toes. I stumble backward.

"Oh, shit. Shit. *Shit!*"

The Cù-Sìth jet toward me, and I turn to run.

That's when the padlock detonates like an atomic bomb.

A pink mushroom cloud ripples through the air, its sheer wrath propelling me back into the hole I crawled from and partially burying me. It's the only thing that saves me. Cathasach's lair doesn't burn; it nuclearizes.

Raucous shrieks and tormented howls clamor along the perimeter. The walls split, and the ceiling collapses at multiple points. The earth quakes, showering me with chunks of dirt. I snake through the hole, digging my hands into the soil to pull myself forward and hanging tight to my chain.

I poke my head out, choking on the dirt-coated air. The hounds that hadn't busted open like flaming piñatas yelp and dash around frantically as my magic eats through their flesh. Souls puncture their limbs through any opening in the hounds they can find, tearing open bellies and exploding through ruptured faces and skulls, rushing to flee.

The quaking begins to subside, but not before a monumental portion of ceiling tumbles down and over an exit. Through the bedlam, clouds of dust, and the crushing noise, Cathasach appears in his human form. He kicks the wounded beasts from his path, his horrid red eyes flaring and fixed on me.

I don't swear often. I do now. "Bloody *fuck*."

"Bring her to me," Cathasach commands. "Bring her to me now!"

He isn't speaking to his hounds. A giant red-scaled dragon bounds my way, scraping his long talons through the debris-riddled ground and stomping over the injured. Sebastian.

My magic won't work against him. It doesn't matter. My body will rot in this crypt before I let him take me. I twirl, spinning my chain and pirouetting across the ground, slowly at first, then faster. I use every bit of momentum, bringing my weapon down on Sebastian's snout with a primal scream.

My kick-ass and graceful attack must have looked really cool from afar. Except my war cry morphs into a whimper when the impact jolts through me and almost breaks my arms.

Sebastian roars, his gold fire singeing the wall above my head. I prance out of the way, over the debris, around the injured hounds, and right into Cathasach's path.

In a crash of furious lightning, Ryker arrives, his scythe high in the air. He slices at Cathasach and severs his newly generated arm and part of his chest. Blood spills, and so do souls.

"Olivia, *run!*"

Ryker's request gives me pause. "I thought I was supposed to fight him?"

I also thought I killed more hounds than I did. An army of Cù-Sìth barrels over the arena of broken ceiling and fragmented stone, charging us. Cathasach retreats in a funnel of green smoke, solidifying just out of reach. He smiles, and in a show of force, snatches two fleeing souls by their throats and feasts.

"Ah, Ryker," I begin.

Ryker knows I'm begging him to get us out of here. "No," he rumbles through clenched teeth. "Tonight, he dies by my hands."

Like a seasoned warrior, Ryker swings his scythe from side to side, majestically and precisely until his movements transform into a blur.

Cathasach answers the challenge with a snarl, his growing number of hounds gathering around him. He's not alone. He's not afraid.

And neither is Ryker.

The bitter scent of primeval magic overwhelms what remains of the arena. Ryker races forward, every stride bulging his muscles against his flexible armor and every movement vowing to mutilate. He's keen on murder. This is the moment he trained for. He'll kill anything in his path.

So will the Ancients who materialize.

Fionn mac Cumhaill, the giant, busts his way in, turning the large chunk of ceiling blocking the exit to rubble with his meaty fists. He's followed by Gwragedd Annwn, the water fairy; Redcap, the goblin; Oberon, the High King; and one very pissed-off Hydra swooping through the air on the back of a gargoyle.

Ryker attacks, cleaving through hounds like a butcher. Jane's venomous serpents spit their poison in a deadly staccato akin to gunfire. The Ancients are all magic. They release the gamut of their power onto the Cù-Sìth, wielding the punishment owed to our people. The power of good meets evil head-on, releasing in a kaleidoscope of sparks.

Command and might overwhelm me, and magic slaps at my skin. The air heats, and souls spout like a fountain as hounds mourn their loss and grieve in pain.

Meanwhile, I'm standing with my mouth open, holding a rusty old chain, and covered in dirt.

Screw this.

My weapon lacks the flare and exactitude of my whip. That doesn't stop me from slamming it onto the ruins at my feet. "*Dhíoghail!*" *Avenge*.

Glowing rays of fuchsia light zigzag across the earth, singeing the advancing hounds and burning their paws. I swing my chain, bright with light, and strike those who break through to attack.

My blows are hard. I feel each one down to my bones, and it hurts—*really hurts*. Yet I keep going. It's not until I bring my chain down and through a death hound's spine that pain explodes into my shoulders, and I drop my only weapon.

My hands throb and openly bleed. I can barely bend my swelling fingers. I try to retrieve my chain. It slips from my grasp. I grunt, frustrated, and try again. Once more, I can't secure my grip. I watch it fall onto the dirt. I stagger, unsure how I'll continue and on the verge of collapsing.

Wretched screaming has me reeling. A horrid gash has cracked open Gwragedd Annwn's skull. Blood pours down her face, plastering her long silver hair against her skin and partially blinding her. She presses her palms against the large open wound across her stomach. The first Ancient is down. I can see part of her bowel bulging through her fingers.

I run to where a pack of hounds have her cornered. Redcap, the goblin, barrels toward her from the opposite direction only to be stormed by a separate pack.

Gwragedd Annwn curses as the pack pounces like wolves on a lamb. She wails, her magic firing. She fights until her last breath, crushing the head of a hound with her bare hands before her soul is hacked from her body.

"*No!*"

I bound through the wreckage and leap onto the hound digging his fangs into her spirit. Bill and Jane sweep in, forcing the others back. Jane's serpents elongate, wrapping around the hounds and tossing them away. Bill tackles a large male attempting to steal Gwragedd Annwn's soul from the hound I'm fighting.

My bloody hands grip the hound's jowls when he tries to bite me. His snout enkindles, and his crumbling jaw snaps beneath my power. I manage to free Gwragedd Annwn's spirit. She falls away. Without thinking, I dive on top of her, gripping her waist and dragging her back to what remains of her body. She's light. I feel her like a warm breeze that passes through just enough to tell the birds it's spring and lulls the rabbits awake.

Live, I plead. *Please don't die, too.*

I swallow the sour taste in my mouth as I stare at the pieces of Gwragedd Annwn that lie before me. It's too late. I'm too late.

Gwragedd Annwn slips from my hold, gaping from me to the

body she once so regally held. Her expression splinters, and she lifts her hands, so translucent her sad eyes see through them and to what remains of her corpse.

Around me, souls propel from the dying hounds. I stagger away, knowing who'll come. "Gwragedd Annwn, you have to go," I stammer. "You have to go now!"

Her heartbroken expression meets mine briefly before she takes to the air. Shafts of green, white, and black smoke surround me, Jane, and Bill, snagging our attention as several hounds stream after Gwragedd Annwn.

My stomach clenches into knots. If another hound consumes her soul, he will raid and steal Gwragedd Annwn's power. I know as much, and so does Cathasach.

He abandons his fight with Ryker, shooting after the water fairy's spirit. Ryker raises his scythe over his head, and with another snap of azure light, he vanishes. Tears sting my eyes. He's going after Gwragedd Annwn to carry her into the Afterlife before the Cù-Sìth can claim her. Except, he's only one being, and no one else can help him.

I stumble forward, seeking something I can use as a weapon, when a giant wing slams into my side. I fly into the crumbling wall, bouncing off my back and crashing onto the wreckage below. Someone screams my name. Oberon hollers. Bill and Fionn roar. Everything hurts, and nothing makes sense. All that remains is my will, and that will wants to survive.

I force myself onto my knees. I barely lift my hands when something cuffs me in the head. I fall back with my leg partially bent and twist my ankle. A reptilian foot covered in red scales comes down on my chest, robbing me of my breath and pinning me down.

My body writhes in misery and from lack of breath. It does it independently, trying to keep me going when my mind simply can't anymore. Sebastian has me, and there's not a thing I can do about it.

Torment consumes every inch of me, yet it doesn't compare to the agony I feel when talons puncture my throat. My ribs crack, and my sternum begins to split apart. I'm certain death will claim me until the weight abruptly lifts in a flash of blue fire.

Sebastian roars, suffering. I cough out blood with my first breath and the next few that follow, unable to draw sufficient oxygen. The pain raking through me leaves me motionless and barely conscious. At first, I don't notice a severed dragon's foot lying beside me. It's only when my head lolls to the side and I blink away the fog claiming my vision that I catch sight of the silver-scaled dragon who saved me.

The silver dragon lifts Sebastian by the throat with his fangs and hurtles him to the ground, using his talons to pierce through Sebastian's scales. Frankie has arrived. He knows what Sebastian did, and now he'll make Sebastian pay.

My body struggles to heal me. It's just not fast enough. I roll to my side, trying to clear my throat of the thick, pooling blood. I cough and sputter and attempt to edge away from the dragons. The stabbing ache tightening my chest and throat make it hard to focus. I'm disoriented and unsure where I'm headed. The only thing I know is that I can't lie here.

I inch away, unable to move fast. Chaos swells, everyone fighting is vicious and angry, their fury pelting me as hard as the pieces of ceiling that continue to fall. I barely notice the Cù-Sìth, who charges, and I only manage to cover my head.

Heat crests like a tsunami, scorching my skin. An orange dragon lands in a deep crouch in front of me, spilling fire as red as blood. The potent flame shoves back the hounds and forces them to disperse into their misty forms. The orange dragon shields Frankie and me, keeping the hounds away. It's not until he kicks back my whip with his hind legs that I realize who he is.

"Stevie," I choke.

I reach for the familiar feel of my weapon. Stevie swirls his large tail, motioning ahead with his snout. Ryker is back. He failed in his mission, and now he's in trouble.

Blood pools around Ryker where he lays gutted and motionless. I gasp. Cathasach reached Gwragedd Annwn first. The water fairy's magic morphed Cathasach's body to twice its size, stretching his muscles against his dense green fur and making him appear unstoppable.

Cathasach hovers over Ryker, ignoring Ryker as he snatches fleeting spirits to feed his mutated body. Dugan and Phillip stand unmoving a few feet away, unable to draw strength from Ryker in his weakened state. Their vacant eyes stare blankly ahead, incognizant to the escalating chaos. Cathasach will seize them next. First, he'll finish off their leader and source of power. I wrench myself to my feet, anger spurring me. Cathasach doesn't see me coming, nor will he likely care. He dives on Ryker and drives his massive claws into his chest. Ryker roars, his back bowing. His armor can't protect him against Cathasach. He's seconds from being cleaved in half.

I stumble forward into a full-out sprint. The Grim Reaper is *not* dying on my watch.

I spin my whip over my head and strike the tip forward, snapping it around Cathasach's throat. Like the rising sun, the earth feels the full mass of my power.

"*Bás!*" Die.

Cathasach reels, jerking his immense body and howling. My feet leave the ground. I clash into a pile of rubble, my knee snapping on impact. Still, I hold tight to my whip, using my rage to surge my magic.

Pink light flares against my scrunching face, encompassing

the whole of the arena. With a scream, I yank the whip taut around Cathasach's throat when he assumes his human form. He rises, his fingers curling over the leather searing through his windpipe.

Every cell in my body burns as I force years of pain, grief, and fury through the braided leather. He fights me. Even as the whip cuts his throat in half, Cathasach fights me.

Die. Just, die!

Ryker, wounded and bleeding, launches himself from the debris. With a crack of his wrist, his scythe appears. He grips it in two hands and drives the point deep into Cathasach's chest.

Cathasach's head soars from his shoulders, and his body buckles. The Alpha. The murderer. The hunter of Fae is dead.

With a deafening wail, the imprisoned souls escape Cathasach's burning body. The Cù-Sìth, so deadly and evil, are mortal once more.

I push up on my battered arms, anticipating an onslaught from the remaining hounds. Instead of killing us for making them whole, they rush toward the exit in a heap, trampling over themselves.

The hounds aren't completely mindless like Ryker suspected. They know if they buy themselves time, their mystical figures will resume, and a new Alpha will rise.

Ryker holds onto his side, panting. Bill and the Ancients tear after the retreating hounds, the giant in the lead, swinging a spiked club. Frankie and Stevie also give chase, burning the death hounds that don't quite reach the exit. Even Sebastian, who lays battered and beaten along the remains of the arena, releases his fire onto the Cù-Sìth. As wicked and conniving as he is, he recognizes the opportunity in Cathasach's death.

Ryker staggers forward, falling to his knees beside me. His blue gaze melts as he takes me in. "You're hurt," he says.

I swallow more blood, my body throbbing like one giant

wound. Between huge gulps of air, I manage to speak. "That's one way to put it."

He reaches for my hand, his hold gentle. "*Beag tuar ceatha,* you were brave, and you were strong. But time is not our ally. Will you join me and finish the hunt?"

I nod, although my tears betray my exhaustion and fear. The Cù-Sìth must die. One pregnant bitch that escapes is all it will take to start this nightmare again.

Blood trickles from Ryker's wounds. My body trembles. I can't be sure what's damaged, bleeding, or broken. I'm not sure I can even walk. The two of us...we're nothing more than prey now. Still, I grip his hand and permit him to pull me against him.

We vanish into darkness. The cold night air pummels me without warning, yet it's the sight before me that leaves me breathless.

Fae, hundreds of them, from trolls to nymphs to sprites and giants, race and fly across the grounds, wielding swords, daggers, and most of all, magic.

The Fae surround the hounds attempting to double back. Dahlia's mother and sister take down a behemoth male. Their nails lengthen to shimmering claws that slice into skin and tear the hound apart.

Scores of souls release, blurring the air. I can barely stand, barely breathe. My kind's valor enlivens me, yet it can't give me the strength I need to fight. But Oberon, the High King can.

Scratches mar Oberon's regal armor, and blood stains his white beard. He's hurt, not that it stops him. This is a Fae who refuses to cower. He points his sword at me and hollers, chanting in ancient Irish.

Power dances around Oberon's hunched frame as waves of energy engulf me. My hands quiver, and I swallow down a shriek. Oberon's magic is strong, except my injuries are too serious to heal completely. My body struggles to knit my wounds and realign my bones. I'm better, but just enough to continue our fight.

So is Ryker.

We leave each other's arms and rush ahead, throwing ourselves at the remaining hounds.

The Cù-Sìth remain lethal, except this time, they're the ones outnumbered, and they won't escape our wrath. I lash out with my whip, searing their flesh and bringing them down. The Fae see me and gather around me, helping me fight, and helping us win.

The night air turns from black to misty white as the freed souls swarm us like a cresting ocean. They don't cry out with pain. They yell in triumph. They glide through my hair, ribbon around my waist, and urge me onward, each pass a sweet touch I sense in my heart.

My whip strikes over and over. I'm briefly aware I'm beating a dead hound when someone clasps my shoulder. My body is so worn, the contact forces me to my knees.

I curl inward, sobbing over the matted creature at my feet. It's not that he's dead. It's knowing no more will die because of him.

Ryker's voice is a mere whisper against my cheek. "Vanessa," he says. "It's time."

I glance up, surprised not to find him against me. The case that houses Vanessa lies open on the ground, but "she" is gone.

Ryker helps me to my feet. He won't look at me. He won't speak to me. He simply walks away.

Bill and Jane trudge to my side. Jane has resumed her human glamour. Dead snakes dangle beneath the hem of her long black dress, indicative of how hard she fought and how tired she feels. Bill retains his Fae form, as do Frankie, Stevie, and the Ancients who flank us.

Poor Stevie. I don't see Sebastian. What I do see is thick black tears running down the length of his sons' broad snout. Stevie knows what his father did, and nothing can spare him from that knowledge.

Bill places his arm around me. "Come, Livvie," he manages through his long fangs.

He holds onto me as I limp. "I'm sorry, Bill," I say.

His frown would send any human running. "For what?"

I sniff. "For ever doubting you."

He smiles sadly. "Livvie, we live in a time where we all have cause to doubt. Take comfort in knowing I'll always stand by you."

I squeeze his hand, trying not to cry.

Bill and the Ancients lead me forward, far from the last hound I killed and toward the parking lot. I keep my head down, everything I feel coming down on me at once.

My body is so raw and aching I can barely move. I take a harsh breath as the path inclines, doubting I'll manage another step. Jane clasps my wrist, keeping me in place.

"Livvie," she croaks. "See what you've done. See what you are."

I turn slowly. All I can do is stare. Around me is a field of the living and the dead. Families and friends of those taken long ago cry as their beloved children, spouses, and lovers gather around them. Their grief is tangible, but it doesn't compare to their joy.

Peace. The dead finally have their peace.

My eyes well, and I break down. I don't notice the throng of souls part, allowing a small group through until Bill helps me to my feet.

"Livvie," Bill says, his voice splintering.

My mother, father, and sisters step forward, crumbling what remains of my resolve.

I cover my mouth when they stop mere feet in front of me.

Tears glisten against their translucent images. They can't touch me or feel me, but I sense their love surging through me.

"Hi, Mama," I stammer.

My sisters, Niamh, Sinead, and Alanna, all as lovely as I remember, smile through their tears. My father, so handsome and tall swipes at his face, trying to stay strong for my mother, who openly weeps when she tries to play with my hair.

It's a moment I want to cling to and never let go. But it doesn't last.

Ryker stalks forward, his presence announcing we're all out of time. With so many souls in our midst, it wouldn't take long for more Death to appear.

Ryker meets my gaze with ice-blue eyes that will never capture the character of the man behind them. "I shall keep my promise," his throaty voice rumbles. "Just as I expect you to keep yours."

With a whip-like snap, he ignites in a blaze of azure, the lucid bodies of every Fae streaming behind him and into the breaking dawn.

I fall to my knees, joining those who'll always mourn the ones they love.

31

It takes me a week and a half to return to work. My physical injuries healed enough for me to function, but the emotional trauma? That's worth at least two Oprah specials and a visit with Anderson Cooper. I cried, a lot, for friends and family now long gone. Mostly, though, I tried to find peace, knowing those I love found theirs.

The biggest hurdle I struggle with is coming to terms with the direction my life has taken. I'm not supposed to be a hero. Heroes aren't scrawny. They have nice, normal hair and don't speak with Jersey accents. They wield weapons without hurting friends, killing pigeons, or falling into stupid holes. I'm no savior. I'm a paralegal and PA, damn it. My typing and organization skills won't save anyone's ass.

So, while I recovered, I ate a carton of prepackaged cakes Dahlia chastised Jane for ordering, listened to a ridiculous amount of bad '80s music, and had deep, meaningful conversations with telemarketers who made the mistake of calling my home. That lady from the credit card company was especially nice, even when she passed on my offer to take her to lunch.

Finally, I called Bill and told him I was ready to come back to work.

The elevators to the 30th floor of Macgregor and Santonelli part. I step onto the polished marble floors with my coffee carrier, purse, and a small vase of flowers. I didn't think anyone would miss me and am surprised by all the polite nods and soft-spoken "welcome backs."

I reach Ryker's office on my way to my cubicle. We haven't spoken, and while I hoped for and expected his presence at night to comfort me, he never appeared. Our last interaction occurred when he escorted my family into the Afterlife. What do you say to someone who does that for you, the same someone who begs you to kill him?

My instincts tell me to play the stereotypical "tough guy," and pretend that nothing so astronomical like taking on an army of death hounds and winning had gone down. In the end, I'm too much the stereotypical girl, ready to talk the incident to death while waving my arms dramatically and accusing him of not listening.

I pause by his door. Death's door. No, I don't miss the irony.

It's as if nothing changed. His broad shoulders hunch forward as he mulls over the legal documents spread along his desk. A silver dress shirt, one flex shy of tearing, covers his stone round muscles. Even with his head lowered, I know that dimple awaits. It's so endearing. Why does it have to be so endearing?

I knock with the point of my pink kitten heels. Ryker grips his pen tightly and slowly glances up. He knew it was me.

"Hi," I say softly.

He nods. "Olivia."

His blue eyes sizzle despite the ice chipping away at his demeanor. Will anyone truly ever know this man?

"You may come in," he adds when I remain in the doorway.

I kick the door shut with my foot and hurry in before I

change my mind. My feet slow the closer I draw. But I can't go back now.

I place the items across his desk and remove a large cup of coffee from the carrying case. "I brought you coffee and a bagel." I fumble through my mammoth purse, pull out a paper bag, and reach in. "I know you like the jalapeño ones with cheddar cheese."

I choke on my last word. Big, thick tears spill out of me. Goodness. I really am that stereotypical girl.

A strong hand gently clasps my wrist. Ryker leads me around the side of his desk to stand before him.

We wait in silence, with nothing between us but our breaths. His fingers envelop my small bones, reminding me how powerful he is, and how delicate I am in comparison.

I watch his fingers slide across my skin to grasp my hand, his thumb teasing my palm in small circles as he releases a surge of his power. As easily as it began, my sorrow eases. It's only then that I dare meet his addicting gaze.

Ryker's intensity softens, leaving only a deep compassion the finest poets would fail to compile into words.

"I'm sorry," I say, tears moistening my cheeks. "I know what I promised, but I can't." I let out a breath. "And I won't. You're my friend and…stuff."

Stars in heaven, kill me.

A flicker of sadness reflects in Ryker's face as he speaks. "When I came into this realm, I was a different man, foolish and bitter. When I asked you to help me find my peace, I only knew emptiness and wrath." He works his jaw. "Since knowing you, I've started to see things in ways I've never dreamed possible." His hand gives me a squeeze. "I've changed, Olivia. I don't dare admit how much, but I have. You…you've given me purpose."

I nod, understanding where he's coming from. "I know exactly how you feel."

Ryker tilts his chin. "Do you?"

I blow out a breath. "Of course. I didn't sign up for all this crazy, either. Now that we're a part of it, maybe we can do more good." I wipe a trailing tear with my free hand. "I'm going to need some serious training. My fighting skills are pathetic at best, and my magic is untamed even during the best of times." I make a face. "There's so much I don't know. With time, maybe I can learn."

"I agree," he says. "And I'll help. But that's not what I mean."

Before I can ask, he lifts my chin with his fingertip. His touch slides along my jawline, sending streams of heat and electricity through my skin, the sensation increasing as his hand cups the base of my skull.

Ryker leans in, his lips meeting mine, soft like silk for a man so hard. His tongue sweeps in for a taste, prodding gently until I allow him in.

My lips part, searching him out. But then my tongue touches his, and I lose my ever-loving mind. The kiss, *our* kiss, that began so light and innocent turns hard and needy.

Ryker's mouth is a dark, bewitching realm that begs my tongue to explore. I regale in his deadly allure. My arms hook around his neck. His hands drag along my back. Heat. Need. Want. This is what it means to lust and desire.

Ryker swears, leaving my mouth. He trails his lips over my throat and tangles his fingers through my hair. My heart throbs against his. My body demands more. I skim my hands down, digging my nails into his—

"Holy *shit*!"

Marco's voice slaps the horniness right out of me. He stands in the doorway with Stevie, clutching files as if they can shield them from the level of whoredom overtaking the room. If that's not humiliating enough, half the staff is gaping at us through the fishbowl office.

I jump out of Ryker's arms, a hell of an accomplishment considering how hard he held me, and, good *God*, were my hands gripping his ass?

"Hello, sir." Ryker clears his throat. "Is there something I may assist you with?"

Is this the best Mr. Harvard Grad can do? I grab the drink carrier, my purse, and the flowers, using all three to mask my severe case of nipple protrudicus.

Ryker calls to me. "Olivia, wait."

I hold out a hand when he reaches for me. "Oh, no. No, no, no, no. So not going there. Sorry about that."

I run out of the office, past the stunned group of attorneys and PAs. Honestly, don't they have murderers to defend?

Stevie chases me, speaking not so softly. "Liv. You like, totally sucked face with Death!"

My face heats. He's so right. What was I thinking? I practi- cally had sex with him across his desk. Forget that I threw my hard work and reputation out the window—I'm Life, and I made out with the Grim *freaking* Reaper!

I reach my desk and dump everything rather ungraciously, spilling some coffee.

"How did he taste?" Jane croaks.

My head slowly swivels in her direction. How did she... We're on the other side of the office.

Jane points to her computer. "Olivia Tongued Ryker" is the subject line on the mass office email.

Nice.

For lack of something better, I sort through the stack of memos and mail overtaking my space. No one lifted a finger to help Marco over the last week. He was likely a total monster to deal with. But as I turn back to the flowers I purchased, I remember why.

I make quick work of organizing the hot mess before me,

giving my racing pulse time to slow. I stack all the documents Marco needs to sign into one pile. With every letter I skim through, I think of Ryker. My better judgment warns that this isn't a man I should allow in my bed.

I slow my movements. It's a shame I've already allowed him into my heart.

Ryker watched out for me, protecting me with his prowess and driving me with his fortitude. Even when I bled, even when I could no longer rise, he didn't fail me or allow me to fail myself.

But he's Death.

"Death is the start of a new life."

I whirl around to find Tobias, the little gremlin who helped me escape. The glamour covering him is that of a little old man with glasses perched on the tip of his pointy nose. He drops several envelopes onto my desk and shuffles along, pushing a small wire cart.

I look to Jane. The small twinkle in her black beady gaze says it all. Death is only the beginning.

"I can't, Jane," I reply.

My little druid priestess simply turns away, lifting her two crooked fingers over her keyboard to resume her typing.

Marco storms by, straight into his office, and slams the door shut. That's my cue.

I tuck the documents that require his signature beneath my arm and reach for the flowers and coffee.

I don't bother knocking. Instead, I walk into Marco's office and place the flowers beside the beautiful photo of him and his wife.

"What the hell is this?" he mutters.

"It's Marion's birthday," I say. "But you already know that."

Marco takes the coffee. He doesn't bother taking a sip. I lay out all the documents, explaining each in detail.

The moment I'm done, I charge his iPad and scroll through his unanswered messages. "Mrs. Shuster caught Mr. Shuster taking a bath with the new maid. She sprayed tub cleaner in his eyes and set his clothes on fire. Mr. Shuster says that he's had it with the psycho and is in love with the maid." I pause. "Never mind, that was Wednesday. Friday, the maid dumped his sorry ass. Now he wants said psycho back." I hurry along, focusing on the calls from the Hudson County Prosecutor's Office and six calls from Jersey City's mayor. A pal of the mayor is in a bit of a mess.

I finish quickly, taking notes of what Marco needs to have done first, who he wants to call back, and who he wants to avoid. Mr. Shuster tops the "avoid" list. I email my notes from his iPad to my computer. I'm ready to start my day, just as soon as I remove the elephant in the room.

My fingers skim over the front of Marco's desk. "About what you saw back there, between me and Mr. Scott." Okay. Why am I calling Ryker Mr. Scott? "I want you to know that nothing that happens or doesn't happen will affect my work. I apologize for my, ah, indiscretions. It won't happen again. I—"

"Do what makes you happy, Olivia," Marco tells me. "Eat good food. Enjoy a decent glass of wine. Talk for hours with someone who can't get enough of your voice and walk with him along the beach, even when you're tired."

Marco sits quietly, his stout body angled in the direction of his wedding photo. "Life's too short," he says, his heartbreak reflecting in the glass. "Just be happy."

I sniff and wipe my eyes. Marco doesn't need my pity. He needs my help and care. Just as he had from the first moment I walked into his office and he yelled at me to get out.

"You're due in court at ten thirty for the San Tomasso hearing," I say. "I'll send for your suits at the cleaners."

I return to my desk, jumping when Stevie drops several

packs of copy paper beside me. "Oops. Sorry, Olivia. I didn't mean to scare you," he says. "I just figured you'd need this stuff now that you're back."

Like the little gremlin, Bill took Stevie under the protection of his powerful wings. Sebastian was sentenced to a life of imprisonment between realms. Until a new guardian can be appointed, Stevie will live with Bill.

I smile, taking in my little fire and ice dragon. "Thank you, Stevie." I don't mean for the paper. I mean for his kindness. I "outed" his father to the Fae community, and he still helped me when I needed it most. Despite his age, Stevie is more courageous than Fae twice his lifetime.

Stevie leans against my gray cubicle, keeping his head low. "It was wrong. What my dad did. I know he was trying to protect me and all, but it was stupid." He shrugs. "I wouldn't have done it. You have to sacrifice for the greater good, you know, Livvie?"

Black eyeliner smears the edges of his soft baby browns, and tiny ruptured blood vessels crawl along the scleras. He's cried a lot and probably hasn't slept well in a long time. "Your father was desperate, Stevie. He didn't want to lose the only family he had left." I think back to the night I lost Dahlia. "Who knows? Maybe I would've have taken the same path."

Stevie lifts his head, smiling softly. "No, you wouldn't, Liv."

He taps the edge of the cubicle, snagging Jane's attention. "Your filing's finally done," he tells her. "You need anything else?"

Jane glances up and blinks her beady eyes. "That sounds good, Jane. I'll pick some up at lunch. Did ya know they have a new raspberry flavor?"

Jane is so excited she shows three of her teeth.

"Package for Olivia Finn."

A postal carrier in a brown uniform jogs toward me when one of the law clerks points in my direction. I lift my hand and

wave. The box he carries is big. Opposing counsel must have
sent everything they have on—

The carrier drops the box as he pulls out a gun. I dive
beneath my desk.

Swip. Swip. Swip.

He fires in quick succession. My computer screen shatters.
Screams blast from down the hall followed by the trampling
sound of feet hauling serious ass.

A shotgun blasts as I reach for the whip in my purse. As my
fingers grip the hilt, my mind screeches to a halt. This isn't a
Reaper. This is a human who can easily kill me. I whirl around,
searching for something to use.

"Jane. Get your wand!"

"Wha?" she crows.

She can't hear me over the sound of a cocking shotgun and
another heart-rendering blast. Rapid fire sprays across the floor.
There's a pause and a clip being loaded.

I cower behind my cubicle. I'm going to die. This time, I mean
it.

Marco's portly body flies over my desk and *kerplunks* beside
me. He rustles through his pockets and loads two more bullets
into his shotgun, rising into a crouch à la Rambo as he fires
another round.

The delivery guy hollers. At least, I hope it's him.

Marco swoops back down, pumping his fist and his rifle. "Got
'em!"

"M-M-Marco?" I stammer.

He frowns at me with those crazy caterpillar eyebrows. "I'm a
criminal defense attorney," he barks. "Do you think this is the
first time a client's tried to kill me!"

Marco's expression is startling and bright with anticipation.
With the skill of someone very, *very* familiar with guns, he digs
into his pocket for two more bullets. My stars, I've never seen

him so alive. I cover my ears just as Jane's magic charges the air.

Papers fly in all directions only to freeze. Marco stops in the middle of rising, one leg bent only slightly.

Jane shuffles to me. "Come," she rasps. She points a crooked finger down the hall. "Know."

I rise on wobbly legs and step around the cubicle. Ryker has the shooter pinned to the floor. The shooter gapes at Ryker, begging Ryker to spare him.

A ribbon of azure mist entwines Ryker's fist. He strikes, punching through the chest to grip his victim's heart. The shooter's breath withdraws. His eyes cave inward, and his body shrivels into a disintegrating mass of muscle and bone.

Whether through Ryker or Jane, this time, I see something more.

Images of the shooter's life flash before me. He was an abused child, a loner, someone who learned to kill because he wasn't good at anything else. I watch him slash the throat of a shrieking woman and beat a man's head in with a bat. It's all I can stomach.

I ram my eyes shut and cover my ears, trying to spare myself from the horror this man committed throughout his life.

Ryker doesn't just eat souls. He endures the darkest aspects of those he consumes. It's not enough to hurt as he does. He gets a front and center view of every last sin.

My hands fall away as Ryker stumbles into a standing position. His murderous gaze shifts my way before he storms toward his office. I follow without hesitation, rushing past everything frozen by Jane's enchantment.

Ryker leans over his desk, breathing hard. I shut the door and draw the shades carefully, trying not to cause a stir. Ryker's nerves are already on edge. How can they not be? I couldn't find the strength to bear through those flashbacks. I closed my eyes and covered my ears because I can. Ryker doesn't have that option. For him, there's no escape.

Even knowing what awaited, Ryker faced his victim's demons to spare me.

I trail my hand along his spine and curl it at his shoulder. He turns his head, revealing the single tear that cuts a line down his face. As I watch, his black eyes dissolve into the ice blue that never fails to capture me. It's all I can do not to join him in his sorrow.

I carry the power to fight Death, yet nothing in my arsenal can lessen the brutality of those memories. I swallow the lump hardening in my throat. "Ryker..."

"Death knows who you are now, and where to find you," he says, speaking quickly through his ragged breathing. "They will continue to hunt you, using humans and Reapers alike. I swear, I will protect you—"

I wrap my arms around his neck and kiss his cheek. "Shhh."

"Olivia..."

I shake my head, brushing my face against his. "Not now," I whisper.

Loss of life brings pain and misery beyond repair. Except those who live aren't the only ones who suffer. I feel it in the Reaper that waits beneath my touch.

I adjust my arms and tighten my embrace over the being capable of causing incomprehensible torment.

What can I say? Even Death needs love.

Read on for an excerpt from Cecy's Urban Fantasy Series,
WEIRD GIRLS

Gone Hunting

A Weird Girls Novel

Cecy Robson

Dear Reader,

The night I was born, a bat swept down in front of my father as he ran along a cobblestone road. My father ignored the bat in his haste to reach the Central American hospital where my mother labored with me. The bat disappeared into the shadows. In its place emerged a man, his dark skin bare, his voice ominous, his imposing form blocking my father's path. "Be wary of this one," he warned in Spanish.

"She's not like the others."

Okay, I'll confess. This didn't happen. But it sounds way cooler than simply admitting my father used to kiss me goodnight wearing vampire fangs and that he was the first person to trigger my overactive imagination.

I've always loved telling stories and getting a laugh. I've also enjoyed hearing stories, especially of the paranormal variety. Being of Latin descent, I heard many tales of spirits who haunt the night, of death lurking in the darkness waiting to claim her victims, and of circumstances that could only be explained by magic and creatures not of this earth.

The stories frightened me. I often slept clutching a crucifix, while my plastic glow-in-the-dark Virgin Mary stood guard on my nightstand. And, still, I begged for more.

Sometimes the beasties of the night bumped too hard and I swear I could see ghosts floating above me. I trekked on, despite my fear, surviving each night with my plastic protector looking on.

On May 1, 2009, I decided to write a story about four unique women, who must trek through their own darkness where super-nasties bump hard and bite harder. *The Weird Girls* series is the journey of Celia, Taran, Shayna, and Emme Wird, sisters who obtained their powers as a result of a backfired curse placed upon their Latina mother for marrying outside her race. Their story begins when the supernatural community of Lake Tahoe becomes aware of who they are and what they can do.

"Weird" isn't welcomed among humans, nor is it embraced by those who hunt with fangs and claws, who cast magic in lethal blows, and who feast on others to survive. I wanted to show that "weird" could be strong, brave, funny, and beautiful.

My "weird" girls will often face great terror, just like my seven-year-old frightened self, except without a glow-in-the-dark icon to keep them safe. Despite their fears, they fight like their lives depend on it, with only each other to rely on.

Sometimes, the darkness will devour the sisters. And, some-times, good won't succeed in kicking evil's ass. But just like glow-light Mary, there is hope. And there is humor—often twisted, a little inappropriate, and always hilarious—very much like a father saying goodnight to his children wearing a rubber ghoul mask and owning a collection of fake fangs no adult male should possess.

Read on and check out my *Weird Girls* series. Maybe you'll find I'm really "not like the others."

~ Cecy

GONE HUNTING: CHAPTER ONE

Her name was Celia. I never saw her coming. I didn't know I'd needed her. But isn't that how love is supposed to work?

I hop downstairs. I don't mean I take the steps one or even three at a time. I mean I hop over the railing and leap from the second floor to the first, landing almost silently in a crouch, the backpack on my shoulders barely brushing against my spine.

I'm a *were*. A wolf to be exact. I can get away with leaping from landings physically, but not so much with my mother.

"Aric," she calls, turning away from the stove. "You're a *were*, not an animal. Take the stairs."

Dad looks up from reading his paper and smirks. "Listen to your mother, son."

I return his smirk and walk toward the kitchen. "Yes, sir. Sorry, Mom."

All eight burners are going on the stove. The smell of several pounds of bacon and more pounds of eggs stirred my senses when Mom first opened the fridge. Yeah, I'm *that* sensitive to smell, sight, sound, taste, and touch. And at fifteen, I'm *always* hungry.

I plop down next to my dad, allowing the pack to fall to my side. "Smells good," I say.

Dad sighs and turns the page. "It always does when your mother's in there. Not so much when we cook."

"Nope. We suck," I agree.

Mom's laugh draws my smile. My parents are supposed to lay into me and drive me crazy, force me to rebel, and scream at me when I do things they think I shouldn't. Except, jumping down a flight of stairs and leaving my mostly destroyed clothes on the floor aside, I'm a pretty decent kid with awesome parents.

I reach for the pitcher of freshly squeezed orange juice, yawning a lot louder than I intend. "Sorry," I say, yawning a second time when I fill my glass.

My knife slices into the butter the second Mom drops several pancakes on my plate. I'm ready to dig in when the scent of fresh buttercream finds my nose. Instead, I blink several times, trying to brush off my fatigue.

I didn't sleep much last night. My head spun with weird dreams that didn't make sense. I was wrenched backward and away from her. No . . . that's not right. *She* was ripped from *me*. They were taking her away from me. Whoever *she* was. I frown, remembering how bad it tore me up. I tried to hold on, tried to see her face. All I could make out were her delicate hands in mine. She sobbed, afraid to let go, while my eyes burned with rage-filled tears.

I was pissed and sad and . . . *broken*, except nothing I felt made sense. I didn't recognize her, and I couldn't fathom why she meant so much to me.

The only thing I'm sure of is that a part of me left with her. And the way I feel this morning, it's still missing.

"Are you all right, son?" Dad asks.

I don't realize how hard I'm gripping my knife until I open

my palm and all that's left is a warped piece of metal. My anger at losing her lingers and I took it out on the stupid knife.

"Sorry. I was . . ." I was what? Angry that I let some girl I didn't know go? "I didn't sleep well," I admit.

Dad folds his paper and places it aside, closely analyzing me. "Did you sleep with the window open?"

I don't remember leaving it open, but I nod when I remember how the cool spring breeze swept against my back when I stumbled into the bathroom this morning.

"There was a bad windstorm last night," Dad says, his dark eyebrows furrowing. "Earth's energy travels in the wind, as well as the memories of those long forgotten."

"The wind also carries magic," Mom quietly adds. She leaves the stove, a large pan of eggs gripped in her hand.

"Yes," Dad agrees. "A great deal of magic."

Mom scoops eggs onto Dad's plate, forming a large pile. "In the future, when the wind is that rough, I'd like you to sleep with the window closed."

The scent of cheese, carefully diced onions, and minced garlic seeps into my nose in a mouth-watering sweep. I dig into my eggs the moment the first scoop lands on my plate.

"Why?" I ask, swallowing quickly.

"You're different, son," Dad reminds me.

My chewing slows. It's the same thing I've heard all my life. Yeah, some things come easy for me. I'm stronger than older and larger *weres*. I'm a better tracker and more agile than anyone around. But I don't feel different. I'm just me, I guess.

"I'm serious, Aric." Dad tells me. "You achieved your first *change* before you were two months old. We went to sleep with an infant between us and woke with a wolf pup. *Two months*. I still don't think you comprehend the significance.

Maybe I don't. The most powerful *weres* achieve their first *change* at six months of age following a full moon. The weakest, closer to a year. If you don't *change* in the first year, you're more human and that's how you'll stay. It's something *weres* who mate with humans deal with. Not pures like us.

My fork hovers over my plate as I give Dad's words some thought. I shove the large helping quickly into my mouth when I sense him noticing. No *were* had ever before achieved a *change* at younger than six months-old. It makes me uncomfortable to be perceived as omnipotent. I'm not. Cut my head off or shoot me up with gold bullets, I'm just as dead as the next *were*. People around here forget that. They look at me like I'll single-handedly save the world, or some other impossible stunt. They fall all over themselves, cozying up to me, filling me with compliments they can't possibly mean. The kissing up, the bowing, the *groveling*...I hate it.

"There's no telling how strong you'll become or what powers you may inherit because of it," Dad says.

"I had trouble sleeping," I mumble. "It's no big deal." I don't want anyone making a big fuss over me. It bothers me more when my parents do it. Aside from my small and close-knit circle of friends, they're the only ones who still see me as Aric, not the savior others have come to expect.

Mom scoops another large helping of eggs onto my plate. Tendrils of steam drift from the pan. "Perhaps. Perhaps not," she says. "But if you're this sensitive to what the wind carries, sleep with the window closed. I don't want to risk a mental attack, or worse, while you're at your most vulnerable."

I open my mouth to argue. It's not that I can't shut the stupid window or that I need it open. I suppose I just don't want to focus on how different I am. I'm already weird enough.

Mom jerks. I cringe. My parents sense my discomfort and move on. Not that I like what they're up to.

"Aidan, behave," Mom whispers.

"What? Can't a wolf show his mate a little affection?"

She slaps Dad's hand playfully off her backside.

I make a face. "I'm right here," I remind them. "Can't that wait until I'm gone?"

"Not at all," Dad replies.

He pulls Mom onto his lap. If she were human, Mom would have spilled the eggs across the wooden floor.

"Eat with me," Dad tells her. "You're doing too much."

Mom kisses his cheek and places the pan on the table, allowing Dad to feed her. It's a mate thing. A protective thing. I've been exposed to it a lot in my life. But it always strikes me as intimate and something I shouldn't watch. I leave the table, returning with a large serving tray topped with bacon. I frown when I find Mom's arms wrapped securely around Dad's neck. Her shoulder length, white hair brushes against his chest with how hard she clutches him.

"You're going hunting again, aren't you?" I ask.

Mom lowers her eyelids as if in pain. Dad smiles softly at her, stroking her hair until she opens her eyes. She doesn't return his smile. It bothers me to see her upset.

"What's going on?" I ask.

"There's a dark witch causing trouble in Lesotho," Dad replies, continuing his slow strokes over Mom's hair.

I reach for more bacon and eggs. "Where's that?" I ask.

"Africa," Mom replies. "It's a territory known for diamond smuggling and dark magic."

"Cue the witch," I guess. Not all witches are dark. Last summer, I met Bellissima, one of the strongest light witches of her kind, along with her daughter, Guinevere, or was it Genevieve? It was something like that. They were okay. But dark witches really suck and give *weres* plenty of problems to chase.

As Guardians of the Earth, it's our job to protect the unsuspecting human populace from things that hunt them. Those creatures that go bump in the night? *We* eat *them*.

I shove a forkful of eggs into my mouth and stab a few more pieces of bacon. "How'd you hear about the witch?" I ask.

"She's protecting the diamond smugglers in the area," Dad explains.

I feel my eyes darken and a growl build deep within me. "In exchange for what?"

Dad doesn't blink. "Sacrifices, mainly human women and children."

I look to Mom, not liking where this is headed. "The women are deeply oppressed throughout the region," she explains. "When you find women fraught with worries of violence and struggling to feed their families, they tend to be more pure of heart and intent, and therefore easier to victimize. The children. . ." Mom straightens, passing her fingertips along the gray peppering Dad's temple. "There's nothing more sacred than a child's soul."

"Which makes the blood sacrifices she seeks more valuable. The purer the soul, the more power each kill will grant her," I finish for her. They nod. "Can I go with you?"

"No," Mom answers at the same time Dad says, "Maybe."

I perk up, my inner wolf totally losing it. "I can go?"

Mom shoots Dad a reprimanding look. "Aric is almost of age, Eliza," Dad gently reminds her. "He's far surpassed seasoned *weres* in strength, ability, and cunning."

Mom leaves Dad's lap, taking the empty pan with her. "No," she says.

Dad and I exchange glances. I know better than to speak up. Mom walks to the large porcelain sink and dumps the pan, gripping the edge. "Our world isn't what it once was," she says. "It's changing in ways even the wisest among us never predicted, Aidan."

Dad gets up slowly, briefly pausing behind her before his hands encircle her waist. He kisses her shoulder. "The world is changing," he agrees. "But it's our duty to maintain it, so good continues to prevail."

"There are many *weres* across the globe now," she reminds him. "Unlike generations ago, when our kind struggled to breed and flourish." She looks up at Dad, her soft brown eyes pleading. "Request that another pack or Leader go in your place. I hate it when you hunt. I hate it when you leave me. Please, my love, don't take our son, too."

"All right," he tells her.

"Wait," I interrupt. "Don't I get a say?" I don't know who's more bummed, me or my wolf.

Dad turns around, keeping Mom against him. "I need you here to protect your mother," he says.

I raise my eyebrows at him. He grins and so does Mom. She's almost sixty and Dad is seventy-five. Although they tried, they didn't have me until late in life. That doesn't mean either couldn't wipe the floor with anyone who messed with them. And if I wasn't around, Mom would be the one hunting alongside Dad, just as they did for years before I came along.

"Aric," Dad says. "I'm not yet sure I'm going. There's already a local pack assigned to track and kill the witch." He looks at my mother. "But in the chance I go, I won't upset your mother further by taking you along."

"Nothing's going to happen to you," I insist. "And if I'm with you, nothing will happen to us."

I mean what I say. My dad is unstoppable. A king among *weres* and my hero.

Dad offers a lopsided smile. "Aric, your mother is worried enough."

"I know, but—"

"*Especially* with all those females knocking on our door, seeking your company," he interrupts.

I roll my eyes. The females I know are annoying at best,

looking to get with me for all the wrong reasons. "I don't even like them."

Dad barks out a laugh. "Not yet. But you will, son. It's just a matter of time."

"I just hope it's not any time soon," Mom quietly adds. She's still upset.

I rise, recognizing they need time. "Where you off to?" Dad asks.

"Hunting," I reply, excited for our plans and that we finally get a few days off from school. "Liam swears he scented elk near Mount Elbert."

Dad leads Mom forward, his fingers threaded in hers. "Is it just you and Liam?" he asks.

"No. Gemini is coming and so is Koda."

Mom exchanges a worried glance with Dad. "How is Miakoda?" she asks.

I shrug. When it comes to Koda, I walk a fine line between betraying my friend and keeping things from my parents. For the most part, I'm allowed free rein. They trust me, and I want to keep things that way. So, I tell them just enough to stay true to my friend.

"Koda's all right. He mostly stays at Liam's. The other night, he was with Gem."

Dad's voice grows an edge. "Do I need to pay his father a visit?"

My gaze lowers to the floor to hide my growing resentment of Koda's father. Except, resentment, anger, *any* emotion carries a scent my folks will recognize as easily as they take their next breath. It's the reason *weres* are so good at sniffing out lies.

Koda's relationship with his dad isn't like mine. Where I'd take a spray of gold bullets to keep my parents safe, Koda would run the other way with tears of agony mixed with relief likely streaming down his face.

"Aric," Dad says, his tone more severe. "Is Koda's father hurting him or his mother?"

"No," I answer truthfully. But only because Koda hasn't been around to let him.

Dad is a pureblood and Leader, just like Mom and just like me. Dad is also our pack alpha, the one who oversees *weres* and their activity within his territory. As formidable as he is, he's often tasked with solving matters outside our region that other *weres* can't handle. But his responsibilities are first and foremost to his pack. The same pack Koda and his family belong to.

"Aric," Dad says, this time more gently. "I'm only trying to help Koda and keep him and his family safe."

"I know." I meet my father square in the eyes, something most *weres* wouldn't dare do. "I'll try to talk to him today and see where he's at."

Dad nods, but he doesn't appear any less concerned. I can't blame him. Not after everything Koda's been through.

"Tell Miakoda he always has a home with us," Mom says.

"I will. Thanks, Mom."

My wolf stiffens when I bend to hug her. We have company. I release her slowly and turn toward the front of the house, my excitement building when I hear the voices of my friends.

"They're here," I say. "Gotta go."

"Be careful," Mom says.

I grin. "I'm going hunting, Mom. What could happen?"

I glide down the steep incline on four paws, digging my claws into the thick forest bed to keep my balance. The weight of my three-hundred-pound wolf form leaves deep indentations in the soil. There wasn't just one elk. There was a massive herd. We separated them as a pack, targeting the eldest and weakest, as nature demands.

The one I'm chasing stumbles down the ravine, his immense

body crashing into the riverbank and sending waves of muddy water to drench my face. I shake off the thick drops blinding me and hurtle forward. I'm almost on him, my excitement of snapping his neck and bringing home a feast propelling me faster.

I bare my teeth at the scent of his fear. Despite his weariness, he's fighting the kill. I can respect him as my prey. That doesn't mean I'll let him go. My supernatural strength jets me faster, ghosting over the slippery rocks when the elk stumbles. He quickly recovers on wobbly limbs. It doesn't matter. I have him. My family will have a sweet meal tonight.

We round the bend as I leap toward his neck. My fangs barely graze his tough pelt before I crash into what feels like an invisible wall. The force flings me backward, slamming me into the riverbed. I whirl up, wondering what happened, and *pissed* that it did.

The sound of beating hooves grows distant as the elk disappears. I ignore his escape and growl with murderous rage.

Something's here. Something different. Something magical.

My paws keep my footing over the uneven and rocky bank as I stalk forward. I poke at the air with my nose, trying to sense the wall or whatever it was that caused my fall.

My nose twitches, latching onto something . . . *weird*. It's not elk, not deer, not even rabbit.

I smell predator.

A challenging growl rumbles through my torso and down my legs, causing a ripple across the water. My eyes sweep my surroundings, up the incline where the woods are thickest and back down where small, gentle waves splash over the river rocks.

Where are you? I growl again.

I angle my body to the left and frown. Something like rot permeates from the forest. It reeks of dead prey and danger, but then it moves further away from me and the predator I seek.

My eyes round with surprise when I home in on a different

scent. In the breeze, cascading along the bank, the fragrance of water misting over roses overtakes the aroma of pine, rich soil, and thick beds of moss, ensnaring me in its beauty.

An excited chill runs down my spine, standing my fur on end. I shake my head, trying to clear a scent that has no business latched to another predator . . . especially one warning me to keep my distance.

My ears perk up and my eyes home in on a thick mound of blackberry brambles a few feet away.

There you are . . .

I prowl forward, my steps quiet and purposeful and my jaws set to sink into bone.

This isn't a cougar. They run from us.

This is hungry.

Dangerous.

Weird.

My body quivers with growing excitement and my thunderous growls echo. I snap my jaws in challenge, letting my prey know I sense him.

It's time to flee or fight. The choice is his. I'm not going anywhere.

The brush shifts. Slowly, very slowly, my prey rises. My lips peel back, yet the next growl dissipates before it can fully form.

Instead of fur, wet, wavy brown hair with streaks of gold catch the faint sunlight, spilling over slender shoulders and flawless olive skin, while droplets of river water trickle around large green eyes and full pink lips.

I stop breathing.

She's young.

My age.

And she's naked.

ABOUT THE AUTHOR

Photo by Kate Gledhill of Kate Gledhill Photography

Cecy Robson is an international and multi-award winning author of over twenty character driven novels. As a registered nurse of eighteen years, Cecy spends her free time creating magical worlds, heart-stopping romance, and young adult adventure. After receiving two RITA® nominations, a National Reader's Choice Award nomination, and winning the Maggie Award of Excellence, you can still find Cecy laughing, crying, and cheering on her characters as she pens her next story.

Connect with Cecy online:
www.cecyrobson.com

CPSIA information can be obtained
at www.ICGtesting.com
Printed in the USA
LVHW030011010921
696579LV00003B/244

9 781947 330313